Her mouth we

He wondered at the ██████████████████ sweetness and thoug███████████████████ She would pull away. She didn't want this.

God knew, he was a man. He was just out of prison. He couldn't handle this.

She tilted her head and moved her lips against his.

She did want it. He'd done the right thing. So right it obliterated all the ugliness he'd seen and heard in the cells. So right it made him feel free.

Her lips moved on his and she kissed him back as if she liked it.

As if she needed it.

She lifted her hand and laid it on his neck, sure and sweet, as if she needed *him*.

What could a man like him have to offer a woman like her?

He couldn't let himself want it. He was free, but not for this. So he caught her wrist, kissed her harder for one more heartbeat, then took his mouth away.

Also by Genell Dellin

CHEROKEE DAWN
CHEROKEE NIGHTS
CHEROKEE SUNDOWN
COMANCHE WIND
COMANCHE FLAME
COMANCHE RAIN
RED SKY WARRIOR
SILVER MOON SONG
AFTER THE THUNDER
THE RENEGADES: COLE
THE RENEGADES: NICK
THE RENEGADES: RAFE
THE LONER
THE LOVER

Written as Gena Dalton

SORREL SUNSET
WILD PASSIONS
APRIL ENCOUNTER
CHEROKEE FIRE
STRANGER AT THE CROSSROADS
MIDNIGHT FAITH
LONG WAY HOME

And coming soon from HQN Books

A PIECE OF THE SKY

MONTANA
BLUE

GENELL DELLIN

HQN™

ISBN 0-373-77044-8

MONTANA BLUE

Copyright © 2005 by Genell Dellin.

This edition published by arrangement with Harlequin Books S.A.

www.HQNBooks.com

Printed in U.S.A.

For Paula Hamilton
and
Karen Crane,
my companions on this journey

ACKNOWLEDGMENTS

I would like to thank:

God, for the story

My agent, Nancy Yost, and my editor, Abby Zidle, for their insights and their faith in MONTANA BLUE

My friends Sheila Forbes, Jill Peale and Robin Miller for their heartfelt encouragement

And my family—my husband, Art, and son, David, daughter-in-law, Julie, and grandson, Gage; my sister Linda, her husband, Luke, and their son, Lance, and daughter, Lucie; Lance's wife, Tamara, and daughter, Elizabeth; Lucie's husband, Joel, and children, Gracie and Waylon Grady; my sister Bonnie, her husband, Gary, and their sons, Ben and Sam; and my uncle Arlen and aunt Clara—for so much love.

Montana
Blue

CHAPTER ONE

THEY TURNED HIM LOOSE on a dazzling, yellow-robed morning ten years to the month—June—since they'd locked him in. The breeze whipped down from the mountains with a wet-dirt smell and the sun struck his face with a strong, hot hand. A crater of need opened in the center of him, the need to rise to meet that life-giving sun, to wallow in its warmth and try to suck it all into the empty sack that was his skin.

"Here," he said, and shoved the bundle of paints and brushes he carried at the last guard, "take this to your kids."

For what he had to do, he sure as hell didn't need them. Besides, they carried the stink of the place just as he did. First thing he'd do was get more clothes and a shower somewhere.

If he could bear to go inside four walls and a roof again.

He could. He could stand anything. He had already been through the worst.

He still could not believe he was free. His sudden release had left him no time to prepare, to adjust his mind to these new circumstances.

On the edge of the road, he stood still, struck blind by the brightness.

"Over here. Take you straight to the bus station in Deer Lodge."

A couple of other men, also newly freed, hurried toward the battered bus, but Blue turned his back and started down the road. He might walk all the way to Bozeman, just to be touching the face of the Earth Mother.

How many miles would it take to join him to her again? His feet were so used to concrete he could barely feel the clumps of grass that made him stumble.

The bus passed and honked but he didn't look up.

Maybe he'd find a waterfall to stand under, wash himself and these clothes at the same time. Live off the land for a week or two. Like he used to do in the Oklahoma hills. He could go into the national forest.

But he'd need a weapon to hunt meat or something to make into snares or fishing lines. He gulped the fresh air, over and over again, and set one foot in front of the other. Could he still survive in the woods?

Not unless he could learn to see in all this color, all this light—the greens of the grass and the leaves on the trees shimmered and blurred because he wasn't used to such richness. For a minute he thought he was looking through tears.

Maybe, in order to get his balance again, he should buy an old truck and go hunt a job riding some young ranch horses or driving cattle to summer pasture. Just until he got his feet under him and made a plan.

He moved his mind away from that. The sight of the high mountains stirred his spirit like a feather on the wind. He was free, for the first time in ten years, and he'd better enjoy it while he could.

Blue walked on and on, letting his mind drift and his body feel. Letting his senses fill.

The whine of a motor started coming up behind him. He moved farther over on the shoulder so the vehicle could pass. It didn't.

A chill touched him. Was it a prison van come to take him back? Had his release been some freak mistake?

He looked over his shoulder. An old, faded red pickup and battered stock trailer moving fast, apparently determined to run over him in spite of the fact the whole opposite lane was empty.

The long shadow of the rig captured him as it pulled alongside. The truck's speed slowed, it drifted toward the shoulder of the road, slowed some more, and finally swerved off the pavement, rolling to a stop.

The open-topped trailer held a horse tied right behind the rusty cab, its head high and handsome.

Blue kept walking. Then he realized he should go to the other side of the road if he didn't want the driver to talk to him and expect him to answer.

The horse drew his gaze again. It'd been a long time since he'd seen one in the flesh.

The door of the truck opened and, rattling, slammed closed. Blue stepped up onto the asphalt, ready to cross to the other side. That put him right in the line of sight of the driver, an old cowboy limping toward the trailer.

"Hey, buddy," he called, "reckon you could help me out here?"

Blue didn't answer. He glanced over his shoulder, saw the way was clear, and started to cross the road.

"Won't take but a minute, pardner," the old man said, "sure would be obliged to ya. I'd hate like sin to lose this here horse."

Blue looked straight at him then. He'd stopped at the rear of the truck to lean on it. He was rubbing his hip and trying to straighten one of his legs.

Well, damn.

"I hit a bump and got skeered this here trailer was about to come off'n' the ball," the old guy said, with an apologetic grin, "and my artheritis is so bad today I cain't hardly bend over to save my soul. Seein' you hikin' along back there was nothin' short of a godsend."

Didn't he ever shut up?

Blue looked away, down the road, and started angling toward the other side. He wanted silence, he wanted to be alone. The old man's troubles were none of his.

"Trailer come off the hitch, this horse would likely git killed," the old chatterbox said. "Be a damnable shame. Never be another one like him."

Blue glanced at the horse again, even though he didn't intend to. The roan was looking at him.

Never be another one like me. Come on. See what you think if you call yourself a horseman.

Blue veered and walked toward him.

"Happened to me and a pardner of mine, oncet," the man said, brightening considerably when he saw that Blue would help.

"Trailer come off on the down side of a hill and left the road going seventy-five mile an hour," he went on in his rusty voice. "Passed us up on the right like we was standin' still. Ol' Skimpy stared and stared at it and finally he turned to me and said, 'Well, damn it all to hell, Micah, looky there. That trailer *and* the horses in it looks just like ours.'"

He took off his hat and slapped it against his leg, laughing, and stuck out his hand to Blue.

"Micah Thompson's the name," he said.

Blue shook with him. His gnarled old grip was hard and strong. His faded brown eyes were sharp.

"Blue Bowman."

"Good to meet you, Blue. And mighty good of you to give me a hand. Won't slow you down for long and then you can get on your way."

Blue stepped in between the truck and trailer, then over the hitch so they could both look at it at the same time. He bent to examine it and Micah stepped down on the bumper of the truck. He bounced it. The hitch didn't come loose. Blue took hold of it and tried it, but it stayed the same.

A safety chain looped around the shaft. The battered bumper had the requisite two holes to thread it through.

"Why not use this?" he asked.

"Couldn't bend over long enough to hook it up," Micah said.

A sharp crack of sound rocked the rig. It jerked Blue's back straight and his head around. Not a gunshot. The horse.

The same noise exploded the air again while the trailer shook some more. The horse glared at Blue with one wild eye.

Blue returned the stare. This was a direct challenge. Personal. He couldn't help but grin.

"Thinks he's King Kong," Micah said.

The red roan kicked again, laid his ears back tighter, and twisted his head to snap at the rusted steel bar of the trailer.

"He might be right," Blue said.

The good smell of horse filled up his nostrils. How strange for it to be real and not just a memory.

Micah laughed.

"We could run on down to my place and find out," he said. "I'm betting you're the man to settle him right down."

The horse still had Blue nailed with one talking eye.

Come on. Try me. I'll dust you, turn and strike you, too. Break your bones.

"What makes you think that?" Blue asked.

He felt Micah's gaze steady on his face but he didn't take his eyes off the horse. Beautiful head. Intelligent eye, but not a soft one. Savvy.

He'd be an interesting way to get horseback, especially for a man who hadn't stepped up onto a horse in ten years.

Micah was still looking at Blue instead of the horse. Blue could feel his gaze on his skin. On the braid of his hair. He turned.

The old man's heavy-lidded eyes were waiting for him, full of knowing, like an ancient turtle's. They met his and held.

"You walk like a horseman," he said.

Blue grunted his disbelief.

Thompson looked at him for another long moment, then he glanced at the horse and chuckled.

"This here colt'll fly you over the mountain, Blue," he said, "but when you get 'im broke and solid, he'll last you for years. Make a hell of a usin' horse and babies just like him, too."

Blue's heart thumped.

"You're selling?"

The old cowboy twisted even more wrinkles into his long neck to turn and spit tobacco juice out of the other side of his mouth.

"Yep. *I* shore as hell cain't break him."

Blue locked eyes with the horse again.

"Two-year-old?"

Micah nodded.

"Yep. Ain't never been rode—but not for lack of tryin'. Started him right after Christmas, with the rest of my string."

As if to show how tough he was, the horse sat back on the rope and started pulling, hooves scrabbling.

"Here now! Here! Stop that, you big fool."

Micah limped alongside the trailer and took hold to climb up on the fender, which made the horse lunge forward into the rattling bars. His rear feet slid up to his front ones and then, fast and impossible as a magician's trick, he slipped his forefeet up between his body and the wall and managed to rear, going higher and higher, one leg on each side of the rope that tied his head up short.

"If he tries to come over the top he'll break his neck," Micah yelled. "Keep him in there 'til I can get another rope."

But the colt had already started choking, eyes rolling. He twisted his head and his right forefoot slid off the top and lodged in between two of the beat-up bars of the trailer. He jerked sideways and wedged it in tighter.

"Forget the rope," Blue called toward the truck, without taking his eyes off the colt. "Come here and hold his head."

He broke out in a sweat. Suddenly he wanted this colt freed safely. It was the first time he'd let himself want anything for a long time.

Micah came back at a lurching run and Blue held out a cautioning hand without looking at him.

"Easy," he said. "Easy, now."

He was talking to all three of them, but mostly to himself.

The small, neat hoof had plunged through a wide space between the bent bars, but now the tender ankle was in a much narrower spot, held tight. Blue grunted comfort to the horse as he and Micah moved slowly toward him.

"It'll take us both," Blue said in a soothing tone. "Stand on the fender, hold his head, and get ready to grab the hoof. I'll spread the bars."

The colt trembled with fear so strong Blue could smell it. His eyes rolled white and his nostrils flared. They didn't have long until he hurt himself bad. No, until he hanged himself.

"Got yourself in trouble, huh?" Blue murmured to him as he climbed up onto the fender. "Huh?"

He began a rhythmic "huh, huh, huh," the old calming sound that mimicked a horse's own talk, and set his feet as far apart as the space permitted. He glanced sideways as Micah stepped up there, too, and took hold of the halter.

The roan colt was on the sharp edge of panic. The air was filled with it.

Blue felt shaky inside. He hadn't done anything—actually *done* anything remotely important in too long. But he had to do this now. He took hold of the two bars and put his back into separating them. It was a lot harder than he expected but when he pulled them apart and bent them out at the same time, he could make enough room. Micah grabbed the hoof and turned it, pushed it back into the trailer, gave it back into the roan's control.

The colt dropped to the floor and stood, trembling.

Micah and Blue looked at him, then at each other. Micah grinned and Blue felt an answering grin lift the corners of his mouth. Micah let go of the halter and checked the tie knot. They stepped down to let the colt have a little space.

"Damned if he didn't nearly hang his ornery self right here," Micah said. "I allus say there ain't no limit to what kind of a fix a hoss can git hisself into."

Blue looked at the roan's shiny hide glistening with the sweat of fear. He knew the feeling.

"Royally bred for a cutting horse," Micah said, as they stood and watched the young horse get his wits back together again, "even if he's too big for one and acts like a crazy no-name on top of that."

"Maybe he never heard the old saying, 'Blood will tell.'"

Micah Thompson didn't answer. When Blue finally looked at him again, his eyes had taken on a glint of humor.

"It will tell sometimes, and then again it won't," Micah said, still studying him.

Then he added, "This sucker hates the sight of a cow."

That made Blue's smile widen and he laughed out loud. He hardly recognized the feeling or the sound.

The horse kicked then, and snorted at them as if they weren't taking him seriously enough. Blue laughed again.

"God knows I'm too crippled up to fork the big bastard," Micah Thompson said. "If'n I kin make a hundred or two on him, he's down the road."

He turned and started walking to the truck as if he expected Blue to go with him. With another look at the chastened colt, Blue followed.

"It's not far to my place," Micah said as he started around to the driver's side. "Couple of hours as the crow flies. I've got a few more for sale, too, if you're thinking you might want somethin' different."

Blue stopped.

"Or if you *can* ride, I could use some help with the whole bunch of twos," Micah said. "That is, if you happen to need a job."

He opened his door and got in behind the wheel. Blue hesitated only another second, then he walked to the passenger door and got into the old truck.

His hands were shaking just a little, so he spread them flat on his knees. In ten years he might've lost his balance and every trick he knew for staying on a rank one.

But he felt his lips curve again in the stupid grin. That roan devil behind him would make him remember how to ride or wish he never had tried. That horse would make him know he was alive again, at least for a little while.

He twisted in his seat and looked back. Horses had been living only in his dreams and his memory for so long and this one was real.

The roan was lifting his muzzle into the wind, real as the cracked glass of the window between them. Blue felt the blood rise in his veins.

The feel of a horse beneath him. That sweet challenge of swinging up onto a new one and finding out how to learn the secrets he had in his heart, what all he could do and *would* do with his four legs and thousand pounds of muscle and sinew. Bronc or ranch horse or cutter or anything else, Blue had never stepped on a new one without feeling that fierce, wild thrill.

"This here's a pretty day," Micah said, pushing down hard on the gas pedal. "Reckon it's good to see summer comin' on again."

Getting hooked up with this old man and trying this colt was all right. He had a job and a place to stay now, at least.

This was okay. He'd known a hundred men like Micah Thompson when he was a kid.

"He's still a stud, you said?" he asked.

"Yep. Reckon that might account for his meanness. A couple of swipes of the knife and he'll likely turn into a pussy-cat."

Blue slanted a look at him. "Not entirely, I'd say."

Micah gave an evil chuckle.

"Told you you was a horseman, didn't I?"

I used to be. I don't yet know what all I've lost. Or will lose again.

Micah began ranting on about the characteristics of a real horseman, giving examples from a long list of the best horsemen he had known down through the years. He was talking as much to himself as to Blue, so Blue tuned him out as the miles rolled past his window.

The power of the mountains began taking him over, filling him up with their fierceness, an excitement nearly as strong as the one that had come with his first glimpse of the roan. Great Spirit of the Earth and Sky, how had he lived ten years without being out among the hills and mountains, the trees and the plains, ten years without laying his hand on a horse's warm flesh?

Or a woman's. Ten years without the touch of a woman.

No mountains and no horses and no tenderness for that long time. It was a miracle he hadn't died.

But he hadn't. That meant he could do anything he had to do. He had already gone through the worst.

He stared out of the truck as if his head couldn't turn. It couldn't. He couldn't get enough of looking.

Or of smelling the wind and hearing it. Or of tasting fresh air on his tongue and feeling the worn paint of the truck door smooth beneath his hand. He wanted to hang his head out the window and soak it all up through his pores. They drove on and on and the farther they traveled, the freer he felt.

The land was huge. The sky was enormous. The day he'd arrived in Montana, following Dannie and her scumbag boyfriend, that was what had struck him. The sky could be big in Oklahoma. The hills there could feel like they were going on and on forever in layers out to the edge of the earth and then lifting into the sky, but when a person hit Montana it was like God had opened up his hand and laid out all the freedom in the world for whoever was brave enough to take it.

Something deep within him, something too unformed to be a memory, awakened from sleeping in his bones. Tanasi Rose had returned to Oklahoma when he was nearly two years old and Dannie not yet born, but his spirit knew this place.

"Always good to see spring, ain't it?" Micah said.

Blue didn't answer. The sun shone with such a yellow power that his eyes watered in its glare. The breeze blew in through the open window and dried the sudden wetness on his cheeks.

Maybe he would take this gift of spring and not think about what else he had to do until later in the summer.

He turned away from the thought and looked back at the roan. The horse was staring off across the wide spaces, thinking of freedom, too.

The old truck slowed at last.

"This here's our turnoff," Micah said. "Be about three more miles to my place."

He turned west onto gravel.

The road led them north and west, winding down, then up and over, each rise a little less than its drop on the other side. It crossed a cattle guard, then a creek, running fast and wide over rocks.

"Looky yonder," Micah said, flicking one gnarled finger toward the windshield as they started uphill again. "White-tails."

Three deer, surprisingly close, bolted. They crossed the road and vanished in among some cedar trees before Blue could realize he'd actually seen them in the flesh, but still his blood thrilled from the glimpse of their wildness.

Micah mashed the brakes as they lurched downward to a low-water bridge over a deeper creek with steeper banks than the first, then gunned the old truck as it labored up the next rising hill. They topped it and picked up speed on the way down as if the rattling trailer pushed the truck to go faster.

Blue looked down into a wide, grassy valley with mountains on the horizon, with trees gathered together in long sweeps of woods, with grain fields and pastures.

With buildings enough to make a town.

Black-topped roads running in every direction made him think for a minute that it was a town. But it was a ranch head-quarters, with barns and bunkhouses, pens and shops and sheds flung all over the place. A big house at the heart of it with flags flying in front must be the main house.

What a dream, set in a sweet, protected valley.

They kept on rolling down the hill while Blue stared, trying to put it all together with the falling-down rig Micah drove. The closer they came to the valley, the more it was clear that this was headquarters to a big operation, one that had been there for many a year, one that was prospering.

Micah sure seemed to be a broken-down cowboy without much in the way of possessions but appearances could deceive. Or maybe, more likely, he just worked here. Lived in the bunkhouse, maybe. He was too stove up to work.

The road took another bend to run along a ridge above the ranch, then began curving in easy switchbacks leading down into the valley. Through the pines, Blue saw a truck with a hay spike on the back driving away from one of the farthest barns. It looked like a toy in the distance.

"That there's where I live," Micah said, as his rig left the gravel road for the asphalt.

He was pointing to a log house and barn nestled onto a low knoll at the base of this west-facing hill. Before Blue could open his mouth to ask who lived in the big house, the sound of a diesel motor came chugging up the last little rise to meet them.

Micah glanced at the driver and slowed to a stop. The other truck stopped, too. It was new and white under the mud that had splattered up onto the doors. Nice truck. One ton flatbed with a crew cab.

The front door bore a brand painted in black and gold, two parallel serpentine lines, elongated versions of the letter *S*, with the word *Wagontracks* arching above them. The driver leaned out the window to glance at the roan.

"Micah," he said, "what are you asking for that hayburner you're hauling?"

Micah grinned and shook his head.

"Save your breath, Pickle. I'm sellin' this one to somebody who can *ride* 'im."

They talked some more but Blue was only dimly aware of the sound and took in none of their meaning. He was caught up in reading the words that formed a crescent below the Wagontracks brand.

Splendid Sky Ranch.

When the other truck had downshifted and gone growling on its way, Blue spoke, even though he had to push his breath past the pounding of his heart.

"Where's the Splendid Sky?"

"You're sittin' on it, son," Micah said. "That's the headquarters right down there."

CHAPTER TWO

MICAH DROVE ON.

"Yes *sir*," he said, "this here's the Splendid Sky Ranch. Gordon Campbell's place is famous all over the West."

He cocked his head and shot a sharp glance at Blue from under the brim of his hat.

"You ever heard of it?"

Blue met his gaze. He had to do it to prove he could conceal his shock and he did.

"Sure, everybody's heard of the Wagontracks horses," Micah said, "and I'll tell you right now, there ain't a line of ranch horses anywhere, including them famous ones in Oklahoma and Texas that can measure up to ours."

Blue couldn't even listen to him. How, in the name of all that was holy, had he ended up here so soon? He didn't have his balance yet—hell, he wasn't even used to trying to *see* in the sunshine.

"I started every horse in the Wagontracks cavvy for fifty year," Micah said. "For the main ranch. How many head you reckon that amounts to?"

Blue's gut clenched as he looked out his window at the main ranch. Gordon could be down there in the big headquarters house right now. Or out there in that pickup zipping down the paved, black road that led away from it. Or he could be that tiny man on top of the tiny horse way off riding across the pasture.

Micah answered his own question. "More'n a thousand

head, and that guess is a little on the low side," he said, pride lacing his voice. "Yessir, Blue, back then, I could ride 'em."

The sound of his own name, a voice calling him Blue instead of Bowman, felt almost as warm as a friendly hand on his shoulder. He turned to look at the old man, who was staring through the windshield into the long distance.

"I was always limber as a cat and I could ride them sunfishin' sumbitches all day long."

"I wouldn't doubt it," Blue said.

Either the words or the sincerity in them drew a flash of a glance from Micah, with some bright light in it that Blue couldn't read.

"You got a good eye if you can see it now," Micah said.

He used both hands to crank the wheel. The truck veered across the road and onto the gravel trail that followed the low ridge above the floor of the valley.

"Long time ago, when he seen he couldn't run me off, Gordon gimme this cabin and barn. Said they was mine as long as I live."

Blue looked at Micah's place as they rattled up into the spot at the edge of the yard where the grass was worn away from years of parking the pickup. Everything there was made of logs a long time ago. Trees sheltered it all and the hill kept it from the north wind. In front of it, the whole West beckoned.

He tasted bitterness on his tongue.

Gordon could give a house and a barn to his wrangler but nothing to his family.

While Micah ground the gears and threw them into reverse, Blue looked again at the Splendid Sky—as much as a man could see of it at one time. There was the headquarters with the house his great-grandfather had built and all its many fine outbuildings dotted here and there, including plenty more nice houses provided for the help. Beneath it all was the land, rolling green and glittering down through the valley like a flung treasure.

This entire ranch should be theirs. His.

He had been robbed of his birthright.

If Gordon had married Tanasi Rose, if he had given his name to her and his children and raised them here, they would be here still. Dannah would never have become a junkie, Rose would never have killed herself, and Blue would not be a murderer.

His mother and Dannie would be alive.

His father had robbed him of them, too.

"You've heard of the Splendid Sky, then you've heard of Gordon Campbell," the old man said.

The name spoken aloud rang strange in Blue's ears, it had been so long silent in his mind.

"He ain't well-liked, that's nothing but the honest truth," Micah said, "and I have to admit that he can be one high-handed son of a bitch. But I'll say somethin' for ol' Gordon. He stands by his friends."

Oh, yeah. And family. Don't forget family.

Blue didn't even want to hear the name again, it made him so bitter. But he said it anyway.

"Maybe you're the *only* friend of Gordon Campbell."

Micah chuckled.

"I reckon not," he said, "there's a few more, here and there."

Blue found himself waiting for Micah to say who they might be, but he didn't. Instead, he cranked the wheel around and started backing up to the gate of the round pen.

"We'll run Roanie in there," he said. "In a good mood, he'll lead some but we ain't takin' no chances. I nearly got mashed to death in a trailer one time."

He pulled forward, turned the wheel some more, and backed into exactly the right spot.

"Well, now, let's get this roan ridgerunner unloaded 'fore he climbs the wall again and breaks his neck or one of them dainty legs of his," he said, throwing open his door. "Then I'll show you around the place."

Blue wasn't sure he wanted that. He wasn't sure what he wanted to see except for this raunchy colt in all his glory. Anything else was questionable. He wanted to see how the colt moved, wanted to know his natural way of going, and beyond that, he couldn't think.

He stepped down. *Dainty* was a good word for the way his own legs felt. They didn't quite want to hold him up and he held on to the seat just for a minute. Feelings were his enemies—that had been so for ten years—and he couldn't give in to them now.

Maybe he should've kept his paints. He'd poured his rage and loneliness into them and slapped it onto the canvas while he held himself completely separate from every person in the prison. That was how he had survived.

He needed to keep separate from Micah, too. It was a pity the old man had passed his prime but feeling sorry about Micah's arthritis was what had brought him to the Splendid Sky on this first day out, and now here he was.

Of course, coming here was giving him a chance at a good horse—and it was putting Gordon in his sights. He had left prison wanting both those things, hadn't he?

Both sides of the coin, that was what this world paid human beings for all the blood and sweat that they put into living. Turn over the good and a man could find the bad; turn over the bad and find the good.

He had already known that when he killed the pond-scum drug pusher who had led Dannah straight to her death. Or had he? Had he just now realized it, which meant it was the good side of the bad ten years in the pen?

He walked on back to the trailer, keeping step with Micah who was on the other side of it. Hell of a note. End up here at the Splendid Sky, first crack out of the box, when he'd imagined it all his life long.

Right now, he'd think about the horse. Nothing else.

He waited on the ground below the horse's head until

Micah had the gate open and had jammed the rusty pin of the trailer door up with his fist. The colt bared his teeth looking down at him.

Get up here. I'll take a chunk out of you.

"Ready?" Micah said.

"Ready."

Blue stepped onto the fender, pulled up on the strap of the halter, freed the tongue of the buckle from its hole and, therefore, the horse from the trailer. Roanie jerked his head away, clattered to the door and leapt out onto the ground of the round pen. Micah pushed the gate shut behind him and then the trailer door.

The two of them stood together and looked in between the logs of the old-time round pen. The colt reared high, came down with a snort and a fart and went ripping off around the circle again, pausing only to buck and rear some more when the notion struck him. After two of those circles, he settled down into a run and tore around the pen so fast he was a blur.

"How'd you get the halter on him?" Blue said.

"I got 'im halter broke," Micah said. "Sort of. But I never could stay on him."

He shook his head, took off his hat and put it back on again. Blue caught the smell of old felt and leather soaked with sweat.

"He's a whole lot worse since I sent him over to the Little Creek Division boys," Micah said. "Gordon oughtta fire every one of them out on his ass. But I found out I'd never be able to stay on him and I was hoping they could get him broke enough for me."

Micah shook his head again, turned it, and spat on the ground.

"Gittin' old is a hoary bitch," he said. "Don't do it."

Blue gave a harsh laugh.

"I won't," he said.

And he probably wouldn't, one way or the other.

He kept looking at the horse and feeling the old, mostly forgotten tug at his gut. The roan thundered by them again.

"Leave him," Micah called over the noise. "You kin start on him tomorry."

Tomorrow. Would he stay here? On the Splendid Sky?

Surely not. But maybe so. Hadn't he been headed here anyhow?

He didn't want to think about it. He turned away, went back to the trailer, stepped up onto the fender, and jerked the halter loose from the rail where it was tied.

He stepped down.

"I'm gonna have to try him now," he said. "Open the gate for me."

Micah did.

"This here pen's built like all the old-time ones—with room for a man to roll out under the bottom log," he said. "Git out if he takes after you. He never done that 'til he'd been to Little Creek."

The warning pricked at Blue's brain, but instead of thinking of himself facing the danger of a charging stud horse, he imagined Micah. The old guy had guts, crippled up as he was, to even try the colt.

Blue walked through the gate and toward the center of the pen. The roan colt blew by behind him, sticking close to the wall. He circled the pen twice more, then half again, slowing, slowing. He started trotting back and forth on the west side, his dappled hide shining in flashes as he went in and out of the sun. Then he came down to a walk.

He knew Blue was there but he wouldn't even glance in his direction.

Blue walked toward him. His fingers tightened around the halter strap as he coiled the rope. Sweat broke out across his back. How could he have sense or skill enough to connect with a terrified horse on this day?

In this *place?*

But he knew how to go about trying it, and that was all he did know.

The roan stood still and turned his hindquarters to Blue. On the outside of the pen, Micah was pacing Blue.

"What all has this horse gone through?" Blue called.

"I ain't sure. Them Little Creek bastards say sell 'im to the rodeo."

"So," Blue said, watching the colt refuse to look at him, "how come you still have him?"

"I know different," Micah said, and the swift certainty in his tone made Blue smile a little. "That bunch of no-counts couldn't tell a good horse from a mountain goat in the bright light of the Judgment Morning."

Blue glanced at him, then back at the roan. The old man was something else. You had to hand it to him.

"So you're hell-bent on dragging somebody in here that *can* ride him?"

"I reckon you're that somebody," Micah said, with a satisfied chuckle.

A troubled horse would spend a great deal of energy avoiding even eye contact with a human being, and this one was surely troubled. Much more so, without a doubt, than if he'd never been tried by anyone but Micah.

Micah read that thought in Blue's head from outside the pen.

"I hate I ever sent him over there," he said.

"Water under the bridge," Blue said.

He bit his tongue. What was this? Keep it up and he'd be as big a chatterbox as Micah. Although, truth to tell, he probably needed to learn to talk again he'd been silent so long.

The prick of pity he'd felt for Micah being too old to ride this colt wasn't excuse enough to try to please him by fixing the horse. He would help this horse for the horse's sake. He was trying to see if he wanted to buy him, that was all.

When he got close enough, still holding on to the end of

the rope, he threw the halter onto the ground behind the horse. Instead of shifting his feet away from it and moving forward as Blue hoped, the roan kicked at it.

Blue took in a deep breath and then another, forcing them out through his mouth, trying to blow the tension out of him so the horse wouldn't feel it. He reeled the halter back in and threw it again.

The roan started backing up, fast as thought, straight toward Blue, kicking, kicking higher as he came. Blue got out of his way and he kicked the fence with a blow that rang through the air. That settled him down a little bit. He whirled to put his head to the fence again and his butt to Blue.

Blue threw the halter. The colt kicked at it again.

Blue pulled the halter to him and threw it again. The colt kicked.

They did that over and over, until Blue lost track of time and of everything except the fact that this horse was so troubled and so defensive that he did not make one forward movement. Until he did, Blue was not going to quit.

Life narrowed down to that one fact and the sun on his back. Time vanished.

Horses knew no time. All they knew was rhythm, the rhythm of the days, and the waxing and waning of the moon. All Blue knew was the look of this horse and the motion of his own arm, the twist of his wrist.

Throw, reel in, throw, reel in.

The breeze picked up and blew on his skin through the sweat in his shirt. The horse's shadow shifted to a different angle. A hawk flew over and tilted its wings into the wind. Blue and the roan colt kept at it.

It took a long time. Dimly, Blue realized that the afternoon was passing faster and later he saw that Micah was perched on the top log of the pen, over by the gate, but he and the roan didn't let that bother them. The colt quit kicking but he didn't move forward.

Blue changed to his left arm to spell the right one, but he did not let up. Finally, the colt took one forward step. One. And that was all.

At first, Blue wondered if he had imagined it, but no. The kicking had stopped. He switched back to his right arm and threw the halter. Reeled it in. Threw it again.

It took a while. The sun was definitely dropping lower in the west when he reeled the halter in again, threw it again, and the horse took three or four steps forward, one more, a few more and then, like held water flowing over a dam, Blue was driving him around the corral.

The roan let himself be driven but he didn't acknowledge Blue in any other way.

Blue didn't care. If they did nothing but this today, it would be a great victory. He let the rising excitement inside him come a little higher and he stayed with the colt.

The roan chose a deliberate pace and stayed with it, and the energy driving the world became the *lub-dub, lub-dub* sounds of his hooves on the ground. Blue's heart fell into that same beat.

The smell of the horse, the fragrance of manure and stirring dirt, the faraway cry of a bird he couldn't name all filled the old round pen. Still, Blue could see nothing but the horse. The horse and the hope for him to leave his fear behind.

Finally, he let him stop.

He tried to walk up to him, but the roan would have none of that. He reared and offered to strike.

Don't come any closer, man. Keep your distance.

Blue drove him some more. He caused the horse to move and then set his own movements in harmony with him. Slowly, finally, their lone dances began to form a bond between them. Both of them relaxed into the rhythm. They stayed the same distance apart—the roan seemed comfortable with exactly that amount of space—and they moved together.

At last, the roan began to acknowledge Blue with his ears, his eyes, and his arched rib cage curving away from him. Blue smiled so wide it felt like he hadn't used those muscles for years. He took a deep breath and moved, this time farther away from the roan.

The colt followed him. The skin on Blue's arms turned to gooseflesh, as if the animal had already come close enough to blow his breath down the back of his neck.

The farther he went, the more the horse closed the gap between them. He had hooked on. Blue made himself take another deep breath. He could hear his own heartbeat in his ears.

He walked toward the middle of the pen. The roan stayed with him. He stopped. The horse came closer, then he stopped, too, ears pricked, watching Blue.

The colt stood still and let him walk up to him.

The old thrill rose in Blue's blood and, with it, memories of other days, other places, other horses. They galloped back to him, flooding through his mind. So many horses and so many days and weeks and months and years without any of them in the flesh.

He still had trouble believing that this was real. It was.

And now was the test of this invisible connection. Now was the time to make it physical, to make it so it would be true and lasting.

Murmuring to the colt, Blue laid a hand on him. He started rubbing him along the top of his neck. He watched both ends of the horse at once and he knew that he could keep touching this colt only if he did it in a way that was fitting to the roan.

That way was going to be very, very carefully. A wrong move could get him a kick in the belly or a hoof upside his head, but if he listened to what the horse had to say to him, that wouldn't happen. He pinched along the roots of the colt's mane as another horse would nibble him, and used the coiled lead rope to rub him, too.

The roan said it felt good. Very, very good. He let his head drop and his eyelids droop. Blue rubbed his back and his flanks and went back to his neck again.

One more time, then he let the halter and rope fall to the ground. He laid his hand on the sweaty withers and let his weight lean on the colt while he held his other hand out for the horse to take in his scent. Slowly, the colt swung his muzzle around, snorting lightly, scattering drops of moisture into Blue's palm like fresh rain.

They settled there. Their breathing fell into an identical, untroubled pattern, in and out. With their warm flesh and blood pressed together, the thunder power living under the hide of the horse flowed through Blue—into his arm and through his heart down into the Mother Earth beneath his feet.

MICAH HELD to the old cowboy custom of eating in silence and that was a relief to Blue. He was able to pick at his food and drink the hot coffee but he couldn't think about anything except the colt and he sure as hell didn't know what to say. He really didn't want to ever talk about it, even if he knew how.

He'd held himself apart, kept himself isolated, breathed and thought and eaten and stayed alone for ten long years, and an outlaw horse had breached the wall. Being connected to another living being, human or horse or dog, was something so new now that he could barely recall how to deal with it.

As soon as they pushed back from the table and started clearing away, Micah's flood of words started again just like somebody had turned on a faucet.

"Tell you the truth," he said, as he limped to the sink with his plate and the skillet, "I ain't never seen nobody git his hands on a horse by throwing a halter at him all day."

He cackled in delight, shaking his head.

"Them boys over at Little Creek wouldn't believe it if they seen it with their own eyes. I'm near eighty years old and *I* never seen nothing like it."

"I can't take credit for the horsemanship," Blue said. "Buck Brannaman gave a demonstration in Tulsa one time when I was a teenaged kid. He worked 'em horseback, too."

He set his plate on the counter by the sink and carried the remains of the loaf of bread in its plastic sack to the battered cupboard where Micah got it. It all felt strange. A kitchen was a foreign country to him now.

"I heard that name," Micah said. "They say he's a hell of a hand with a horse."

"He is."

Blue glanced around the room after he closed the antique cupboard. He slid his fingertips over its punched tin door as if he were reading Braille.

Any part of a home was unknown to him now. This one smelled rich and ripe with age, with the ghosts of long-dead wood fires drifting out of the chimney and the gleam of low lamplight in the front room.

It recalled Auntie Cheyosie's cabin way back in the woods in Oklahoma. Way back in another life. Way back when Tanasi Rose was alive. She had taken him with her to see the wise old woman many times during his childhood.

Rose wouldn't have killed herself, maybe, if Auntie Cheyosie had still been alive. Or if Dannie had been.

But *he* had been.

Yeah, Bowman, but you might as well have been dead. What comfort were you to her, locked up in a cage a thousand miles away?

"I'm gonna wrangle these here dishes," Micah said suddenly, "you go on in yonder and clean up."

Blue glanced at him. The old man's sharp gaze met his. What had Micah seen on his face?

Micah set the skillet down with a thump.

"Here," he said, "I'll show you the room and what's in it. There's duds you can wear instead of them sweaty ones."

He limped past Blue and gestured for him to follow.

"We've had ever' size of hired hand in the world pass through here one time or another and I reckon half of 'em left somethin' behind. Boots, hats, coats, warbags, you name it, we got it."

Blue crossed the hallway behind him and Micah led the way into a room with two windows, a bed, a chest of drawers, and a closet with the door standing open. Assorted clothes hung on hangers and a jumble of boots covered the floor.

"Help yourself," Micah said. "Gordon's known for running 'em off pronto if they give any lip or if they ain't up to working fourteen hours a day seven days a week with a smile on their face for a wetback's wage. If they leave somethin' behind, ain't no way they come back after it when he told 'em never set foot on the ranch again."

"Nice guy," Blue said.

Micah chuckled.

"Oncet in a great while," he said. "Oncet in a high lonesome blue moon, you might say."

He limped to one of the windows and banged on the sides of it with his fists to loosen it in the frame.

"You ain't workin' for Gordon, remember that," he said. "I got my own operation here."

He wrenched at the bottom of the window with both hands and then slid it up. The fresh, cold night poured in.

"Air this room out a little bit," the old man said.

Two windows. One open. Doors open all the way to the front porch.

If he couldn't sleep inside the walls, he could sleep outside—blankets were piled on the bed. He was tired. Tireder physically than he had been for years. It felt good.

But before sleep he needed the feel of hot water sluicing

down his back and the smell of clean clothes—not prison clothes—in his nostrils.

"Bathroom down the hall," Micah said, and limped past him to the door. "Holler if you need anything."

"Right. Thanks."

The old man stopped and made a quick turn of his stiff body so he could see Blue.

"You've got him now and he's gonna make you a mount that won't quit," he said. "You done a helluva job today."

His voice held traces of envy and regret. But mostly happiness, satisfaction.

"Thanks," Blue said. "It took a while. You didn't have to stay out there all that time."

The old man's bushy eyebrows lifted.

"Never know when I might could lend a hand," he said, with a shrug.

That touched Blue. Nobody had been concerned about his safety for a long, long time.

Micah hesitated, then he said, "Whenever you want, we can get horseback and take him to a bigger pen."

We.

"That'll work," Blue said. "If you furnish the horses."

Micah grinned.

"Get some sleep," he said. "Don't worry, this is your deal. I won't get in your way, son."

Blue returned the grin as Micah left him.

Blue thought about the old man while he unbuttoned his shirt.

Son. We.

Being robbed of a ranch—even this ranch—was nothing. Not compared to being robbed of a father.

CHAPTER THREE

BLUE WOKE in the middle of the night in a cold fit of fear. He sat up, hands fisted, until the memory drifted up out of his sleep. He had turned over without hitting the wall and it had scared him awake.

A bright fall of moonlight poured in through the window. The sturdy old room lay peaceful around him.

A real bed, standing on legs, instead of a bunk hanging from the wall. Real quilts, instead of a scratchy blanket. Micah's house.

The whole of yesterday came flooding back to him.

The Splendid Sky. He was on the Splendid Sky for the first time in his life. He had thought about how that would be since he was old enough to imagine anything—how the land and the house would look and how his father would act. When Blue was really little, in most versions of that daydream, Gordon would explain that he had inadvertently lost track of Rose and her children, and rejoice at finding them again.

Blue hadn't been very old when he'd trashed that little fantasy.

He stared into the curtain of moonlight. Gordon was out there now. Within striking distance.

Blue reached for the clothes Micah had given him and dressed. Loath to risk waking the old man, he ducked out through the window, crossed the porch on the balls of his feet, and stepped off into the space and the brightness.

The night was all space, calling to him like a talking drum. It pumped power into his veins, it set a steady beat going in his blood like the need to dance. Dances and women and horses. Those had made him feel so alive, sometimes he'd thought his heart would burst with the joy of breathing, of being. Until now, he had forgotten completely how that felt.

But he might have a chance to come back to it. The inside of his body hurt as if his heart and all his organs were almost gone to atrophy and the night had begun forcing life back into them. He had horses again, and if luck and God stayed with him as they had in bringing him here, he would have dances and women in his life once more. Maybe even joy.

When Gordon was gone from the face of Mother Earth, then he would feel joy.

He crossed the yard through the shadows of tree limbs floating on the grass. The breeze ruffled his still-damp hair across his shoulders. It sent such a cool freshness into him that he gasped a quick, shivery breath.

Last night he'd been buried alive. Tonight he could fly. Last night he had only memories of moonlight and starlight. Tonight he could fill his eyes with them and rub them into his skin.

Tonight he could look down right at the place where Gordon Campbell slept. He could bail off this hillside and run all the way to the main house and confront him with his sins right now. He savored the thought. But first, he had to plan. He was not going back inside for killing someone who needed to be killed.

Dawn was coming in the air. He felt it as he walked across Micah's road and headed for the edge of the west-facing bluff. Far away, down the valley, a cow bawled. Another one answered. Then, from still farther away drifted the lingering, lonesome howl of a coyote.

Gooseflesh popped up on his arms. Twice blessed by the wild ones—by the sight of the deer and the sound of this coyote—he didn't know how he'd survived so long shut up inside. The beat of his heart quickened again.

He was here, through no plan of his own, so it was meant

to be. He was here in the perfect place to find out Gordon's habits and the best way to get to him. The perfect place to do what he had to do.

Here where he should've lived all his life. Where, if that had happened, his mother and sister would be at this very moment. Alive and beautiful.

Here in this enormous land that smelled of pine trees and sweet grass and snow on the mountains and dust and horse from the pen where he'd left the roan. He walked to the edge of the bluff and looked down. The moonlight glinted off a long body of water on the west side of the valley. All over the east side, man-made lights shone like harsh imitations of stars. The arms of the mountains formed a cradle to keep it all safe.

Had his mother ever seen this? Had Gordon ever brought his young lover to this spot on the bluff to look down on his kingdom?

Had she been happy while she was with Gordon? Had loving him made her happy? When she was a seventeen-year-old on her first job, falling in love with her boss?

Even if it did at the time, why didn't she quit loving him later, when she was so alone and unhappy? She could've stopped if she'd tried. Over the years, she could've married—and loved—any one of a half-dozen good men.

Blue pushed away the old grief and guilt and stared down into the valley at the scattering of steady-burning farm lights standing guard over every building. Security lights.

Gordon was in there behind them. Feeling secure.

For a long time, Blue stood watching, memorizing as much as he could see while the stars faded and the moon began to set. As soon as he could ride the roan outside a pen, he would take him up along the ridge that crossed the road from the highway. That lowest crest circled to the west and south from Micah's place to form the rim of the valley. He would learn the lay of it and every road and trail into and out of the head-quarters.

He would gather some gear in case he had to run into the

mountains and some cash money in case he didn't. He would have Micah take him up on the highway and into town one of these days soon and leave him for a while so he could start pricing things. He hadn't bought anything in so long he didn't remember how to make a deal.

He turned and started back to Micah's. The rising sun was painting the sky pink. The wind reached out to blow his hair back from his face. It was going to be a fine, free day, and a man could never tell how many of those he would be given.

He watched the streaks in the sky go from pink to red, then to orange and purple and blue. This dawn made all of the colors, every color, seem like a separate wonder. His fingers itched to paint. He needed to buy more supplies.

Yes, he'd have a chance to paint a little bit before he took care of Gordon.

And he wanted time to get the colt going well, whether he got to keep him or had to sell him. Whichever way that went, he would need the most he could get out of the horse, in either money or performance.

He stopped and stood quiet for a while, watching the sky's glory dissolve until the tints were as faint as a watercolor, then he walked on toward the barn, thinking about how much Micah might ask for the roan. The few thousand dollars he'd earned off the paintings he'd sold from prison over the years would be enough, he hoped, to buy the roan and a rig of some kind.

Of course, Micah would pay him something for the job riding the colts.

Blue glanced into the round pen as he passed. The colt was standing near the water bucket, eyes closed in a doze.

"Rest up," Blue muttered. "I'll be with you after breakfast."

He took another long draught of morning air off the mountains. Crisp and fresh enough to crackle in his lungs, it carried the promise of a whole new life.

It gave him a fleeting thought of roaming with the colt through the mountains that were turning to purple crystal in the rising light. Roaming, not running. Wandering with no one on the back trail trying to hunt him down.

But when he stepped into the barn and stood in the midst of its aromas of manure and horse and hay and sweet feed all mixed with the smells of aged wood and oiled leather, he wanted not to run *or* roam. What he wanted was to have no reason to leave and, instead, every reason to stay in a place that felt this much like a home.

Micah kept his barn clean and neat and the horses in it were all hanging their heads over the stall doors looking at Blue with trusting, gentle eyes. They talked to him.

Where is it? The morning feed? Are you here to feed us and turn us out?

The peace. For a minute, Blue could feel it like a hand on his shoulder. There was nothing better than an old barn and animals depending on him to center a man.

But there was no peace for him. Not yet. Maybe not ever.

If not, so be it. Rose and Dannie never knew peace.

He went to pull a bale of hay down from the stack. There was a lot of satisfaction in feeding hungry animals. He reached for the wire cutters Micah had stuck by the handle into the cross-timber supporting the wall, and snipped the baling wire. While he broke off flakes and carried them to the stalls, he looked over the horses and kept his mind on them. There was a cute sorrel mare with a wide blaze and a tall gray gelding with black points. Last night, Micah said they both belonged to a friend of his.

The stalls across the aisle held a stocky gelding that Micah said had been his best mount for fifteen years and a young filly who'd been easier for him to start than the roan. She bore a vague resemblance to him. Half sister, maybe, since she had some gentle blood from somewhere.

He liked his roan colt better, though.

That thought made him grin but it also bothered him some. He hadn't even bought him yet, but he must be getting attached to the ornery rascal.

Once they all had fresh hay and water, Blue stopped at the sorrel mare and, murmuring to her, started scratching her nose. Her neighbor, the gray, stuck his head out, too, and reached over to nudge Blue on the shoulder.

"Demanding your share of the attention, hmm, buddy?" Blue said, petting him with his other hand. "I'm thinking Micah's friend has spoiled you both."

They made him laugh, both of them, with their signs of pleasure as he pinched along the toplines of their manes and rubbed their polls. The mare had a sweet spot behind one ear that made her moan when Blue caressed it. She curled her top lip and let the bottom one tremble.

Blue petted them for a long time, not letting himself think, only being. Being with friendly horses, exchanging breaths with them, letting the feel of them comfort his hands. The sun poured into the barn and streamed down the aisle to paint all of them warm and yellow-gold.

GETTING UP and getting outside right before dawn, greeting the morning and the mountains and the horses, became a habit with Blue, if four days in a row could be called a habit. Micah usually slept until daylight and had breakfast ready when Blue went back to the house. After they ate, Blue helped clean up the dishes and then they both went on to their hard day's work—Blue with the roan and the toughest of the twos, and Micah with the ones he'd been able to start on his own. The comfort of the routine was already beginning to ease into Blue's bones.

This morning, he puttered around the barn as if it belonged to him, rearranging the saddles in the tack room and spreading fresh bedding in the stalls. He had fed Micah's friend's horses and they and the roan were about finished with their hay. It was time to get to work.

He knew that but instead of leaving the barn, he fell into a mindless reverie, sweeping out the aisle and feeling the sun on his back through the wide-flung doors. Finally, he roused himself.

"All right," he said, petting the sorrel and then the gray, "I need to get on that ornery roan and you two need to be outside. Ready?"

He turned to take their halters from the wall.

His gaze swept across the west door of the barn and he froze.

From the corner of his eye, he'd caught a glimpse of movement, he would swear it, at the edge of the opening. But he waited and no one stepped into his line of sight.

The hackles lifted on his neck. He kept watching the doorway.

Micah was still in the house, as far as he knew. If not, he certainly wouldn't come to the barn and look in without saying something. That old man liked to talk too much for that. Besides, he wouldn't be sneaking around on his own place.

Maybe it was an animal. Blue crossed the aisle to the opposite side of the door with two silent strides.

He listened. Nothing.

He took a step forward and looked out. No one.

But when he turned to look toward the house out the east end of the barn aisle, he saw him.

Gordon.

Blue knew it the way a horse knew a storm was coming. He knew it, even though all he could see was his back as he strode toward the house.

Walking away, Gordon gave off the feeling that he was advancing instead. He wore ordinary clothes. A battered Resistol, faded jeans, and a plain white shirt made him look like a thousand other men, but every line of his substantial body gave that the lie. Tall, broad-shouldered, with hair as white as his shirt curling at his neck, he walked with a rare authority. The way his feet touched the ground told anybody with eyes to see that these acres belonged to him.

It was an easy arrogance he wore, simple as his clothes, one that never expected to be challenged.

Blue's gut stretched, then tightened like a guitar string. His hands were trembling. Gordon had looked in on him as he would a horse in a stall, and had walked away without a word.

Which was one step up from the way he'd treated him his whole life.

It wasn't until Gordon had reached the porch, walked up on it and shouted for Micah that Blue realized how shaken he was and how tangled his thinking. Gordon didn't know him. Gordon had no clue that his son was there.

Or that now it was Blue watching him.

THE ROAN COLT KICKED the trailer just as they were pulling out of the yard with him. Kicked it so hard it sounded like the metal split in two.

Micah shook his head and flashed a grin at Blue.

"Just like old times," he said.

Blue moved on over against the door and sat sideways so he could look through the back window at the colt.

"Aw, now, cut us some slack," he said. "We've not had our hauling lesson yet."

"That's what you get for babyin' him along," Micah said. "Seven or eight days of playin' games and pettin' and such carryings on. That's liable to ruin any horse. Why don't you just tote him around on a pillow?"

"Yeah," Blue said. "Reckon I ought to tie his nose to his tail or whatever it was that the Little Creek boys did to him. That's the way to get control of this outlaw."

"On second thought, take your time," Micah said.

Blue chuckled, too, as the old rig straightened out on the gravel road and headed for the asphalt one that ran between the highway and the valley. Then his stomach clutched.

He might see Gordon today. Face to face. The big indoor arena wasn't very far from the main house. It was Gordon's arena.

It galled him to use anything of Gordon's. Yet it had occurred to him that he was entitled, after all—as the son and heir.

Yeah. Right.

"Micah," he said, "do we pay a fee to use the indoor? You said your operation's separate from Gordon's."

Micah shot him a narrow-eyed glance while he shifted gears.

"It is," he said. "But I done paid that rent. Years ago. Workin' for nothin' but grub and bed them first coupla years and short pay for five or six more."

"That's you," Blue said. "This is my horse."

Micah shrugged. "Then you can pay the same way," he said.

"Hell'll freeze over before I work for Gordon."

Micah gave him a look. "I meant pay me."

"With which? Working for only grub and bed? Or short pay?"

The old man grinned and mashed his foot down on the accelerator.

"Ain't my cookin' worth every dusty, bone-jarring minute of every ride?"

Blue squinted back at him. "I wouldn't go so far as to say *that*."

Micah raised one scraggly eyebrow. "Think about my biscuits," he said. "They're better'n any canned biscuit you ever did eat."

"Canned biscuits don't set the bar too high," Blue said.

"Stubborn man," Micah muttered to himself. "Hardheaded as a mule."

He shook his head sorrowfully, then turned and fixed Blue with one of his piercing looks.

"Why're you in a fret about using that arena?"

"No way will I be beholden to Gordon."

"How come?"

"I don't like him."

"How do you know that? You ain't even met the man."

"I despised him the minute I laid eyes on him."

"You didn't even know who that *was* the minute you seen him. Not 'til I told you."

"I knew him. Who else would step up on your porch and holler for you like you'd damn well better appear right then and be all ears when you got there?"

Micah clicked his teeth and looked out across the valley. "Sounds like prejudging to me. Or jumping to conclusions, I'd say."

"I knew I didn't like him the same way you'd know a horse you didn't like."

"Lotsa times, a man has to get close to a horse to know that."

"If there's gonna be any question at all about me bringing my horse into that arena, I'd rather haul out to the fairgrounds," Blue said. "I saw we passed them that day on the way in."

"Look, son," Micah said. "You can set your mind to rest. Every horse in my barn and in my pastures is my deal. I ain't started a horse for Gordon for right at ten years and he ain't got a dime in anything I own."

He gunned the motor and pushed it up to sixty, but when they got close to turning onto the road that ran out to the highway, he sucked in his breath and started pumping the brakes. "Hey, what the hell?"

Blue turned toward the noise of another vehicle coming. Another pickup, a big white one, was roaring downhill into the valley.

Micah got their rig stopped just before the dually reached the intersection. It swerved to the right as it passed them, as if they were still moving into its path.

Blue caught a glimpse of long blond hair beneath a cowboy hat and a woman's slender hand on the wheel, then all he could see was the rear end of the truck fishtailing. Ahead of it, he saw why.

A fawn, with the doe too far ahead, flashed across the road in a blur of tan and white and away into the trees in the blink of an eye, the truck missing it by a hair. The woman ran off the asphalt onto the shoulder of the road and corrected too fast back up over the edge of the pavement.

"That's Andie Lee," Micah said. "God *damn it*, that girl's

gonna kill herself to save a *fawn* and I'll have to set right here and see it."

The big pickup spun around in a full circle twice, ran astraddle of the right-hand edge of the pavement for a hundred yards or so and then left the road for good, headed south in its original direction. The woman managed to run it down the ditch awhile, then it took a jump or two and hit a bank of earth, slowed, finally jarred to a stop, lurched, lifted on one side and rocked as it threatened to roll. Finally, it landed and stayed upright on all six tires.

Micah started shifting gears. "Maybe she ain't hurt, after all," he said.

He didn't take his eyes from the white truck as he sawed on the steering wheel, gunned the motor and started toward it.

Blue stared at it, too, hoping that the woman wasn't hurt—for her own sake but also, selfishly, for his. He didn't need to get involved in anybody's upset. He didn't even want any contact with anybody but the roan and Micah.

They plunged downhill as fast as Micah could push his old rig, but the woman was faster and she opened the driver's door before they could get there. She half jumped, half fell from the running board down to the ground, a distance of about three feet since the truck was angled high on the left.

She had lost the hat and her golden hair caught the light from the sun. Her legs were long and slender in jeans and boots. Clinging to the door for only a second to get her balance, she looked to see them approaching, pushed her loose hair out of her face, and started climbing up the side of the ditch to meet them on the road.

Micah slowed, Blue opened the door, and she got in before they even came to a stop. Her eyes met his for one direct instant, as if to see who he was. Or whether he could help her.

They were gray, storm-cloud eyes with a sure purpose. That was clear even through the fear and relief.

"Girl, you are mighty lucky," Micah said. "I thought you was a goner for sure. Scared me half to death."

"Baby," she said, gasping for air. "Couldn't bear to hit it."

She pointed down the road while she dragged in enough breath to talk more. "Go, Micah," she said. "Shane's in trouble again."

Her voice was a little bit low, with a catch in it.

Micah blurted, *"Damn,"* and stepped on the gas.

Blue reached behind her, with the truck already moving again, and slammed the door closed. The woman's slender body fell into the curve of his arm. That was such an unfamiliar sensation it roused his instinct to really hold her. That and the fact that she was shaking. Her back pressed against his taut bicep, but she didn't seem aware of him.

"He got drugs again?" Micah asked.

Sympathy twinged in Blue. She cared about somebody like Dannie.

"He's got a *gun* and he's holding his girlfriend hostage. We've reached a whole new low."

Now her voice sounded cold as a rock on the bottom of the river. Anger. It was anger that had her trembling.

"That stupid-ass Jason is no di-rector at all," Micah said.

The woman bent over and slammed her thighs with her fists. Her hair fell forward and pooled in Blue's lap, then she raised her head and it whipped past his face.

It smelled like flowers. That and the woman-scent of her skin went all through him. Fragrance from another universe.

She arched her back, twisted up to fish something out of her pocket, dropped back down and scraped her hair away from her face with both hands. She pulled it all together and fastened it flat against her neck with a heavy silver clip.

"I have such a *rage* in me I could wreck the world," she said, slamming her fists on her thighs again.

Micah shot her a sideways glance.

"You done wrecked your truck," he said. "Ain't that enough?"

She shook her head and stared straight ahead with her lips pressed together. Too near tears now to talk, probably.

Or not. With her hair out of the way Blue could see the pure line of her jaw. Hard and determined.

Blue moved his arm and braced his hand against the door frame to hold himself away from her, trying to give her some room and still keep his legs out of the stick shift but they were all three jammed together in the narrow old cab and there was no space to put between them. Her thigh trembled against his.

"What the hell else am I supposed to do?" she cried. "What *can* I do?"

"Honey, you're doin' all you can," Micah said. "It's like a man who's a slave to whiskey."

She whipped her head around to look at him and leaned across Blue to get even closer as if Micah had to see her lips to hear her.

"I can't come this far and fail," she said. "I can't. I won't. I've given everything I've got to this fight for two years and I'm not quitting now. What else can I do?"

Her face was so close to Blue's her breath was warm on his chin. He could see that she was not wearing one speck of makeup and she was beautiful.

He also could see that her eyes were full of tears but she wouldn't let them spill out. He admired that.

Like her jawline, her cheekbones showed strong underneath her light tan. Her eyelashes were long and thick, much darker than her hair, and the wing of her brow made a perfect arch that he wanted to trace with his fingertip.

"Who called you?" Micah asked.

"Tracie. She said it all started about two hours ago. Gordon told her not to call me but she couldn't bear it—she thought I had a right to know."

Andie Lee's breath came more easily now.

"I just went to the post office," she said. "I can't even go to town for two hours without getting a call that he's in trouble again. Micah, I want to *throttle* him. I have worked twenty-four/seven for years for his sake and he has no more gratitude or appreciation or consideration for me than my hateful cat does."

Micah drove faster. The trailer lurched along behind them with the roan standing quiet for once. Blue wished he would act up just to draw her attention away from all this pain.

"Shane and the girl may only want a little time together," Micah said, trying to soothe her.

"Not if Lisa's begging for help and Jason's calling the highway patrol in here."

The words snapped off her tongue.

"Then let the highway patrol handle it," Micah said.

She flashed him a look that would melt metal.

"They—and *wise Gordon*—have been trying to handle it for over an hour."

Blue took a quick glance at her face. Evidently she didn't think much of Gordon.

"I'm his *mother*," she said, with that same natural dignity that held back her tears. "They should let me talk to him."

That shocked Blue. His mother? How old was she, anyway? This Shane must be a teenager or nearly so if he was taking girls hostage at gunpoint.

If he'd thought about it, he would've guessed she was in her twenties. He sneaked another look while she leaned across him toward Micah again.

"They should let *me* talk to him. Gordon's been trying to do it himself, since they don't have a professional negotiator in here yet. Tracie said he's so furious with Jason for calling in the law that he's about to strangle him."

She could be thirty, maybe. There were tiny crow's feet at the corners of her eyes.

Micah drove faster. They careened around a turn that led off to the west long before they got near the main headquarters.

"What kind of gun is it?" Micah asked. "Where in hell did he get it?"

"A handgun, a twenty-two," she said. "Where and how

he got it, I don't have a clue. I know the counselors can't watch them every second, but they could do better than this."

Now the whole length of her leg lay smooth and warm against Blue's.

"He's a big boy and nobody can control him, honey," Micah said.

Andie Lee jerked away from him and leaned forward in a sudden movement as if to make the truck go faster. She stared through the windshield into the distance.

Blue felt a chill. The line of her body reminded him of Rose's long ago, yearning into the dark from their tiny front porch in Tahlequah, willing her darling Dannah to appear out of the night.

CHAPTER FOUR

"I TOLD GORDON instead of building that goddamn rehab center he oughtta put them boys to work," Micah said. "That'll cure 'em. Let 'em buck hay bales when it's a hundred in the shade and then load 'em up again and haul 'em out on the ice and bust 'em for the cows when it's twenty below and they'll be too tired to go looking for dope or guns."

Andie Lee didn't answer.

Taking advantage of her silence to try to distract her, Micah said, "This here's Blue Bowman, Andie. Blue, Andie Lee Hart, Gordon's daughter."

Blue took a breath that dragged her flowery woman-smell deeper into him. Gordon had a *daughter?* A daughter other than Dannie? Another daughter—one he was helping in her time of trouble.

It fit. She looked like a rich rancher's daughter. She had that air of position and privilege. Her jeans were faded Wranglers and her boots were broken-in and battered, but there was nothing ordinary about her. The boots were fine and custom-made. That silver clip. Shiny hair, silky-looking skin.

Then it hit him as they both turned at the same time to look each other full in the face. This woman was his half sister.

"*Step*daughter," she said, quick and hard. "Gordon's not my father."

She looked deep into his eyes to make sure that he got it.

Then she gave him the barest nod and turned away to begin boring a hole with her gaze through the windshield again.

"I just hope they don't shoot him, Micah," she said, too quietly.

"They won't," he said. "You're gonna talk him into giving up."

Stepdaughter.

So. Gordon must've divorced the first wife he'd had back when he'd refused to marry Rose.

"Shane's never done anything violent before," Andie Lee said. "Never. You know that, Micah, as well as I do."

"And he ain't yet," Micah said, with a forced calm in his voice.

He did drive even faster, however. Too fast around a curve in the winding road. The roan kicked the trailer again—so hard it rocked the old truck and Micah cursed, just under his breath.

They headed downhill again, toward another cluster of ranch buildings. A sign beside the road came into view.

GORDON CAMPBELL RECOVERY CENTER

Blue ran his eye over the neat, low buildings—bunkhouses, cottages, barns and pens—all built to seem rustic but they were fairly new. Good lord. Gordon was trying to work his way into heaven.

Did he build all this just because Andie Lee's son had a drug problem?

"Shane's in the recreation hall," Andie Lee said, pointing it out.

Then she added sarcastically, "Naturally, he's not in a classroom or a barn."

"That's what I mean—They want to straighten these kids out, they got to learn 'em what work is," Micah said.

But now his voice sounded shaky. Micah was worried. Micah really cared for Andie Lee and her son so they must be worth liking.

They started driving past the first building, one with Gordon's name on it.

"Tracie said Shane and the girl are in the game room," Andie Lee said. "It's on the back of the office."

"I'm going with you," Micah said.

She gave him a quick smile, the first smile Blue had ever seen on her.

"Park over there," she said, pointing. "I want to surprise them and get in before they try to keep me out."

Micah pulled into a paved area that held another patrol car and several more vehicles, mostly pickup trucks, and parked his rig parallel to one of the landscapings of bushes and small trees. He turned the key off and opened his door.

Andie Lee was out of the truck and around the front of it, reaching for his arm by the time he could get his stiff limbs out from behind the wheel, and they took off at a hobbling run up the little hill toward the rec hall. Blue watched them go.

So. Gordon's stepgrandson was dealing drugs and holding girls hostage. Sins of the fathers visited, as usual, upon the children and the children's children—because, judging from the way Andie Lee said Gordon wasn't her father, he hadn't tried to be a daddy to her, either.

He and Dannah weren't the only ones. There had been other children Gordon had neglected. Knowing that made him angry for her, too.

The roan stamped and nickered. Blue looked around just in time to see him sit down and halfheartedly twist on his tie rope. That'd be trouble nobody needed right now.

Blue opened the door and got out.

"No sense in choking yourself again," he said as he walked up to the trailer. "That will get you nowhere, buddy. You know that."

The colt did it again.

"Aw, come on," Blue crooned. "You'll have to get over

this hating to be tied. But later. I'm not set up for that lesson today."

Still talking to the horse, he stepped up onto the running board near the roan's head. The colt rolled an eye at him and listened as if he understood every word. But the stubborn look in his eye didn't change any and that made Blue chuckle as he untied the rope and let it drop.

A sharp scream tore the air. The roan, loose in the trailer now, threw up his head and listened.

A second scream, this one closer. Blue leaned out backward to look toward the rec hall.

"No! Sha-a-ne! Stop!"

A girl's high voice, terrified. For an instant he couldn't see her and then he did, her face bobbing out from behind the boy running toward him, brandishing a handgun over his head with one hand while he dragged the girl along with the other. Blue's pulse leaped, his gaze fixed on the gun. Somebody could get killed right here, right now. For no reason.

Farther back, four or five men were jostling out through the doorway of the recreation building, rushing past Andie Lee and Micah who were both white-faced and wide-eyed. All of them were chasing after the kids.

Except for Gordon. Within the commotion, Blue saw him walk up to Andie Lee and take her arm.

"Hey! Stop! Stop where you are!" somebody yelled.

It was the man at the head of the pack, the other one besides Gordon who wasn't dressed in a law-enforcement uniform. Unlike Gordon, though, the front-runner wasn't dressed for the ranch—he wore slacks and a loose-fitting shirt.

Andie Lee's Shane kept barreling toward Blue. His eyes, wilder than the roan's, strained toward the vehicles parked down by the cedar trees. He actually thought he could take one of them and get out of here, that determination was in every line of his tall, coltish body.

Blue flattened himself against the side of the trailer, murmuring to the horse, who, in spite of the girl's continued screams had become surprisingly calm. For Roanie. All he did was stand there and paw the floor.

"Turn loose of the girl and the law'll go easier on you!" yelled one of the men who was chasing Shane.

Blue leaned out far enough to see where they were. The kid had his mouth open now as if to reply but instead he was using his breath to keep running. He had lowered the gun and was waving it back and forth in front of him, ready to aim at any second. When he reached the nose of Micah's battered truck, not slowing, jerking the girl around like a puppet, Blue got ready.

Shane passed the bed of the truck.

Blue stepped down into his path.

"What's your hurry, son?" he said.

Shocked, eyes rolling white, Shane slowed and tried to swerve away.

Blue grabbed the gun.

Shane came after it. The girl slammed into his back and they stumbled into Blue with Shane's long, skinny arm still reaching for the weapon. Blue stuck it into the back of his own waistband and took hold of the boy.

The kid was wasted. His upper arm was nothing but a stick of bone, yet he was nearly as tall as Blue. He was just like Dannie when she'd lost so much weight her skull showed through her face.

The clutch of breathless men swarmed all over them. They separated the two kids, surrounded each one, and took the boy from Blue. Gordon parted the crowd as he brought Andie Lee to her son.

With her face pale as milk, she took the boy's arm in both her hands as if to pull it away from the lawman who was cuffing his wrists behind his back. She was saying something to him but Shane ignored her completely.

"Thanks a *lot,* man!"

It took a second for Blue to realize that he was the target of the sarcastic remark, shouted over the buzz of voices and the girl's loud sobs. The hateful, fearful look in the kid's eyes was fixed on him.

"You're right to thank me," Blue said. "Kidnapping might be a charge even your grandpa can't fix."

"He's not my grandpa! And I don't want him to fix anything—I want him to throw me out. Then Andie Lee couldn't keep me here."

He turned the poison glare onto his mother. She stared back, anger tightening her face over the worry. She let go of him. Then he lifted his chin defiantly and moved his eyes to Gordon.

"You stupid little *shit,*" Gordon said. "You ought to be horsewhipped."

Shane, even though he was trembling, didn't look away from Gordon's piercing blue glare.

"I'll take that weapon," one of the lawmen said, as he stepped up to Blue.

Blue took the gun in his hand, broke it open, and tilted it, but no rounds fell out into his palm. He spun the chamber. Nothing. The old gun was well oiled and in good condition but it wasn't loaded.

Blue offered it and the lawman took it to perform the same ritual all over again.

"Empty!" Andie Lee cried. "Shane, you mean you used an empty gun to make Jason call out the highway patrol?"

"You want me to kill somebody? Shoot up the place?"

He looked away from Gordon to sneer at her. His curled lip reminded Blue of the roan colt.

"You don't want me to embarrass *Gordon,* right? That's more important than Jason listening to lies about me and me being falsely accused and deserted by my *girl,* right?"

He turned his malevolent stare on the weeping girl, who lifted her face from her hands to stare back.

"You're an asshole, Shane Hart," she screamed. "I hate you. In your *dreams* I'm your girl—and don't you ever say that again!"

That hurt him but he covered it quickly.

"Shut up, stupid Lisa," he said. "All I wanted you for was a hostage, don't you know that?"

"Fine. And now you don't have one anymore."

"It's all your fault, anyhow," he said. "You started this with your lies."

"They weren't lies! I saw you, I heard you, I *bought* from you!"

"Lisa the liar," he said scornfully.

It came out weak, though, because his voice broke on the last word. He was so young, Blue thought. Fifteen, maybe.

"What were you thinking, son? Where were you headed when you ran out of there?"

It was the lawman who had hold of his arm.

"To find my dad."

He'd managed to recover his hateful tone, but it was sheer bravado. He wouldn't even turn to see who had hold of him. His eyes filled with the panic of knowing he was trapped.

He lifted his head and stared his challenge at Blue again.

"It's all *your* fault," he said. "If you'd minded your own business I'd be on the road, headed to my dad right now."

The look in Shane's gray eyes was so raw Blue couldn't look away. The wings of his collarbone stuck up through his T-shirt, sharp enough to poke through his skin.

"My dad would b-break your face if he was here," he said to Blue.

"You don't *have* a dad to do jack for you, boy," Gordon boomed, scornful of Shane's fantasy. "You haven't noticed that yet?"

Andie Lee gasped. Shane flinched as if from a blow.

Gordon held him with a terrible glare.

"If you *did* have a daddy you'd be nothing but a disgrace to his name," Gordon said. "It's your mother who's killing herself trying to help you."

"Shut up!" Shane yelled, his voice panicky.

But Gordon was relentless.

"You haven't got the sense God gave a wooden goose. Look at you—fooling with that stinking dope again, stealing guns and kidnapping girls like some little outlaw wanna-be."

Gordon took a threatening step toward the boy.

"And telling me to shut up is another piece of stupidity. If you ever show disrespect like that to me again, I'll hang your hide on the fence just like any other coyote's."

That took the sand out of Shane. His jaw sagged and tears sprang into his eyes. Helpless, he pulled at his hands anyway, but all he could do was stand there with his face naked in front of the world.

Blue stepped up closer, set himself between the kid and Gordon and all the rest of them. Gordon was one cold bastard.

The boy held his own, kept on trying to stare Blue down until his eyes were so full of tears he had to blink them away.

He was tough enough, though, that he never let them fall.

That gave him strength. He got a handle on himself and the tears went away but his gaze stayed on Blue's.

Don't get in my way again. I hate you. You can't stop me next time. Nobody can stop me next time.

Those eyes held another message, too, though.

I'm scared. I'm caught and I'm handcuffed and I'm scared.

Not half as scared as he would be at the end of the road he was taking.

Gordon pushed in between them.

"You could be in jail for weeks—for years, maybe," he said. "I'm gonna leave you there. *I'm* gonna decide when you get out. *I'm* gonna decide when and *if* you come back here. Think about it."

"*You* think about *this*," Shane said, his voice strengthening with each word. "Chase Lomax is my dad and he'd do anything for me. Insult him again and it'll be the last time you insult anybody."

Andie Lee cried out and grabbed his arm again. She talked to him some more. In a low tone that held a whole world of fury and sorrow.

Blue stepped away. He couldn't bear to hear it.

Gordon made a gesture to the highway patrolman, who took Shane and started toward the patrol car. Andie Lee stuck right with them and so did Gordon, talking in a low voice to the lawman.

Shane's shoulders sagged and he hung his head so far down he couldn't see ahead of him while he walked. The guy in the slacks and silk shirt followed and touched Shane's shoulder.

Shane threw his head up like a spooked deer and twisted toward him. "Jason," he said, his voice louder than before. "Thanks for nothing, dude."

"Get back," the lawman said, motioning Jason away, keeping Shane moving.

Andie Lee kept her shoulders straight and her spine stiff, yet the way she looked at her wayward son reminded Blue of Rose again. Money didn't always make a difference, after all. Not after the addiction took hold.

"Shane. Man. When you get back, we'll talk about it," Jason called. "We can adjust your…rewards, Shane. In your treatment program. And I'll…"

The other three went on toward the patrol car, but Gordon turned and started back for Jason, his sardonic voice lashing out like a whip.

"Don't worry your pretty little head about it, Jason. You're gone, too. Hit the road."

Jason's head turned around fast. He stared at Gordon and backed up a couple of steps.

"Mr. Campbell, it isn't my fault that Shane…"

Gordon grabbed hold of his collar at the back of his neck and shoved him forward into a stumbling stagger.

"Make tracks off this place and don't ever let me see you again," he yelled. "If you can't keep drugs out of here you can't get these kids off of 'em."

He pointed at the office building with *GORDON CAMP-BELL TREATMENT CENTER* written above the door.

"Get your stuff and get out. Ten minutes."

Jason flushed bright red. He whirled around to face Gordon but he didn't stop moving, walking backwards, glaring and pouting like a kid. He looked nearly as young as Shane, but Blue judged him to be in his late twenties, maybe.

Only six or eight years younger than Blue, but it might as well be a hundred—one glance and a man could see that Jason'd had it soft all his life.

"You're just angry," he said, "because I called the police. That's it, isn't it, Mr. Campbell? You want to be the law and the judge and the jury all by yourself. But kidnapping and threatening someone with a gun is a serious matter, one for the authorities, and—"

"On this ranch I *am* the goddamned law," Gordon roared. "And no judge or jury on earth can save your job, so shut your trap and do what I tell you, boy, before I stick my boot up your worthless ass and kick you into the next county."

Jason was scared but he was as stubborn as Gordon. He, too, was accustomed to being the boss. He'd probably grown up a spoiled brat.

"There's no need for you to use abusive language," he said, his eyes blazing, his cheeks even redder with fury and embarrassment. "I'm afraid I'll have to report this to the board and…"

Gordon went after him.

"I've been paying you big bucks and this kid's still an addict, just like he was the first day you saw him," Gordon yelled, pointing at Shane. "You're worthless. Not get the hell out of here while you're still able to walk."

Jason turned around, fast, and started toward his office at a jog trot. Finally, everybody else moved, too.

The lawman opened the door to the back seat of his car and didn't even bother to put his hand on Shane's head, it was already bent so low. Shane got in and Andie Lee moved as if to get into the front seat, but the highway patrolman shook his head and Gordon went to talk to her. The other authorities started back up the hill to the recreation center.

Micah turned and walked slowly to Blue, heavily favoring his bad knee.

Once there, he stood looking back at Andie Lee. Blue looked at her, too.

She stood with her hand on the door handle, still trying to get a grip on the situation by talking to the patrolman across the top of his car. Gordon, scornful and fierce, was bent over to look in at Shane and berate him again.

"Damn shame," Micah said. "It's nothin' but a goddamn shame. Andie Lee was the sweetest girl ever lived and she's growed up to be a good, hardworking woman. She don't deserve such hell."

"Not many people do," Blue said.

"No, and them that does don't seem to catch it," Micah said. "Leastways, not on this earth."

Blue stared at Gordon. "Once in awhile they do," he said.

"I figure we orter help each other through the rough patches," Micah said. "No tellin' when we'll hit one of our own."

Blue whipped his head around. Micah had him locked in his sharp sights.

"Helpin' somebody else can take a man's mind off his own trouble."

"What're you talking about?" Blue said. "I can't help Andie Lee, if that's what you mean."

He tasted her name on his tongue.

"You can help that boy," Micah said. "You seen that look he give you, and don't try to tell me you didn't. Shane has some respect for you when he don't have none for nobody else."

"You heard him," Blue said. "He hates my guts for getting in his way."

"Yeah, but he admires you for it, too," Micah said. "Ever'body else chasin' around like a bunch of chickens with their heads cut off and you put the kibosh on the whole deal in a heartbeat. He's glad you done it, he just won't admit it."

Blue turned toward the truck.

Micah came along behind him. Blue could hear his boot-heel scrape against the dirt.

"Your horse is loose," Micah said. "You know that?"

"I untied him to keep him from hanging himself again," Blue said. He strode to the truck, jerked open the door, got in and slammed it shut.

Micah stopped at his window. "You'd do that fer a horse but not fer a boy?"

Blue ignored him.

Micah went around and got in on the driver's side. He closed his door, reached for the key and fired up the old truck. Then he just sat there.

The roan kicked the tailgate of the trailer hard enough to knock it down.

"The horse is mine," Blue said.

"Because you're the one can handle him," Micah said.

"Because I paid money for him."

"No," the old man said, shaking his head to lament Blue's

willful blindness, "it's because you can bring him along to be all the horse he's made to be. You're the one he can connect with, so he is your horse."

Blue turned and glared at him.

Micah met his look with one just as unyielding, shifted gears, and put the truck in motion.

"Ownership," Micah said. "It's a funny deal. Is it who holds the papers or who's got the know-how to put a thing to use? Gordon holds the papers on this ranch. He uses a lot of it and he's a top hand at breeding and raising cattle and horses and feed. Lots of jobs connected with them things he can do better than any other man on this place."

He swung the truck around to head back to the road, pausing in his sermon only long enough to spit out the window.

"But there's parts of this ranch Gordon don't even know *how* to use. So who's the real owners then? Jemmy in the machine shop. Toby in the show barn. Me in my wranglin' pen and my garden spot."

"I don't own Shane just because I stopped him from running away," Blue said. "He belongs to Andie Lee."

Micah shook his head.

"She holds the papers on him," he said. "But you're the man with the juice when it comes to that boy."

Blue snorted. "You're smoking something besides tobacco," he said.

Micah shook his head. "Nope."

Amazingly enough, for another minute, he didn't say a word. He just looked at Blue, his hands loose on the wheel while the old truck followed the road.

"I may never get another thing out of that colt," Blue said. "As far as we are now may be as far as we go."

Micah nodded and broke into a grin that made his eyes crinkle at the corners. "Sounds like plain old life to me," he said.

He slapped Blue on the shoulder as if they had just come to an agreement and pulled the rig back from the edge of the Center's gravel road.

"Yessir," he said, speeding up a little, "from where I sit, looks like the best any of us can ever do is just go ahead and hook up and hope for the best."

Hope for the best wasn't going to cut it for Shane.

Blue raised his voice to carry over the rattling of the rig. "What could I do for him, anyhow?"

"For starters, let him ride with you," Micah said. "That roan colt could teach him as much as he's teaching you and you could teach Shane more, too."

Blue's stomach tied into a hard knot.

"You heard Gordon," he said. "The kid could be gone a long time—maybe he'll use his influence to get him sent to reform school."

"He'll bring him home in a day or two," Micah said. "Gordon aims to be the one that gets him off the dope for Andie Lee. Gordon likes to prove he can do what nobody else can."

"The way he's going about it, he'll drive him to it instead."

"How would you go about it?" Micah asked.

Blue sensed the trap. "I wouldn't."

"Horses heal a lot of wounds," Micah said, completely undeterred. "Shane likes horses but he never has stayed with 'em because he likes them drugs more."

He drove on out to the main ranch road, then stopped and looked both ways as if the traffic was terrible instead of nonexistent.

"You still want to go down to the arena?"

"No," Blue said. "Let's go see about using the fairgrounds."

"That haulin' is a waste," Micah said. "And you won't spite Gordon any by not usin' his facilities, if spite's what you're after."

Blue shrugged. "I'll get my own rig soon. 'Til then, I'll pay you mileage."

"Gas money ain't what I'm talkin' about and you know it," Micah said, wheeling out onto the road. "They'll never let the boy off the place to go up there to ride with you."

To find my dad.

Blue could still hear the crack in the boy's voice. Shane had been lost in those same fatherless feelings Blue had felt at that age—although he had been too proud to ever try to go to his dad.

That had been Dannie, always wanting to go find Gordon. And then, when she had finally ridden all the way to Montana on the back of a drug dealer's motorcycle, she had ended up dead before she ever saw the Splendid Sky.

Micah glanced in his rearview mirror.

"Looks like we're leadin' the parade," he said.

Blue turned but the roan colt filled his vision.

"Who is it?"

"Patrolman with Shane. Follered by Gordon's truck. Andie Lee's talked him into bringing her to be with her boy as long as she can."

The patrolman passed them. Shane still had his head down. But when the car pulled directly in front of them, he twisted around and looked back. Straight at Blue. Their eyes met.

I'm so scared. I don't know what to do. What can I do?

Then Gordon's truck passed them and whipped in between the trailer and the patrolman. Andie Lee sat in the passenger seat, staring straight ahead, looking at Shane.

"Boys fifteen, sixteen, twenty years old think they've got the bit in their teeth," Micah said. "They don't know they can get hurt bad or die."

Blue could remember how that felt, too. He'd been immortal. He could do anything.

And he *had* done a lot of it—he'd ridden the worst ones

in all the rodeos, he'd fought the biggest bullies out behind the chutes, he'd driven the old trucks the fastest and dived off the highest bluff into the river. He'd danced with the wildest girls in the honky-tonks and made the best love to them in the grass.

But he had never fought the demon of drugs that had hold of Dannah. If he had gotten into dope back then, he might've proved to be mortal, too.

That same demon had hold of Shane.

Blue hadn't been there for Dannah, not when she'd needed him the most. Because she wouldn't let him. Would Shane let him?

If he could make a difference for Shane, it would be for Dannie's sake. All he'd been able to do for her was avenge her death.

Andie Lee's truck came in sight, its nose buried in the soft earth like an ostrich trying to hide its head in the sand.

Rose had been in such despair that she'd driven her car off the road, too. Into a tree.

If Shane went to prison, Andie Lee would share another great grief with Tanasi Rose. And if the boy got hold of another gun, he, too, could very well be in there for murder.

The roan whinnied and ran from one end of the twenty-foot trailer to the other. That rocked the truck and it pulled to one side. Blue turned to look through the back window just in time to see the colt brace himself and kick the side with a cracking blow.

"Onery sucker," Micah said. "You'll play hell trying to ride him out in public."

"What was that saying of yours about all we can do is hook up and hope for the best?" Blue said.

"Huh," Micah said, "I'm jist glad you remember what I tell you."

"It's not easy," Blue said. "You talk so much it wears out my ears trying to sift for nuggets of wisdom."

"Here's another one," Micah said. "Look off down there at that valley. Then let your eyes drift up and up over them mountains. You won't ever see as handsome a place anywhere—not on this wicked old world, you won't."

Blue looked.

They drove on in silence. There, to the right, stood the old round pen, the house and the barn that belonged to Micah because he was the one who put them to use.

Straight ahead lay the highway.

The rig slowed on the uphill grade.

"Which way?" Micah said.

Blue threw him a slant-eyed look.

"Fairgrounds," he said.

Micah drove all the way on out to the highway and turned toward town in silence. A miracle.

Blue was thankful for it. He pushed back his hat and leaned into the open window to feel the wind on his face. Ahead, the highway stretched empty.

But he kept seeing the patrolman's car and Shane looking back at him.

They'll never let the boy off the place to go ride with you.

Good. He didn't want to get involved with the kid. And he hadn't been free long enough yet to *choose* to do something he hated—like seeing Gordon humiliate Shane.

The irony of it struck him in a hard revelation. All Blue's life he'd wanted Gordon to be his daddy, yet he'd probably been better off without him.

Micah slowed, then pulled off the road into a wide gravel parking lot filled with trucks and trailers of every kind and size, some empty, some full of bawling cattle. An auctioneer's voice echoed from inside one of the barns.

Micah cut the motor and folded his arms on the wheel to wait.

"Secretary in the sale office is who you need to see."

Blue got out and closed the door, his boot heels crunching on the gravel. But after he'd stepped away, he turned back.

"Micah. Does Gordon talk to Shane like that all the time?"

"Yep."

Blue turned and looked off down the road.

Finally, he reached for the door handle.

"Aw, hell," he said. "Let's go."

CHAPTER FIVE

"DO YOU ALWAYS have to talk to Shane that way?"

Andie Lee turned on Gordon the minute he pulled his truck away from the police station. She shouldn't. Shane was at Gordon's mercy and Gordon tolerated no questioning, ever.

But she couldn't pull together enough caution to stop herself. She wanted to punish him for telling Shane—and in front of half the world, too—that he had no father. She wanted to be rid of Gordon Campbell and never have to be indebted to him for another thing as long as she lived.

He took his time getting onto the road, then threw her the briefest of glances, one that slashed her with scorn.

"You mean do I always have to tell him the bare-assed truth?"

"No, I mean do you always have to deliberately humiliate him?"

"There's the reason your kid's in trouble today," he said. "You."

She turned cold all over, when she'd just been hot.

Pray God it wasn't true. But of course, she had been afraid that it was, ever since the trouble started with Shane.

Surely, surely, since she'd tried so hard, she wasn't as bad a parent as Gordon and Toni, her mother, had been.

"A boy needs somebody to grab him by the collar, yell at him, shake him and scare the shit out of him once in a while," Gordon raved on, "that's what makes a man out of him."

"Destroying his pride makes a man out of him?"

"Stay out of this, Andie Lee. You came to me for help, so I'm helping you."

He clamped his mouth shut in that tight, straight line she remembered so well. For Gordon, the subject was closed.

Well, he'd have to get used to the fact she was no longer a little girl who wanted his approval.

"Oh, right. You've got him to the point of kidnapping girls and trying to steal cars, and in only three weeks. I could never have accomplished that all by myself."

He ignored her.

"And now you've left him in jail for the whole night."

"More than one whole night," he said. "Know that."

Fear struck, all through her. She tried for a reasonable tone of voice.

"That'll only make things worse, Gordon. Shane—"

He interrupted in his usual vicious way. "I got him in a cell by himself. You know that. I saw you hovering around with your ears flapping in the wind while I arranged it."

She wished with all her being that she hadn't asked him for help. If only she'd made the decision to sell her practice before she ever dialed his number! Then she could've had money to buy help for Shane. But the practice was her livelihood and the only asset she hadn't already poured into this battle against addiction.

Her reasoning had been that her practice was as important to Shane's future as it was to hers. So she had destroyed her considerable pride and broken her fifteen-year-old vow never to be at Gordon Campbell's mercy again. For four days and nights, she had thought about it and agonized over it but in the end she had decided that any amount of pain would be worth the suffering if it could save Shane's life and sanity.

She would do anything to save Shane. How could she even think about sacrificing this chance of help for him just to cling to her pride and the word of honor she had given to herself?

Gordon had the resources to help the one she loved. She would swallow her pride and call him.

And so she did.

It was still hard to believe that she had broken her vow. That vow, coming out of fury and fear and the unspeakable shocked hurt of a child betrayed by its mother—a feeling she had sworn at his birth Shane would never know—had held her upright while she lived in poverty as a teenaged, single mother. It had driven her to travel with Chase Lomax on the rodeo circuit, painting designs on leather chaps and shirts for a living while he tried to win the big prizes riding roughstock. Later, she waited tables to take care of her baby and pay her way through college and veterinary school.

That vow had pushed her to borrow a lot of money to set up her practice, even after Gordon had offered, at her mother's funeral, to help her get started. That had been some kind of temporary sentimental aberration—not because he felt guilty or generous toward Andie Lee but because he'd felt suddenly lonely without Toni.

Theirs had been some kind of devil's pact. They had fought like tigers all the years they'd been married but they never separated. They both thrived on the conflict, even though they both knew that it would come out, always, with Gordon on top.

Only one thing had ever brought them to agree. That was the idea that Andie Lee should date Trey Gebhardt, scion of another prominent family, a political family that could do Gordon some good at the national level. Trey had raped her on their third date and Shane had been the result.

Her mind drew back from the memory fast as a damp finger from a sizzling burner. Her life hadn't turned out to be all that bad—not until Shane started going downhill. Before that, he had been her greatest joy.

One good thing was that she'd had Chase to help her—although not with money, because back then he'd had none, either—and she still loved him for being the only daddy Shane had ever known. And she loved him for loving her. He just hadn't loved her enough to quit the rodeo life and make a real family, and she hadn't loved him enough to keep going down the road with him.

Now she was a professional, accustomed to making life-and-death decisions and giving orders that were obeyed. She'd made another bad choice by asking for Gordon's help, but she was a grown-up now and she wouldn't let him push her around.

"I'm taking him away," she said. "As soon as they let Shane go, I'm taking him someplace else."

He pressed his foot harder on the accelerator.

"He's staying here," he said. "Either on the Splendid Sky or in jail."

"This is all about your ego," she said, "and we don't have time for that. I've got to save him before it's too late and that point's coming closer by the minute."

"Andie Lee," he said, letting a full measure of disgust come into his voice, "I'll take care of your boy. Go back to Texas and see to your practice before you end up losing it."

He looked at her again and this time she couldn't read one single trace of emotion in his blue eyes.

"You've put a lot of money and energy into veterinary school," he said "You'd be losing that, too."

"My life's over anyway if Shane goes down the tubes," she said. "And there's no way I can leave him here since your idea of taking care of him is to tell him he doesn't have a daddy to do jack for him."

"That's the truth. He doesn't."

"And whose fault is that?" she asked, surprised at the depth of bitterness she heard in her voice.

Andie Lee, you'll fool around and make him really mad

and he'll leave Shane in jail to spite you. He has all the power around here, and you know it. Take care.

But the words were already said and on the table and she would make him acknowledge them. She should have said them to him long ago.

"Yours," he said. "It's your fault he has no daddy. I gave you choices. I would've arranged for you to get rid of the baby or to marry Trey Gebhardt, either one."

"Surely you can understand why neither was an acceptable choice," she said dryly.

"Don't cry to me," he said. "All you had to do that night was stay out of the back seat and tell Trey no."

That accusation stirred the old shame and frustration hidden deep inside her. She pushed it away. No time for that when Shane was hitting rock bottom.

But she couldn't let it go.

"All I had to do was tell *you and my mother* no," she said, "but I didn't have the guts. I was a silly, seventeen-year-old girl who couldn't help wanting to please her mother and the stepfather she'd always hoped would be her daddy."

"Did we tell you to let the boy into your pants?"

She should never have brought this up. It was stirring the rage deep inside her. No way could she tamp it down and think about Shane at the same time.

"No," she said. "You did not. I made my own choices and—now that I think about it, true to what you always preach—I've done a very responsible job of living with the consequences of those choices. The problem right now is that I made another bad choice in asking you for help."

"You just said you always wanted me to be your daddy."

"I did. A long time ago. When I was a silly kid whose real daddy had never been around much. A silly, lonesome kid who was eager to please."

But all that was old news.

Shane was locked up in jail. Shane was skinny and weak

and sweating for need of a fix. Shane was in misery and it was all her fault.

But his further misery would be Gordon's fault. Gordon had had the power to bring him home in this truck with them right now.

"You didn't have to leave him there overnight."

Gordon wouldn't look at her. He was driving like a bat out of hell.

"I got him a private cell." He bit the words off like bullets.

"We're not talking about the Marriott!" she cried. "He needs to be out of there."

"He *needs* to stop and think about what he's doing," Gordon said. "Hard experiences teach hard lessons."

"He's defenseless! His arms aren't as big around as your finger."

"He'll survive."

Andie Lee stared out her window at the landscape hurtling past.

Shane hated her. Shane hated himself, too. She had to save him.

"I'll call my cousin Boone," she said. "He's an attorney and he'll get Shane out of there."

"An army of attorneys can't get him out of there, Andie Lee."

Now Gordon's voice was flat with the knowledge of a sure thing. He was king and he knew it.

"He will learn," he said crisply, "or he will die. The only way human beings ever learn a damn thing is by taking the consequences of the choices they make."

"Oh, yeah," she said. "Yeah. That's your mantra, all right."

"Right it is."

Her lips parted and she started to say something else, then she thought better of it. There must be a way to work him if she'd stop and think.

She'd been going about this all wrong. She'd known that from the beginning because she'd known Gordon Campbell almost all her life. Since she was ten years old and her mother brought her to live in his house. That had been just like Toni: she'd met Gordon at the big cutting horse sale in Fort Worth in December and by April she was married to him and moving to Montana, turning Andie Lee's life upside down.

Twenty-three years Andie Lee had known this man. And in all that time, she'd never seen anybody who'd directly faced him down and managed to win.

"Gordon," she said, "you've been most generous to have Shane accepted into your center free of charge. But it isn't helping him. I have to look for another treatment center that might fit him better."

"Free of charge?" he said.

"No, I'm sure I couldn't find that anywhere else. I'll have to sell my practice."

"That's the dumbest thing I've ever heard. That's your livelihood."

"Don't worry," she said. "I won't be asking you to support us. I can always work for somebody else. I can even go temporary and fill in for veterinarians on vacation. There are plenty of them in North Texas. "

"On a salary you'd never get his bills paid," he said. "This drug-treatment business costs a freaking fortune."

"Tell me about it," she said wryly. "It just about broke me before I ever called you."

"And it's a damned good thing you did, no matter what you say."

He actually sounded almost hurt that she'd said that.

"Get over it, Gordon," she said. "You're not God and you can't have power over everything. Face the fact that you hired a snake of a loser to run your rehab center and it's doing more harm than good. I made a mistake bringing Shane here."

"I *fired* the goddamned loser snake of an SOB, didn't I?" he growled.

He drove even faster. Why not? He wasn't God, but around here, he was king. Speed limits didn't apply.

"It won't take two weeks to get the whole program turned around," he said. "I'm on it."

"I'm out of here," she said. "If you won't do it tonight, go back tomorrow and get Shane out on bail. We'll leave Montana and be out of your hair."

"Forget it," he said, in that tone of unbreakable ice she'd also known since the age of ten. "The kid stays where he is until I come back and get him. When I do, I'll sober him up."

"As if you know how to do that."

"I can find somebody who does," he said. "And I'm going to add some ideas of mine to their program."

"Sounds like a winner."

"Come on, Andie Lee, cut the sarcasm. Don't I always do what I say I will?"

"A combination of a world-class employment agency, plenty of money, and some good, hard, rancher's common sense will do the trick, huh?"

"Guaranteed. Every time."

"So which one of those did you leave out last time? When you hired Jason?"

"Will you shut up about Jason? What I left out was work for those kids."

He clamped his jaw shut tight as a vise.

"I cannot believe it's come to this," she said. "I can't even think. I'm so scared and so mad at Shane I cannot even think."

"Leave it to me. Quit your worrying."

"As if I could."

"You were right about one thing," he said.

She jerked around to stare at him. That was a rare statement, coming from Gordon. He skewered her with his hard blue eyes.

"It *is* my ego," he said. "You won't find another rehab center on the face of the earth where the owner's got his ass on the line for your kid to sober up."

Andie Lee couldn't say a word.

"He'll be gone some day," Gordon said. "Sober or stoned or dead, he'll be gone. You're gonna have to make yourself another life. You've worked too hard to throw your practice away."

That was one thing Gordon respected. Hard work.

"It's no skin off your back. I'd never ask you for help."

"You never have," he said, his eyes boring into her again. "Except for this once. You know I refuse to fail at anything I do. Cut me some slack and I'll save your boy."

He went back to staring through the windshield, one big brown hand resting easy on the steering wheel of the speeding truck as if he could rule the world with one hand tied behind him. Andie Lee couldn't stop looking at his chiseled profile.

The man had no earthly clue of how monumental this problem was. He didn't know the size of the dragon he was promising to slay. The most aggravating thing about Gordon Campbell was his arrogance.

"You might," she said, "if Micah's new wrangler stays around to catch him for you."

He turned, slowly, and gave her a long, straight look that she couldn't read.

Then he laughed. Gordon didn't laugh often and when he did, it was always a shock to her.

"You sound like Toni," he said.

Oh, great. On top of everything else, she was turning into her mother.

But maybe she always had been like Toni—selfish and driven. Maybe she should never have spent all those endless hours and untold amounts of energy on veterinary school instead of pouring them out on the growing Shane.

Gordon had a point, though. Gordon always reached his goals and Gordon always got his way. Shane's recovery was a point of honor with him now. This wasn't something Gordon could will into being, but he would put more effort than any stranger would into trying to get the right help for Shane. He would hire a proven professional to replace Jason and he would spare no expense.

It didn't matter whether his motives were selfish or not. If anyone on earth could do it, Gordon could make things happen so that Shane would recover—if Shane would cooperate.

Gordon was a busy, busy man. He wouldn't be around Shane all that much to talk down to him.

And she had been half-serious in her sarcastic remark. Micah's new hired hand might be good for Shane—if their paths could ever cross again. She could arrange that, maybe, with Micah's help.

What a thought! She didn't know one thing about the big, blue-eyed Native American with the braid and the muscular shoulders. He could be an axe murderer for all she knew. Truly, she was desperate.

Micah's instinct for trustworthiness in human beings was usually faultless. Even though he'd been hiring a horse wrangler, not a friend or counselor for Shane, when he brought Blue to the ranch, he wouldn't want a bad man living in his house or working with his horses.

He had a power, Blue did. She'd felt it this morning, sitting beside him, even with her whole concentration on Shane.

THE ROAN WAS both disrespectful and scared all over again. Whoever said that a horse, like a person, is different every day and therein lies his charm, sure knew what he was talking about. However, at the moment, nothing about Roanie brought the word *charm* to mind. He was thoroughly pissed after his trip to the fairgrounds.

When Blue walked up to the fence, the horse gave him that "Go to hell" look of his. Then he turned his hindquarters to him and stood all sulled up, looking out across the valley.

He'd been hauled way more than he liked, so he'd kicked all the way back to the ranch and fought the leadrope coming out of the trailer. Blue had left him alone in the tree-shaded pasture to relax for a while. But Blue hadn't been able to relax, either.

Even while he was riding some of the other horses, all he'd wanted was to get back to the roan. That was a bad sign. It was less dangerous to get attached to a horse than to people, that was for sure, but Blue needed to keep his emotions clear and his mind clear so he could truly be free and focused. An attachment to anything would get in his way.

Probably, though, it wasn't attachment that drew him to the colt. It was the fact that he owned him now. And the fact that he was the most challenging horse he'd ever known.

He couldn't let himself get attached to Shane, either. He'd only given in to Micah's pleas about the boy because if, on some off chance he could help him, it'd be doing something positive in memory of Dannah. *If.* So what if the boy did offer Blue some slight respect as compared to none at all for anyone else? That wasn't much to build on in a fight with an enemy as strong as addiction.

He wouldn't let the boy get him any more tangled up with Micah, or with Andie Lee or Gordon, either. One thing always led to another.

The aggravating thoughts wouldn't leave him alone. They were still buzzing in him right now, after they'd stirred him up so much that he skipped lunch and the break and kept working. They'd made him feel just as sour as the colt looked.

Blue waited a little while to clear his mind and his mood, then he opened the gate and went in. As he closed it again,

Roanie kicked out, so Blue took his time. The colt knew him, yes, but he didn't fully trust him and he might not for a long time. He had a suspicious attitude that was partly natural to him and partly manufactured by the boys over at Little Creek.

Rhythmically, slowly, Blue moved to approach and then retreat, approach and retreat so the prey animal instincts in the horse wouldn't signal alarm. From a horse's point of view, anything that comes at him in a straight line is behaving as a predator would.

Roanie was making it perfectly clear that he didn't intend to be touched again. Blue started thinking of something to use as an extension of his arm. He found a thin tree limb about three feet long and, holding it down by his side, started working his way to Roanie again. When he finally got close, he stood back the full length of it so the horse wouldn't feel crowded.

"I'll just scratch your back a little," he told him as he took hold of the leadrope with his free hand. "Remember how you like that? Remember how you like for me to rub you with the halter? With my rope?"

He began to scratch him with the limb. Slowly, gently, along his back, over his croup, down to the hock, then up again and along the base of his mane.

Blue watched the horse carefully and concentrated on the best spots again and again. Soon, Roanie admitted that Blue meant no harm. He let his head drop lower and allowed Blue to touch him everywhere he wanted.

Blue replaced the stick with his hand. He could feel through his palm and through every one of his fingers that the colt was really beginning to relax, so he rubbed him all over several times.

Then he concentrated on massaging his legs. He moved the touch on down below the knees and caressed the tendons where the legs were the most sensitive, too sensitive for the stick.

"All I want to do today is pick up your feet," he told the horse. "That's all. Then I'll let you be."

Gradually, finally, Blue closed everything else out of his mind and they both relaxed into the companionship they were beginning to build. He didn't know how much time passed but, at last, the roan let him pick up all four of his feet.

Blue whistled as he patted the sleek, warm neck again and again, then he moved to the horse's head, unfastened the halter he'd left on him all day, and slipped it off.

The roan rolled his eye at him and moved away at a brisk trot. Blue backed up against the fence, hooked one heel in it and leaned back to watch him as he lifted into a lope. He moved so smoothly through the shade and the sunlight that he reminded Blue of water flowing, turning his speckled hide to one liquid color. Red.

In Cherokee lore, red was the color of victory, of success.

The color blue meant failure, disappointment, or unsatisfied desire.

He'd had ten unsatisfied and lonely years to wonder if his mother knew that he would fail her and disappoint her when she named him Blue.

What made him think there was even a chance that he would help Shane after he'd failed Rose and Dannah so completely?

FOR THE SAKE OF positive thinking, Andie Lee went for a long, hard run late that afternoon, trying to clear her head of the negative thoughts that had lived there for so long. While she ran, she reviewed the whole day in her mind, hoping to banish those images forever once she got back to the house.

She hadn't realized, through these last weeks, that she'd fallen into such a habit of despair until she and Gordon drove into the yard at the main house and he said, "I'll take care of the Center. And of Shane. Forget him for a week and go find something that'll make you smile."

Surprised, she'd leaned back against her door and watched him as he parked and turned off the motor.

"What's different, Gordon?"

He looked at her. "What are you talking about?"

"You never cared if I smiled before now. You never insisted on helping me with anything until now. What's the deal?"

He shrugged. "Things change."

As he threw open his door and got out, he said, "I've got a truckload of money sunk in that drug rehab center. Why wouldn't I want it to produce results?"

She got out and they walked toward the house.

"The question is why did you build it? It's not something you'd do."

He shot her a look.

"How do you know? You don't know squat about me."

"I know some," she said. "Or I should say, I did know some about who you used to be. Any kid who wants a parent's love knows more about that parent than either of them realizes."

He shook his head.

"You always did read too much," he said. "You've let your imagination run wild."

With that, he went straight to his office and closed the door.

She went up to her old room and looked at herself in the mirror. It hurt her to look at herself. She looked horrid. She looked exhausted and haggard and old and wrinkled and sad, sad, sad.

She forced a smile. It hurt her muscles. It looked fake. It looked so false that it still hurt her to look at herself.

How could she help Shane to believe in hope for recovery if she looked so hopeless?

She felt like crawling into bed, pulling the covers over her head, and never coming out to be seen again. The thought was scarily tempting.

She stared at her image.

"You've never given up," she told it. "Don't start now."

Gordon was in control of Shane. Gordon was talking to her—a little—and listening to her. A little. She wanted some influence over what Gordon did to Shane.

The work, for example. He was finally going to take Micah's advice and find a director who'd put the inmates to work. She wanted Shane to be with horses because they had great healing power.

Certainly more than hauling hay or digging ditches would have.

So she'd put on her shorts and running shoes and hit the road that ran across the valley to the river. Once there, she walked for a while and then sat for a while and made herself think, for once, about something besides Shane. It was an exercise in will that made her brain feel as stiff as her face had done when she forced a smile.

She looked into the water and tried to see her plans for the future, the ones she'd had two years ago when the nightmare began. Before her every thought had been fixed on Shane and his problems.

Right now, her dreams of buying a cabin in Wyoming where she would go to rest and read and think and learn to paint landscapes—in other words, to actually discover who she was and what she wanted for the rest of her life, since she'd never had a minute free to figure that out since she was seventeen—were hopeless.

Her profession was one she loved, but other than that, what did she want to do? Gordon was right. Someday Shane would be gone. What would be the most important thing to her then?

Her savings had vanished like snow in the sun, along

with all the money she'd raised by selling the few luxuries in her life: her show horse and saddle and her sporty little car. Gordon was right about that, too. She couldn't recover financially if she sold her practice.

She couldn't let Shane's troubles take everything else away from her because the stronger she was for herself, the greater the chances she could help him. She'd made the right decision. She'd hang on to her practice, stay here and deal with Gordon the best way she could.

He really was different toward her, and she thought about that. In the past, he would've exploded and then chewed her up and spit her out for questioning him and arguing with him on the way back from the jail.

He would've been furious at her asking him why he built the Center.

As far as she'd observed, he was still his old hair-trigger self with everybody else. Did he pity her so much that he was trying to be kind to her? Act like a father to her twenty years too late because she was such a lousy mother?

No. Negative thoughts. She was doing, and had done, the best she knew how. That was all anyone could do.

She got up and started slowly jogging back toward the house. No negativity. It was self-fulfilling.

Only positive thoughts. This was the turning point. Shane had hit rock bottom this morning and his only direction now was up.

She would hold that thought.

The houses, barns, pens, arenas, all passed by in a blur. For the first time in what seemed a lifetime, she was comfortable in her body and her mind. For these few minutes. Her blood was pumping warm in her veins and hope was growing in her heart.

When she got back to the house, Gordon's truck was gone. Andie Lee pounded up the stairs, pretending she had more energy left than she had thought. In her childhood room, she stripped and stood in the shower for the longest time, willing the hot water to wash away the traces of tension left in her muscles and her mind.

Tonight, for the first time in a long time, she'd have a chance of getting some sleep.

She was standing at the window drying her hair when the big white truck came rolling into the glow of the dusk-activated yard light. Gordon got out and slammed the door behind him, but she never heard him come into the house.

When her hair was only damp, she pulled on some soft pants and a T-shirt, stuck her feet into some flip-flops and went down the stairs. All the rooms were still dark except for the lamps they always left on in the huge old living area. She walked out onto the porch. He was standing down on the north end of it, one foot propped on the railing, staring out into the night, smoking a cigarette. He didn't turn around.

"I guess you know that stuff'll kill you," she said.

After a heartbeat he answered. "Somethin' will."

She walked halfway to him and sat down in the swing.

"Hmm," she said, "I thought you considered yourself immortal, Gordon."

He gave his little bark of a laugh, set his foot on the floor, and turned around.

He looked at her. In the faint lamp glow that came through the window she couldn't see his eyes.

"That was before the doc said cancer."

She gasped. "What? You have…"

"Turns out he was wrong," he said. "Even the experts can't win 'em all."

He walked to one of the leather rocking chairs, turned it to face her, and sat. He rocked it slowly back and forth.

"Made me think, though," he said. "What'll happen to the Wagontracks when I'm gone?"

The question stunned her. Gordon had never talked to her about anything personal before. He never talked to *anyone* like this. Not even Micah, as far as she knew.

"I'm thinking that would depend on your choice of an heir," she said.

He gave a bitter chuckle.

"Just think, Andie. I'm the sixth generation Campbell in Montana, counting the first one who came directly from Scotland. Six generations. We've kept this ranch together through droughts and blizzards, Indian wars and rock-bottom cattle markets. Kept it together and added to it, Andie Lee."

"You're a famous breeder who believes the bloodline is everything," she said, "and there's no seventh-generation Campbell to carry it on."

He grunted and took another drag on the cigarette.

"Ironic, isn't it?"

She nodded.

"The bloodline *is* everything," he said. "Besides, a woman could never manage this ranch in a million years of trying."

Anger flashed through her amazement to flare in her voice.

"That's not what I meant. I don't want anything from you," she said. "I wish I'd never asked you to help us this time, but here we are."

"That's *why* I'm helping you now," he said. "You put yourself through college and took care of a baby and graduated veterinary school and wouldn't take money when your mother offered it. I respect that kind of guts."

"Then respect my need to see Shane in the morning."

"No. A week with nobody fawning over him will work wonders."

"A *week!* You said overnight! I never thought you'd leave him so long! That's way too long…"

"It'll help make a man out of him. Every boy needs a time as a kid when he's scared shitless and has nobody to depend on but himself."

"You justify everything you do," she snapped. "You could justify torture or rustling or *murder* for your own purposes. You've always done that!"

He shrugged and deliberately crossed one leg over his knee to put out his cigarette on the sole of his boot.

He had said a week when they first got back. When he'd told her to forget Shane for a week and find something to make her smile. She just hadn't really heard it then.

"So. You can't resist being the great dictator. I ought to leave here."

"I thought we settled that, Andie."

"*I* never said so. You always assume that when you make a decree everybody else agrees."

"Because I'm always right," he said. "Now calm down and go on up to bed. Get some sleep. The week'll be gone before you know it."

She wanted nothing more than to leave him, but she sat stubbornly in her place and pushed the swing into motion with her toe.

"I'll go when I'm ready."

She pushed the swing again.

"What do you know about that wrangler Micah hired?"

He jerked his chin up to look at her and she saw his eyes glint in the dark.

"You got a thing for Indians?"

She ignored that. She also ignored the little voice in the back of her head whispering that she should drop this whole idea because she knew nothing about Blue.

"Micah says Blue's a real horseman," she said, "but that wouldn't keep him from also being an axe murderer."

"Look, Andie, if you're desperate there're a few single ranchers around and a judge and a doctor I could introduce to you."

"Let's not repeat past mistakes," she said tartly. "All I'm looking for is a good male influence and some hard work for Shane, like you and Micah are always talking about. Horses can help heal him."

Gordon was watching her with his sharp eyes. She could feel them on her, boring into her, as if he didn't believe her.

"Ask Micah," he said.

ANDIE LEE PULLED UP to park at Micah's place in her own truck. She'd told herself that she was driving it instead of a ranch vehicle because she'd already wrecked one truck of Gordon's, that she didn't want to owe him any more than she had to. Of course that made absolutely no sense, considering that, as he had said so eloquently, Shane's treatment was costing a freaking fortune.

Therefore, the real reason, which she was just now able to admit to herself, was that she wanted to be in her own truck with its veterinary box in the back to give her confidence and courage. Pathetic. This was what it was like to be desperate and down to her last chance.

And she didn't even know if it *was* a chance. She didn't know this man from Adam's off ox, as Micah would say.

But she'd seen with her own eyes that Shane had connected to Blue in some way. He'd been furious with him, yes, but even in the shattered state he was in, he had looked at Blue with respect. Shane hadn't looked at anybody that way for two years. It was as if he'd refused to respect anyone else ever since he'd lost respect for himself.

She cut the motor, took a deep breath, and opened her door. Micah wasn't the kind to pick up some day laborer off the street in Deer Lodge to break his horses. He was bound to know something about Blue Bowman.

Even if he didn't think Shane should ride with the man, she ought to thank Blue for what he'd done yesterday. If he hadn't stopped Shane, the whole deal could've turned into an even bigger disaster.

Andie Lee was on the ground, closing the door behind her, before she noticed that Micah's truck wasn't there. For a minute, she just stood and looked around, then she headed for the barn anyway.

She could talk to Blue herself and begin to form an opinion of her own, couldn't she? She would get Micah's later.

Blue could be gone with Micah but it was more likely, considering Micah's eternal determination to get his money's worth, that Blue was there working. She would thank him and try to get him to talk to her for a little while.

As soon as she glanced into the barn she saw it was empty. She walked the length of it down the center aisle and stepped out the other end.

Her horses nickered as soon as they saw her and ran to the corner of the pasture nearest her but she ignored them for the moment to look at Blue and the roan colt.

She narrowed her eyes and watched the horse. Yes, it was *the* roan colt. No mistaking him for anything else.

But he was behaving like a broke horse—paying attention to Blue and moving on cue at the end of a long, soft rope. She watched for a minute. Blue was using natural horsemanship, communicating with the horse through that rope. The roan colt was so wild he was already a legend. Who would have believed that anyone could bring him this far this fast?

How long had Blue been here? She'd been so wrapped up in Shane she hadn't been coming up to Micah's to ride every day, but she and Shane had only been here three weeks and Blue certainly hadn't been around when they arrived.

Out in the middle of the unfenced meadow that looked across the valley, Blue was allowing the roan to drift away and then was bringing him back to face him, making serpentine lines through the dewy grass. He was letting him have his space but he was getting his respect from a distance.

After a little while, Blue stopped the horse and approached

him, then stopped and moved in another direction. He worked his way closer and closer and finally, he was at his head, petting his neck and rubbing his poll as if they'd been friends forever.

Finally, he let his hand drop to his side and just stood there, looking out across the valley. The colt did the same. Against the purple mountains, they looked like a statue of a cowboy and his horse in repose.

Andie Lee couldn't stop staring. Her heart beat faster and her hopes started rising. Blue had power. If he could do this, in this length of time, with such an incorrigible colt, he could do some good with Shane.

No. Not necessarily. He could be a doper himself. He could be an alcoholic. He could be any kind of a bad influence that would make Shane even worse.

At last, Blue stroked the nose of the colt and turned to lead him toward the barn. The roan jerked back and Blue held on, going with him as he backed and backed and backed some more. Andie Lee held her breath. If that colt panicked, they both could go right over the edge of the bluff. They weren't far from it.

She needn't have worried. The roan settled down and followed Blue's lead as if he were an old hand at being a working horse. Like a puppy dog.

Blue walked straight toward her at a leisurely pace and stopped a few yards away.

"Don't let me hinder your work," she called. "I can ride my own or play with them until you're done."

Blue flashed a sharp look at her. Even in the shadow of his battered hat's brim, his blue steel eyes were as remote as she remembered. Looking into them was not going to tell her one thing about him.

His glance followed her gesture toward her own horses.

"So you're the one who spoiled those two," he said.

He didn't smile as he said it but he wasn't censuring her,

either. He was stating a simple fact—one that meant he knew her horses as individuals. Maybe it was horses that would give her the key to getting to know him.

"Guilty," she said. "They're my friends."

He answered with the barest of nods, then just stood there, looking at her, waiting for her to state her business.

"That's amazing, what you've done with Roanie," she said. "I held my breath when he pulled back on you. I know Micah's had quite a time with him."

"Anybody willing to listen to him can work with this horse," he said flatly, and that was the end of that line of talk.

Blue had a low, melodious voice. It was a shame he didn't use it more.

He had a presence, too, that held her captive. He stood easy in his skin, waiting.

The roan was getting restless.

"I came to thank you," she said quickly. "You may have saved Shane's life yesterday.…"

Saying the words out loud made her throat go tight. She swallowed and went on, "…or Lisa's. Or both."

He didn't say a word.

"Many people in your position would've refused to get involved," she said. "Thank you."

He touched the brim of his hat. "No problem."

He clucked to the horse and led him away.

Andie Lee caught her breath so fast it made a knot in her stomach. No. She wouldn't let it go at that.

But whether for Shane's sake or her own, she couldn't have said. Something about the man fascinated her.

You know nothing about him, Andie Lee. Let him go. Wait until you can talk to Micah.

Blue and the colt disappeared around the other side of the old round pen. She turned and went back through the barn.

I know that he's great with horses. I know horses can help Shane. I know that much.

When she reached the gate, he was just going in.

"Blue," she called, "please give me just a moment. I need to talk to you."

At first she thought he would keep going, but he stopped. He turned around and looked at her.

Behind him, she saw that there were five or six other young horses already in the pen, saddled and tied around with their heads to one side. Some were playing, others were chasing each other, bucking, wandering around or standing quiet.

"Wait there," he said to Andie Lee.

He led the roan into the middle of the pen, coiled up the lead and slipped the hand-tied halter made of the same rope off the colt's head.

He hung it over his shoulder. Roanie ran away from him and started to buck, but he was halfhearted about it. A couple of the other young horses approached him, but he kicked out and then whirled to bare his teeth at them. They left him alone. Blue watched them all for a minute before he headed for the gate.

He came out and, with a last look at the horses, latched it behind him.

"You tie them around to make them flexible?" Andie Lee asked.

"And humble," Blue said.

"With the roan, that may take a while," she said.

He gave a rueful chuckle that sent a sudden warmth into the cold center of her belly. She met his eyes as he turned to her.

Awareness leapt between them like a spark from a fire.

"Maybe a *long* while," he said, with a gentle quirk of his mouth.

Then, suddenly deadly serious, he kept looking straight into her eyes as if to make sure she'd listen.

"If you're ever around here when I'm not, don't mess with him. He's still biting and striking at everybody but me."

"Don't worry," she said. "I have enough trouble with an outlaw boy without taking on an outlaw horse."

One corner of his mouth lifted again. His lips were nice. Finely shaped. She tried not to look at his mouth too long.

Blue leaned his shoulders back against the wall and bent one leg to hook his boot heel onto a log.

He was waiting to hear what she wanted with him.

She started talking, fast.

Watch what you say, Andie Lee. Wait until you check him out with Micah.

She threw caution to the wind with her very next breath.

"I wanted to thank you for stopping Shane," she blurted, "but I also wanted to ask if you…might…maybe show him some of those natural horsemanship techniques you use."

The look in his eyes sharpened.

"He might even talk to you," she said quickly. "He won't open up to anybody else, not even the counselor."

"I told Micah I'm not taking your boy to raise. I'll tell you the same thing."

She stared, trying to take that in.

"Micah asked you to…?" She didn't know how to finish the sentence.

But Blue wouldn't fill in the blank. He just inclined his head slightly and waited for her to go on. She was too busy getting her mind around it all.

Micah had mentioned Shane to him! He'd suggested that Blue let him hang around or work for him or something! So Micah knew that Blue was all right. Her hopes grew.

"Shane needs the horses," she said. "If he'd start riding every day and get emotionally involved with them and start listening to them, it'd make a lot of difference in his outlook."

"Micah asked me to let Shane come ride with me," Blue said. "I agreed."

"You did?"

She sighed with relief, then caught her breath again.

"But wait! What are you riding, the colts?"

"Mostly. And anything else that's too much for Micah."

"The colts might be too much for Shane, too. He's really weak right now and he's never been on a horse that wasn't broke."

In her imagination she saw Shane leaving the saddle of a bucking colt, his thin body flying up into the air, flopping like a rag doll's before it slammed into the ground.

"I won't put him on any horse at all until he's drug free and stronger."

"But he needs to start in your barn as soon as he gets out of jail."

"What he does depends on me."

"Well…and on me. I'm his mother. I have to decide…"

The look in his eyes stopped her tongue.

"Have you noticed yet that whatever you do makes no difference in what Shane does?"

The question came out of his mouth as a statement. The cold, hard truth.

She hated it.

"How do *you* know? You've only seen him—and me— once. And that was in a very extreme situation."

He just looked at her.

"Listen," she said. "I know there's a limit to what I can do for Shane. I've had two years of pure hell to teach me that. But I cannot, I *will* not, give up trying."

Completely against her will, her voice and her temper had risen on every word she'd just said, so she didn't say any more.

She felt a terrible anger overcome her.

She wanted to scream at him for saying she had no influence on Shane. But her hunch—and Micah's—might be right, and he might be important for Shane's future. And no man wanted to deal with an hysterical woman, especially one who was a stranger. She would not be one.

She wasn't one. She was calm. She took a couple of deep breaths to prove it.

He was still looking at her, his eyes hard and sharp, willing her to admit to the truth he'd spoken. She wouldn't. She couldn't.

"Shane is all I have," she blurted. "He's my heart walking around out there in another body. Gordon says I'm his problem—that he needed to grow up with a daddy in the house."

The line of his square jaw hardened.

"I can't be his daddy," he said. "If that's what you want."

Stung, she snapped, "I'm not that deluded."

She took a deep breath while she searched for the right words.

"I'm glad you said yes to Micah's plan to let Shane ride with you. Thanks, Blue. And I hope you'll let him talk to you, too—eventually he might do that."

Andie Lee bit her lip again so she wouldn't rave on and on. She had already said too much, seemed too desperate and been too verbal about her feelings. Men didn't like that.

If she had caused Blue to change his mind and say no to Micah now, she would never get over it.

CHAPTER SIX

YOU'RE THE ONLY ONE who can help him.

She might as well have spoken the words. It was clear as spring water that that was what was going through her mind.

Little did she know that it had been many years—too many—since he'd helped anyone. Himself included.

Blue pushed his hat back on his head and wished she'd step aside so he could walk away. This was way more than he could handle. And this woman was in such a passion of trying to save her son that she would never give up.

What the hell am I getting myself into?

Damn it. He knew the minute Micah said the first word to him that he should've stayed out of this.

He'd tried to stay out. He'd thought of Dannie and that had pulled him in, which was stupid. There was nothing he could do for her now.

Andie Lee turned away, walked to her truck, pulled the tailgate down, and sat on it. Long legs dangling, she stared off across the valley.

He had given his word to Micah. No way could he take it back.

What he had to do now was make Andie Lee see the limits of what he could do for Shane.

He hitched the loose halter and the coil of leadrope higher onto his shoulder and walked over to her. She didn't move, didn't even glance at him. Maybe she hadn't intended to strip her feelings quite so naked and now she was embarrassed to look at him.

"I'll make a horseman out of him," he said. "If he wants it."

She didn't look at him or say a word. No matter. She could still hear.

"Horses are dangerous," he said to the side of her face. "No guarantees."

She didn't turn toward him. She just held her pure profile still against the blue of the sky and looked at the mountains.

Finally, she sighed. It was a pitiful sound if he ever heard one.

"If *he* wants," she said. "I can't make him want it."

"Nobody can."

That little bit of agreement made her turn to him, with her eyes flashing and her tongue loosened again.

"It's ironic that I panicked at the thought of him riding the colts," she said. "Ironic and stupid when he's out there trying to kill himself every day of the week with drugs and guns."

"Not stupid," he said. "With the right horse he could get it done."

Shock showed in her face, but she had to already know that. She'd grown up on a ranch.

Her eyes softened in a silent plea.

He wanted to look away but that'd make him feel like a coward. He knew what the plea was and he knew only God could give her what she wanted. Blue hadn't even been able to help his own mother when she looked at him like that.

"I'll not put him on the roan," he said.

She searched his eyes, quick and deep, the way she had done in Micah's truck when she said she was Gordon's *step*daughter.

Because she didn't know if she could trust him. It made her seem so vulnerable he wanted to reach out and touch her. Reassure her. Comfort her.

It was an unaccustomed feeling. A long forgotten one.

"I'm thinking maybe Shane's been snorting cocaine and

stealing guns and whatever else he's been doing partly for the danger itself," she said. "Maybe breaking horses will be enough thrills to satisfy him."

She held his gaze again. Her eyes were beautiful. They told him she was a woman with a lot of heart.

"I only hope being in jail won't finish killing his spirit," she said.

It could happen, especially to a kid. Fear could kill a weak spirit and Shane had been scared.

Blue could remember the unreasoning, blood-freezing fear of being so close to pure evil in so many bodies committing so many acts of unreasoning cruelty. When one prisoner had reached around Blue with a lightning strike of his hand to knife an enemy in the back and brought it back to slash Blue for no reason except that he was there. When two of the Pureblood Brotherhood had jumped Blue in the showers and tried to cut off his braid.

Defending himself from such insanity was enough to make his fear explode into a cloud big enough to smother him.

But those fights had been a relief from the bigger fear pent up inside him. The fear of no escape from the relentless noise of strangers forever invading his ears, reaching for his mind.

And fear of no escape from the endless silence of every minute passing without one real, personal word addressed to him that carried a meaning for his heart.

Those two fears would be instilled by a county jail as well as a state prison.

Blue had stood up under the fear and conquered it. Shane didn't look able to fight off a fly. The fear Blue had seen in his eyes must be heavy enough by now to crush Shane's soul.

"Gordon arranged for him to be in a cell by himself," she said, talking to herself again. Anything for a shred of comfort.

"You going to see him?" he asked.

Andie Lee glanced at Blue quickly.

"No. Gordon arranged it so that only he and his lawyer are allowed to visit Shane."

Blue's gut clenched. He wouldn't let himself think about Gordon. He wouldn't let himself think about this woman's misery. He'd only gotten into this for Shane.

"Shane'll have to put his back into the grunt work," he said, "or I'm not fooling with him."

"Well, it certainly won't do any good for *me* to tell him that," she said. Then, wryly, she added, "As I believe you so thoughtfully pointed out a little while ago."

"Stay out of it," Blue said.

"Well, thanks a lot."

She meant to be sarcastic but she sounded hurt, too.

"A kid his age needs something of his own without his mother in it," Blue said.

"He already has that," she said with a wry chuckle.

She was scared to death herself for her boy, but she was still hanging on to her sense of humor, which took guts. He could see why Micah was hell-bent on helping her. She drew a man's eye to her, yes, but her spirit appealed to him, too.

"Gordon said every boy needs somebody to grab him by the neck and yell at him and shake some sense into him," she said. "I told him humiliating Shane like he does is going to make him worse instead of better."

"Gordon won't be hanging around this barn."

Andie Lee looked at him. She heard his own dislike of Gordon in his voice.

"Good." A little smile played on her lips when she said it.

Blue felt the corners of his own mouth turn up as if they were co-conspirators. He took a step back. No need to get in any deeper here.

"Work's waiting," he said.

"Don't let me keep you," she said. "And don't worry. I'll stay out of it and I'll stay away when Shane's here."

He nodded, turned and walked away, his hand closed hard around the loops of rope. He slapped them against his hipbone in rhythm with his steps.

THE NEXT DAY, Andie came up to the barn to ride her horses for the first time since Blue had been on the ranch, and three days later he decided that she was planning to make a habit of it. Late in the morning, she'd drive in and park her truck beside Micah's, go straight to the barn and saddle up. She'd ride off into the trees behind the house or go across the road and climb the hills to the west or ride down into the valley and disappear, becoming a smaller and smaller dot as she headed for the river.

One day she'd ride the gray horse and the next she'd take the sorrel mare. Some days she rode them both. Every day she talked to Blue a little.

Not for long, because twelve colts took up his whole day and she was careful not to interrupt his groundwork or bother him if he was busy in the barn, but they fell into a little conversation every day. About the horses, mostly.

Around the fourth day or so, she started sitting in the shade of the barn and watching him ride when she came in tired from her travels. He didn't care. When he was mounted on a young one, he was thinking about that horse and listening to him while he taught him to listen to Blue. He didn't even remember that Andie Lee was there.

Who are you kidding, Bowman? You always know she's there.

Well, he *tried* not to be aware of her. He didn't *want* to be aware of her.

When he was done, sometimes she had a remark or two about that horse and they compared opinions. When he was in the barn, sometimes she talked about what she'd seen on the ranch that day and he asked questions.

After all, he needed to learn the lay of the land and the locations of the hands and the work. Not to mention what all she could tell him about Gordon, if she ever felt inclined to say anything about him.

When Blue and Micah were working on the fences or the trailer or the tack while she wrangled tools for them, sometimes she talked about the past. And Shane.

That was why she came up there every day, Blue decided. Shane was why she did everything she did. The woman was obsessed, just the way Tanasi Rose had been.

She was hanging with him and Micah out of loneliness while her son was jailed, but she was also trying to make Blue sympathize with the boy before he came back. Andie Lee was leaving no stone unturned.

Sometimes it irritated him. He had told her plainly what he could and would do for her wayward child. Trying to make friends with him or trying to brainwash him would not change that one bit.

Yet he understood it, too. She had that glossy look of a woman used to getting what she wanted, but she was trapped in a low-down problem that she was as helpless to solve as any mother accustomed to poverty and prejudice. Helpless as Tanasi Rose.

In fact, he and Andie Lee were surprisingly alike. They were from entirely different worlds but they both had a passion. She wanted to save Shane just as much as he wanted to destroy Gordon.

And he couldn't stay aggravated with her for long because she didn't overstay her welcome or intrude in any way. She just offered and took a little companionship every day. In spite of how he tried to control his mind and his emotions, he began to look forward to it.

By the end of that week, Blue had to admit that the best times were when Micah was off somewhere else and Andie Lee was around when he was done riding for the day.

She would help him turn them out, each of them leading two tired two-year-olds from the round pen to the pasture with the big trees scattered over it and the grass darker green in the shadows thrown by the passing clouds. He loved that walk. Two people and four horses together after the work was done.

Blue wasn't alone then. It was as if, for the first time in his life, he wasn't alone. It was hard to explain to himself. He didn't let himself try to figure it out. If he let himself think about it too much, he might start wanting it all the time.

Always, after they'd slipped the halters off and let the horses go free, kicking up behind and throwing their heads around, he and Andie Lee would stay there for a little while, leaning against the fence.

When the horses settled, some of them, always including Andie Lee's two, came up to get a little scratching and petting. Then he and Andie Lee were just two simple humans feeling the warm hides beneath their hands and the silky muzzles against their faces, looking off across the homey valley and up at the beckoning mountains. Saying only a few words now and then.

Not wanting ever to move again.

THE DAY AFTER they brought Shane back to the Center, Andie Lee woke before dawn, her hopes rising even before the sun. She got up and went out on the long second-floor balcony that ran along the east and south sides of the old house to think about why that was so. No way could she afford to set herself up for a new disappointment. She had to be realistic and logical.

But Blue was going to help Shane, she just knew it. True, Micah claimed to know little of his background, except that Blue was from Oklahoma originally and he'd worked with horses most of his life. He said he'd hired him because some friend had known Blue was looking for a job and Micah needed somebody.

And Blue had told her nothing about himself or his past. But she had been around him almost every day, trying to get a sense of his character, watching and feeling his quiet ways with horses and with Micah and with herself. She had found no reason not to trust him with her son.

Her son, who had already known more lowlife scum than she would ever meet.

Her son, whom she would see in just a little while. She was scared to death he'd be in worse shape than ever after a week in jail.

Andie Lee watched the sun come up, then she dressed to go over to the Center. Lawrence, the new director, had told her she could have a private breakfast with Shane, who'd begin his new regimen today. It included getting up early.

When she arrived at the recreation building that housed the dining hall, Tracie, the assistant director, showed her to a rough-hewn table out on the deck. It was set with old-fashioned enamelware on serape-striped woven place mats.

Trees grew up close, and the pine smell and the fresh sunlight made it seem a whole new world to her, as well as a new day. She hoped Shane would feel the same way and behave like a new boy.

Tracie brought him out of the back door of the dining hall. Andie Lee wanted nothing more than to go to him and put her arms around him. But the set of his head warned her off.

"Hi, Shane," Andie Lee said, happy that her tone came out bright but neutral. "I'm glad you're back."

He actually responded. If you could call it that.

"Huh," he said.

He looked horrid. Pale as death.

He sat down and began fiddling nervously with his silverware. Two people from the kitchen came out with plates of hot food, pitchers of coffee and juice and a basket of fruit.

Shane blurted, "Gordon said I've got a job."

"Right."

Andie Lee picked up her fork and took a bite of scrambled egg to set a good example. She hated this distance between them with the whole core of her being. She was scared to say too much, scared to say too little, scared to say the wrong thing and sick to death of the caution.

And the situation. He had opened the conversation, though. Maybe this was the beginning of the end of their stint in hell.

"A job breaking colts," he said, clanging his knife against his plate. "And I'm telling you now that as soon as I get out of here, I'm goin' on the circuit with Dad."

She took a bite of toast and made herself chew and swallow it.

"I've been trying to get hold of him," she said. "No luck so far."

Shane picked up his glass and gulped his orange juice, frowning at her over the rim.

"Don't tell him I was in jail."

"You can tell him that yourself."

The scowl deepened.

"I'm gonna ride with the Indian guy."

"He's a good horseman."

He set down the glass and glared.

"How do *you* know?"

Ah, yes. To him, anything she touched was poisoned. How could they have come to this when they used to be buddies? How much of it was his age and how much the drugs? *What* had she done wrong?

She wanted to scream but she shrugged and spoke casually.

"My horses are in his barn, you know. I go up there to ride. I see him working."

He eyed her suspiciously and jabbed the fork at his eggs. He ate one tiny bite.

"I'm gonna travel with Dad pretty soon," he said. "Get ready."

"I'm ready now," she blurted, and her tone said she meant it.

Shane's eyes jerked up to meet hers, surprise written all over his face.

She smiled at him. She wanted to laugh. It was the first time in two years she'd actually roused his full attention.

It surprised her nearly as much as it did him, and it gave her hope. Maybe somebody could get through to him now. Even if she couldn't, maybe Blue could.

If Blue couldn't, maybe Chase could. Maybe someday Shane would be on his own and healthy and she wouldn't have to worry about him anymore.

At that moment, she wanted to lose that horrible burden more than she'd ever wanted anything. It made her feel new guilt on top of old, but it was true.

BLUE WAS riding one of the twos out in the open for the first time when Micah came out of the house and headed in his direction. He was motioning with one creaky arm for Blue to come to him.

He rode the little bay filly over to meet him halfway. She was going to be a sweetheart—she stopped on the whoa just as pretty as a finished horse. He patted her on the neck.

"Jist got the call," Micah said. "I'm goin' down to the Center to pick up the boy."

"Wait up," Blue said.

He had thought about it and decided that he should keep a sharp eye on Shane any time he was in their care. He'd only been back at the Center for two days after spending a week in jail, so that was nine days without drugs.

Blue led the filly to the round pen, tied her around, and put her back in with the others.

Micah had said that Gordon threatened the personnel at

the jail with death and dismemberment, not to mention loss of their jobs, if so much as a whiff of marijuana made its way to Shane's cell. So Shane probably still had the shakes and his snaky attitude.

He would be looking for money. He might be furious because he'd been jailed in the first place and blame Micah as well as Blue. He might still be on the prowl to steal a vehicle. In any case, he'd not be at all happy. He was a skinny, out-of-shape kid, but Micah was an old man and stove up and it'd be a shame if he got hurt.

When Blue got to the truck, Micah had it running.

"You're taking this here babysittin' job mighty serious," he said.

He was pretty sharp.

"Don't want you to mess with my new helper," Blue said lightly. "You're liable to tell him I'm a pushover."

"Hopin' to see his mother's more like it," Micah said, shifting gears. He gunned the truck out into the road. "Well, you're hopin' in vain this time, son. Andie Lee said the new director ain't lettin' Shane see her 'cept fer a half hour at breakfast this mornin'. No other visitors."

"So we don't count as visitors?"

"Nope. Reckon not. Reckon we must be em-ployers."

Blue looked at him.

"You can't be an employer, Micah, unless you pay wages."

"Well, I cain't even pay room and board to that boy Shane," he said, wagging his head. "Wouldn't do to have him around night and day 'cause we couldn't get no sleep fer fearin' he'd sneak out on us."

"Don't even think about it," Blue said.

"It's a shame, a cryin' shame he ever gotta hold of that dope," Micah said. "He was a fine little boy."

"We all were," Blue said, and Micah laughed.

"I'd go see 'em anytime Chase was rodeoin' in this part of the state," Micah said. "Shane was a pistol but he never had a mean bone in his body and Andie Lee was a fine lit-tle mother, too. She kept that trailer spotless and cooked ever' meal and watched over that boy like a mother hen."

Blue looked at him.

"They lived in a trailer?"

Micah squinted at him as he shifted gears and started down the hill to headquarters.

"Fer years," he said, nodding sagely. "Seemed odd to see her in it, after she'd growed up down here at the big house, but back then Chase never could win enough to git a place of his own."

Blue waited for him to say more.

"That's what hurts me so bad and makes me so mad at Shane," Micah said, "the way he talks to his mother. I may whip his ass over it yet. She has tried to be a mama and a daddy to him and this is the thanks she gets."

"I thought Chase was his daddy."

Again that squinted look from Micah.

"She left the rodeo road when Shane started to school. Said he was gonna have a good eddication, no matter what. Now he's fried his brain so bad he likely can't learn another damn thing or remember what he did know."

Did she leave Chase, too, or just the road? Is she still married to him? Will he be likely to come here to see her?

But Blue didn't ask any of the questions rattling around in his mind. In fact, it irritated him that he wanted to know those things. Andie Lee's life was none of his concern.

And Micah actually quit talking then, clamped his lips to-gether in a disapproving line, and glared through the wind-shield at the road.

Blue watched the mountains and looked at the cattle and the grass all the way down to the clinic and tried not to think about what he'd gotten himself into. Whatever he could do to help Shane would be in Dannah's memory and it'd only be a few hours every day.

No matter what the end result, it wouldn't be a waste. Just being outside and around the horses would do the boy good. Just using his muscles to clean stalls and throw hay and accomplish something he could see would do him good.

Micah drove to the building at the Center that Gordon had indicated when he told Jason to get his things and get off the ranch. He rattled up there, opened his door, said he'd be back in a minute, and limped off up the walk. He was an independent old coot and he'd guessed that Blue was trying to take care of him.

He felt bad about that but not bad enough to wish he hadn't come. It was unnecessary, maybe, but maybe not. No sense in letting anything bad happen if it could be prevented.

Blue got out of the small truck cab to stretch his legs. And to put Shane on the inside and himself by the door. One time, in a fit of depression, Dannie had tried to throw herself out of a moving car.

It was hardly a minute before Shane, scowling, stepped out the door with Micah right behind him and a tall, thin man probably in his midforties following them. They all walked toward the truck.

Shane looked sick and pale. As they came closer it was clear that he did still have the shakes, too.

"I'm Lawrence Cotton," the thin guy said, coming forward to shake Blue's hand. "I'm the new director here at the Center."

He met Blue's eyes squarely as Blue introduced himself. His handshake was firm and his gaze was direct. He was dressed in jeans and a starched shirt. He was not only older but also much more impressive than Jason had been.

"Hey, you've got a classic truck here," he said, walking around it.

Blue said the truck was Micah's and Micah began to brag about how many miles she had on her and how good she was still running.

Shane stood there, moving restlessly and never quite meeting Blue's gaze.

When Micah paused for breath, Lawrence clapped him on the shoulder and said he'd like to drive the truck sometime. He caught Blue's eye, nodded goodbye, and turned to Shane.

"See you this evening, Shane," he said. "Work hard and pick out a horse for me. I'll come and ride with you one of these days."

"They're two-year-olds," Shane said. "They're not broke."

"You can coach me," Lawrence said. "Or maybe you could find me one that *is* broke."

Shane rolled his eyes. Blue felt like doing the same. That was all he needed—another pilgrim in the saddle. Lawrence seemed okay, though. Nothing phony about him.

Micah went around to the driver's seat and Shane stood where he was. Blue opened the passenger door and waited for Shane to go ahead. He hesitated for several seconds, so Blue said, "Get in, Shane."

He did, but he wasn't happy about it.

"I feel trapped in here," he said, when they were all wedged in and the doors closed.

"Won't be long," Micah said. "Jist up to my barn."

"I *hate* sitting in the middle."

"Cowboy up," Micah said. "There's a five dollar fine for whinin'."

"You always say that," Shane said. "Sue me. I haven't got a cent."

"You can work it out," Micah said.

Shane glanced up at him sideways, the first time he'd looked at either one of them.

"I'm not whining. What I'm saying is a fact. And I'm not working for you, Micah. I'm riding with Blue."

He had the shakes bad enough that his arm jerked against

Blue's as he looked up at him then and finally met his gaze. His eyes were bloodshot and not as hostile as when Blue had put a stop to his bid for freedom. Now they hid his feelings beneath a flat, angry glare and a glimmer of uncertainty.

Shane jerked his gaze away.

"And Blue works for me," Micah said. "So you can figger it however you want it."

"Let me outta here," Shane said. "I'll ride in the back."

"No ridin' in the back," Micah said. "It's agin the law."

"Aw, and we're really worried about the law," Shane scoffed.

"So jail's not bad, huh?" Blue said.

Shane jumped at the unexpected sound of his voice. It took him a second, but he shot back, "Not if you're tough."

He glared at Blue to make his point.

"You're pretty tough?" Blue asked.

"Tough enough," Shane said, and managed for a couple of heartbeats not to look away.

He sulled up and stared out through the windshield the rest of the way. At Micah's, he spilled out onto the ground as soon as Blue was out of his way but then he just stood there, blinking in the sun, as if he wasn't quite sure where he was or what came next.

Micah looked across the boy to Blue and shrugged, as if to say, *He's all yours.*

"Come on," Blue said, heading for the barn.

Shane came along, walking fast, trying to match Blue's stride. Micah stayed where he was. Blue was glad. He didn't need a lot of talk while he tried to get a feel for the kid.

As they stepped in at the east end, Blue said, "I'll get you started on your chores before I ride the next one."

"What do you mean, chores? Gordon said I'm riding with you. I'm gonna help you break them."

"Gordon's not the boss of this barn. You're not straddling anything until I see what kind of a hand you are. Don't even be messing with the twos from the ground. Especially not the roan."

Shane stalked past him, walked fast down the aisle and out the other end of the barn.

"Look out there," he said, raising his trembling arm to point, "I'll ride if I want to. My mom owns those two horses out there and she's always telling me to ride."

"Nope," Blue said. "No horses to ride until you're clean and sober."

Shane came back to him.

"I am. I haven't had a hit in a week."

"Keep that up and we'll see about it next week," Blue said. "You oughta be over the shakes by then."

Shane stuck his hands into his pockets.

"I wanta ride the colts," he said. "My dad's a roughstock rider. If I get good enough, I can rodeo with him."

"What I try to do is get 'em started in a frame of mind where they *don't* buck," Blue said.

He gestured at the manure fork standing in the corner.

"Start by cleaning the stalls," he said, "and don't throw out too much of the shavings."

Shane's sullen expression fell over his face again and he glared at Blue.

"I can ride," Shane said. "I want the worst one you've got."

Blue ignored that nonsense and went into the little corner tack room. He came out with a headstall and a bit he wanted to change to, noticing from the corner of his eye that Shane still stood in the same place.

Blue changed the bit without saying a word to him. Finally, just as he finished, Shane went to get the fork and the wheelbarrow.

After he put the screwdriver away, Blue left the barn and headed for the round pen. Andie Lee was just driving in.

Damn it. All he needed was for her to go in there and start

sympathizing with her baby boy, who had just taken his first step in the right direction.

Maybe she didn't know he was already here.

She cut off the motor and turned to get her hat off the seat.

Blue lengthened his stride and got there just as she opened the door. He put one hand around the frame of the open window and stood in her way.

"Don't get out," he said. "You can ride later."

A flicker of guilt in her eyes disappointed him. She did know.

"You said you weren't coming around when Shane's here."

"I know," she said. "I know I said that."

The hurt in her voice made him sorry he'd been gruff. That made him mad at himself. It also made him mad that he liked being this close to her. And that he'd love to touch her.

"You lied."

"Not *then*," she said quickly. "I'm just making myself a liar *now.* I need to see him working, actually *doing* something, Blue. I'll saddle up in five minutes and ride away."

"*You* need to see him in action," he said, "but *he* doesn't need that. You've got to let him have this for his own. Go to the barn now and you'll screw up everything."

"You, too?" she said. "Now Gordon and you think I'm Shane's biggest problem? I thought you were my friend, Blue."

Her voice caught when she said his name, like she was going to cry. But she wasn't. His hand tightened around the window frame until the edge dug into his fingers.

What the hell did he care what she thought of him?

"Listen to me," he said, from between his teeth. "I told you that boys need something of their own. There's a real possibility that Shane might take to this."

She gasped a little and her eyes bored into his.

"Why? How do you know that? What happened?"

"He's picking stalls, is what. When he thought he never would. Because he wants to ride the colts."

"He does? He's never been horse crazy. What did he say…"

"Nope," Blue said. "No tale-carrying between the two of you."

He glanced in to see that her feet were out of the way and pushed the door closed.

"I just need to see him."

He squatted down so his face was level with hers. Oh, God. This was too close. He wanted to kiss her.

"Andie Lee," he said. "Give him this chance."

Then he stood up and walked away toward the round pen.

He didn't realize he was holding his breath until the engine of her truck fired up. He heard the tires on the gravel and knew she was backing around in the driveway.

As she drove out into the road, he lifted the latch on the round pen gate, stepped inside and closed it behind him.

He'd done nothing all morning except babysit—first Micah, then Shane, and now Andie Lee.

He had to get a handle on himself. All this entanglement was nothing but a hindrance to the purpose that had brought him here.

CHAPTER SEVEN

NOT COMPLAINING—no matter what—was one of Blue's points of honor with himself. He didn't whine, not ever, not even silently in his own head. Fix it, ignore it, walk away from it—do something, even if it was wrong—but shut up about it. And don't be having regrets. Thinking back and being sorry about something was just another way of crying.

He followed that credo religiously. For ten years in the pen, that careful practice had given him a portion of peace. It had let him see beauty in his mind and paint it on canvas instead of thinking about being trapped where he was. It had kept him from going crazy.

Now a loser kid and a gabby old man were causing him to break his own code.

Lying there along the edge of Micah's porch with one boot crossed over the other knee and his hat down over his face, trying to get his twenty-minute after-lunch siesta, his gut was in a knot and his brain was sounding a steady drumbeat of bitching. How had he ever gotten himself into this? Why had he let himself be roped into this deal with Shane? He'd been doing all right with just the old man around and now he'd gone and given in to Micah's ideas about how to help this obnoxious kid.

He'd been an idiot to run Andie Lee off like he did. He should've let her stay here for the day and ruin her own plans. One day of the humiliation of his mother hanging around telling him what to do and Shane would've refused ever to leave the Center again.

She was expecting Blue to take Shane to raise, even though she said she wasn't and he said he wouldn't, and he should've backed out of the agreement the instant he knew that. He had to find a way out of this.

"My tomatoes will outdo any medicine when it comes to healin' a body," Micah said. "You better be eatin' that sandwich and don't you peel them offa there, neither. Put 'em back on. And that leaf of lettuce, too."

"What'll *it* do? Give me the power to fly?"

"Don't use that sneer with me," Micah snapped. "If one mornin's work wore you out so bad you can't eat then you'll starve slap to death, 'cause come suppertime, you'll be too weak to lift a fork. You're actin' like a foolish young'un, Shane."

Silence.

Good. Maybe they'd be quiet for five minutes.

"Git up," Micah said. "If you won't eat, then you ain't settin' around like a prince on my porch. Git out there and pick the rest of that manure outta them stalls like I told you the first time. You ain't half did your job and your mama ain't raisin' no slacker. Now hit it."

"Andie Lee…" Shane began.

"I won't hear it," Micah said.

"What I'm trying to tell you is that *my mama* ain't raisin' no slacker at *riding*. She wants me to ride, not shovel manure. She asked Lawrence to let me come up here so I can ride. She wants me to learn to ride, Micah, and roughstock, too, so I can go live with my dad and get out of her hair."

"You heard Blue this mornin'. Next week you can ride. *If* you're clean and sober."

"I'm sober now."

"Mebbe so, but from time to time you're shakin' like you got the palsy."

"What's the palsy?"

"A shakin' disease. Now get the hell to the barn."

Blue listened to the squeak of the woven leather chair and boot heels on the floor and then the steps. Shane got up. He went.

"Reckon he's got a stash on him?" Micah said in a low tone. "If he was to light a match in my barn, Blue, I'd have to kill him and tell Andie Lee he died."

Blue swung his legs off the edge of the porch and sat up. He ran his hand through his hair and settled his hat.

Damn. No sleep was what he got for getting mixed up with everybody he met.

"I'd say not, or he'd already have used it," he said. "He's been in the barn by himself enough times this morning."

"You're right," Micah said, watching Shane from beneath his hat brim. "He surely would be in a more mellow frame of mind if'n he'd had some dope."

Blue watched the boy, too. Shane walked into the barn with a weak, but insolent, swagger and disappeared down the aisle.

It'd take a lot to influence that little idiot for the good. Something along the lines of a miracle.

And he was not the man who could perform one. Andie Lee was a foolish woman for even thinking he could help save her son. Right now Shane hated his own guts and considered himself to be a worthless piece of flesh and blood. She had no clue what it would take to overcome that, and Blue didn't, either.

"Well," he said, "I've got six more colts to work. You coming out to supervise your barn boy?"

"In a while," Micah said. "I gotta clean up this mess and give it to the dogs. *They* like my tomatoes jist fine."

Blue turned and looked at him.

"They eat three-day-dead guineas, too, Micah."

Micah tried to look offended, but he grinned. "You had no call to point that out," he said.

He gathered up Shane's scattered remains of a sandwich.

"Dang it," he said. "I shoulda made him clean this up before I sent him to the barn. I'm gonna take some tomatoes down to the big house and when I come back, I'll work his little tail off. I aim for him to learn to pick a stall today if has to stay at it 'til midnight."

He went into the house, letting the screen door slam closed behind him.

Blue stood up and stretched. He would quit wasting time even thinking about Shane. He didn't owe the kid any more than a few minutes here and there. Micah was the one who'd had the idea to bring him up here, so Micah could take care of him.

Deliberately, he moved his thoughts to the roan colt. And to Gordon. He had to have a plan put together for Gordon by the time the colt was solid and dependable.

Too bad he and the roan couldn't be together for a long lifetime. Of course they might, if everything went the way he planned it and he planned well. He'd been caught before because he'd been in a blood heat.

That, and the fact that he couldn't leave Dannie's body to run.

But surely he could make a plan that would let him stay free. Andie Lee could tell him lots about Gordon and his habits, since she was staying down at the big house and since she'd known the big SOB for so long.

If Andie Lee would ever speak to him again.

All generative power resides in thought. That was an old Cherokee truth, but right now he had to quit thinking. Time to get something done.

He walked through the barn on the way to the small catch-pen out back where he'd been putting the twos for the last day or so. He still brought them all into the round pen for a couple of hours so they could get used to being worked with other horses in there, and at night he still turned them out into the pretty pasture with the trees, but today he was holding them in the pen just for something different. Variety was good. He ought to know.

Shane wasn't in the barn. Blue glanced into the stalls and the tack room but he wasn't there.

Micah didn't put his two using horses in for the night except in the very coldest weeks of winter, so Andie Lee's two head were the only ones who'd messed up any stalls. The bedding in both appeared to have been stirred a little, but there were still piles of manure scattered on top of it and wet spots, too.

Lousy job. Shane'd probably never done a day's work in his life. Evidently he didn't have the will to do it, either. He was probably lazy. Years of doping sure went hand in hand with laziness.

Dannie had had lots of energy as a young girl, but as soon as she got on the stuff every scrap of ambition had left her. Permanently. Even in the few short weeks that she had lived sober in the year before she died.

Andie Lee ought to know that this whole effort with Shane had less than a snowball's chance in hell.

When he reached the west end of the barn, Blue looked out and saw the boy.

With the roan.

Instinct sent his adrenaline surging. Worry that Shane could get hurt. Anger at the blatant disobedience. He'd told him to stay away from that colt, damn it.

He started toward them, moving slowly so as not to startle them. The colt was still more than skittish—downright nervous and mean—with everybody but Blue.

Which was why he couldn't believe what he was seeing.

Shane was at the fence, standing very still...with his head leaning against Roanie's neck. Unbelievable. The horse wouldn't let anyone get near him but Blue.

He stared, closed his eyes and looked again—at a loose-limbed scarecrow made of sticks propped up against a statue of a horse. He couldn't even see them breathe.

Boy and horse stood full in the sunlight, soaking it up through their skins. That was the only thing that made them real. Watching them made Blue feel it, too, even though he was in the shade.

It brought back the memory of the day he stepped out into the sunlight, free. This was a side of Roanie he would never have predicted.

A horse could tell the difference between an adult and a vulnerable young one—of any species. But the roan colt was very young, himself, to be trying to act on that recognition to offer support.

Especially since he'd had such a rough history with people. Shane wasn't all bad or all crazy, if any animal, especially this one, accepted him to such an extent.

It'd be an irony for sure if Roanie eventually developed into the rare babysitter kind of horse. Anything could happen. Horses were full of contradictions just like people.

But probably this was a fleeting moment, the first sign of the slightest trust between the colt and any other person. It probably happened because Shane was weak and wandering.

Remember this lesson, Bowman. You can't know all there is to know about a horse any more than you can about another person.

Shane stepped back. He backed up another step, bent double, and began to vomit into the grass. Roanie backed up, too, watched Shane for a minute, then dropped his head and began to graze along the fence.

Blue pulled the handkerchief from his hip pocket.

You can't know all there is to know about yourself, either. Who'd ever have thought you'd be out here on Gordon's ranch playing nursemaid to a junkie?

Shane had his hands braced on his trembling thighs.

He straightened up and wiped his mouth on the sleeve of his shirt. Blue dipped the cloth into the watering trough as he passed and wrung it out as he approached the boy. He held it out to Shane, who waited a while and then took it.

This is a deal-breaker. If you can't depend on him to follow orders you can't have him around horses. Send him packing, right now. He can ride down the hill with Micah when he goes to headquarters.

"I told you to stay away from this horse," Blue said. "He could've killed you."

"I know." Shane wiped his mouth again. "I was hoping he would."

He meant it. The low, flat tone of his voice rang true to despair.

"I'm such a fuck-up," Shane said.

Blue's anger flared.

"That's your choice. Don't be."

Shane raised his eyes to meet Blue's.

"My dad thinks so, too," he said. "I've not heard from him in a real long time."

His face flushing pink with embarrassment, Shane turned away. He stuffed the wet handkerchief into his own back pocket and tried to regain his swagger as he walked as fast as he could toward the barn.

Blue knew it well: Shane's blood was racing through his veins in a prickling flood of hopeless, helpless desire. Blue could feel it, too, fast and fresh and bitter as if he were still fifteen and wanting a father.

Micah's truck started up with a roar and drove, rattling, out onto the road in a cloud of dust.

ANDIE LEE ARRIVED before the middle of the afternoon. When Blue opened the gate of the round pen, leading the palomino filly out, Andie Lee was standing right there in his way.

"Blue," she said. "I need to talk to you."

Here she was again. How could such a beautiful woman be so stupid?

"The deal's off," he said.

She froze in place so he couldn't get past her.

"No! Why? That's what I came to see you about. Micah said you're riding and Shane's picking stalls. *All day.* I thought it'd be just for a little while and then he'd ride."

Blue's anger flared.

"You think Micah was lying?"

"No! Of course not. But you said you'd ride with Shane. You're not doing it."

She stepped up closer and he caught the smell of her flowery hair, even with the dust and horse and scent of pines from the mountains.

It still shocked him deep inside to realize he was looking at a real woman. Standing this close to one. She was breathing so hard, her breasts rose and fell under her shirt. He wanted to touch her, with a fierce desire that was an entirely separate thing from anything she was saying or doing. Her just being within his reach caused it.

Years. It had been years since he'd been with a woman.

Her eyes were full of worry.

He shouldn't be mad at her. He should be thanking her instead. She was giving him an excuse not to have to go through this torture again.

"You said you'd stay away. You've been here twice on Shane's first day."

"I know, but—"

He interrupted. He wanted to get past her.

"You don't trust me. I can't do you any good."

He took a step forward but she didn't back up.

"I *do* trust you or I never would've asked you to help me with Shane."

"I'm done."

"No! You can't be."

They were standing way too close now. The shape of her face was all strong lines that called to his hands—determined chin and high cheekbones and delicate jaw. Her skin looked soft as a foal's muzzle.

"Get out of here, Andie Lee. Take your boy back to the Center. Now step aside, please, and let me get by."

"Not yet. You have to give me a real reason for going back on your word."

Anger flashed through him like heat lightning.

"Neither you nor your son can take direction," he said. "You're proving that again standing here in my way."

She fell back.

He walked out, and Andie Lee fell into step beside him before the filly even cleared the gate.

"Please," she said. "Think about it some more before you send Shane away. He's already failed so many times. You're the one who said he's interested in the horses."

"As a way to try and get attention from his dad," Blue said. "That's all."

Andie Lee was silent. Evidently, she was thinking about that. They walked around the barn to the west end. He stopped and began to unsaddle the filly. Absently, Andie Lee picked up a comb and started working on the mane.

"Blue," she said quietly, "Shane's dad is hardly more than a dream anymore. He hasn't been to see us in a long time because he's so absorbed in his own goals. You're the only real man in Shane's life that he shows any respect."

"And that's not enough to obey me," he said, as he lifted the saddle off and dropped it onto the rack standing outside the door of the barn.

He took off the blanket and threw it wet-side up over the saddle. Then he began to scrape the sweat from the horse's back.

"I'm sorry I keep coming up here when I promised not

to," she said thoughtfully. "This morning I had *such* a feeling that Shane's hit bottom now and is going to go only upward from here. I guess I'm just trying to watch him do it. Trying to hurry it along, so I'll be free of all the burden and sorrow."

He didn't answer.

"Give him two days," she said. "Please. Today and tomorrow."

He looked up at her. She was watching him with those big gray-sky eyes, her bright hair shining in the sun. Her lips were slightly parted, waiting for his answer.

Her face was beautiful, yes. But her mouth went even beyond that word and he wanted to do things with it that he couldn't even put words to.

Many more talks with her and she, too, would be making him break his code. It wouldn't be the part about whining, though. In her case, it would be the part about blowing himself all to hell over a woman.

He would be playing this sight and the sound of her husky voice over and over in his mind and it wouldn't be long until he was crazy for more. For a guy in his position, there was no way he could take that.

No. No. I won't have any more to do with Shane or with you. There is no hope for your son.

She didn't push him. She waited for him to speak, working the tangles out with her long slender fingers before she pulled the comb through the blond hair of the horse that just matched her own. Finally, she shook hers back and turned to look at him.

The look in her eyes must be the same one that desperate mothers everywhere took on when their children started to go down. Tanasi Rose had looked at him just that way.

And he had failed her. That right there was the real reason he had to say no. He, too, had failed at a lot of things.

Big things. The real reason he was sending Shane away was that he couldn't save him, so he didn't have the heart to try.

Besides, it'd do more harm than not if he *could* get a handle on Shane. Blue would disappear from here for good someday. Then Shane would see that as another desertion.

Anyhow, he was a killer. That was nobody for a kid to admire.

"No," he said, his frustration and his own despair starting to rise. "If you and Micah want Shane to ride your horses, that's your business, but I'm having nothing to do with it."

He would not let himself look away from her like a coward. He was relieved to see no change in the expression in her eyes. Desperation was desperation. Maybe, once there, it couldn't deepen any more.

BLUE RODE every one of the twos longer than usual, making himself be patient, making himself concentrate, making himself focus on the individual facts about that particular horse. And making himself take each horse one more step forward in its training before he let it go and got on the next one.

He had so much going on in his mind and his heart that it was all he could do to ride intelligently, but if he hadn't made himself do it, he would've punched a hole in the barn wall. Andie Lee had been gone when he came out of the round pen after his next ride and Micah had pretty much stayed on top of Shane, so he didn't know if they'd talked or not.

He was fighting an onslaught of memories, and a whole new wave of rage against Gordon. If he hadn't talked to Shane like he did, Blue would never have gotten into this in the first place.

Now he felt like a quitter and he hated that. But better now than later, after going through a whole lot more frustration from Shane and putting time and thought into him that needed to go into the plan for Gordon.

Except that he'd cut himself off from any information about Gordon that Andie Lee could've given him.

"Blue!"

He turned to see Micah at the round-pen gate and rode over to him.

"I'm gonna run down to the machine shop fer twenty minutes, no more," the old man said. "Gotta pick up my tiller. Shane's straightenin' up the tack room."

"I'm not watching over him, Micah."

"I know. Andie Lee told me." He kept his face neutral but his voice had a trace of an aggrieved tone in it.

"I caught him with the roan colt after I told him to stay away from him."

"I know. I seen it all from the back porch," Micah said. "I can't fault you for a minute, Blue. He could get hisself killed and there ain't no call for you to have that on yore conscience."

As if Micah knew anything about his conscience.

Micah meant it, but he was disappointed, too. Well, so was Blue. He should've known before he ever said yes the first time that Shane was too far gone in rebelling. He and Micah both should have known.

Blue felt his gut crank one notch tighter. Damn. That was no good because the little paint horse he was on had already sensed it and was refusing to listen to him.

And it was no good because he was breaking his code again.

Micah's truck roared to life and he left and Blue opened the gate to ride outside. A change of place and a look at the mountains. That'd help him and the colt both settle down.

He rode out along the edge of the yard, following the road until he came to the thick trees, then swung the paint to the left to go up the hill a little and around behind Micah's house. By the time they almost got around it, the colt was settling down nicely.

"You're gonna be all right," he told the horse. "Everything's gonna be all right."

And then he rode out to where he could see the barn and the pens again. Everything *wasn't* all right. Shane was horseback, riding on the patch of soft dirt between the round pen and the road.

Blue smooched to the paint and got a faster trot. At first he thought the horse was one of Micah's older ones, but it wasn't. It was one of Blue's twos, the big bay colt.

Shane hadn't quite had the nerve to pick the roan. Or maybe Roanie hadn't let him catch him.

This open defiance proved he was right to wash his hands of the boy.

However, it hadn't done him much good because now he was the only adult on the place and it was up to him to stop Shane before he got hurt. He did have the horse saddled. Blue could only hope he had it cinched down tight.

Blue couldn't see Shane while he rode along the side of Micah's house and around the end of the barn. When he came out where he could see him again, the bay was bucking. Not too hard, but he was getting wound up.

"Over-and-under him! Give him some encouragement if you've got the guts!"

Blue swung around in the saddle to see Gordon on a big, heavy-muscled white horse charging toward Shane, coming up off the road with a scatter of gravel and dirt. Blue'd been so intent on Shane he hadn't even realized someone else was near.

The fury was already roaring in his ears, threatening that that was the last calm thought he'd have. He took a deep breath and tried to get control. Shane was his responsibility whether he wanted it or not. He had to be careful what he said and did so he could try to help the kid get out of this.

The horse wasn't broke and he and Shane could get into a terrible wreck.

"Use the ends of your reins," Gordon yelled. "Damn it, boy, don't you know what I mean? Hit him on the hip and the withers."

Shane had a hold on the saddle horn with one hand and it was all he could do to hang on to the reins with the other. The horse bucked harder with every shout Gordon made and he began to shy sideways to get away from the oncoming horse.

Blue could've killed Gordon that minute with his bare hands.

"*Make* him buck," Gordon yelled. "Whip the snot out of him, boy! Help him get it out of his system."

Blue guided his horse around the round pen, hoping to head Gordon off, but he was too late. Gordon pulled up at the edge of the dirt and kept up the barrage.

Shane lost a stirrup and slid sideways, then pitched up over the horse's neck. By some miracle, he didn't come off, though, and he came back down about half in the saddle.

"You'll never make a cowboy," Gordon sneered. "Turn loose of the horn and ride with your hand in the air. What's the matter with you, anyhow?"

Blue ached to get his hands on him. He got around the action and rode up next to Gordon.

"Shut up," he said.

Gordon flicked a scornful glance at him as if he were a fly. The bay colt slowed down and came to a sudden, jarring stop. Shane fell forward and grabbed him around the neck, then, when the horse stayed still, the boy sat back up in the saddle.

He found his stirrup and stuck his foot into it. He turned to look at Gordon, his eyes blazing in his paper-white face.

"I rode him, didn't I?"

His yell was loud but not strong. His confidence was

gone. He wasn't giving up, though. That was a point in his favor.

"Because he *let* you," Gordon said. "That horse knows when a baby's on his back. He *let* you stay there."

Shane shook his head.

"If you wanta rodeo so bad, fork the saddle on that roan colt," Gordon said. "Show *him* you're the boss and I'll call you a roughstock rider."

Who cares what you call him?

Blue held his tongue. It'd only shame Shane further if he didn't let him fight his own battle.

"The roan colt likes me," he said. "I can ride him, too."

"Yeah. Like pigs can fly." Gordon was even more scornful, if that could be possible. "You're always full of brag. If you ever get where you're not hungover, you'll have to back that up or eat your words."

Shane managed not to look away from Gordon. He fought it, but he resisted breaking their locked look, just as he'd done the day he tried to run. This time he didn't show any tears, which was another point for him. His chin trembled, though.

Blue kept his eyes on the boy so he wouldn't reach over, drag Gordon off his horse and have at him right there.

Shane's lips parted but he couldn't speak. The best he could do was to pull the bay around and ride toward Gordon, then past him, so he wouldn't be turning tail and running. He didn't look away from Gordon's glare as long as they faced each other but every line of his body said he had to get out of there because he'd had all he could take.

Blue said, "Nobody rides up to this barn and insults my hand. Get off this hill."

Gordon laughed. "That's one thing I like about you, Bowman. You've got a hell of a nerve."

"Make tracks."

For a long minute Gordon sat and studied him, almost as

if trying to decide whether to bail down off his horse and pull Blue off his. Yet a fight wasn't what was in the air.

Gordon looked at him with eyes the very same deep blue color as Blue's own.

"I may like your nerve," Gordon said, "but it's a sad day when a jailbird can come onto my ranch and tell me where to go."

Jailbird. The word sent a bolt of shock through Blue.

"And there'll be another sad one for you," Blue drawled, "because someday even the great Gordon Campbell will go to the Ghost Country."

Gordon waited, holding his head cocked with the air of the big boss man looking down his nose at a lowly beggar.

"Am I to take that as a threat?"

Blue held the blue-steel gaze and pierced it with his own.

"Take it for the truth," he said.

CHAPTER EIGHT

SOMETHING FLASHED in Gordon's eyes, like a shaft of sun striking ice. Not fear. Anger, yes, but also some kind of approbation. Could that be?

"Here's another truth for you," he said. "I'm God. On the Splendid Sky, any man who forgets that is in a world of hurt."

Blue had a sudden remembrance of his little-boy daydreams about meeting his father. None of them went anything like this.

Gordon turned his back on Blue and rode away. Naturally. So he'd have the last word.

Blue watched him go while the dust-devil of turmoil in his gut grew into a tornado.

He turned his own horse away from the sight and looked to see if he could tell which way Shane had taken the colt. The bay would make a good horse if he didn't get away with too much. But if he had very much time to run over Shane and take advantage of him, he'd be ruined.

Blue tried, but he couldn't turn his thoughts.

How did Gordon know he'd been in prison? Of course, that could be a guess. Micah had told him where he picked Blue up, probably. And they had both rightly assumed that a man on foot not a half mile down the road from the gates— a man who, when offered a job, had no other place to go— had just been released.

That would only be logical thinking.

It didn't mean that Gordon knew who Blue was.

What *had* that been in Gordon's eyes?

Surely not approval. But for a split second that's what he'd seen.

Blue didn't want to think about it. He wanted to slam his mind shut and think about something else. Because…he had to admit that he wanted it to be.

That shocked him. How could he care what Gordon thought of him?

It was a horrible knowledge. The worst feeling in the world—worse, even, than regret. Which, come to think of it, was nothing but helplessness of the past.

The helpless little boy still lived in him. The little boy who'd wanted a daddy more than anything else in the world. This weird feeling was nothing but the natural desire of any child to please a parent.

He dismissed the thought and tried to concentrate on the beauty around him but the encounter with Gordon filled his mind. Gordon Campbell didn't deserve to smell this fresh grass scent on the wind or see the mountains white-topped against the sky.

Blue had to get control again. He had to find Shane.

He clucked to the paint and headed toward the hills that rose along the edge of the road west of Micah's pastures. To get completely out of sight this fast, the kid must've headed for the trees. He'd probably let the bay scrape him off on a low-hanging limb somewhere and the colt would try to do that to every rider from now on.

But he couldn't stop thinking about what Gordon had said to him. Really, it was stupid of him to be surprised.

If he'd thought about it, he would've realized that Micah had assumed all along that he was just out of prison because Micah had asked him no questions at all. Of course, Micah was one of the old-timers who considered it rude and danger-ous to ask a man about his past, but still, the natural thing would've been to have asked him if he needed to go pick up some clothes or anything when Blue accepted the job and they headed out to the ranch.

Micah must've known. That's why he'd made that remark about Blue's conscience this morning.

So, if Micah and Gordon knew Blue was just out of the pen, did they know what he'd been in for? Did they know who he was?

He doubted that. Gordon would've had to be the one to look into it and Blue wasn't that important in his life. Yet.

Wake up, Bowman. Remember every human and every horse is an unpredictable individual. Don't take anything for a fact until you know that for sure.

He'd keep that in mind, but he was pretty sure that on the Splendid Sky he was nothing but an ex-convict horse wrangler.

Blue turned in the saddle and looked down along the bountiful sweep of the river valley, warming in the sunlight. That valley was like a little heaven in itself.

And beyond it, the mountains. Medicine mountains.

To look at them every day of his life would heal a man's soul.

If he'd grown up here looking at these mountains, he wouldn't be carrying all this anguish in his heart.

Blindly, Blue rode past the round pen and up along the fence line of the pasture. How much time had passed since the kid and the bay had been gone? Not long. It couldn't have been very long but it seemed forever.

Fresh hoofprints in the dust showed where Shane rode up the side of the hill. He saw them but he couldn't quite think about them.

He hadn't heard a thing since he'd been here about Gordon's son. Where was he? Rose had said he had a son, which was the main reason he wouldn't divorce his wife and marry her.

Blue headed the paint toward the hoofprints. One more hard pitch from the bay, and that little pissant would be on the ground, maybe with his head knocked against a tree or a rock.

Serve him right for going against everything Blue told him. It might knock some sense into him.

Lawrence ought to lock him up down at the Center and make him scrub pots and pans in the kitchen. Anything more than that, Shane would mess up.

Now, that'd be a skill he could use in prison. Except that inside, he wouldn't last a day.

Yes, if Shane didn't watch out, some day soon he'd be trading good old, affable, educated, reasonable Lawrence for ugly Stud Dedmon, who'd slam him up against a cell wall just to make himself happy. And he'd *be* the screaming little girlfriend instead of dragging poor Lisa around at gunpoint.

At fifteen, fatherless and scratching to ride the bad broncs to prove his manhood, Blue had been just as ignorant as Shane but at least he'd grown up pretty rough and he'd been twenty-three when he went to prison. He'd been big and strong and tough enough to protect himself instead of being a wasted wimp like Shane.

But he did have to hand the kid one thing. He had stood up to Gordon as best he could. He never had let the spirit-killing words cut his legs out from under him. There was still a shred of self-respect somewhere down in that skinny frame of his.

And it wasn't just that one time Gordon had been slashing at Shane, either, since he'd made himself the only visitor allowed all week down at the jail—and that after the public mortification he'd laid on him right before he went in. But in spite of that kind of a wearing down, today Shane hadn't looked away from the arrogant old bastard once.

Behind Blue, Micah's truck roared into the yard. Blue

turned back and trotted to meet it. The horse wasn't too happy to go toward that noise, but he did.

"Where're you headed?" Micah yelled, climbing out and settling his hat again once he was on the ground.

Blue rode up to him.

"Looking for my good bay colt," he said. "That damn Shane's trying to ruin one of the best horses we've got."

Micah squinted past him.

"What the hell is Shane doin' *on* the bay colt?"

"Proving he doesn't have to do what we tell him," Blue said.

Micah squinted past Blue. "Looky yonder," he said.

Sure enough. Shane was coming downhill out of the pine trees, afoot. He was limping and he was dusted up some, but he was walking.

"He's all right," Blue said, "and that colt had goddamn well better be just fine, too."

"I'm takin' him back to Lawrence right now," Micah said. "We cain't have him loose on the place. The boy ain't strong enough yit in his mind to be foolin' with horses."

He pushed his hat to the back again. "Matter of fact, I'm beginnin' to think his mind may never come back to him."

Blue thought about Toby Clark hollering and yelling through the night, losing his mind from being locked up so many years. He wasn't the only one. And for some of them, it didn't take years, either. Micah didn't know any more than Shane did about how easy life was on the Splendid Sky.

"The kid did do one thing right today," Blue said. "He looked Gordon in the eye all the time he was putting him down."

"Gordon? What's he got to do with it?"

"He dropped by to give Shane a little advice about riding a bucking horse," Blue said. "But he wasn't real tactful about it."

"Well, then," Micah said happily. "No wonder the kid went haywire. We cain't expect Shane to..."

"Shane was already mounted and the horse was pitching when Gordon rode up," Blue said. "The little hardhead saddled and got horseback as soon as I let him out of my sight."

Micah shook his head mournfully. "That's twicet today he disobeyed a di-rect order about the horses," he said. "He ain't ready to work up here…"

"No," Blue said.

"…yet," Micah said.

Blue looked down at Micah and waited until he looked up at him again.

"I need to go find that colt."

Shane was stumbling, clearly exhausted. It would take him a little while to make it into the yard. Micah would be fine alone with him.

"Serve Shane right if we made him go find him," Micah said. "Except that it'd be teetotally im-possible for him to git within spittin' distance. He'd spook the colt clear into Canady."

"Hell, no," Blue shot back. "I won't put the colt through that. Besides, I'm done trying to clean up somebody else's mistakes raising their kids. Shane's Andie Lee's deal. I'm out of it."

Don't know why I ever got in it. Looks like I'd have learned to say no, since trying to clean up after Gordon's fatherly neglect got me sent to prison.

Micah thought about it for a minute, then shook his head sorrowfully. "Cain't fault you there," he said. "Go on and git the colt. I don't need no help to haul that bony little carcass back where we got it—but man, I jist hate havin' to tell Andie Lee and ruin her dream."

EARLY THE NEXT MORNING, the steady peal of a bell wove itself into Blue's dream. It turned into the clanging of cell doors and took him from dreaming he was in the round pen with the bay to believing in his bones he was back inside.

He sat bolt upright in a light sweat, eyes wide open. The sturdy old room in Micah's house surrounded him.

"Git yer boots and britches on!" Micah yelled. "Somethin's happened. Let's go!"

In no time they were in the truck, bouncing out into the road, straining their eyes down toward headquarters where the bell was still ringing. Daylight filtered into the valley but the sun wasn't up over the mountains yet. Lights were coming on all over the ranch, looking paler than they would have if the dark still ruled.

"The bell's at the big house," Micah said, grumbling. "Looks like Andie Lee coulda took time to call and tell us what's goin' on. See any smoke?"

"No," Blue said, buttoning his shirt against the cold air on his bare skin. He was scanning the valley as best he could. "But with the mist in the low places, it's not easy to tell."

They were some of the first to get to the main house. Somebody was running on foot from a house across the road as they drove into the yard, and another man was heading there horseback from the big arena.

Everybody was looking at Andie Lee and Gordon. They were arguing toe-to-toe beneath the bell on its wrought-iron frame with the big SS on top that stood in the west end of the yard. Micah pulled up onto the grass and parked not far from it.

Andie Lee was dimly aware that the Splendid Sky hands were gathering but she couldn't see them for Gordon, looming in her face, yelling at her as if she were deaf. He jerked the bell rope from her hands so fast it burned her palms.

"What the hell were you thinking? Andie Lee, goddammit, you've alarmed the whole ranch."

She yelled right back at him.

"This is the emergency bell, Gordon. That's its purpose."

"We don't have an emergency here."

Her heart lurched. He was going to be really difficult. Shane had hurt Gordon's ego, and that was going to be hard to face.

"Yes, we do," she said, as calmly as she could. "We need to find them fast. Check all the trails, just in case Shane's not headed for the Lininger. Look where there aren't any trails. That horse could kill him, Gordon."

"Too bad. He asked for it."

"You could probably see him if you'd go up…"

"No. I'll not take the Piper up to look for him. It's not cheap to put a plane in the air. Do you know much it costs?"

Gordon was so angry he couldn't even say more than a simple sentence without sucking in a fresh breath. He was even more furious than he looked.

"You fly around all the time spying to see if your men are working, looking for fence down, looking for cattle out, looking for elk and moose and wolves and coyotes and who knows what all else? My son isn't as important as any of that?"

"I've spent a God's plenty on your son. And it's all been money down a rat hole. This is how he repays me and I'm mad as hell."

"I'm embarrassed," she said. "I'm mortified that Shane has invaded your house and stolen your gun. But, Gordon, we have to put all that aside until we find him."

He gave her a glare of pure disgust and turned away to stride to the steps where he could be on a higher plane than the hired hands coming into his yard to wait for his orders.

When Gordon stomped off, Micah got out and limped toward Andie Lee. Blue went with him. Men on four-wheelers, in trucks, on horseback were gathering, all fully dressed and ready to roll. They'd obviously been up way before daylight, already starting their work. Gordon got his money's worth and more than twelve hours a day out of them, that was for sure.

Blue had never been this close to the big house. It sat there, part of the earth, rising behind Gordon solid as a mountain, welcoming all comers with a porch lined with benches and chairs, potted plants blooming among them as if this were the most hospitable home on earth.

The difference between it and the rented houses Rose and her children had lived in was the difference between heaven and earth.

Micah took Andie Lee by the shoulders.

"What's the matter, honey? What's going on?"

"Shane," Andie Lee snapped, her husky voice cooking with anger. "What else? He ran off and took the roan colt with him to prove to Gordon he could ride him."

Blue stepped up, staring at her in disbelief.

"*My* roan colt?"

She fixed him with her direct gray eyes. "That's the only one I know of on the place," she said tartly.

Blue's heart dropped. The roan colt. He had just started to whinny to him, calling to a friend, whenever he caught a glimpse of Blue.

"I'd like to get my hands on that little cokehead," he said, from a jaw nearly too tight to move. "That's a damn fine horse. He better not get him hurt."

Andie Lee paled and her eyes widened as if he'd struck her. Watching her face, Blue realized it was because she couldn't come back with, "and that's a damn fine boy."

And because Blue should be putting Shane's safety ahead of the roan's.

"The *horse* has good sense," he said.

Micah interrupted. "Used up as the kid was yesterday, he must've got rested in a mighty hurry. Or maybe he got some of them uppers pills. He could've had 'em hid."

"Yes," Andie Lee said. "I wouldn't be a bit surprised if that turned out to be exactly what he did."

Her eyes were bright with the anger that flushed a pink

streak across her cheekbones. She was still beautiful. Even more so.

"I'm going to wring his ungrateful little neck, Micah," she said. "I promise you. And Blue, I'm sorry about your horse. I'm mortified."

"Where'd he go?" Blue asked. "Are you sure he even caught the colt?"

Her hot gaze flashed back and forth between him and Micah. "Was the horse there this morning?"

"Well, we didn't hardly stop to count heads in the pens," Micah drawled. "Not with you ringing the clapper outta this bell."

Her hair was pulled up in a high ponytail that stretched the skin over her cheekbones and sent loose strands falling across her face. She was pacing around, constantly in motion, wearing tight leggings and a huge sweatshirt that hung off her slim frame and a long shirttail sticking out from under that.

Maybe that was her pajamas. They looked like they'd been slept in.

Even dressed like that, she still looked like the rich rancher's daughter. One who wasn't getting her way right then but intended to have it soon.

She stepped closer to talk to Blue and Micah, keeping her voice low just as if the rest of the men didn't need to know why they'd been called out at the crack of dawn. The scent of her hair was still flowers but her skin smelled like sleep. Warm and cozy. Blue took an involuntary breath that pulled the smell to him again.

"Shane came in here last night and took Gordon's daddy's rifle down off the fireplace and some supplies out of the kitchen and left a note on the refrigerator that said he was going to get the roan. He vowed to prove Gordon wrong that he couldn't ride that horse."

Micah laughed. "I wisht I'd been a little mouse," he said. "I bet seein' that note put a double kink in ol' Gordon's tail."

"He found it while I was out here ringing the bell," she said. "I don't know which made him more furious."

"How come? This here's an emergency," Micah said.

Before she could answer, Gordon's voice boomed across the yard.

"I'll make this fast, men, so you can get on to work," he shouted, and that put an end to all other conversation.

Gordon looked around to make sure of that, though.

"Andie Lee's Shane has run off with the roan colt and some firearms and food," he said. "Keep an eye out for them today as you go about your business."

He waited for that to sink in.

"And do *not* blab about this on the radios and walkie-talkies."

Somebody called, "What about notifying the other divisions?"

"I doubt he'll get as far as any other division," Gordon said, "considering the disposition of that colt. Shane's no horseman. The fewer people who know, the better. This time we're having no police, no highway patrol, no outsiders of any kind. Word of this is not to leave the ranch. Running your mouth when you oughtta keep it shut could mean your job."

"So we're getting up our own search parties, then, Mr. Campbell?"

The question came from one of the young men sitting on a four-wheeler, chomping at the bit to fire it up and run.

"No, Crockett. This may finally be the lesson that'll straighten that boy out," Gordon said. "I'm gonna let him take the consequences of his actions today."

"What?"

Andie Lee turned on him like a mother bear. She ran to the steps and up them in a flash of long legs. She had on some kind of clog shoes, sort of cutoff boots, and they slammed on the wooden steps like blows from a hammer.

"What do you mean? It's bad enough that you won't take the airplane up. What are you *thinking?*"

He barely glanced at her as he said to the crowd, "Nothing else we've tried has made a bit of difference in Shane's behavior. If nobody rescues him, he'll learn enough today that he'll be a different boy by dark tonight," Gordon said.

"If that horse hurts him, he could be dead by dark," she said.

Gordon said, "Just remember—we're not calling in the authorities this time."

That should be enough to satisfy you was the message in the look he gave her then.

She turned to look at the men who had come here for orders.

"I think Shane is headed up to the Lininger cabin where Jason used to take the kids for outings," she said. "It's the only trail on the ranch he knows."

"Any of you working between here and there today, keep your eyes peeled," Gordon commanded.

He was furious. Blue could see and hear that beneath the surface. The boy had got Gordon's goat—he'd made him the subject of talk and the butt of many a joke that'd be told today on the ranch. A kid stealing his gun from him while Gordon was asleep in the house. That was an exploit bound to enter the legends of any ranch, much less one where the owner was not generally well-liked.

Yep. That was the real reason Gordon was so determined to try to keep the story on the ranch. His own ego.

Blue watched Micah, knowing that he didn't care how mad Gordon was.

"There's a horse been stolen," the old man said loudly. "That right there used to be a big deal around here. It's worth a couple of search parties."

Everybody turned to look at him.

"It's not my horse," Gordon said.

"It's a dangerous horse with a sick boy," Micah said. "Time was, that would've meant somethin', too."

"Time was that stealing a horse meant a man went to jail or to his own hanging," Gordon snapped. "But this is a special case."

He looked as if he thought it was generous of him not to hang Shane.

"I won't throw good money after bad," he said. "I've already invested a great deal in that boy with no return. I won't pay wages for my men to hunt for him. This ranch won't run itself."

"Then I'll go alone!" Andie Lee said. "I don't need any help."

But, of course, she did. Blue knew it and so did every other man there. An out-of-control kid with a gun and a horse with the rep of a budding outlaw made a combination that was way too much for any one person to corral.

A tenser silence fell over the yard for one short minute as the men fought their gallant impulses to volunteer to help a woman in distress. It deepened as they then thought about the value of their jobs, instead.

"I'll go with you, honey," Micah said.

He started toward her.

"Well, then," Gordon said quickly. "That's settled. Let's get to work, men!"

The crowd started dispersing before the words were out of his mouth. Gordon's men didn't let any grass grow under their feet.

Blue turned and walked away.

This was one time he actually agreed with Gordon, much as he hated to admit it. Letting Shane take his lumps was the only way to get it through the kid's head that horses and the land were bigger than any person and neither one could be fooled with lightly.

No telling what condition the roan would be in when he found him.

That colt was going to make the best horse ever to cross Blue's path. Bar none. When he was old—if he lived to be old—the roan would be the horse he always held as special—as the best one in his life. He'd known that by instinct when he first saw him and he had a feeling the roan had felt it, too. Horses knew a lot more than most people thought.

He'd like to grab that worthless, trouble-making kid by the scruff of the neck right now and shake him until his teeth rattled. Roanie had come so far. If Shane got him badly hurt or killed, that boy had better be hunting a hole.

Drug addiction had taken everyone he loved, and now it had his horse. It was a hell of a thing. Why was it that only marijuana was called "weed"? All drugs should be called that because they were everywhere, sucking the good out of the soil.

Out of the people. People who turned and ran to hide inside a fake-happy, poison haze every time they had a little problem.

He probably should take one of Micah's guns with him in case the roan was hopelessly down. The thought made his gut go tight. He'd never let him suffer and never leave him there alive. Best to go prepared.

If there was trouble, the sooner he found it, the sooner it'd be behind him.

Blue turned on his heel and kept walking, feeling his way with his feet while he held out his thumb to the truck coming up the hill from headquarters driven by one of Gordon's good men, headed for work up in the hills. It slowed.

"Ride up to Micah's?" he called.

"Hop on."

Two men sat on the back of the flat bed. Blue jumped up to join them as the truck kept moving at a crawl.

"Tell me how to get to the Lininger place?" he said.

Both of them told him, one giving one detail, the other adding the next. They were young kids, probably hired for the summer. He wondered how they knew so much about it.

"Y'all been working up there?"

"Moving cattle," one of them said. "Summer pasture's on past that cabin."

"Gonna help the old man and the lady hunt the kid?" the other one asked.

"No," Blue said. "It's my horse."

They nodded and watched him, trying not to let him see the curious glances they threw at him, at his braid hanging out from under his hat and his face beneath the brim.

"It's a red roan? Ain't that what Mr. Campbell said?"

"Yeah. Two year old. Don't try to catch him, though. If you see him, just drive him downhill towards home."

The word stayed on his lips after the sound of it died away. It felt like a foreign language on his tongue. He hadn't used that word in a long, long time.

He didn't know why he'd said it.

No, he wasn't going to hunt for that miserable addict of a kid any more than Gordon was. But be damned if he'd let the druggie little devil take the roan colt off into the mountains and ruin him.

What he was going after was his horse.

CHAPTER NINE

ANDIE LEE STOOD on the porch and stared at Micah without hearing a word he was saying. Her insides had gone stone cold the minute she heard the news. How could this be happening to her? And her son? She was Andie Lee Hart. Her life was not supposed to be this way.

Growing up, she'd been given whatever she wanted. Except love and attention, of course, but she'd always believed that those treasures would be granted to her someday, by magic.

After she grew up overnight at seventeen, she had *done* whatever she wanted—waitressing and leather-painting notwithstanding. She could've walked away from that life any day if she'd let Toni send her money. Even after she kept the baby, Toni had begged her—not to come back to the Splendid Sky, of course, but to settle in Texas near her relatives and let them find her a respectable rich man to marry.

Andie Lee had refused. She had proved she could succeed in everything she'd started by using her will and her brains and her pride.

But dealing with Shane had worn every part of her down to nothing. Using up every one of her strong qualities had not moved her one millimeter closer to saving him.

From the corner of her eye, she saw Gordon driving his pickup out of the circle drive that surrounded the house, going off to his usual day's work. The yard was empty. Gordon. Acting like the ass he was. Why had she expected anything different?

Because he'd been different lately. Somehow. To her, at least.

Not really. Hadn't he left Shane in jail for a whole week? Gordon would never really change. It was only the pathetic little girl still living inside her that had thought that he would. The little girl who'd expected magic to happen.

She looked over Micah's shoulder one more time but there was no sign of Blue near the old truck. And *why* was she looking for him?

Because he seemed to have the guts to go against Gordon and he didn't like Gordon and he didn't work for Gordon. Now why was she thinking that when Blue had already cut Shane loose?

Expecting magic again. A knight on a white horse. Well, on the Splendid Sky it was the wicked stepfather who rode the white horse and the little girl who'd been all alone was now a woman alone.

Except for her surrogate grandpa.

"So I'll pack us a horse," Micah was saying. "Thataway, we'll have another mount, jist in case we find the boy afoot—or, God forbid, hurt."

"Micah," she said, turning toward the door, "I'm gone as soon as I grab some clothes and a medical bag. You don't have time to pack a horse."

His face fell. He was so dear and she did not want to hurt his feelings, but he'd be another burden for her.

"You think I'm too stove up to ride, don't you?"

"Well," she said, "Shane's got a good head start and you can't stay in the saddle all day."

"Time will tell," he said, turning toward his truck. "Git your gear. I'll meet you at the barn."

All the time she was running up the stairs and then while she was pulling on jeans and a shirt, she took slow, deep breaths and tried to get her thinking under control. The trouble was, she could understand Gordon's reasoning and his refusal to help. He had a huge ranch to run, work that was never done, and Shane had given him a symbolic slap in the face.

She needed an additional someone to be furious with—someone to blame besides Shane—but there was no one.

Except herself.

Gordon was right. He had invested a lot in Shane, including a portion of his ego and his reputation along with the money and time, and in return he had lost Old Ian's rifle, a precious possession that no amount of money could replace.

It was unfathomable to her that anyone would refuse to look for an impaired child on a wild horse in the wilderness, but when she stepped back and looked at it rationally, the man was certainly within his rights. He owed her nothing. It was too late for him to be a father for her childhood and maybe he had never even owed her that.

What if he cut his losses now? What would she do?

Andie Lee jerked a pair of jeans off the hanger in the ancient armoire, rolled them up and stuffed them into one of the saddlebags, then crossed the room to its little closet. She'd hidden in there as a child, covering her ears against Toni and Gordon's fights until she fell asleep, and now she wished she could crawl in there and not come out for a week.

A whole new series of decisions was looming and she didn't want to make them. She'd done nothing but make the wrong ones for two years now.

She jerked her mind off that useless, well-worn track and tried to think of tactful reasons she could use to make Micah stay home. That was better than thinking about where Shane was this minute and what he was doing and whether he'd tried to fire that ancient gun and whether the horse had killed him yet.

Or what she was going to do and say when she found him. This latest bad behavior had driven her to the limits of the amount of humiliation she could take. If she were very honest, she'd have to admit that she'd never been so furious with Shane in all his life.

Micah. First, she had to get away from Micah. He would slow her down considerably.

But she did need help. One thing she meant to do today, if it were humanly possible, was bring Blue's horse back to him. That would ease her debts a little. The man was working sixteen hours a day for the pittance Micah could pay him and he needed his horse back.

If she found either the horse or Shane hurt, she would more than have her hands full. Micah knew that and he did not mean to be dissuaded.

That was one of Micah's basic traits. He felt perfectly comfortable butting into anybody's business and he had always felt especially free to jump right in the middle of hers. She might as well forget about leaving him behind. Knowing him, he'd follow her even if she rode off without him.

She pulled out her quilted Carhartt jacket because she might have to stay out overnight, and threw it over one arm. With her saddlebags over one shoulder, she stood still for a second and tried to think if there was anything else.

She'd need her binoculars. They were in her truck.

Andie Lee was out of the room and into the wide, dim hallway when she brushed back a strand of hair and realized she still had the ponytail and her silver clip was lying on the dresser. She had to have her silver barrette.

Chase had given it to her on that starry Montana night so long ago when they'd run off from the Splendid Sky. He'd bought it for her at the Plaza in Santa Fe when he went down there for a rodeo. Before they'd ever even kissed or flirted very much at all. Soon after he came to the ranch, soon after he saw her for the first time.

When he gave it to her, it was in a solemn, almost ceremonial way, as if it were an engagement ring. Neither of them had mentioned marriage—not until many years after that night—but the gift he had shined on his jeans before he offered it to her had been like a promise between them.

When she'd tried to give it back the day she left him in San Antonio, he had refused to take it.

Keep it, Andie. Then we'll still be together even if we're apart.

Chase had loved her, in his own selfish way. He still did. And she would always love him in *her* own selfish way because he was the only person who'd helped her keep her baby without having to marry Trey Gebhardt.

She picked up the barrette and looked at it.

He had helped her keep her baby, who didn't love her any more. Chase still loved her but Shane didn't. Shane couldn't love anyone, he hated himself so much.

To think that she'd never considered anything else but that she would keep him and raise him. She'd done it so she'd always have someone of her own, someone to love her.

The weight of the old Navajo silver in her hand was a comfort. The worn edges of its hand-worked pattern caressed the pad of her thumb and soothed her a little. It was her worry-stone. Pretty soon, if Shane didn't get well, she'd have the ancient Two Gray Hills pattern worn away.

She thought about what Blue had said. Shane only wanted to ride so he could impress his dad.

Maybe she should find Chase wherever he was and ask him to come. He would do it—unless he was really high up in the standings or had an especially important ride coming up. Even so, eventually, he would appear, world-stopping grin and all.

But that would only reinforce the myth that Chase was Shane's biological father. She had let Shane believe that far too long. Obviously, that had been another of her major mistakes.

And maybe refusing to marry Chase four years ago when

he had finally asked her had been another. Shane had never forgiven her for saying no.

Maybe if she'd sacrificed it all for Shane one more time it would've made him happy.

But she and Chase were both too bent on doing what they wanted to have time to make a home—she was trying to be the most famous, sought-after, successful equine lameness specialist in North Texas and he was trying for World Champion in both saddle-bronc and bareback. Homes had to be built on compromises and give-and-take and the two of them could never do that.

If they'd tried and failed, Shane would have suffered even more.

She pushed the clawing thoughts away and ran downstairs, boot heels clattering on the bare oak steps. On the way up to Micah's she tried not to think at all. She tried not to feel, either.

There was a big job before her and she'd better steel herself to get it done. She needed to go into surgery mode: calm, clear and ruthlessly analytical. All feelings locked away. Every part of her brain on alert.

Micah was at the barn, cinching a pack saddle onto a horse. Bedrolls, packs of food and a big canteen rested on a nearby hay bale. On top of them lay Micah's personal war bag and his jean jacket.

"Well, I see you haven't slowed down any on your packing, Micah."

"No, nor on my ridin', either," he said testily. "The food's all dried stuff and the canteen's water. No time to make coffee but I've brought the pot."

As he moved around the horse, his limp was worse.

"Micah…" she began.

"I won't hear it, so save your breath. You got your medical bag packed?"

"I need to check it," she said, and went to her truck.

"I've put my gun in the pack," he yelled after her. "If we need to put that roan colt down, you cain't git close enough to him fer a needle."

Damn. But it was true. Anything could've happened to either the colt or Shane or both by now. Somehow, in the heart of the selfish child deep down in her, she was glad Micah was going to stick with her, whether he'd slow her down or not.

When she went back in with her two bags and the jacket, she dropped them with the other packs and went to saddle her horse.

"Where's Blue?" she asked.

"I dunno. I thought he'd wait for me at the truck but he warn't there."

"Which one of your horses do you want?" she asked.

"Shorty, a'course."

She picked up a halter and went to the pasture to get the gelding who was nearly as old in horse years as Micah was in human years. He was in good shape, though, and as dependable a horse as ever lived.

While she caught him and led him back to the barn, she thought about her own choice. She would take Sinn Fein. He was bigger boned and stronger and faster if they saw something that needed to be reached in a hurry.

If they saw Shane in danger and needed to save him.

What an irony. How long had she been trying to save him?

She pulled her mind back to the horse. She had no idea who'd bred the tall gray and given him his Irish terrorist name or exactly what his training history was. She'd bought him on the spot one day when she'd been the veterinarian on call at a hunter-jumper show. He'd been too thin, which was considered stylish then, and one reason she'd bought him was to feed him. The other was that he simply struck some chord in her, even though he'd been jerking at the bit and giving a hard time to the young girl who was his owner.

Maybe *because* he'd been jerking away from her hands. The rider had been quite the little bitch. Sinn Fein had showed patience and restraint by not dumping her.

They worked fast and Andie Lee saddled both the riding horses while Micah loaded the packs. He had taken her and her friends on pack trips while she was growing up, and he was a wizard at judging what to put where in order to get the same amount of weight on each side of the tree.

"I see you've performed your usual magic," she said, when he'd lashed the last rope into place and tied the knot.

"Thank'ee, ma'am. Now go in the house and pee whilst I leave a note for Blue. I aim to ride. I ain't stoppin' for no bathroom breaks. *Ain't* no bathrooms in the mountains. This here's yore last chance."

She laughed and did as she was told. When she came out onto the front porch again, she noticed a rider in the distance, crossing the big hay meadow at the foot of the hill across the road from Micah's.

That was the way she and Micah would take to hit the trail to the old Lininger place, which was still called by the name of its original settlers although it'd been part of the Splendid Sky since before Gordon was born. She watched for another minute, then ran to the barn.

"Micah, there's a rider headed west across the meadow. At the foot of Butte Hill. Do you suppose Gordon changed his mind and sent somebody out to look for Shane?"

He came out of the tack room with a tattered yellow paper, probably an old feed bill, in his hand.

"Must be Blue," he said. "He left me a note instead of the other way around."

He hurried to the west end of the barn and looked out.

"You can catch him," he said. "Go on."

He turned and untied her horse.

"What do you mean *I* can catch him?"

"I gotta stay here now, don't you see? Nobody to do the chores."

She opened her mouth but he held up his hand to silence her.

"No. I ain't askin' for none of Gordon's hands to see after my place. He cain't afford to pay his men to do nothin' but run his ranch, remember?"

She stared at him, trying to take in this quick change of heart.

"I hate to send you off alone with a man you don't hardly know, honey," he said. "But I'd trust him further than I would a lot of other waddies around here."

That made her smile.

"Are you worried about my virtue, Micah?"

He looked at her sharply. "I recall one time I oughtta been."

The old sorrow in his tone struck her in the heart. She felt her smile vanish.

"Oh, Micah, please don't worry. I'm a grown woman now. I can take care of myself."

"You've got my forty-five," he said. "Don't hesitate to use it if he gives you any trouble."

"I won't," she said. "Don't you worry now. I've got my cell phone and there might be a few spots where it'll find a tower."

He looked at her a little bit longer, with love in his eyes. Micah loved her and Chase loved her. Two people in the world loved her.

But she felt sick to her stomach. If her child didn't love her now, would he someday love her again? Ever?

"You're the one said I cain't ride all day," Micah said. "Blue'll be a whole lot more help to you than I can."

It was true. Blue was strong and in his prime and in any situation, he could do more to help her than Micah. And she didn't think he'd give her any problems.

"Note says he's gone after his horse," Micah said. "His horse is with your boy."

"We hope."

He grinned up at her. Then he pushed back his hat and stared at her, hard, with narrowed eyes.

"Right. And Blue loves that horse like you love your son."

He was saying that to himself as much as to her.

"Don't worry, Micah. Don't be sitting here worrying about me the whole time. I'll be back soon."

"Ride safe, honey," he said.

Andie Lee kissed Sinn Fein.

"Bye, Micah," she said. "Just hold a good thought for me."

"I'm already prayin'," he said. "And I don't hardly ever do that."

THE LAND WAS MORE SEDUCTIVE than any woman or any whiskey. It was making Blue drunk to ride through it, this boundless world of dun and green and blue, with white clouds and trees looking black from a distance. It stirred up longings shut away so deep in him that he didn't even know them anymore.

All he needed more was the feel of the roan between his legs.

That thousand pounds of pent-up power who hated all people except Blue. And, evidently, Shane. He would never believe that the boy had even caught the colt if he hadn't seen them together that once.

Blue scanned the ground again but still he saw no sign. He lifted his gaze to the purple mountains to rest his eyes and tried to fathom the mystery of the colt. How far would he go as a babysitter, this angry horse with the intelligent eye who had caught Blue's attention and Shane's?

Andie Lee was right. If Gordon would take his airplane

up, it would help so much. It could save Shane's life and it could save the roan colt's. The two of them together were nothing but a wreck waiting to happen.

Could it be that whatever happened would make Shane straighten up? It could, but it was doubtful. Dannie had gone through hell on earth and hit rock bottom a dozen times and none of it had swerved her one inch to the right on the road she was on.

Well, no matter. What happened to Shane was nothing to Blue. He just wished the kid had picked a different horse, that was all.

He took a deep breath and tried to clear his mind and open all his senses so he could hear and feel any direction that might come to him. The boy had done a remarkable thing already—if he really was still astride the horse.

Did he think about the horse and try to read him? Did he listen to the roan and the roan to him? Or did the roan just let him mount and carry him around like a sack of potatoes because the boy was young and sick in heart and body?

If he lived and didn't get hurt, the roan would prove how special he was. If he was still with Shane, the horse was already proving it.

Blue saw the two horses when they topped the ridge behind him, silhouetted against the sky. His heart gave a little jump. He didn't want company in this good country. And he didn't want to take care of anybody or anything but the roan.

A minute or two later, he checked back again.

It was still too far to identify the rider but the lead horse was tall with a long stride to match and he was gray—white, almost, from this distance. The other was a packhorse.

Andie Lee, no doubt, and prepared to stay out for a week from the looks of her outfit.

So much for his hope that he'd be too far ahead for her to catch him.

He couldn't push his horse any faster and have enough

left to keep going all day. And it probably would *be* all day, since there was no loose horse or limping boy in sight.

Blue cast another glance over his shoulder. Damn. She was gaining on him on that ground-eating gray horse. His mount, one of Micah's using horses, was built for stamina and not for speed.

He rode on, scanning in almost a 360, looking for any sign that Shane had not made it all the way to the Lininger Trail. But it was big country, way too big to catch a glimpse of a blond head or a dusty red hide without being right up on it. If Andie Lee was wrong and Shane *hadn't* started for that cabin where the kids used to go, it would take blind luck or an act of God to find him.

He took a deep breath and tried to forget that she was coming behind him. Thinking about her might make him miss something. Shane—especially if he was high, as Micah had guessed—could've headed in any direction. And anything could've happened between him and the roan.

She caught up with him at the end of the meadow.

"Hey, Blue," she said, her husky voice low-key.

Then, "Seen any sign yet?"

Just as if they were in this together. She slowed her mount to the pace of his and rode right beside him with the packhorse trotting along on her other side. Her perfect breasts bounced a little at the jog. He would *not* be distracted.

"No," he said.

His hard tone didn't faze her.

"Micah found your note."

Blue looked straight ahead. One glimpse at her face and he wanted to look at her all the time.

"He said since you were headed out, he had to stay there to do the chores."

Damn. The old fox never quit.

And neither did she. She just kept on talking to him in that musical voice that stirred him as sure as a hand stroking his skin.

"He packed everything we'll need," she said, "in a heartbeat. Micah always could pack a horse like a magician doing tricks."

We. She'd said *we'll* need.

No. Talk about torture.

They rode along for a minute.

"Oughtta find 'em before dark," he said.

It was nothing but a wish out loud. Normally, he didn't let himself have wishes, much less speak them, but he was *not* going to let himself start thinking about being with her.

"I can't believe Shane being able to ride that horse for this long."

She was looking straight ahead now, the lines of her body falling into that posture of straining ahead, her eyes scanning the horizon and everything in between.

"Can you?" she asked. "Wouldn't you think the colt would've thrown him by now?"

"Even afoot, all night he'd cover some ground."

"Gotta find him. Soon."

She glanced at him.

"Them, I mean. I want to get your horse back to you."

Then anger edged out the worry in her tone.

"I'm so mad at Shane, I cannot even think what to do with him. *To* him."

He knew how that was. There were times he'd wanted to walk away from Dannie and never look back, but before he did that, he wanted to shake her until her teeth rattled.

The times she went back to that motorcycle-riding dealer and the rest of the scum of the earth and the drugs. Always, eternally, the goddamned drugs.

The times after he'd carried her, kicking and screaming, into some treatment center or other.

The times his mother had looked nearly as bad as Dannie, worn to the bone, to the soul, by worry and fear.

Tanasi Rose, though, had gone to silence during the worst of it. Andie Lee was talking too much instead.

"The day I had to face the fact that my suspicions were right and he was using was the most terrible day I ever had," she said. "That I ever *could* have, I thought. But all this today has shocked me that much all over again."

Her profile looked chiseled out of china. She had her hair pulled back in that big silver clip now, hanging flat down her back like a spill of sunlight coming out of the shadow of her hat brim.

"Somewhere deep inside I must've believed a week in jail would scare him straight," she said. "When I saw that note this morning, it froze every cell in my body."

She turned to meet his eyes.

"My blood just stopped."

He nodded.

"Internalizing the fact that he might never be cured—that's what I was doing. Admitting to myself that I may fail, after all I've done and spent and prayed and hoped and tried. Blue, everything else I've really wanted in my life, I've done but now maybe I can't pull this off. I may not be able to save him."

She rushed on as if he would interrupt and stop her too soon.

"I'm determined to win. I still am, at the core. But I'm so scared and so embarrassed and I am so damn *pissed* at that little wretch I don't even know how to *think*."

She surely was blunt about her feelings. She didn't know him. And here she was, telling him her heart. And letting it show in her eyes.

"All I know is I'll show him what tough love really means," she said.

Like a vow.

Then she hushed and looked away again, staring at the mountains through her horse's ears.

Staring off into the far distance like she'd done that first day in Micah's truck. Like his mother had done, sitting silent on the front porch looking for Dannie.

It made him want to help her.

She was good-hearted, Andie Lee was. She was even feeling responsible for getting his horse back to him.

Don't you go feeling responsible for her, Bowman. Get a grip.

"Any idea what time of night he took off?" he asked.

"Lawrence said he was there at bed-check, completely exhausted. Then his bed wasn't slept in, so he probably got hold of some meth or something."

"Hope we're on his trail."

"So do I, but how could I possibly know?" she asked, spreading her free hand palm up, helpless. "Jason only took him there once. I just keep going back to the fact that Shane hasn't been anywhere else on the ranch."

"Would he be trying to get off it?"

She thought about that.

"Shane's devious, like any addict, but I believe the note. He'll try to prove to Gordon he can ride the roan."

Gordon. Every bit of this mess was made by Gordon. If the roan or the boy got hurt or killed, it'd be on Gordon.

Blue's legs tightened on the horse and he obediently picked up speed a little. Her horse kept pace.

"The Lininger is the only trail Shane knows. But I don't know if Jason took the kids from the trailhead at Two Fork or if he used the shortcut."

"There's a shortcut?"

"Not far from here," she said, and turned to look at him full on.

Her fine mouth maybe trembled just a little. Or maybe he imagined it.

Whichever, a sudden urge to kiss her struck through him like a laser light.

"How'd you know which direction to take?" she asked.

"Couple of the hands," he said.

Her gaze held his. Yes, her mouth was trembling.

Not your deal. You're not responsible for her. And you're not going to kiss her. You've got enough to deal with without adding that kind of trouble.

He had to stop looking at her.

"Wanta take the shortcut?" he asked. "Cover more ground?"

She hesitated an instant, then she set her jaw and looked away. There was something so quickly lonely in the movement that it stabbed him.

"It'd probably be a good idea."

She legged her mount into a short lope and rode out—as she threw him a quick backward glance.

With a spark of regret in it. He would swear that was there.

Stop thinking about how she feels or doesn't feel, Bowman. Find the roan and ride the other way.

CHAPTER TEN

THE LOWERING SUN HIT it again. The glimmer that had caught Blue's eye, up ahead beside the trail, shone at him for the third time.

The breeze moving the aspen leaves shaded it sometimes, but when the light came through, whatever was glittering looked like something new. He rode up to it and saw that it hadn't lain on the pine needles for long.

He got down, picked it up, and turned it in his hands. It wasn't new. Its sheen of old steel is what had attracted him, the sun catching the edges of the blades of an old-fashioned pocketknife, covered in worn-down hide with the hair on. Several blades and a perfect size and heft for fitting in a man's palm.

Most men carried one and most felt about their pocketknife the same way they felt about their hat or their horse. Blue hadn't held such a personal article as this for ten years. No knives, no steel, no weapons, no tools, nothing fine that would give a person the feeling he could *do* something. None of that allowed in prison.

A piece of brass set in the middle with tiny brads had some writing on it, but even by turning it to the sun, he couldn't read it. The words were gone to only scraps of letters.

Didn't strike him as the kind of thing Shane would be carrying.

But it hadn't been here for twenty-four hours. Blue would

bet on that. No leaves or pine needles covered it and it showed no signs of weather.

He dropped it into the front pocket of his jeans and stuck his toe in the stirrup. Maybe Andie Lee would know if Shane had carried it. Or maybe not.

An addict's life was not an open book. Shane might've stolen it.

Or Shane might not have been the one who dropped it.

Blue bent his head to duck the pine branches and got Micah's horse moving again, faster this time, but still looking for tracks. There were so many pine needles he couldn't see any clear hoofprints, but broken needles and scuff marks in the dirt made him think someone had come this way recently.

And not Andie Lee. Her shortcut had to come in farther up the main trail because he hadn't seen its juncture yet.

He traveled another half mile or so with no more sign of another person, then he topped an incline and saw Andie Lee at the bottom, watering her horses. She stood between them, holding the reins and the lead rope, looking down into the fast-running creek. She didn't know he was there.

She didn't move while he watched her. She had fastened on to that look again. Fallen into it. This time it was at the bottom of the creek instead of the mountains, but it was the same.

Searching for answers in the earth. In the sky. In the water and the air, and tonight in the fire.

Like Tanasi Rose. Like his great-grandmother, Quaty Lucinda.

He remembered Auntie Cheyosie's stories about her. His great-grandmother, who, after her husband died, had taken to stirring the fire for hours at a time—most nights all night long—staring into it for answers while, most days, her tired boys fell asleep on the porch after their long day of hunting and plowing and scratching out a living, waiting for her to get up and cook their suppers.

Instead of stirring the fire, Rose had run her car into a tree. What would Andie Lee do?

He nudged his horse and started down the hill.

Show her the knife and get back on the trail. Don't linger.

Not to scare her, he called, "Hello."

She was far gone into her thoughts. She didn't even look up fast. Finally, she raised her head and turned to watch him come.

"I haven't seen a single trace of them," she said.

At the creek, he got down to let his horse drink, too.

"Look at this," he said, and pulled the knife from his pocket.

She gasped and stared at it.

"It's Shane's," she said, her hand to her heart, excited in an instant. "Where'd you find it?"

"Half mile back."

"Oh, I'm so glad you found it—it's his most prized possession."

She frowned, staring at it, trying to make it talk.

"He's had it hidden somewhere—and drugs, too, no doubt," she said. "They don't allow weapons in the Center."

"Like the handgun that got him sent to jail," Blue said.

Shane's about to go back there for a long time. He'll lose the privilege of having a prized possession, much less this one.

She knew that. He didn't have to say it, even if he would.

"But how'd he lose it? Is anything on the blade? Was it open?"

Blue stuck his thumbnail into the slot of the biggest blade and pulled. It came way too quick and easy. The tip sliced open the side of his bent forefinger and his blood welled in the same heartbeat.

Andie Lee gave a little cry like she was the one hurt.

"Oh, no! Oh, I'm so sorry—here, Blue, let me see that."

She was reaching for his hand with both of hers but he

closed the knife against his hip and, switching it to his other hand, turned away.

"It's nothing."

He heard her boots in the rocks of the creek bank as he dropped the knife into his front pocket and reached into the back one for a handkerchief that wasn't there. It was bleeding pretty freely. Trying to staunch it with his other hand, he turned toward the hasty pack he'd put together.

There was nothing in there but another shirt, though.

"Don't touch anything," Andie Lee ordered.

She was at her horse, untying a bag from the saddle.

"Stand right there," she said. "Keep your hand in the air."

He let go, jerked his shirttail out, and used both hands to tear a strip off the bottom. She was unzipping the bag, digging around in it, but she looked up over her horse's back at the sound of the tearing.

"You heard me, Blue. Get your hand up. I've got sterile bandages right here."

The concern and familiarity in her voice hit his ears as so strange. The worry in her eyes was for him.

He only glimpsed it before he put one end of the ragged strip of shirt in his teeth and wound it around the bleeding cut but it stayed with him.

"You are one damn-stubborn horse wrangler," she said, angry now.

She came around the back of his mount with the open bag, laid it out on the rump of his horse.

"Step up there and rest your arm on your saddle," she said, mean as a bad dog.

On his account. It brought back the wish to touch her as surely as an endearment could have done.

"Not your deal," he said, and tucked in the end of the strip so it'd stay in place.

Her gray eyes flashed hot at him. "Step up, I said."

"I'll take care of myself."

"You'll take a shot of antibiotic into that neat butt of yours if I have to ride up behind you and slap it into you in the saddle."

He felt the heat rush into his face. Heat rushing from the bursting of crazy feelings in him. He wanted to laugh, it was so unexpected. He was a little shocked and embarrassed at her bald talk, he couldn't believe she was this determined to take care of him. He couldn't even think.

She backed him up against his horse where he couldn't get away without brushing against her—her feet set outside of his—and took hold of his arm, which he did have in the air at the moment. He hated it.

Her hand was surprisingly strong. And her fingers were long, nearly long enough to circle his wrist.

Anger surged in him. "Step aside," he growled.

"All right, then," she said, unfazed. "No shot. *If* you'll hold still for a minute."

She was everywhere at once, taking hold of his arm, reaching past him to get something from the bag, nearly getting close enough for those perfect breasts to brush his chest. He was furious.

He tried to lift his hand too high as she unwound his bandage and slapped something cold and alcohol-smelling onto the wound, but she was tall and long-armed, too. And really mad now.

Her eyes burned into his for a second before they went to the wound.

"Watch out," she snapped. "Knock my supplies off this horse and you'll be sorry if we find your horse hurt."

He forced his panic and anger down. He never had liked feeling trapped, even before prison.

And he never had liked to be this close to a beautiful woman if he couldn't touch her. What man would? But this time was okay. He was nothing but furious, now, with this one.

"You're worse than a broncy horse," she said, from between her teeth. "I should've brought my twitch. Use your brain, Blue."

The sound of his name on her tongue again hit him with a deep, sharp sting like the alcohol had done. It was still a surprise to hear it from anybody. Micah called him son most of the time.

"I am going to clean this wound and bandage it," she said, "so you might just as well stand here and take it like a man. What a baby!"

He stood there like a stubborn boy resisting his mother and a willow switch. He felt ridiculous.

Yet his anger was slipping a little.

Her breath was warm and sweet-smelling and the feel of her fingers when they brushed the inside of his wrist woke the sleeping skin all over his body.

Damn her.

"I meant what I said about the shot," she said. "I'm not going to carry the guilt of you getting really sick on top of everything else."

"I can take care of myself."

"I'm nearly done."

"Get away from me, Andie Lee."

She worked quickly and she didn't waste a motion. She smelled like a woman. No, like herself. He'd never known a woman who smelled or acted like this one.

All of sudden, she was done. And gone.

She gave him back his hand and stepped aside to get the bag, moving on behind his horse quicker than she'd trapped him.

His finger was wrapped with something pretty thin. It wouldn't hinder him too much.

"Let's get going," she said. "Shane may be camping at the Sevenmile. Or we might even catch up with him between here and there."

"How far?"

"Not more than a mile but part of it's steep."

They mounted and he let her lead the way. He had to tamp it all down inside and focus on the hunt again.

She felt guilty that he was hurt.

She had been hell-bent to take care of him.

She thought he had a neat butt.

Idiot. She'd have done the same for any horse or dog she came across.

Just keep your neat butt in the saddle and ride.

ANDIE LEE PUSHED her mount harder than she normally would have done, straining her eyes through the lowering light, her stomach nothing but a hard knot. Then, as she led the way into the clearing that was Sevenmile camp, she wanted so much to close her eyes that she almost did it. She couldn't bear it if Shane wasn't there.

But she kept them open and knew in a flashing, circular glance of trees and burnt-rock fire ring and stacked firewood that he *wasn't* there. No one had been there for a long time.

"Let's push on a little farther," she said, starting to ride a half circle to head her horses toward the upper trail. "We might squeeze another hour out of the light and we can camp anywhere."

Blue rode into the camp, stopped his horse and got down.

Just like that.

"Whoa," she said, stopping to face him. "Blue, didn't you hear me?"

"As someone once said, use your brain, Andie Lee. Dusk won't last fifteen minutes now."

"Well, but the moon'll be up in a little while and I know the way," she said.

She was behaving like a silly greenhorn and she knew it. This country was far too rough to be stumbling around in the dark.

In spite of that bit of good sense, she said, "Micah packed that flashlight with the big square battery."

She sat there for a minute, unable to give up, her legs refusing to take her out of her saddle.

"Go ahead," he said.

He turned his back to her, unbuckled the latigo strap on his saddle, and pulled it loose.

"What if he's hurt?" she said. "He can't be that far ahead of us. We know he came this way."

"He had most of the night. He could be all the way to the Lininger cabin by now."

Blue went to work in earnest, unsaddling, taking hobbles out of his meager pack, putting them on the horse and starting to brush him down. When he walked around to the offside, he looked at her across the horse. It was getting dark fast. She could hardly see the details of his face under his hat.

But she could see his eyes flash.

"You're a damn stubborn veterinarian," he said. "No sense taking the chance of killing a couple of good horses."

She gave it up.

"What about me?" she asked, standing in her stirrup and throwing her leg over.

He had better talk to her tonight. Or at least listen. She could not sit here for hours in the dark with these images of where Shane might be at this moment and in what condition assaulting her mind every moment.

"What about taking the chance of killing me?" she demanded.

At first she thought he wouldn't answer.

She began to unsaddle her own horse.

"You're too mean to die," he said, right behind her.

"Thanks a lot," she said sarcastically.

As she turned, he took the weight of the saddle from her hands.

His teeth flashed in the gathering dark. A rare, quick grin from him.

Her fury at Shane choked out her fear. Only now was she realizing—along with the fact that she might not be able to save him—how much pain and havoc he had caused and to how many people.

Not only to her and to Gordon and a dozen others, but even to this good man who tried so hard not to admit that a cut from a knife would make him bleed just like anybody else.

"THIS IS THE FIRST PLACE I ever camped out," Andie Lee said. "And when full dark fell that night it felt like the end of the earth. If Micah hadn't been here, I'd really have been scared."

She was talking a lot. She'd talked to him, off and on, while they'd set up camp and cooked and eaten supper. It didn't bother him, though. Her low voice was good to hear, even when she was nervous like this, and she didn't seem to care if he listened or not.

"Are you a camper, Blue? Do you like to hunt and fish?"

His name on her tongue had a little hint of Texas in it that never failed to come to the surface. But he wasn't going to be drawn into this memory-sharing talk.

"We'll bank the fire after these burn down," he said, arranging two fresh sticks of wood on the ones that were crumbling. "Won't be long 'til morning and you need to rest."

"I can ride as long on as little sleep as you can."

"Not if you don't rest your jaw some."

She laughed a little.

"All your fault. You who won't answer any question I ask you."

She smiled and, with a sigh, leaned back against the trunk of the big pine where they'd eaten, sitting cross-legged on a bed of dry needles. For the first time since they'd met up, the tension was easing in her. Just a little. He'd like to take her in his arms and make her smile a lot more.

Would she? Would she smile or would she push him away?

"Micah brought us up here," she said. "Me and my best friend from back home, Lacie Marie. It wasn't long after we moved to the Splendid Sky and I had missed her so much."

He stood up and took the coffeepot off the hook. It certainly didn't need to boil again—it was already stiff enough to keep a horseshoe from sinking. He turned and offered it.

She held out her cup and picked up his with her other hand.

"Let's split what's left," she said, smiling up at him.

Her mouth was even more beautiful when she smiled.

He poured the coffee, returned to the fire to set the empty pot down on a rock, and then walked out to the edge of the light to get a glimpse of the three horses grazing near the creek. They were fine.

"Your coffee's getting cold," she said. "Blue."

As if she liked to say his name.

"Good thing we brought heavy jackets 'cause it gets colder at night even faster up here."

He went back to sit beside her beneath the tree. As he sat down, he felt the knife's weight against his crotch and stretched out his leg so he could dig it out of his front pocket. He handed it to her.

"Didn't mean to keep it."

She tilted her palm as she looked at it. The fire's light caught the edges of the blades the way the sun had done.

"Chase would be devastated to lose this," she said. Almost like she was talking to herself.

"Thought it was Shane's."

"Chase won this knife riding bareback right after we ran off together. First prize he ever won that they engraved his name on."

She held the little brass plate toward the low glow of the fire.

"Now it's worn away. That all seems like it happened a hundred years ago."

Her voice grew huskier.

"And it seems like yesterday. As a baby, Shane loved to play with this knife and stroke the hide smooth, and when he was a little bigger he'd pretend to read 'Chase Lomax' on the plate. When we left, Chase gave it to him to remember him by."

"How old was he?" Blue said.

She turned to look at him, lifting her chin in that way she had. "Chase? He's five years older than I am...."

"Shane."

Chase was on her mind. Maybe she still loved him.

"Oh. Five, turning six. I'd already kept him on the road until he missed kindergarten. I had to get settled in one place and put him in school."

"That's young to carry one."

She jerked back and stared at him for a minute. "The *knife?* Do you think I'm *insane?*"

Then, with a bitter chuckle, she answered herself hotly.

"Well, why not? Look at how well-brought-up my son is now. Kidnapper, horse-thief, burglar and druggie. At least I suppose he could be called well-rounded."

"I had a pocketknife and a .22 BB gun when I was six or seven. I hunted the woods behind our house every day. Squirrel's good when it's the only meat on the table."

Surprised, she stared at him. "I'll bet you were as responsible then as you are now."

He bit his lip and looked back at her.

Keep your mouth shut, Bowman. She already thinks you're something you're not.

He needn't worry. He'd lost her attention again. She took a sip of coffee and stared off into the distance. For too long.

"I probably should've stayed," she said. "But, damn it, he still wouldn't have had a daddy in the house unless we'd stayed on the road."

She turned and looked a question at Blue as if he could tell her if she'd done right or not. The firelight barely reached them but her hair still caught it.

"I was sick to the bone of traveling," she said. "And of no space. That trailer was way too little to live in and raise a child."

It was none of his business and he couldn't care less but he'd damn sure rather she talked than not. She looked too sad when she didn't.

"Sounds pretty cold," he said. "From where this guy Chase was sitting."

She stared at him, surprised again.

"If that was all he could afford," he said.

"It was— He wasn't winning much back then," she said. "But I couldn't ask him to settle down and get a job and change his whole life when Shane wasn't even his kid."

It was Blue's turn to be surprised. He threw the rest of his coffee into the dark.

"Chase offered to try to quit rodeoing, but I knew he'd never last," she said. "I was scared to death to be on my own with Shane but I had to do it. And I had to *know* I could do it, if that makes any sense."

He listened, his breath tight in his chest. She sure was one to blurt out her deep feelings to a stranger.

"I'll always wonder if it would've made a difference with Shane if we'd gotten married then instead of waiting another eight years to even say the word out loud."

She turned her head to catch Blue's gaze and hold it.

There was some light from the moon beginning to rise. Her eyes glittered with the passion of her thoughts.

Five and eight made thirteen. Shane was fifteen now. Two years ago.

"Shane never forgave me for saying no to Chase," she said. "He started with the drugs around then."

She watched Blue, waiting for his opinion. How the hell could he know what she should've done?

Did that "no" drive Chase away forever, or do you still see him sometimes?

"They like to blame it on somebody else," he said.

"Kids, you mean?"

"Addicts."

She knew it. She didn't wince. She had faced that truth, at least. Rose never had. With Rose, Dannie's addiction had always been somebody else's fault.

"For thirteen years, Shane was my joy. I'm still glad I didn't have the abortion."

Shock shot through him. Was there nothing she wouldn't say? He'd never known that women could just open their mouths and say what they thought and felt about such private business like they were talking about the weather.

And to a man. A stranger.

Or maybe it was just Andie Lee. Neither his mother or his sister had been like that.

"Gordon and my mother tried threats and bribery and locking me in my room and everything else they could think of, but I wouldn't give in," she said. "I knew before I ever asked for Gordon's help with Shane that he'd bring up the fact that I'd had choices. I knew he'd say he'd been right."

"I'd bet the roan that Gordon *always* thinks he's right."

"How horrid is that?" she said. "Saying it would've been better if Shane had never been born?"

Horrid or not, he had had that thought. He had thought it about Dannie, trapped in her slavery and suffering.

But then he'd recalled those summer nights when they'd chased lightning bugs and looked at the stars with Auntie Cheyosie. To live one night like that, wild and free and surrounded by the dark in a place that was safe and full of love was worth being born. Years of growing up like that were worth a lot of suffering.

"The thought has occurred to me, though," she said, "much as I hate to admit it. No matter what hell it's put me through, Shane's the one suffering the most in this. Caught in a trap, so completely demoralized he can't even struggle to get free."

"Don't listen to Gordon," he said. "You didn't do what he told you. Even fifteen years won't make him forget that. He likes to make people do his will."

She looked toward the horses making snuffling sounds as they grazed.

"Then I think about his baby fingers stroking my cheek and Chase playing horse with him bouncing on his knee and later teaching him to ride and the way Shane used to say 'Mom' with so much love in his voice and I know it's *not* true, no matter what a nightmare these last two years have been," she said. "Shane could be happy again if he'd try to get off the drugs. He's not trying."

Anger rang in her voice.

"I don't mean to sound like an addict here," she said, "but it's Gordon's fault—and my mother's—that I got pregnant at seventeen in the first place."

"What?"

"No, no, I don't mean he molested me. But he pushed and pushed me to date Trey Gebhardt because Trey's dad was also a powerful man and the two of them together could make the legislature do what they wanted on some agriculture bills."

"Bastard."

"That's the word he kept using," she said, "as he tried to make me agree to marry Trey."

And a word I've heard applied to me a few times. Thanks to Gordon. The hypocrite.

"Now it's called date rape," she said "Back then it was

'boys will be boys if you let them.' Or, 'It's the girl's responsibility to hold the line.'"

Her face was half in shadow, but her voice told the whole story. Here was another piece of that load of guilt she'd mentioned when she doctored his hand. She was staring off into the darkness, sitting with a hopeless stiffness to her shoulders.

"All kids make mistakes," he said.

She nodded without turning.

"I was trying to please Gordon and my mom," she said, "by keeping Trey happy. But by the time I got back to my room that night I knew it wasn't worth it. I was so upset I couldn't even turn loose of myself to cry."

Don't tell me this. I can't do anything about it. I don't want to hear it.

"Later, when they were furious about the baby, I got courage that I didn't know I had. I thought that my baby would always love me. All I'd wanted all the time was someone to love me. In fact, I might've even thought on some level that letting him have his way would make *Trey* love me."

That hit Blue in the gut. At least he'd always known that Rose loved him. And so did Dannie.

"You don't have any brothers or sisters?"

She shook her head.

"No one to turn to," she said. "Except Chase. He was breaking colts for the ranch and we were flirting like crazy but Gordon wouldn't let us date. He called Chase a saddle bum."

She turned to look at Blue again and leaned toward him. The scent of her hair filled his nostrils.

"To be fair, I must tell you that Gordon offered more than once to make Trey marry me," she said. "And it was only when I refused that he said I had to get rid of the baby."

She held his attention to her story with every line of her body. She needed to tell him all about it.

"I climbed out of my window one bright, shining midnight and ran to Chase's room in the barn. I told him everything. We left the Splendid Sky that night in his old truck with six hundred dollars between us."

"Different kind of life for the princess," Blue said.

"Better believe it. But Chase and I loved being wild and young. Freedom went straight to my head like the stars had done that night. I never saw such a splendid sky as the night we left the Splendid Sky."

"Didn't Gordon send somebody after you?"

"No. Come to think of it, he had the same attitude then that he had toward Shane this morning: Let me learn my lesson. Let me get what I deserved. Toni began coming to the rodeos to find us and begging me to let her help me, begging me to come back to the ranch, but I wouldn't."

She stared into the fire. For a long time, she sat, far-gone and silent. And sad to the bone. Like his mother.

Then she looked at him like she wanted to say something. Her full lips parted, but instead of saying whatever it was, she shook her head.

A strand of hair slipped across her mouth and she brushed it away to take a sip of coffee. Her eyes never left his, though, as if promising herself she was going to make herself say whatever it was.

She leaned a little bit closer as if to see the look in his eyes when she said it. The heavy silver clip at the nape of her neck was losing the battle on both sides of her face.

She reached up with one hand and took it out, then shook her hair back over her shoulders.

"I wanted my baby so I'd have someone to love me forever," she said. "But now he doesn't love me at all. He won't even say the word 'mom' anymore."

That wasn't all of it, so he waited.

"Micah insisted I bring a gun with me," she said. "He said it was because if the roan had to be put down I couldn't get close to him with a needle. There's that, and other reasons, too."

She paused as if he would name some other reasons. He kept his silence.

"On the way up here I had a thought I can hardly bear," she said. "One of those reasons might be that Shane has a gun. Micah's wise and he's had a lot of years to see a lot of human behavior. Do you suppose Shane would actually shoot at me, Blue?"

Her voice broke on the word *shoot*. In the growing moonlight, her eyes glistened with tears. She lifted her chin so they wouldn't fall. Her breath felt warm and it smelled of coffee. Her lips trembled.

Blue leaned forward and kissed them.

CHAPTER ELEVEN

HER MOUTH WENT STILL beneath his. Even the fire went still.

He wondered at the warm softness, tasted the coffee and the sweetness and thought he'd done the wrong thing. She would pull away. She didn't want this.

God knew, he was a man. He was just out of prison. He couldn't handle this.

She tilted her head and moved her lips against his.

She did want it. He'd done the right thing. So right it obliterated all the ugliness he'd seen and heard in the cells. So right it made him feel free.

Her lips moved on his and she kissed him back like she liked it.

Like she needed it.

She lifted her hand and laid it on his neck, sure and sweet, like she needed *him*.

What could a man like him have to offer a woman like her? Gordon had given her everything she wanted and that expectation was ingrained in her as a child, never mind a few wild young years in a rodeo trailer.

When she touched his lips with the very tip of her tongue, he let his meet it.

What he had remembered all those years had not been one thousandth of the reality. Memories fade over time—he'd known that but hadn't realized how much.

She got up on her knees and reached to put her arms around his neck, leaning to him, asking to come into his arms. He wrapped them around her and pulled her onto his lap while they deepened the kiss.

Andie Lee settled into his crossed legs and laid her palm against his face, brushing her thumb like a feather across his cheek while she stroked the line of his jaw. He couldn't remember when he'd last felt any caress, any at all. It cut through his body like the blade of a knife and into his mind.

He couldn't let himself want it. He was free, but not for this. He had forgotten how much just a kiss could do to a man.

So he caught her wrist, held her hand against his chest, and kissed her harder for one more heartbeat, then took his mouth away.

She gasped and collapsed against him. The light of the moon was strong enough to make dark pools of her eyes and gold of her hair.

"Sorry," she said. "I wasn't going to knock your hat off."

He was still holding her wrist. He couldn't seem to make his fingers open to let go.

"My hair," he said. "Don't touch it."

Not yet. Not ever.

"Why not?"

"It's my power. No one but me touches it."

"Ever?"

"Only someone who walks in my soul," he said.

She didn't ask, just questioned him with her eyes.

"Lots of Indians have that tradition, not just Cherokee."

"You're Cherokee?"

"Less than half blood."

"Less than half of anything doesn't compute with you," she said, sure as if she really knew him.

He let go of her wrist and used both arms to pull her closer, for just one instant.

She nestled against him like she needed a place to hide and he held her a little longer. She was no longer looking at him. She'd tucked her head under his chin and was staring out into the night.

"That's a beautiful way to say it," she said. "'Walk in my soul.' But it sets the bar too high. Who ever finds a soul mate? How many of you men find somebody who can touch your hair?"

He held her a little closer, just for one long breath.

"You're asking the wrong man," he said. "We'd better get some sleep, Andie Lee."

"Yes," she said, dryly, and turned to glance up at him with a little grin. "I need to rest my jaw."

He opened his arms and she left him.

Once they lay in their bedrolls, it wasn't long until her breathing evened out and slowed for sleep. She must be worn to a frazzle from her feelings alone, much less the long ride.

Anybody could tell by looking at her that she hadn't been raised working in the saddle all day. Gordon had given her her every heart's desire—she had grown up in a life of ease down at the big house while Blue had been starting colts for the public at the age of twelve and riding in the youth rodeos for money prizes.

Gordon hadn't cared one whit about him or what his heart's desires might be. Andie Lee had spent all her childhood in a life of luxury where she expected everything she wanted to be handed to her and he had scrabbled and risked his neck for everything his family needed, not wanted. The wants that he'd been able to satisfy had been few and far between.

The end result of those two, far-different childhoods meant that he and Andie Lee would always be on completely different paths of thinking and feeling and going about living life. It was like two horses trained to different purposes.

Blue stared up at the moon and stars. Tonight, up here on

the mountain, every one of them looked close enough to put his hands on.

Andie Lee looked close, too, over there in her bedroll, and she had felt close in his arms. But she was every bit as far away as those stars. If he reached for one, the impossible distance between him and them would strike him like a lance to the heart.

His code was all he had left. It demanded that he see the truth and face it.

He was alone. His loneness lived all through him, in his flesh and bones and soul as deep as the stars and moon stood high above him. That would always be. He was a natural loner and most of the time it felt right to him.

Yet, tonight he wished it wasn't so.

BLUE MUST HAVE SLEPT, but not very deep or very long, because when he woke with a startle he knew instantly where he was.

The moon rode high. The grass smelled fresh with dew. He could hear the creek running. Somewhere, far off, an owl hooted. But none of that was what had waked him.

He turned his head and saw Andie Lee's bright hair against the dark of her bedroll.

Do you think Shane would shoot at me?

Both of them were clearly lit by the moon. He had no weapon and no idea where her gun was.

He listened. The owl again, then nothing but a light breeze in the limbs.

He sat up.

A pale ghost horse came walking. A spirit horse, materializing out of the dark, heading straight toward him. Its hooves made no sound on the thick grass.

The roan? He was asleep, dreaming the roan.

Blue's throat locked on his breath.

Already it was within six or eight yards of his bed. It was

his horse and it was real. Coming from the north, the direction of trouble.

Blue crossed his ankles and got to his bare feet in one motion, already reaching to touch the horse. The colt had been through no telling what kind of hell to get back to Blue.

Roanie carried his head low and a load on his back. He looked to be lame on the left front but he walked faster, anyway, when Blue stepped off into the wet, cool grass to go meet him.

The smell of blood stung the sharp air.

Moonlight poured over the sack with a stick in it that was tied to the saddle, but even with that much light it took Blue's eyes and brain an instant or two to make sense of what he was seeing. A person's rump and skinny back with…an arrow through it? Yes, that was the fletching and the shaft protruding from a body tied hanging facedown over the saddle like somebody dead in a Western movie.

The head and arms dangled in the shadows on the near side. Light-colored hair, skinny arms. Here was Shane.

The colt came up to him and stopped, immediately resting that leg. Murmuring to him, Blue stroked his neck and moved along his side until he could lift Shane's head with his other hand. Blood ran from his nose, but not heavily. His cheeks were rubbed raw from hitting the rough old saddle leathers. His eyes were closed.

"Andie Lee!"

No way to break it to her gently. His fingers found the pulse in Shane's neck. Weak and thready, but definitely moving there beneath the thin skin that was cold enough to be dead.

His face looked dead. The arrowhead had gone all the way through his thin body, back to front. That dark river running down the roan's front leg was blood. Damn it to hell, the point had stabbed Blue's horse with every step he'd taken.

He lifted Shane by the shoulders, thin and delicate as bird bones. The rope held the rest of his limp body hard to the saddle.

"Bring the knife, Andie Lee."

"What? What is it?"

He glanced back and saw that she was awake now and scrambling to her feet.

"My horse and your boy. Shot up and cut up, but alive." She screamed. "Shot?"

"With a crossbow. And tied to the saddle. Bring me that knife."

When the boy came to, *if* he did, he'd be in as much or more pain as the horse. Depending, of course, on how he'd medicated himself before getting into this new bit of trouble.

Blue supported the kid's head with one hand and stroked the horse with the other. At least Shane would know why he was suffering but the horse never would.

He stepped back and aside so the moonlight would show him the shoulder of the colt.

It was chopped to a sickening, bloody pulp. He glimpsed raw muscle and bone.

Fury flared so hot from his gut he couldn't think. Stupid, stupid waste. More waste, even more needless waste piled on top of the fried brain in this boy's hollow head that he held in his hand.

Weak, goddamned, stupid drug-addicted worthless ungrateful piece-of-shit junkie kid.

Hours. There was dried and drying blood as well as fresh. Hour upon hour this good horse had suffered. Despite the pain, he had not tried to rub Shane off on a tree. He'd taken hundreds and hundreds of steps, *thousands* of steps—for the small tip of the arrow to do this much damage one jab at a time.

God*damn* all drug dealers to the lowest, hottest hell. If

Shane hadn't been high enough to be running around climbing out of windows and stealing guns and horses, none of this would've happened.

He reached over the saddle and felt the scabbard on the other side. Gordon's rifle was still there.

"Here." Andie Lee, barefoot and breathless, holding out the knife, ran to him, her eyes straining to see Shane. "How bad is he?"

She slipped her hand beneath Blue's to take Shane's head and shoulders.

"I've got you now, Shane," she murmured. "Mom's here. It's gonna be okay, son. It's okay. Hang on. Hang on, now."

She found the pulse for herself as she threw one quick glance at Blue.

"An *arrow*? In the middle of the night?"

He shrugged as he worked on finding a place on the rope loose enough to slip the knife under.

"Could've been before dark. There's dried blood beneath the fresh."

She bent to look at the boy's face and the arrowhead.

"Did he go to meet someone? Who? Do you suppose he met some new lowlife in jail and was going to meet him? Is this a drug deal gone bad? If Shane had a supply of drugs hidden with the knife..."

She straightened up and looked at Blue across the saddle.

"He was in a cell by himself," she said. "But he could've talked to somebody in another one, I guess."

"Could be anybody," Blue said, bending over to cut the rope from around Shane's ankles.

"Maybe campers, poachers, anybody who didn't have permission from Gordon to be on his property," Andie Lee said. "He's known to be tough about that, and if they were doing something illegal..."

She stopped talking to concentrate on feeling Shane's pulse in his wrist.

Blue cut the last section of rope and pulled at one end of it.

"If he slides, I'll catch him," he said, but Shane lay as if glued to the saddle.

"Careful," she said, helping to lift him. "Don't disturb the arrow *at all.*"

"It's rocked up and down with every step this horse has taken for God only knows how long," Blue said, spitting the hard words out from between his teeth. "The damage is done."

"Believe me," she snapped, "there can always be more damage done."

Blue lifted the knotted reins from the saddle horn and threw them over Roanie's head to ground-tie the colt, although he doubted the poor horse would want to take another step.

"Let me have him," he said.

Andie Lee leaned over the saddle and kept Shane's head supported until Blue gathered the limp body into his arms. He held him out away from his body so as not to bump against the arrow as he carried him.

"Hurry," she said, barely breathing the word.

The boy felt too far gone for hurry to do him a bit of good.

Anger surged in Blue. Damn it, here he was again, saddled with an impossible responsibility.

All he had to do now was get a desperate mother, a wounded kid and a lame horse down the mountain before the boy died on them. How many rough, steep miles were they from any real help?

Andie Lee ran ahead and pulled her bedroll closer to the fire as she headed to her pack for her medical bag and the flashlight.

Shane hardly weighed as much as a sack of feed. Who would guess he could do, and did, as much damage as a three-hundred pound gorilla every time he got a chance?

"Lay him there and we'll get him warm," Andie Lee called, looking back over her shoulder. "On his right side."

When Blue bent over the bedroll with Shane, she came toward them, saying, "Careful, careful. Slow and easy."

Blue dropped to his haunches and followed her orders.

She knelt to look the boy over, opening her medicine bag without glancing at it. Lightly, she touched his chest near the arrow.

"Yes, the blood on his shirt's been there awhile," she muttered.

She adjusted the light and looked at the situation some more, then lifted Shane's lids and looked into his eyes.

"I don't know what all's in his system," she said.

Then she turned to look at Blue with worry all over her face but her jaw set against it.

"Your bedroll," she said. "Blue, will you bring it? We need to cover him."

Blue brought the blankets to her and then went to add more wood and stir up the fire.

"We need heat," she said, "but I hate to draw attention. Do you suppose whoever did this is still after him?"

"No," Blue said. "Not if they left him alive and tied him to the saddle."

She lifted her head and stared into the distance for a minute.

"Right," she said, nodding. "That almost makes it seem like it might've been an accident and they wanted the horse to take him home."

"Or just didn't want him found anywhere near the place where they were."

She thought about that, too.

Then she said, talking to herself more than to him, "I can't worry about that now. Blue, I've got a quilted brown Carhartt over there in my pack. Would you get it so I can prop Shane up with it?"

He got it for her and watched her roll it up and wedge it into the small of Shane's back.

"That'll keep him from falling over backwards," she said. "We'll have to use something else in the front."

Quickly, still kneeling beside her boy, she pulled a cell phone from her jeans pocket and turned it on. Staring at it, she shook her head. She turned it to another angle in the light as if that might show her something different.

"Damn it," she muttered, punching in numbers anyway, and held it to her ear.

"No hope," she said, stuffing it back into her pocket. "No service. We'll have to get back to the head of the shortcut to use it. I checked that out on the way up here."

"We need one of Gordon's radios."

"Nobody in the vehicles this time of night," she said.

She looked at the sky.

"I hope and pray we can get him out of here alive," she said. "It's a good thing there are two of us—I'm so glad I don't have to try to get him onto a horse by myself. How long is it 'til first light?"

She didn't expect an answer. She wore a watch on her arm. She dropped to her knees beside Shane and reached for her bag.

"Damn it" was right.

Blue went to get the roan horse.

It's a good thing there are two of us.

The connection he'd felt when they kissed tugged at him. He pushed it away.

He should've stayed at the ranch and let Micah come with her, let the roan horse take its chances. If he had, he would've missed the kiss, too, and that would've been for the best.

Andie Lee didn't need *him,* Blue Bowman. There was nothing personal between them.

She had needed to kiss him in the same way she needed

him to lift her boy onto a horse and get him safely to a doctor.

In the way of any human being seeking comfort from another.

In the way of a woman needing a man. Any man.

Well, what was wrong with that? Hadn't he kissed her only because it'd been so long since he'd been near any woman?

BLUE HELD THE HORSE and watched the boy while Andie Lee gave the roan a shot of Banamine and flushed the wound with water. He listened for possible bow-shooters in the woods because, no matter what he'd said to Andie Lee, lowlifes who would shoot a kid in the back were hard to predict.

They both watched the sky, waiting for the moon to set and the sun to rise. Willing the light to come.

She'd quit talking, except for what was necessary, and had gone tight-lipped and scared. Not his problem. Not his business. All he could do was try to take her son down the mountain alive.

After that, they were on their own. He was fighting such a fury at the boy and worry for the horse that it was almost too much to keep inside. It hurt Blue to look at Shane in this condition, and it made him sick to think that the foolish kid might not live through this latest escapade of his, but damn it all to hell, he could hardly contain his anger at him. The roan colt was an innocent victim of all Shane's insanity. Not only was he suffering, but he might always be lame. He might even have to be put down.

"The pack saddle's best for Shane," he said. "The high crossties will hold him better. We can pad the seat."

She jerked her head up.

"Tie him on? We can't do that."

"You're the one who said not to disturb the arrow."

"I won't," she said. "I'm not as big as you are and I can sit at an angle."

"He'll still have to be tied. You're not strong enough to hold his weight all day long."

"Yes, I am," she said.

She worked on the roan some more, then threw her things back into her box and stood up to look at Blue.

"If Shane was lashed on to a separate horse that spooked and got away from us, I'd never get over it," she said. "His head would be smashed into a tree limb in a heartbeat. No."

Her flat tone fired his anger and he welcomed it.

"Well, then, if you don't trust my decisions, make your own," he said.

She turned, fast, and looked at him. "Shane didn't mean for your horse to get hurt. Look at him. He couldn't protect him if he was unconscious!"

"He wasn't unconscious when he took him," Blue said. "Just crazy from whatever drugs he was pumping into his system."

The look on her face made him wish he'd kept his mouth shut. But she might as well face the truth. Her little plan to have Blue and the horses save her child accomplished nothing but the ruination of a good horse.

"Time to break camp," he said.

They put food and water for the day into their canteens and saddlebags, wrapped the rest of the packs, and saddled the packhorse first, arranging the burdens evenly but not nearly so neatly as Micah had done.

Andie Lee went to get Shane ready. Blue banked the fire and covered it with ashes.

First light was creeping silently in over the grass as he saddled the riding horses. He brought Andie Lee's horse to her.

"Get on," he said. "I'll hand him up."

She mounted, then shifted to sit behind the seat. She

helped steady Shane's shoulders as Blue set him on the horse.

"Let's wedge him in with the blankets and that jacket," she said, and, as Blue gave them to her, she arranged them in the saddle with Shane one at a time until she got it all the way she wanted it.

They left the Sevenmile camp before good daylight, riding single file with the packhorse tied to Andie Lee's saddle and the roan to Blue's. At least he had his horse back alive. For now.

He didn't see how he could come out of this sound. If a bad infection set in, he might not come out of it at all.

With one horse carrying double and the roan horse lame, it was slow going. Blue tried to push the worries out of his mind and concentrate on what had to be done. He watched the way ahead, looking for overhanging limbs and rocks that would slide, warning Andie Lee when he found them. She was game, he had to hand her that. She never once called for a rest until they reached a spot where she thought her cell phone might work. It didn't.

He made them stop a couple of times, to give the roan a breather, but not for long. The kid still hadn't made a sound and every time Blue glanced back, Shane's head was lolling worse. Andie Lee was trying to steady it with one hand, hold him upright with the other, and still not hit the protruding arrow or let it hit her.

The first day he'd been in prison had been the longest he could ever endure. That had been his judgment for a long, long time but as the years stretched on and on, he'd decided that he might've been wrong. Somehow, the very sameness had made some of the later prison days seem nearly eternal.

Now this free day seemed to be a contender. He hadn't carried such a burden since he'd tried so hard to fix Dannie for Rose.

He remembered his rule about regrets and pulled his mind

back from the past. He looked at the roan horse, who was his present—at least for a little while—and more regrets attacked him. He couldn't think about it. He could not, would not, let himself think what might happen.

He had to keep his focus on the present, on the moment, and on the good instead of the bad. He had this marvelous country to ride in. He was free. Before sundown, he'd be free of this damaged, pitiful boy and his mother, too.

"Stay with us, Roanie," he said. "We're on the cutoff. Won't be long now."

It was, though. He judged the way ahead, he glanced back to make sure they were both still on top of the gray horse, he gauged the roan's strength. Over and over again.

He probably did it more times than he threw the halter at Roanie that first day.

He did it until they came within sight of the open valley below and Andie Lee hollered for him to stop.

Blue turned to see her put the cell phone to her ear again. As he watched, she threw up her head, eyes shining, and started talking into it, one hand holding on to Shane's shoulder. In a minute, she was done.

"I got Micah!" she said, as she dropped the phone into the pocket of her vest. "He's calling the rescue helicopter to meet us on top of Butte Hill. Then he'll bring the truck and trailer up there by the logging road so your roan colt doesn't have to walk so far."

"Give me directions," Blue said.

"Take the left in the fork up ahead," she said. "It's less than a mile."

From then on, things happened fast. From the fork, it was more than a mile, but not a lot more to the small butte that rose above the valley. It was a natural landing pad—open tabletop hilltop ringed by trees on the mountainside.

They could see headquarters from there, in a much smaller version than from Micah's hill, and, as they rode out onto the top of the butte, they thought they saw the old man driving up the road with his truck and trailer to come to meet them.

They talked about it like two yearning little kids.

"I don't know," Blue said. "It's been a while since you called. Micah would've left sooner, I'm thinking."

"It's taken him a while to make the arrangements," she said. "And besides, why get here before we could?"

Something inside Blue let go and his tension eased a little bit. Help was coming.

But something even deeper in his gut tightened still more. Hurt. Shane had really hurt Blue and it wasn't all about the horse. He hardened his jaw and his heart. He wasn't going to give anybody that power over him, ever again. Yet this time, it was already done.

He made himself look at the still, silent boy.

"At least we got him here alive," he said.

Now, if the emergency crew would hurry, he'd be able to hand him off to them still breathing. That'd be one point in the column opposite all Blue's failures.

Yet the very fact that they were here was another one on the minus side, wasn't it?

"It's a road with a lot of switchbacks," Andie Lee said. "It'll take Micah a while."

Blue got down and held Shane in the saddle while she slid off the gray's rump and took one of the bedrolls with her to lay Shane on. When it was ready, she came back and helped Blue take him off the horse.

Once the boy was stretched out on the ground, Andie Lee started checking him out all over again.

"Doesn't seem any worse for the ride," she said. "Everything's about the same. Oh, Blue, his pulse is so weak! It's steady, though."

On her knees, she twisted around to look at Blue and the roan.

"Do you suppose he's in a coma for *life?*" she asked, her voice cracking.

Blue shook his head.

"Not in my line of work," he said. "You'll have some expert help here any minute."

"Any hour," she said, turning back to look at her unmoving son. "They fly out of Helena."

Blue couldn't bear to look at either one of them. The boy did look dead and Andie Lee looked like she could believe he was.

"Is the horse bleeding again?" she asked.

She started to get up and go to him, but she couldn't leave the boy. Somehow that one tiny hesitating motion made his heart hurt for her. That pity eased his anger a little.

"Some," he said.

"Well, it has to heal from the inside out," she said. "It'll have to be flushed and cleaned every day to prevent infection and he'll need to be hand-walked. Of course, keep him stalled."

She looked down at Shane.

"I'll take care of Roanie when I'm there, but you'll have to do it while Shane's in the hospital, which may be quite a while."

Blue realized that he knew her well enough to read the message underneath the words.

She was *hoping* he'd have a long stay. Instead of one just long enough to put a tag on his toe.

"I'll do it," he said. "You can't heal him, anyway."

"Shane didn't mean…" she said, but her voice trailed off.

Blue saw in her eyes that she knew that the old "Sorry, I was too drunk to know what I was doing," excuse was all she had.

He would've said that but he didn't want to be as mean as Gordon.

They looked at each other while the rattling, banging sounds of Micah's rig began to float through the air.

"You were right," she said. "That wasn't Micah we saw."

"No," he said.

"Before he gets here and starts doing all the talking, I want to say how grateful I am to you," she said.

He didn't even want to hear it. He clenched his teeth together so he wouldn't yell at her about how completely unnecessary every bit of this pain and trouble was.

"Anybody would've done the same," he said.

"No," she said, "because not just anybody's unbroke two-year-old would've done what yours did."

He looked at her.

"I'll always be grateful that you're the horseman you are. I'll never forget it."

Well. Damn. He wasn't just any horseman but he was *just* any man. One she might think back and remember once every ten years or so.

That thought made him mad at himself. Why should he care what she thought of him or whether she would ever remember him?

He didn't.

CHAPTER TWELVE

MICAH ARRIVED in a rattling, banging hurry and drove off the road to bounce into the open meadow at that same speed. He slowed as he reached the trees on the north side of the butte and stopped there, next to the mountain, leaving plenty of room for the helicopter to land.

He got out and hobbled toward them, making a beeline for Andie Lee and Shane. He acknowledged Blue and the roan with a nod and a wave.

"Hold on a minute," he called. "I wanta look at that colt before you put 'im in the trailer."

He limped straight to Andie Lee, who was kneeling beside Shane, and laid his hand on her head, lightly, just for a moment, as if she were still a little girl. Blue couldn't hear what they were saying but he didn't need to. It must be a comfort for her to have somebody like Micah, who clearly loved her and would do anything for her.

That was another way his path and hers were forever different. Andie Lee expected that support from Micah and probably from some other people in her life, too. Even Gordon, who, though he might not love her and had already proved he would not do whatever she asked, still was someone she could depend on for help.

There was no one like that left alive for Blue.

He concentrated on flushing the wound again with the last of the water they had left in the canteens. It looked horrible, with the muscles laid open and the skin chewed up and blood everywhere. The roan stood, trembling all over from exhaustion. It was a good thing he didn't have to walk the rest of the way home.

Not home. Micah's.

Blue made himself look at the wounds in great detail. Deep in, he thought he could see the bone, but Andie Lee said it was bits of pale skin imbedded by the arrow's point. He hoped she was right.

The colt stood with his head turned a little toward Blue and his ear bent.

"Now's the time to prove it, Roanie," Blue said, glancing up at the knowing eye fixed on him. "That brag of yours that you're double tough."

The main thing would be to keep out infection. Keep the flies away. Keep it clean every morning. Maybe he could heal without any permanent damage but right now, Blue couldn't see how.

His heart twisted. Such a good horse. Such a spirit. It would be doubly unfair if he died or turned out permanently lame.

"Son," Micah said, "come give me a hand? Andie Lee wants us to turn Shane over."

Blue got up and went to them. He took Shane's shoulders, Micah lifted his feet, and they turned him to his right side, the way he'd lain all night.

"It's hard on the heart to lie on the left side too long," Andie Lee said.

She was constantly hovering, washing Shane's face to bring down the fever, trying to get him to swallow a bit of fresh water from a folding tin cup, and checking his vital signs over and over again. Her arms were shaky from exhaustion, like the legs of the roan.

"This waiting," she said, not taking her eyes off Shane. "It's harder than holding him in the saddle and bringing him down the mountain."

The noise of a powerful, throbbing diesel motor made them all turn to look. One of the ranch rigs, pickup and stock trailer, was coming around the last bend in the road. It roared into the meadow and growled down to a stop behind Micah's rig. The big white horse stood saddled in the trailer. Gordon was the driver.

He got out, fast, slammed the door behind him, strode to the door of his trailer and unloaded his horse. Holding on to the reins with one hand and dialing his cell phone with the other, he walked toward them.

"Hold on," he said into the phone, then raked that blue glance of his over Shane on the blanket, Andie Lee on her knees and Micah and Blue standing over them.

His gaze came to rest on Shane. "Pale as milk and his lips turning blue," he said. "Well, Andie Lee, if he doesn't make it, just remember it'll probably save you a whole lot of grief."

She jerked around and stared up at him, her eyes wide with shock.

"What direction did the roan come from into your camp?" he asked.

She turned her back on him and leaned over Shane, propping him up with blankets and jackets again.

"Blue knows," Micah said.

Gordon looked at Blue.

"North."

"Send the Little Creek men to the Lininger's," Gordon barked into the phone. "Split 'em—some uphill from there, some down. Let headquarters fan out from the Sevenmile. I'm headed up from the Butte."

He dropped the phone into its holster at his belt and held his icy gaze on Blue.

"I thought Indians were supposed to be some hellacious trackers," he said. "So why are you standing here instead of heading back up the mountain to find this bow-shooting, trespassing, poaching son of a bitch?"

Anger took Blue by the scruff of the neck and squeezed him hard all the way to his gut.

"Not my job."

"Right," Andie Lee said. She was recovering enough to be angry, too.

She sat back on her heels to blaze a look up at Gordon. "You're a day late with your search, Gordon."

Gordon ignored her and kept his piercing eyes locked on Blue.

"I can have you a fresh horse here in fifteen minutes," he said, needling Blue with the challenge.

"Your poacher's in Idaho by now," Blue said.

"And that's right, too," Andie Lee said. "You're sending fifty men on a wild goose chase when you wouldn't send one to try to prevent this disaster. Every time I look at my child I hate myself for ever giving you so much control over his life. You made him waste a whole week in jail and it may be the last whole week of his life."

Gordon finally looked at her.

"Yes," she said fiercely. "You wanted him to take his consequences and now he has, Gordon. Look."

She made a sweeping gesture down the length of the boy.

"If you'd mounted a search at first light yesterday, somebody would've found him before all this happened. The other day, I thought you were changing, Gordon. I thought age was mellowing you and actually causing your heart to do something besides pump blood, but I was wrong."

"You could've called the law, Andie Lee," he said roughly. *"They"* would've mounted a search."

"And brought them onto your ranch against your specific orders?" she said. "When I am so indebted to you that I'd need three careers and two lives to ever be able to repay you?"

He walked around his horse and stuck his toe in the stirrup. He pulled up and swung his leg over.

"Imagine this," he said tightly. He glared down into her eyes as he settled into the saddle. "What if you'd owed me nothing? Better yet, what if I'd never given that order? Would you have called the sheriff or the highway patrol then, Andie Lee?"

She didn't look away from him but her cheeks reddened.

"Hindsight, yes, you would. But without knowing what you know now. Would you have called in the law?"

"No," she said. "I wouldn't have. I don't want Shane back in jail. Ever. If the authorities ever knew he was stealing horses and breaking into your house on top of the kidnapping and drugs…"

"Thank you," he said, his voice heavy with sarcasm. "For your honesty. Now you know what I mean about taking the consequences of your decisions."

She looked as if he'd kicked her in the gut. She turned away and clapped both hands to her middle, bent over her motionless boy.

Guilt. She'd said she carried a load of guilt.

Gordon knew that. He was a mean-spirited son of a bitch.

And he'd probably been just as mean to Rose when she asked him to help her with Dannie.

He backed his white horse up several steps and turned him.

"At bottom, this is all Shane's doing," he said. "Remember that, Andie Lee."

"Not all," she said. "He never had a daddy in the house."

Gordon looked at Blue, then. For one electric moment, Blue thought Gordon was thinking about himself. And Blue.

"If you won't hunt," he said to him, "keep your eyes open."

There was real disdain in his voice and he turned away with an air of disgust that he dared Blue to challenge. Another try for power over him.

Blue's gaze bored into his back as Gordon put the big

white horse into a long trot. Gordon would never believe he couldn't intimidate Blue. It was Gordon's place in life to be the big dog.

He was probably disappointed. He'd wanted to see Blue perform an Indian trick and be the one who made him do it. As if he were a pet monkey.

Blue tasted bitterness with the thought.

Halfway to the trees, Gordon stopped the white horse in midstride and turned in the saddle.

"Andie Lee," he called. "I've seen men shot up worse than that and they lived."

She didn't answer. The sound of rotors in the distance had her attention and she stared at the sky to see the helicopter come.

Blue went to the roan colt.

Gordon wheeled the white horse and rode on.

Blue led the badly-limping colt to Micah's trailer. He was lame and in pain and exhausted but the helicopter at close range might make him run anyhow.

He went into the trailer with no trouble and Blue tied him in at the front. Blue closed its door and went back for the packhorse and his and Andie Lee's mounts to tie to the outside of the trailer. Inside it, they could all get into a terrible wreck if the roan came unwound.

But if he could see them nearby, their company might keep the colt calmer, although he was a loner at heart and had paid them very little mind all day. Blue's own presence, too, would help.

Sitting on Micah's tailgate where Roanie could see him, he watched the copter come in and land in a great rush of wind and noise. Three emergency technicians spilled out, surrounded Shane, and went to work.

Andie Lee stepped back to give them room. Micah limped over to stand beside her, touched her arm, and when she looked at him, pulled his wallet from his hip pocket.

That was smart. Andie Lee probably didn't have much, if any money on her for the trip up the mountain, unless she'd thought ahead to this moment. She'd be going to town with Shane and she'd have to eat.

The crew didn't spend long stabilizing Shane. Nothing could be done for him until that arrow was out and that would have to be done in an operating room. They lifted him onto their stretcher and replaced Andie Lee's blankets with their own, then they carried him on board. She gave Micah a quick hug and followed, reaching up to twine her arm with that of the guy waiting to pull her up into the belly of the machine.

Once up, though, she stopped in the doorway. She turned, looked for Blue, and raised a hand to him in goodbye.

Then somebody closed the door, the noise and the wind grew bigger and bigger, and the copter lifted off into the endless sky.

With all that was on her mind, she'd stopped and turned to look for him.

Forget it, Bowman. To her, you're nothing but muscle-power. To Gordon, you're a trick monkey. Which is about the same thing.

You got the kid down the mountain alive. Now step back out of this and take care of your horse.

THE ROAN DID REAL WELL with all the racket. Once the helicopter's noise was fading away, Blue went to help Micah gather up the blankets.

"Well," the old man said, "I reckon I might's well git me a big Bible and take to preachin'."

"How so?"

"I'm still a-prayin'," he said. "That girl cain't take no funeral or boy in a coma, neither one, and keep in her right mind. You think Shane'll come out o' this?"

Blue shook his head. "No way to know."

For that moment, pity overcame his anger. What a mess. What an unnecessary waste of horse and boy and a mother's strength.

They stuffed the bedding into the cab of the truck and loaded the other three horses, tying them as far from Roanie as they could. He didn't seem to care what any of them did.

That worried Blue a little. He'd heard of horses, like people, who just gave up and died.

Micah got in behind the wheel and Blue squeezed in on the other side. He untangled the blankets from the gearshift and held them out of Micah's way.

"Gordon feels bad about it all," Micah said, as he turned the key. "He's worried about Andie Lee."

"I didn't notice," Blue said.

"You don't know him," Micah said, raising his voice over the noise of the truck.

"I know he didn't hesitate to tell her that her boy probably wouldn't live. And that it was her fault."

"He's a funny duck, Gordon is."

"Makes *me* laugh."

Micah ignored the sarcasm and kept on talking while he drove the rig around in a big circle to head back down to the valley.

"He never could show he loved somebody," Micah said. "Not even his son, Ian. Gordon took it hard and he grieved for years when that boy died, but nobody ever knowed it. Includin' his wife. She finally left him over it."

Blue listened. So that was what happened.

"Gordon let Ian hunt by himself—encouraged it—and he wasn't but ten or eleven year old. Tryin' to make a man outta him, you know."

"How'd he die?"

"Avalanche. Gunshot set it off, we think."

Micah shook his head as he shifted gears.

"It's been thirty years, but now that Gordon's older, sometimes it's jist like yesterday to him. I can always tell when it's on his mind."

He'd had a brother he'd never known. When he had been five years old, just learning to ride the neighbor's ponies in Oklahoma, his brother had smothered to death under a pile of snow in far-off Montana. At that moment, neither had known the other existed.

Micah headed for the mouth of the one road that led down into the valley.

"No," he said, "Gordon's not heartless. Lots of folks think he is, but it ain't so. Like today. You seen him stop to tell Andie Lee he'd seen men shot up a lot worse that lived."

Blue looked at him.

"He meant it for comfort. For her not to give up hope."

"He sure wasn't trying to comfort her when he made her admit she could've gotten out a search party on her own."

"Gordon can spit out the hard, cold truth when a person least needs to hear it," Micah said. "People mistake his intentions but that's all it is—telling the facts."

"His intentions are to be cruel, and that's no mistake," Blue snapped. "What the hell good could it do to say any of that to her now?"

Micah looked at him. Blue looked back. His jaws felt so hard with anger he didn't know if he could open his mouth again.

But he could.

"Except to try to take the heat off himself," he said. "Andie Lee was telling *him* the truth and he didn't want to hear it."

Micah shook his head. "Gordon ain't cruel. Not on purpose."

"To say what he said just now to a woman with a child in that condition was nothing but cruel," Blue argued. "He knows she already carries a load of guilt over Shane being a druggie, and that he was adding to it."

"He tells the truth to try to help people change their ways," Micah said.

Blue grunted disdainfully. "To hurt them. To show he can get away with it because he's the head honcho and everybody else is dirt under his feet."

"You're as stubborn as he is."

Blue jerked his head around to look at the old man.

"If he was half human, he'd think about how somebody else feels," Blue said. "How would he have liked it if somebody'd said that to him when his son got killed?"

"Genevieve did," Micah said. "I heard her myself."

"She was Ian's mother?"

"Yep."

"Then he knows how it feels. He just wanted to make Andie Lee hurt the way he did. If he's even capable of pain."

"He can work his hands the hardest with the sparest praise, he can squeeze a dollar 'til it hollers and drive a bargain so sharp it'll make the other man squeal. Few people like him and he don't like even them few. But I'm tellin' you that Gordon Campbell ain't bad at heart."

Micah started down an even rougher hill, braking and letting up, braking again, and Blue realized how truly steep the road was. The weight of the horses behind them made too much of a load for the rig.

"I'll ride one and pony the others," he said. "You can haul the roan."

"Too late now," Micah said. "Cain't stop before we hit the turnback."

He shifted gears, pumped the brake, and took up his lecture again as if they were flying along on a flat, straight road instead of a crooked mountain one.

"He's hard on horses, but he don't never abuse one. He don't lie, he don't carry tales, he don't cheat and he don't sneak."

"I'll bet he's a lot sneakier than you know."

"You think what you want," Micah said, "but Gordon cares about Andie Lee. He'll hire the best doctors in the country to take care of that boy."

"He said down at the house yesterday that he was through throwing good money after bad."

Micah waved that away. "This's different."

The truck tried to pull toward the edge of the road. Micah wrestled the wheel with both hands and shot Blue a knowing look.

"Wal," he drawled, "at least we know one thing. You'll take Andie Lee's side in a fight."

Blue thought of the kiss. Micah was trying to get him to talk about her. About their time alone. Nosy old sister.

"What you know," he said, "is I'll take the side against Gordon."

Micah, thank God, shut up then and put his mind on his driving. If they ever got down from here, Blue would never ride with him on such a road again.

But he thought of Andie Lee in spite of all his efforts not to. She was up there, spinning through the sky in the helicopter, burning up with love for Shane and the need to help him, but powerless. Exactly like Blue when he'd stood looking down at Dannie's body on that motel room bed.

Except that she was even worse off than he had been that day because she had no one to strike out against.

Or maybe that made her better off than he'd been. At least she wouldn't be looking at prison.

THE WHOLE TIME Andie Lee was finding her way from the elevator where the hospital staff had closed Shane in and her out to the surgical family waiting room where they'd told her to stay, she felt somehow loose from reality, disconnected from gravity, in danger, somehow of drifting off into space never to return.

It made her think of an old Robert Frost poem she'd liked

in high school, the one that said living life was like riding
bareback on the earth. It was. And she'd just been thrown
from her horse and bit the dust.

When the helicopter lifted off the butte and went spinning
high into the enormous sky, all she could think about was
the fact that the two years of pure hell that she and Shane
had fought their way through had come to this end. Shane,
still in the clutches of drugs and madness, impaled on an
arrow.

And her, still trying to save him and even more helpless
now.

She could hardly believe that this was the end result of
all the sacrifices she'd made, tears she'd shed and treatments she'd tried.

Not only that, but now her load of guilt was heavier, too.
Guilt for what Shane had done stung even worse than the
part that came from her own actions. Blue's horse truly was
an innocent in this. He'd never know why he was hurting so
much. And maybe lame for life.

The memory of the horrible wound swam in front of her
eyes. How could she defend Shane when he'd caused something like that? But he hadn't intended such a disaster—for
himself or the horse.

Andie Lee turned the last corner and saw the large space
up ahead which was not really a room at all. It was a long
bulge in the hallway filled with armless soft chairs, vending
machines on one side, restrooms on the other side of the hall,
and windows across the end. Two bunches of people were
there waiting to hear the fate of whoever they had in surgery,
one group quiet and worried, the other noisy and worried.

She walked to the farthest corner and sat in a chair facing
the last window, one with its back against the wall that held a
bank of three telephones. She needed a wall to anchor her to
the earth or a corner to hide in, she didn't know which. Her
head felt so light it seemed no longer to be attached to her body.

As she settled in, a whiff of her own odor broke through into her consciousness. The other people would be happy that she chose to stay away from them because she smelled like a campfire, like a horse, like sweat and dust and blood. Who cared? She didn't.

She'd just been thrown, like Chase on a particularly bad night at the rodeo, but she wasn't even going to bother to dust off her jeans and hat and raise a hand to the people watching from the stands. Without an announcer to balance her loss with tales of her past exploits and victories on her way to this place, she had no reputation to uphold.

And she wasn't going to smile at the crowd, either. Chase, even when he lay flat on his back on a stretcher, would always light up the arena with that smile of his just to prove how tough he was. And to get the applause to prove that everybody knew it.

Well, she didn't feel tough at all anymore, but she wasn't dead yet. She wasn't giving up. She couldn't. She wouldn't.

However, her body was too drained to support her mind. Her arms sank into her lap and she sat there slumped, huddled inside her jean jacket, staring into space.

She had to call Chase. He needed to know about this. But she couldn't make herself do it just yet.

Chase wanted to fix things for her and Shane and it galled him that he couldn't. Now they had an even bigger problem he couldn't fix.

She tried to make a blank of her mind.

She wished she smoked so she'd have something to do with her hands. She made herself take some deep breaths.

Then she fished her cell phone out of her pocket past the wad of bills Micah had pressed into her hand.

"No cell phones in here," a woman called to her. "You have to use those phones over there."

Andie Lee made herself get up again and walk the few

steps to the phones. She needed to hear a warm voice more than she needed to rest.

She read the instructions and dialed Micah's number for a collect call. He answered on the first ring and accepted the charges.

"Andie Lee?" he said. "Are you on the ground?"

The sound of his voice and the sound of her name melted the cold center of her the least bit.

"Yep," she said, "we didn't crash a single time."

"That means our luck has turned," he said.

Micah had never flown and he swore he never would.

"Shane's gone to surgery," she said. "They don't know how long it'll take."

"I'll come up there and sit with you, honey."

Because of his night-blindness and reluctance to enter any town larger than Deer Lodge, the offer was a formality and they both knew it, but they argued about it for a while anyway. Just to stay connected.

Dusk was falling and it was making Andie feel even more loosed from gravity. Except for the weight of her worries which was certainly sufficient to hold her to the earth.

"Is Blue taking care of the roan?" she asked.

"Yeah. He's gonna sleep in the barn with him tonight."

"Tell him I said thanks again for everything."

"Will do."

"Has Gordon found the shooter yet?"

"Ain't heard a word from him."

After a moment of silence, he asked, "Any message fer him?"

That made her laugh a little.

"He means well, Andie," Micah said. "You know Gordon."

"Yes," she said.

But neither of them wanted to talk about him.

Finally, she promised faithfully to call the minute she had news and they hung up.

She looked up and stared at the Charles Russell print on the wall next to the phones. It was the one of the five cowboys riding their horses into the saloon.

Chase had to be told. He would come to see about them.

Maybe she should've married him. Maybe that would've prevented every bit of this trouble.

He loved Shane and he hated it that "his boy" was so messed up on drugs. He came to see them three or four times a year now instead of twice and called every couple of months.

But it wasn't the same at all. Not the way it had been in the beginning. Chase was like a brother to her now, or a cousin. A kissing cousin.

It'd be heaven right now to have someone to hold her. Strong arms to hold her and a shoulder to cry on. That would be such a comfort.

Blue's kiss on the mountain had been a comfort. And a gentle, stirring, tingling thrill. And a melting heat. And an unspeakable temptation.

How long had it been since she'd gone to bed with a man? Years. The night Chase proposed to her.

She'd better not let Blue kiss her again. She'd better not kiss him back anymore.

She needn't worry. He was so disgusted and angry about what Shane had done to his horse he'd probably never speak to her again.

Yes, she must tuck that kiss away somewhere into her memory and not think about it for a long, long time.

She didn't even know Blue. And she'd be willing to bet that getting to know him would be a long, hard road through deep woods. Even if his anger dissipated, she didn't have the time or the heart or the guts that would take. Not now.

Now, more than ever, weary of the fight as she was, she had to give everything she had to Shane.

She punched Chase's number in and held the phone to her

ear. It rang twice and then quit. The tinny message twanged in her ear: "The customer you have tried to reach is roaming out of our service area."

That would be Chase, all right.

She let her hand fall toward the holder for the receiver— all of a sudden, it felt like it weighed a ton.

She walked back to her chair, dropped into it, and closed her eyes. She tried not to think. She tried not to shiver, even when she got that chill of goose bumps for no apparent reason that Micah always said meant somebody was walking over her grave.

CHAPTER THIRTEEN

A FEW DAYS LATER, Blue woke up thinking about his argument with Micah and wondering why he couldn't just forget it. He'd gone over it and over it almost every day as he rode, and that wasn't like him at all. Technically, it wasn't a violation of his code, in that he didn't regret anything about it, but it was a stupid waste of time and energy.

Did part of him think there could possibly be some truth to what the old man said? Or was he trying to figure out whether Micah really believed his own argument that Gordon had good intentions?

It wasn't like Micah to tell a bald-faced lie. At least, that's what Blue's instincts told him.

He liked Micah. Probably that was what was really bothering him, because he had intended never to let his guard down enough to like or love anybody again. Any entanglement would be nothing but a hindrance to his purpose—for that, the only strong feeling he needed was hatred for Gordon.

It didn't matter one whit whether Micah really thought there was some good in Gordon. Blue's own family history told the real truth about the man.

He threw back the covers and set his feet on the floor. No sense staying here if he couldn't sleep. Might as well go check on his colt.

He'd been letting himself have feelings for the ornery roan, too, even though he knew their days together were probably numbered.

But no man could train a horse to his full potential without a bond between them. The painful healing process the colt was going through just naturally created even more of a connection.

He reached for the clean jeans he'd laid out across the chair and thought about that some more while he stepped into them.

Trust. That was the real creator of feelings. And it had been such a leap for the roan to trust Blue that, once he did it, Blue trusted him in return. The colt was honest, right down to the ground. Nothing counterfeit about him.

Roanie was a smart horse, too. No matter how much pain he was in, he knew Blue was trying to help him. The whole process was settling him down a lot.

He still wouldn't let Micah come in his stall, though. Time would tell whether he would ever really trust anyone but Blue. It'd be interesting to see what reaction Roanie had to Shane—if he ever saw him again. Blue certainly wasn't going to let the kid ride with him again.

He got up, went to get a pair of socks out of the battered chest of drawers and sat on the chair to put them on. First light was just creeping over the ranch. The breeze blew in through the west window smelling of pine and sweetgrass, juniper and…water. Running over rocks somewhere.

As if he could know that just from the smell. He grinned. Well, it never did hurt a man to have a little imagination. After all, his had brought him through ten years of hell.

The roan would throw up his head and snort when he caught all those tantalizing aromas in his nostrils. He might be at the window of his stall right now, pawing to get out.

Blue hated to keep him penned up. He'd like to take him out and hand-walk him around, but he didn't trust him not to bolt. It'd take a while longer in the box stall for the wound to heal enough for that.

All in all, the roan was accepting his captivity fairly well.

Probably partly because he was smart and partly because he felt so wounded.

Blue's stomach clutched. God willing, the horse wasn't permanently lamed. It would be awhile—a long while, really—before he'd know.

Blue padded to the kitchen in his sock feet to start the coffee and found it already made. Through the kitchen window, he saw Micah puttering around out back, picking fresh tomatoes for breakfast.

Micah had lived here for fifty years or more. He'd probably told Blue what a good guy Gordon was at heart because he wouldn't want to admit that he'd spent that much time working for a man with a rotten soul. Even if he knew it was true, he wouldn't let himself see it.

What'd they call that? Denial. Humans were damned good at denial. Probably because lots of times they had to be to keep from going crazy.

Blue went back for a shirt, found a fresh wild rag, too, and went out on the back porch to knock the extra dust off his hat.

"I'll do your chores," he said, raising his voice so Micah could hear him.

Micah answered with a lift of his hand.

Blue went back inside, filled a plastic mug, snapped the lid on it, and headed for the barn.

As soon as his boot heels hit the front steps, the roan called to him.

He smiled. Here was a sweet summer day of freedom to spend with his horses. Forget about people.

But he had barely started across the yard when Gordon rode past the corner of the barn. Forget about forgetting about people.

Apparently, he didn't notice Blue, though. He was headed for Micah.

For a little while, as Blue threw the hay and started portioning out the grain, he thought he'd be left in his usual morning's peace, but soon Gordon and Micah strolled into the barn.

"We leave for the hospital at one o'clock, Bowman," Gordon said. "We'll stop at the Co-op and you can run in for the supplement Toby ordered. Mrs. Beall's there alone for the rest of the week."

Blue stared at him in disbelief. Suddenly he was errand boy for Gordon?

"So she can't load it? Is that your point?"

Gordon answered with a short nod. "It's ten cases. I'll call and tell her we'll pick it up on the way back from the hospital."

Blue said, "I've got horses to ride this afternoon. Your arms aren't broken."

Gordon whipped around and looked at him as if he didn't believe his ears.

"The hell you say."

Blue held his gaze. "I don't work for you."

"Good god," Gordon said, almost sputtering in his surprise, "what's your problem? Don't you want to see the boy? He's been asking about you."

What was this? All of a sudden Blue was a member of the family? So he could do the heavy lifting?

All of a sudden Campbell was worried about Shane's feelings? Half the time, the man made no sense.

"Shane doesn't work for me," Blue said. "Not anymore."

"What's all this 'work' business? You can't do a man a favor? You can't visit a hurt boy?"

"The amazing thing is that *you* can visit him," Blue drawled. "After you wouldn't mount a search until you had an intruder on your precious ranch."

Gordon ignored that. "And Andie Lee," he said. "She's asking about you, too. She feels responsible because your horse got hurt and she doesn't need to be worrying about that."

Blue smiled coldly. "Your rep's all wrong," he said, with soft sarcasm. "You've got a heart big as Dallas, Campbell."

Gordon's eyes drilled into Blue's. He tried to move Blue by the sheer strength of his look and the force of his will. Clearly, he expected that Blue would give in.

And why not? He was the boss. Everyone always did what he said.

Blue said, "Drive safe."

Gordon turned in disgust and left the barn.

Micah made a little whistling noise and shook his head.

"*Now* who's actin' like a mean sumbitch?" he said.

Blue whirled to defend himself. "What the hell's he doing, pretending to worry about Andie Lee's state of mind? Going to see Shane when he wouldn't even look for him before he got hurt? He's the biggest counterfeit on two legs."

"He does care about Andie Lee and Shane," Micah said. "And they both have asked about you."

"I don't want to hear it," Blue snapped, and walked away.

He didn't want Andie Lee and Shane asking about him, he didn't want to hear Gordon's bluster, he didn't want to like Micah. He'd stick to horses.

TWO DAYS LATER, as soon as Blue opened the colt's stall door, he saw he had trouble. The roan hadn't called to him when he came out of the house and now he knew why.

Roanie stood without moving, his head hanging low. One glance at him told Blue that he was really sick. Blue watched his flank. The colt's breathing was much too fast.

Blue moved toward him, murmuring, "Well, now, what's the matter, Roanie? Let me see your shoulder. Let me look at you now."

He didn't know or care what he was saying because he had to concentrate on what he was doing. He didn't want to rile the colt in any way.

The artery along the jaw was a place Blue liked to take a pulse, and he stroked Roanie's face until he could get his finger on it, but before he even started to count, he was thinking he should be heading for the house to the phone to call Barry, the ranch veterinarian who lived on the Splendid Sky.

Blue gently urged Roanie to turn so the light from the window would fall on the wound and bent to look at it carefully. It was a great, raw bloody mess with a yellowish, pussy discharge coming from several places in it.

He urged the colt toward the water bucket and Roanie jerked to life, pulling away and kicking out. He didn't try to kick Blue, but he didn't want to be bothered, either. Blue got behind him and worked him around into the corner where the water bucket hung. Roanie stuck his nose in it, but he wasn't interested in taking a drink.

The colt needed antibiotics and pain medicine as soon as he could get them.

Blue left the stall and started for the house, since Micah had no phone in the barn. Andie Lee was driving into the yard as Blue stepped outside the barn. She parked in her usual spot, got out, and walked toward him as if they'd arranged to meet.

"I came in last night to get some clean clothes and a breath of air," she said. "I want to check on your horse before I head back to the hospital."

Blue felt a fine relief, not only for his colt's sake, but because she no longer had the haunted look she'd worn when he last saw her. Which was none of his business. Which he did not want to care about at all.

He also did not want the feelings she roused in him with her long, sure legs striding toward him and the steady way she looked directly at him. As if they were old friends.

"Infection's set in," Blue said. "I didn't see it last night."

She walked faster, straight past him, headed for the stall. He followed.

"Have you done anything yet?"

"No. I was on my way to call Barry."

"Barry's on vacation."

When she laid her hand on the stall door, Roanie lifted his head to look at her and kicked the wall.

"Well, he's not dead yet," she said dryly. The word *dead* echoed in Blue's ear.

"Let me go in first," Blue said.

In a couple of tries, he positioned Roanie where she could look him over. The colt wasn't happy that Andie Lee was in his stall. Not happy at all. Yet he felt so rotten he only made halfhearted attempts to object. Blue stayed by his head and soothed him with his hand and his voice.

"I talked to Barry about him after he treated him that first day," Andie Lee said. "He told me he shot him full of antibiotics and that he'd already had tetanus. Ranch policy."

"Right," Blue said. "He's been coming along fine and I didn't notice anything wrong when I left him last night."

"Yeah. The problem is that we have to leave this kind of wound open for it to heal," she said. "That makes it so susceptible to flies, manure and everything else."

She, too, looked at the colt's flanks and watched his breathing.

"I'll go get my bag," she said, "while you put him in the stock."

Blue immediately tried to judge whether that would upset Roanie to the point that he'd hurt himself more. He'd feel trapped in the stock, but he'd been in it before. Andie Lee had to be able to get close to him and he had to hold still.

He'd stood in the horse-size space made of pipe for Barry to work on him when he first got him back to the ranch. He hadn't given much resistance then because he'd been so exhausted. Today, he seemed nearly as weak.

So Blue took down the water bucket and held it under

Roanie's nose until he reluctantly drank a little, then he led him out of the stall and into the stock which was just inside the east barn door. The colt did trust him. He didn't even offer to bolt when they left the stall and he resisted the stock only a little.

Which scared Blue even more. Roanie hardly had the strength to lift his head.

Once Andie Lee had taken the horse's temperature and pulse and respiration, she gave him shots of antibiotics and Banamine. Then she squatted beside Roanie's shoulder and began to work on the wound itself, flushing and cleaning it.

She didn't talk, just concentrated on her work. Blue watched her.

He thought about how she'd never complained on the way down the mountain holding Shane in the saddle.

"How's Shane?" he said.

"Much better," she said, glancing up at him. "I guess Micah told you about the surgery and all."

"He said the arrow took a piece out of one of his lungs and broke a couple of ribs."

"Yeah," she said, "he was really lucky."

Roanie jumped back from something she did and tried to pull away from her but the pipe across his butt held him in. A fear-filled trembling ran through his hide for a moment, but Blue stroked his neck and Andie Lee stopped working and talked to him. He settled back down.

Blue stared at the raw mess that looked like somebody had cut a steak off the roan's shoulder.

"Well, how's he taking it?" he drawled.

He hated the bitterness in his tone because it made him feel petty but there it was.

She looked up at him questioningly, then glanced at the roan as if he could see for himself how the horse was taking it.

"I mean Shane," he said. "Does he appreciate his good luck?"

Andie Lee flashed him a sharp look and went back to work on the horse.

"Say what you mean, Blue," she said in a calm tone that made him regret his sharp one again. "Considering what you and I have been through together, we're entitled to be honest with one another."

"What d'you think I mean?"

"Shane doesn't deserve his good luck. Isn't that what you want to say?"

She stood up and looked him straight in the eye.

"I know how you feel," she said. "I don't blame you and I cannot tell you how sorry I am. But Shane's just a kid and he did *not* mean to get your horse hurt. Even high on whatever it was, he didn't want that. He asks about Roanie—and you—all the time. He's worried about it."

Her calm reasonableness only made Blue's temper flare.

"Don't talk down to me," he said, "and don't try to get my sympathy. That kid's had every advantage in the book and thrown it away. He had no reason to ruin a good horse but he did it anyway."

Her face flushed red across her cheekbones.

"I'll take care of your horse," she said, "if I have to drive back and forth from the hospital every day. And it won't cost you a cent."

"Forget that," he said, his blood as hot as the look in her eyes. "I'll take care of him myself."

THE NEXT DAY she came rolling in around noon. Blue was riding the bay colt in the meadow at the edge of the bluff. His first instinct was to ignore her.

Which was ridiculous, since she was so stubborn he knew she'd go into Roanie's stall and try to work on him, whether Roanie wanted her in there with him or not. He rode back to the barn and then past it at a short lope to pull up at the end of her truck. She was already getting her stuff out of the veterinary box built into the back.

"I told you I'd take care of him," Blue said. "I meant what I said."

She looked up, solemn for a second, then she gave him an infuriatingly calm and pleasant smile.

"So did I," she said.

She went back to her task, gathered up what she needed, threw it all in her bag, and carried it toward the barn.

"I flushed it out this morning," he said. "The fever's down. I can give him the rest of the antibiotic."

"I need to clean the wound myself," she said.

No surprise there.

Blue got down, tied the bay around, and turned him loose in the round pen. By the time he got into the barn, Andie Lee was standing at Roanie's stall with the door open, offering the horse a carrot. To his surprise, Roanie had come close enough to her to sniff it.

As Blue walked up, the colt's tongue flicked out for a tentative lick.

"I don't give stuff like that to my horses…"

Roanie snatched the carrot from Andie Lee's hand and began to chew.

"…because it's not good for them, damn it."

"I don't normally give treats to another person's animal without asking permission," she said, cool as if she were queen.

His anger flared.

"So how come I don't rate that same courtesy?"

She glanced from Roanie to him.

"In this case, it's part of his treatment. I assure you that it's not bad for him."

Fury rose in Blue.

"Well, it's not part of his *training*. You just want him to like you so you can work on him without my help. So you can work on him even when I tell you not to."

"Don't you think he deserves a little pleasure? Something new to take his mind off his pain?"

She looked at him, waiting patiently for his answer.

Awareness of her washed over him in a powerful tide. Her scent and her mouth—oh, God, her mouth. She was close enough to touch. As close as she'd been when he kissed her up there on the mountain.

He wanted more than he wanted his next breath to kiss her again.

"You're a bad actor," he drawled. "And I mean that in more ways than one."

She laughed then, and he couldn't help but smile. He could not help himself. It scared him. He had no control anymore.

"So are you," she said, smiling. "You've just blown your cover as Grizzly Gruff."

They looked at each other. Neither of them moved. Her gaze drifted to his mouth. She *wanted* him to kiss her.

"Andie Lee," he said, "get out of this barn. You can ruin every bit of training I do faster than I can get it solid."

Her eyes wouldn't leave him.

"I promise not to touch—or treat—any other horse on this place."

"Cold comfort," he said. "You've picked my best one."

My only one. Who used to be the best. Who may be lame from now on. Your taking care of him won't undo what your stupid son has done.

But he bit his tongue on the words.

Get over it, Bowman. You sound like a baby. Where's your code? No looking back.

Roanie turned away, chomping slowly on the carrot. He was stiff. Every movement he made hurt him and he had no energy to spare.

The horse deserved the best care and she was the only veterinarian within miles and miles of the ranch.

"All right," he said, "let me in there. Don't ever go into his stall without me—he's too unpredictable."

"I've been around a lot of horses in pain," she said.

He held the horse's head while she bent over and looked at the wound.

"Let's put him in the stock again so I can trim this dead skin away from the edges," she said. "And I'll take his vitals again."

Blue haltered Roanie with no trouble and led him into the stock once more. Andie Lee took the vital signs, announced they were all much better than yesterday's and then squatted down beside the hurt shoulder and looked at it carefully before she started to work on it.

"I can't give you a prognosis yet," she said. "Except to say there'll be a lot of scar tissue for sure and very possibly some lameness. I'm surprised he can walk as well as he can so far."

Blue didn't answer. He was trying not to think about Shane.

She worked in silence for a little while and Roanie stood it pretty well.

"How was Shane when you went back yesterday?"

"Better," she said. "I'm excited that he's responding to the treatment they're giving him. That doctor came to see me yesterday, and after hearing what he had to say, I'm really getting my hopes up that Shane's hit rock bottom and it'll all be up for him from here."

Blue's heart twisted. Foolish woman. She sounded just like his mother. How many times had Rose gotten her hopes up for Dannah?

But he didn't want to care—he wasn't *going* to care—whether Andie Lee's hopes would be dashed like Rose's.

"I'm happy for once in a blue moon," she said. "And I'm

so glad you aren't ruining it by not letting me help you with Roanie. If I couldn't take care of him, I'd feel even more in your debt, Blue."

"You don't owe me," he said.

"Yes, I do. Not only for helping me with the search and bringing us safely down the mountain, but for taking Shane on in the first place. He admires you. He's asking about you."

He didn't want to hear that, either. The next thing he knew she'd be asking him to take Shane back again.

"As soon as Roanie's all clear of infection, I'll take care of him," he said.

Their gazes locked when he said it. They looked at each other as if that was not at all what he'd expected to say or what she'd expected to hear.

They looked at each other while Andie Lee got to her feet, caressing Roanie's back, murmuring to him about how good a patient he'd been. The horse stood still between them while Blue longed to feel her touch on his own skin.

ANDIE LEE APPEARED at about that same time, sometimes a little later, every day for the next three days. Blue had usually ridden half his horses when she got there.

They fell into a routine of taking care of the horse—after he ate a carrot—while she talked about how Shane had slept and what the doctors had said about him on their morning rounds. Then she talked about Shane's behavior, which included lots of television watching, sometimes even a little conversation, and much less belligerence towards everyone. Blue tried not to hear the hope in her voice and refused to worry about the disappointment that was probably waiting for her.

Then came the morning when he went to the barn at dawn, as usual, and found Roanie's wound already cleaned and the greasy pink fly repellent already applied. He turned on his heel to look. Andie Lee's big gray horse was gone from his stall.

There was no sign of a truck and he hadn't heard one. The sound of a motor outside his window would've waked him.

He latched his horse's stall door closed again and walked to the end of the barn with Roanie hanging his head over and watching his every move. Blue went on outside and stood, sipping his coffee. Finally, he saw them. Halfway down into the valley, the horse and the woman looking smaller than life but not like tiny toys yet.

Andie Lee's hair and the near-white hide of the horse caught the first climbing rays of the sun.

She had mentioned that she was going to quit spending her nights at the hospital so she could get a room in the big house ready for Shane. He could understand that she didn't intend to make the trip back to the ranch in the middle of the day, but why not wait until evening to treat the roan? Or why not tell Blue she was coming to do it at dawn?

Maybe she'd just wanted a sunrise ride and had worked on the roan because she happened to be there. But he didn't think so. Or maybe she had lots of things to do all the rest of the day.

But he thought this had been deliberate, this coming up before daylight to try to help pay the debt she felt she owed him and disappearing before he came to the barn. She didn't want to see him any more than he wanted to see her.

Because she, too, was beginning to fear the pull of attraction that was always between them.

Which told him that she'd felt the power of that kiss on the mountain, just as he had, and didn't want to risk another one.

Didn't it? Could that be true or was he imagining it?

Bowman, you're losing your mind. Whatever reason doesn't matter. Be glad she won't be here for one day, at least.

He made himself turn and go back into the barn to start his workday. He set the coffee down and broke off a couple of flakes of hay.

"Hey, you," he said softly to the colt, as he carried them in to him, "so you let Andie Lee work on you, huh? I thought you didn't trust anybody but me. You going soft just because you like a carrot once in awhile?"

Andie Lee had taken a chance. But the colt would remember her making him feel better up at the Sevenmile camp, too, and her ministrations every day had made him used to her.

Despite all that, she had a lot of guts, Andie Lee did. And a big sense of responsibility.

It was sad that she felt so responsible for everything Shane did. It wasn't her fault that he made the choices he made.

Hey, wait a minute, Bowman. Wasn't it Gordon's fault that Dannie made the choices she made? Then how come you're making him pay for her death?

That was an entirely different deal. Andie Lee had been there for Shane, loving him every single minute of his life, trying to do everything she could to make him grow up right. Gordon had never come around or even acknowledged that Dannah was alive. That had made him such a huge, exciting mystery that she'd hooked up with that scumbag dope peddler again to come and see her fascinating rich rancher daddy.

Those thoughts set such a fire in his blood that Blue banished everyone human from his mind as best he could and filled it with the horses and what he needed to accomplish with each one of them that day. Until he went in for breakfast and found Micah in fine form, serving up lots of talk while he cooked scrambled eggs and bacon.

Thank goodness the food would be ready in a minute and then there'd be silence while they ate.

"You'll have to cook for yourself pretty soon," Micah called through the back screen door. "When I go into town today fer my supplies, I'll git yours, too."

Blue finished washing up out on the porch, dried his hands and came in.

"You movin' out and leavin' me or what?"

Micah opened the oven door and looked in at the biscuits.

"Fer a few days. Gordon's decided to take me along to cook fer the hay crews so's they can camp and not take the time to go back and forth every night."

"No problem," Blue said.

"I aim to take the chuckwagon instead o' tryin' to clean up the kitchens in any of them old cabins," he said. "Gordon don't know it yet, but I am."

The biscuits came out, Micah put it all on the table and they ate without talking, as always. As they got up from the table, Micah said, "I told Andie Lee to call on you if she needs anything when she brings the boy home."

Blue stared at him. "When's that?"

"Don't know yit. But I'll be gone at least a week, startin' the day after tomorrow."

She wouldn't ask him. Not if she was avoiding him now. There were a dozen men living around headquarters whom she'd known for years. If she made sure not to see Blue when she doctored his horse, why would she call on him for help?

The day turned out to be hotter than any they'd had so far this summer, but Blue didn't cut himself any slack. He worked the colts in the round pen, then rode each one all around Micah's and down the road a little. Andie Lee never did bring her gray horse back. When Blue and Micah did the evening chores, the gray's stall stood empty

Micah noticed it, too. "Told me she can't sleep," he said. "I told her she needs to start ridin' again. That'll help her more than anything."

Blue felt a sharp stab of what must be jealousy. A feeling of betrayal. She hadn't said anything to *him* about any trouble sleeping.

"Hard thing, not being able to sleep," he said, thinking of that first endless year he'd been in prison.

"You can say that again," Micah said. "Miserable. I never was troubled with it but once or twice in my life."

"'Cause you talk all the time you're awake," Blue said. "When you close your jaw, your eyes close, too, and you're so tired you go right to sleep."

Micah laughed. "Bad-mouth me all you want," he said. "You're gonna miss me when I'm gone and you're cookin' fer yourself."

The next morning, the gray was in his stall, Andie Lee's sorrel was gone and Roanie was cleaned up and doctored once again.

It gave Blue the strangest feeling. As if the barn wasn't completely under his control anymore. As if he were invisible. Or so important she would go to such great lengths not to see him.

It felt like an insult, somehow.

What was the matter with him? He ought to be relieved.

The third morning it was the same, except the sorrel was there and the gray was gone.

Then Blue felt foolish. As if she were playing a trick on him and he couldn't do anything about it.

No, he felt insulted. She had chattered away to him for all those days in a row and now she was treating him as if he didn't exist.

Micah came out to the barn to saddle Shorty for the trip, explaining that somebody else would drive the chuckwagon because he wanted to explore a little as he went. He hadn't been over to any of those parts of the ranch in a long time. Since last year.

He glanced at the gray's stall.

"Andie Lee still ain't sleepin'," he said. "Ramon said she made him move all the furniture out of the room next to hers and put in a hospital bed and she scrubbed everything down and put up pictures on the walls and I don't know what all. She didn't tell me all that 'cause she knew I'd give her hell about doin' too much."

He fixed Blue with his sharp old eyes.

"If Shane don't straighten up after all this, I aim to call the law to come and git him," he said. "Or else run him off so far into the ranch he'll have to fight a bear to git back here."

Then he swung up stiffly into the saddle and, after only two more orders for Blue about things to do while he was gone, he rode away. Blue settled into the quiet. He worked harder than usual all morning, enjoying being alone with no one around to bother him.

But he took a shorter lunch break than usual because he never could relax enough to lie down on the porch. That evening, although it was nearly nine o'clock when he finally quit work and showered and ate supper, he sat outside watching the stars until it must've been way after midnight.

Still, he woke early the next morning. Way early.

Probably because he was alone in the house. Most mornings, he could hear Micah thumping around.

It hit him, then, that he had changed. He'd already become accustomed to being in a real house with someone else always there. He'd gotten used to sleeping in a real bed and living like a regular human being.

He *wasn't* a regular human being, though, because of his plans and he had to keep them in mind. He'd be gone from the ranch one of these days, probably by the end of the summer.

So he might as well get up now and enjoy its beauty. Dawn wasn't any prettier anywhere—he could never get enough of the way the dark mountains on the west side of the valley lit up and turned to rose when the sun came up.

He pulled his jeans, then his boots and shirt on, and went to start the coffee. Then he stepped out onto the front porch to feel the morning.

A light was on in the barn. Andie Lee.

The thought that he'd waked early because he'd intended all along to catch her there drifted into his mind and floated through like a leaf falling to a bedrock of truth. It couldn't be true, but it was. He had feelings, not only for Micah, but for Andie Lee, too.

Foolish feelings of liking and desire that could lead nowhere but to trouble for them both.

He'd take care of that right now. He'd tell her he didn't need her for Roanie anymore. After all, the infection was gone.

He took the steps two at a time, long strides to the barn, and walked in through the east door. Roanie nickered a greeting and stuck his head over. Blue touched his nose in answer, but his eyes were on Andie Lee.

She was standing in the other end of the aisle with her back to him, looking out across the dark valley. Maybe she, too, liked to see the rosy light wash over the mountains.

It wasn't until she turned around that he remembered he hadn't buttoned his shirt.

"Blue," she said, surprised.

He thought, again, that no one else had ever said his name the way she did.

Quick desire rose in him at the sight of her face.

He'd have to be strong.

"If you're gonna run all over the country by yourself all night, you'd damn well better know it when somebody walks up behind you," he snapped.

Her eyes widened, then narrowed, as she looked him over. A smile touched the corners of her mouth.

"That's sweet of you to worry about me," she said.

"I'm not."

The smile vanished.

"Well, then," she said sharply. "Don't talk as if you are."

She walked toward him.

"I don't like anybody in my barn when I'm not around," he said. "Roanie's healing. I'll take care of him and you can stop sneaking around."

She stopped, just within his easy reach.

"Go back to bed," she said. "You got up on the wrong side of it this morning."

When he didn't answer, she searched his face.

"This strikes me as something akin to looking a gift horse in the mouth. I'm taking care of your horse for free and you're fussing about when I do it."

"I can do it."

"I need to check his wound every once in a while. And I'm just trying to relieve you of one chore out of your day. I owe you, and you know it."

"No," he said.

"Alone, odds are that I'd never have brought Shane down off the mountain alive," she said. "I told you. I'm happy to do something for you."

She started past him, reaching to open the door of Roanie's stall. He laid his hand on the top of it and caught her against his arm.

"Give me a break," she snapped. "What's the matter with you?"

"It's *you*," he said, and then he realized how that sounded. He added, "Something's wrong with you, coming in and out of here like a ghost every night."

She took a step away from his arm and stood with her back against the stall door. He left his hand where it was.

"I wanted to see you, Blue," she said, as if not seeing her was what he was bent out of shape about. "But…"

He waited, but she didn't finish the sentence.

"That's not what I meant," he said.

He snapped every word off his tongue, crisp and strong.

She waited. He didn't say anything. He couldn't quite think what to say that he *did* mean.

They just stood there, looking at each other, in the harsh circle made by the overhead light. Roanie bumped restlessly against the wall but they ignored him.

He wondered what she could see in his eyes. He was trying not to let her see anything in them—especially not that he wanted to hold her more than he'd known he could want it until this very minute.

"I…was getting afraid that if we were alone again," she said slowly, "I would shamelessly throw myself into your arms the way I did up there at the Sevenmile."

She actually said that to him. With her beautiful mouth.

It stopped his breath in his throat. She *did* want him to hold her again. She *did* want him to kiss her.

She hadn't forgotten that kiss on the mountain.

"I was afraid," she said, and she came closer to him, "that if I got half a chance I'd do something like this."

She slipped her hands underneath his shirt and up over his ribs. From the first brush of her fingertips on his bare skin, Andie Lee's touch traveled all the way through him like sudden sunshine melting his bones.

Blue let his arms fall to surround her. He knew, somewhere in the back of his mind that holding her would only make it harder to step away from her before things went past a kiss. He knew that this way lay trouble, much trouble, but he let himself hold her.

It was so new to him—touching her shoulders, her back, resting his hands at her small waist. He didn't add any pressure. He didn't pull her closer because he didn't want to be responsible. On her own, she came in against him with a sigh.

"Blue," she said, and laid her face against him, twining her arms around him to press her body against his.

She gave a relieved sigh and stood very still.

She wore a long-sleeved shirt against the early morning chill, but she had the sleeves rolled up and he could feel the soft fabric at the small of his back and then the even softer skin of her wrists. And her hands. They held him, cupping his sides as if she were holding him together.

That and her cheek on his chest created so many sensations he hardly knew where to put them. So many tender touches and warm embraces. It was as if he'd walked into a different world.

Scraps of memories flew into his head here and there but the desire rising in him erased them and then there was only reality. This moment. He wanted to live it. He was living it now, after so many like it had been nothing but dreams.

He looked down at the top of her head. Her hair gleamed bright against the darkness of his skin.

"I saw you the other morning on the gray," he said. "That trail's too steep and rough to ride before sunup."

He said it before he even knew he was going to speak and then he wished he hadn't.

She lifted her head and looked up at him.

At least it put a little space between them. Maybe it was good he said it. He had to break this up, one way or another.

Yet he couldn't open his arms and let go of her.

"Aha, caught you," she said, her eyes smiling. "I thought you weren't worried about me."

"I'm not," he said again.

She grinned. "That's your story and you're stickin' to it, but now I know that at least in the *past* you worried about me."

Lighthearted. She sounded so lighthearted. This was a different Andie Lee.

He couldn't resist grinning back at her, even while he was shaking his head at her silliness.

"Why were you riding that trail? You could've gone around by the road."

She let her arms drop to step back and look at him. His whole body disagreed with him. It didn't want to break this up at all.

"Trying to prove I'm still alive, I guess."

Solemn. She offered that without a smile. With an air of waiting.

As if wanting to hear his opinion of the idea.

"You might prove you aren't if you keep riding down that hill in the dark."

"There you go, worrying again."

He didn't answer. He only looked at her.

She looked at him. Waiting for something else. Waiting for his opinion of her other idea.

As if he'd never thought of it himself. He could almost feel her hands on his skin again.

Her gaze drifted to his mouth and lingered there.

"Now and again, everybody needs to put a little edge on their life," she said.

She wanted him.

He wanted her.

Watch yourself, Bowman. Even one time will be trouble. You're gonna want another time. And another. And what more will she want?

She was waiting, still looking at him as if she didn't want to look at anything else.

"I put some coffee on," he said.

They walked to the house without talking. Without touching.

You're letting your guard down, Bowman. You're losing your control. You're letting your pecker lead you around, which never is a good idea.

Up the steps and across the porch. He held the door for her and she walked in. The minute he stepped into the house behind her, they stopped and turned to each other.

She came into his arms. They seemed to have opened and reached for her all on their own.

"Blue…" She whispered his name against his lips, which seemed to have parted all on their own.

He held her closer and then closer still, bending her slender body back until he cradled her head in one palm and filled the small of her back with the other. He brushed her lips once, lightly, just for the taste, and then traced the shape of them with the tip of his tongue.

Deliberately he explored her mouth, dropping one small kiss at the corner and another in the middle where her upper lip made a perfect bow and the lower one was fullest. He took his time, savoring the moment. Kissing her was even sweeter when he knew for sure she wanted it.

But she wrapped her arms up under his shoulders and pressed herself even closer and he took her mouth in a long, slow kiss that she returned with a passion.

He broke the kiss and pulled back to look at her face.

There was such a vulnerable look in her eyes that it seared him.

"You don't know me," he said. "Maybe..."

"All I want is to be a woman for a little while. Just a woman, not a mother or a veterinarian or a stepdaughter. I'm about to lose myself, Blue."

He took her shoulders in his big hands. Her muscles were small but strong as her will.

He knew how she felt. He was pretty damned strong, too, but there'd been a time or two he thought he might lose himself.

"Hold on," he said, and kissed her again.

She parted her lips and gave him the heat of her tongue. She bit his lower lip gently and pulled on it, gave as good as she got until they both had to have breath.

"Keep that up and you'll let the coffee get cold," he said.

She turned away, and as she did, flashed him a look that pierced him with desire.

"Can we see the mountains from your bed?"

"That depends," he drawled, and took the hand she held back for him.

It'd be okay. She wasn't getting attached to him or anything like that. She just needed a little help getting through a rough patch right now.

She was right. People did need to keep an edge on their lives.

CHAPTER FOURTEEN

SHE LED HIM straight to the same bed he'd just gotten out of. Hard to believe.

"Sit down," she said. "I'll pull your boots off."

He laughed. Andie Lee herself was hard to believe.

"Don't be shy, now," he said. "Come right out and tell me what you want."

He swung her around and lifted her into his arms, just to taste her again, hold her, just to realize that she was really here.

"How about first we have all the fun we can have with our boots on?"

"Mmm," she said, grinning, then pretending to frown. "I dunno. I s'pose we could give it a try."

Her beautiful face so close to his.

"I want to kiss you," he said, "but I'd have to close my eyes."

She wrapped her arms around his neck and turned into him as if she never intended to move again. He took her mouth with his.

He let himself fall into it, into the warmth and the closeness and the sweet, sweet taste of her mouth. They kissed until desire almost overcame him and he had to see her again. When he drew back, she made a wordless murmuring protest.

The gleam in her eyes tested his control. He pulled at the side of his shirt that was bunched in between them to get it out of the way. To feel her. He wanted to feel her with every inch of him, yet he couldn't bear to set her down.

"No fair," she said, and lightly kissed his bare chest, ending with a tiny lick with the tip of her tongue. "I want my shirt off, too."

"I'll get to that."

He kissed her again, as slowly and thoroughly as he knew how while he set her on her feet, straddled her legs with his and let his hands work their way over her back. He let them start to memorize the feel of her—the slender curve of her neck, the shape of her shoulders, the small, slender waist.

When he ran his thumbs over the sides of her breasts, she moaned into his mouth and stuck her hands down the collar of his shirt to get to his skin. She pushed it back, over his shoulders.

Andie Lee wanted him. She wanted him and she needed him to help her not lose herself.

He broke the kiss to look at her. She opened her eyes and looked at him the same way she had done in the barn. As if he were the only thing she wanted to look at.

Blue reached for the buttons on her shirt. He undid the first one. By the time he got to the last one the look in her eyes had almost broken the short rein he held on his desire. He was thankful there weren't very many.

He pushed the shirt off her shoulders and down her arms, pulled the tail of it out of her jeans and threw it away while she stood perfectly still and her eyes smoldered at him. She wore a low-cut white bra that held her breasts exactly right and perfect for his hands.

He cupped them in his palms and rubbed his thumbs across the nipples through the thin cotton. They were already risen to his touch. He was already yearning for them bare.

"Please, Blue," she said, her voice huskier than ever.

"Hold on."

He slipped both hands to her back and unfastened the garment. Let it fall.

They were beautiful. More perfect than any fantasy he'd ever had.

She reached with both hands and pushed his shirt off his shoulders. He let it drop from his arms and stood without touching her, both of them naked except for boots and jeans. They looked at each other.

Andie Lee reached for him. "Blue…"

"One more thing," he said, although he knew he was coming to the edge of losing control. "One more minute."

He held her shoulder and cradled one bare breast that fit his hand as if made for him, and bent his head to suckle. She cried out and writhed against him and held him there with both hands.

The pleasure of it blazed through him but it wasn't enough, not nearly enough, and he knew he'd almost caught himself in his own trap. He needed more, he needed all of her with a need that burned his blood.

It had been ten years and more, after all. There was a limit to the torture that any man could lay on himself and survive.

When he lifted his head, her eyes were glazed and her lips were parted and she was clinging to his belt.

"Let's get rid of these boots," he said, and his own voice surprised him, it was so hoarse.

"What?" she said, dropping down onto the bed and lying flat on her back as if her knees were gone from under her. "That's all the fun with them on?"

"For this go-round," he said.

Weakly, she held up one leg. He turned his back, stepped over it, took hold of her boot heel, and bent over.

"Wait," she said. "I think I'm able to sit up after all. I like the view."

He threw a look over his shoulder that made her laugh.

"What?" she said. "Don't look so surprised. I've re-marked on your cute butt before."

He shook his head as he pulled off the boot.

"Blue, if you didn't know what a good be-hind you've got before you met me, you've been hanging out with the wrong women," she said.

If she knew where you've been hanging out, Bowman, this'd be a whole different story. And what the hell did you mean by "this go-round"?

He dropped that boot and she held up the other foot.

"That's not your only sexy feature, either," she said. "I could talk about your eyes, and your muscles, and your…"

"Andie Lee…" he said.

"You are so funny, Blue. I think compliments embarrass you. I don't think you're used to them."

She planted her other foot on his behind to give him leverage and he pulled off that boot.

"Now you know I didn't come up here this morning intending to seduce you," she said. "Since I wore my new boots."

That made him laugh out loud.

He turned to look at her as he toed off his own boots. He'd never known a woman like her.

"You coulda fooled me," he said. "I think you wore them on purpose so they'd give you an excuse to grope my cute butt."

"With my *toes,*" she said, laughing. "Let me tell you something, mister, when I *really* grope you, you'll know you've been groped."

He felt very powerful. Not only could he make her moan but he could make her laugh.

"Get your socks off," he said, and pulled off his own while he stood on one foot and then the other. "Quit foolin' around here, girl. Comin' up here before daylight and wake me up and promise me the world and then lay there and talk, talk, talk."

He unbuckled his belt and started unbuttoning his jeans.

"No, no. Hey, stop it. I'm planning to do that."

He grinned at her. He'd never been so overcome by desire and so happy at the same time.

"What about having all the fun we can?"

"I changed my mind," he said. "Now it's *without* our boots on."

She sniffed. "How come you get to make all the decisions?"

"I do it. I don't waste a lot of time talking about it."

Her gaze devoured him as he shed his clothes and he loved everything her eyes told him. What had happened to him? He felt as if he'd known her all his life. But yet she was a surprise a minute.

"Blue Bowman, you get in bed this minute."

He did.

"Now," he said, and reached to trace the shape of her mouth with his fingertip, trying to hold on to the anticipation just one minute longer, "let's see if you'll put your money where your mouth is, cowgirl."

Smiling, she let him see the raw desire in her eyes and draped her arm across his shoulders like a sign of possession. She scooted into him and laid every inch of her heated skin against his that could possibly touch.

"You just get ready, cowboy. It's been a long, long time."

Their gazes locked.

"A long time," he said.

As if they were talking about the last time they'd been with each other. As if they had known each other for all that long, long time.

He wondered about that, but only for a moment because the time for thoughts and words had flown away. They sank into each other and it took them both to separate Andie Lee from the rest of her clothes without breaking their kiss.

When she was as naked as he was and underneath him, smiling, in his bed, when he was inside her and she was holding on to him with her arms hooked under his as if she'd never let him go, her body arched to him and shuddering, her eyes wild with pleasure, Blue was free as he had ever been.

BLUE WOKE with the sun beating in through the window, on his side with Andie Lee spooned into him, her head resting on his arm, her silky hair spread over his skin and the pillow. As relaxed and unaware as if they'd always been together. He pressed his lips to the top of her head. She slept on, her breathing deep and slow.

He lay there for a long time with his arm numb, feeling the warm magic of her body curled against his. Her hand lay open at her side. He touched it with his fingertip in the center of her palm.

Waking up beside her was like a dream, but she was real.

Gradually, she began to stir and stretch, then she turned over—careful to nestle her head into the crook of his arm again—and smiled up at him.

"Hi," she said.

She gazed at him in that intense way of hers, in spite of the drowsy glaze in her eyes. They looked at each other. Smiled at each other. Blue could feel his own heart beating.

"I can't believe I slept," she said. "Sleep came easy in your bed."

The melody of her voice, sweet and low and sleepy, settled into the sinews of his body.

"Oh," he said. "So that's how it is. The bed gets all the credit."

That made her laugh and he felt that surge of power again.

Watch yourself, Bowman. This is a one-time deal, remember?

"Not true," she said, and she reached up to lay a hand on his neck—sliding her hand underneath his braid—and raised up to kiss him lightly on the lips.

He could get used to this. He *wanted* to get used to this. To all of it: the sex, the laughter, and, God knew, the closeness. Especially with this woman.

Only with this woman.

What the hell's the matter with you? Get up. Get out of this bed.

He wanted to kiss her back. He ached to gather her up and kiss her senseless and start up all over again.

You can't have feelings for anyone. Remember Dannie and Rose. Gordon. Think of Gordon.

Andie Lee was concentrating on his mouth, tracing the shape of it with her fingertip.

He wouldn't hurt her feelings for the world—she got enough of that from Shane and Gordon—but if he didn't do something, and do it now, they'd be right here all day and all night and then they'd be making plans for the next time. He had horses to ride today. He had plans for revenge.

Which contradicted any plans with a woman, no matter how temporary.

"How about some breakfast?" he said, and let himself kiss her on the forehead.

She hesitated, her lips parted. Finally, she said, "Sounds good."

Then she glanced at the window and the sun streaming in.

"I've got to go soon," she said, but she didn't move a muscle. "They're releasing Shane tomorrow morning and there's a lot I have to do today."

"Micah said you'll take care of him at the headquarters house."

Somehow he couldn't make himself call it Gordon's.

She sat up and reached for her clothes. Blue did the same.

"What kind of supplies do y'all have here?" she said. "I'm in the mood for an enormous cheese omelette and a gallon of coffee."

"You got it."

So she didn't want to talk about taking care of Shane. Was he already giving her trouble again?

They dressed quickly, without looking at each other, and Blue wondered whether it was for the same reason on her part as his. If he really looked at her, he'd never *let* her get dressed.

"I'm a fair cook," he said as they headed for the kitchen. "Not as bad as Micah, though."

They laughed and joked about Micah's high opinion of his own cooking and talked about the roan and the paint colt and the bay one and some of the others while she made the omelette. He made the coffee and the toast and watched her.

He loved her graceful, competent hands and the way they always found what they reached for, always did what they set out to do. In a heartbeat.

Andie Lee never looked hurried but she got things done. It was a shame so much of her time and energy had to go into trying to drag Shane back from the brink.

They ate in near-silence, joking a little about Micah's customs rubbing off on them. Blue was glad for the quiet. He wanted to soak in this amazing experience of sitting across the table from her, eating food that she had cooked for him, his body still imprinted by the shape and feel of hers.

Words would be good only to tell him whether that was what she was thinking about, too. Either way, he didn't want to know. If she wasn't, it'd hurt him a little and if she was, he'd have to take her right back to the bedroom before they had their second cups of coffee.

When they'd finished the meal and started cleaning up, Andie Lee said, "Would you give me a ride back to headquarters in Micah's truck? I want to leave both my horses here."

He nodded. Her mind was already turned away from him. Good. That was good.

But he felt the loss.

"You're a much better cook than Micah," he said, "but if

I tell him that, he'll try to prove he's the best and no telling what I'll have to eat."

"Yes, and he'll tease us unmercifully trying to find out exactly when and why I was cooking for you," she said, laughing. "No, no, don't say a word."

And she turned from the sink with her hands still in the soapy water to look at him. In that studying way again.

His hands tightened so hard on the plate he was drying that it broke right down the middle. That created a good enough distraction to get them moving again.

This business of one time and no more was not going to be easy. Not for either of them.

Tell her. Tell her you're a killer, Bowman. That's guaranteed to do the trick.

They finished up in the kitchen and headed for the truck, walking side by side across the yard.

"The other day when you wouldn't let Gordon goad you into joining his wild goose chase," she said. "I just want you to know I really admire you for that."

He jerked his head around to look at her.

"Where'd that come from?"

She shrugged. He followed her around to the passenger side of Micah's truck and opened the door for her.

"I just happened to think about it when I saw the butte over there. The man who can blow off a challenge from Gordon is a rare one."

Blue thought about that as he went around to the driver's side. She admired that. Really admired it.

"Gordon's so accustomed to dominating and pushing people around that he's astounded when he can't get it done," she said. "He's trying to make me hire a nurse for Shane instead of taking care of him myself."

Blue hated to agree with Gordon on anything, but he thought that sounded like a pretty good idea.

None of his business.

But he ventured into it anyhow. She deserved some help. Blue loved to see some justice in the world, no matter how small.

"Micah said you haven't been sleeping much…."

She interrupted him. "I know. But I am *not* going to have anybody in between me and Shane. He's talking to me again and I want to keep that going."

She was looking at him, waiting for agreement, he supposed, so Blue nodded as he turned the key. The old engine roared to life.

"I'm still thinking this has been rock bottom for Shane," she said, raising her voice over the noise. "I believe he really has learned from all this pain and from knowing he could've been killed."

Blue nodded again.

He could feel her gaze on the side of his face like a touch. He turned to look at her.

"I'm scared to death that this is my last chance and I can't save him," she said, all in a rush, her voice teetering on the edge of trembling.

The pain in it stabbed him like a blade.

"You can't," he snapped. "Give it up."

"As if you know," she snapped back. "Have you ever had a child?"

Tell her. Get out of her life. Get her out of yours.

"I watched my mother try to save my sister," he said, measuring his words as he tried to marshal his thoughts and blunt his feelings. "I tried, too."

Andie Lee went quiet, still staring at him.

He couldn't make himself turn to look at her as the old truck barreled down the hill.

She needed emotional support from him. He needed never to have that close of a relationship ever again.

Finally, she said, in a smaller voice, "What happened to your sister?"

"She died. Of an overdose."

All the old guilt and frustration came flooding back. All the bitter bile rose in his gut. All the fury and hatred.

"It's between the addict and the drug," he said, knowing as he did so that he was talking to himself as much as to her. "Nobody else can get in there."

But knowing, at the same time, that it was true.

"The only person who can save Shane is Shane," he said.

She lashed out at him. "I happen to know that some kids have been saved by different programs or counselors or treatments. If nobody *ever* was, if every one of them *always* failed, all the rehab centers and hospitals would be out of business."

Blue didn't answer. He just drove. The sooner he got her out of this truck, the better. Her pain was such a palpable thing that he was nearly overwhelmed by the urge to put his arms around her and try to make it go away.

Yeah. Make the pain go away. Help her save her son. You're a helluva good hand at that, Bowman.

The only way he could help Andie Lee now was to make her see reality.

"You said it yourself," he said. "He has to want it."

He was driving along in the valley now. It wouldn't be long until he could be rid of her.

She was quiet for a minute. "Yeah. I did say that when I asked you to let him ride with you."

She waited a minute more.

"Blue, if he really does want it, now…to be a horseman, I mean…and if he stays clean and sober…"

She interrupted herself.

"They've helped him a lot while he's been in the hospital. I think he really thought he was going to die and that's what scared him straight. Right now, he's clean and he says he feels different and wants to get off the drugs."

"Sounds like Dannie."

"Your sister's name was Dannie?"

"Dannah."

Somehow just saying her name out loud comforted him—
and hurt him at the same time.

"How old was she?"

"Twenty-two."

"I've wished over and over that I could've raised Shane
to be eighteen without trying drugs and then I think he would
have had more sense. He was a good kid, he really was, until
he got sucked in."

Blue slowed as a rabbit ran into the road and when it was
gone, sped up again.

It wouldn't be long now. He'd pull up into the driveway
at headquarters and let her out.

"What age was your sister when she first got addicted?"

"Seventeen or so when she started smoking a few joints.
Nineteen or twenty for the hard stuff."

"I just always thought… Shane was such a good kid…"

"So was Dannah," he snapped.

"Did she ever go into treatment?"

"Four or five times. I carried her in, kicking and screaming a couple of times. A couple more, she asked to go."

It was good, this thinking about Dannie. Bringing back
all the fury and frustration was even better. It'd get him focused on Gordon again.

"All the same program?"

"No."

"All different?"

He nodded.

"I still think one person or one technique or one insight
can be the key," she said, stubborn to the core.

Blue turned into the driveway at the big house and drove
to the middle where it curved in front of the porch steps. He
stopped but he kept the motor running.

Andie Lee scooted around and sat sideways in the seat to

look at him head-on, her knees against the stick shift. They were touching his hand on the knob.

His mind flashed back to the first time he ever saw her, when it was his legs against the gearshift and she sat hard against him on the other side, smelling of her flowery scent and soap and sweet woman. He could remember exactly how it felt for the length of her thigh and his to be pressed together.

After this morning, he had a whole lot more than that to remember.

He turned his head to look at her but didn't move another muscle. He left his hand where it was.

"Blue," she said, searching his face, "if Shane does stay clean, will you take him back? You're that one person who's the key for him, I know that for sure because of the remarks he's made about you. Deep in my gut, I know it."

He shook his head, piercing her with his most direct look, willing her to believe what he was going to say.

"Your gut's wrong," he said. "He already rode for me and look where he is now."

"He was on uppers that night," she said. "He admitted that he'd had a stash hidden. But that was before he nearly died."

"No."

"Would you turn off the motor? Please? Just for a minute," she said. "I know you need to get back and ride."

Do it, Bowman. You chicken. Turn it off, listen to her, and then tell her the real reason she shouldn't be asking you to help her with her son.

He moved the gearshift, she moved to put her back against the door, and he cut off the motor. No touching. No more.

"He's changed now, Blue. It's as if he has a purpose for the first time in a long time."

"He said that?"

"No, but I sense it and I think it's about the horses. He talks about the roan colt and worries about him a lot."

Blue shook his head.

"He looks up to you, Blue," she said. "He's been quoting you to me."

"I never said a damn thing worth quoting."

"About the horses. About being a horseman. He wants to be one and if we don't encourage that now…"

He interrupted.

"There're hundreds of good horsemen in Montana. Plenty more in Texas."

Coward. Trying to send her and the boy back to Texas.

"I don't want anybody else but you, Blue."

That flat statement held a world of meanings and so did the look in her eyes. A thrill ran through him.

For a couple of heartbeats they looked at each other as if they were back up on the hill and in his bed.

No. Don't reach for her. One time, you said, and it's over now. Open your mouth and tell her what you did so she'll go her way and you can go yours.

"I can't afford to hire anybody else," she said. "I'm barely hanging on to my practice now."

"He could work it out. Anybody in the horse business always needs extra help."

"True statement which applies to you, too," she said. "You could ride an extra two or three a day if Shane did all the chores."

She smiled. She let her gaze wander to his mouth and he came within a split hair of reaching for her.

But he had a job to do and a score to settle. And he wasn't about to be a liar about any of it.

It's a lie not to tell something just as much as it is to tell a lie in words.

"Andie Lee," he said slowly. Even now, with his mind made up and his resolve strengthening, he was picking his words to lessen the impact.

When he should be shocking her out of her shoes so she'd never speak to him again.

She'd sensed something was coming and she'd lost the smile. She was waiting, looking to him. For help. Help with the son she loved so much.

God damn all the sorrow that lived and grew in this world.

"You don't want me around your son," he said. "Or in your bed."

Her stormy eyes widened. They never left his.

"The day I came here was the day I got out of prison."

The shock that came into her face made him go cold all over. The blood drained from her cheeks.

"What?" she asked, the word no more than a breath. "What did you do?"

"I killed a man," he said.

CHAPTER FIFTEEN

ANDIE LEE SEEMED to lose her voice completely and Blue didn't have another word on his tongue. They sat there in silence while she looked at him, searching his eyes as if expecting him to say it wasn't so.

A terrible hollow opened in him, the old, familiar emptiness that had made him nothing but a shell of a man for the last ten years. He hadn't known this new life had been filling it up so much. Not until that instant.

"Who? Who was it?"

He couldn't have heard her if he hadn't been looking at her lips because the sound came out as less than a whisper. Her face was turning pale. He had shocked her.

"Dannie's drug dealer." The words came out quick and hard.

"Oh." Again, it was hardly a sound.

Her eyes never left his, but she narrowed them. As if she could see that.

"The piece of garbage who got her hooked," he said. "Her boyfriend. Major supplier to the kids of the county."

Shut up, Bowman. Don't try to justify it. You want to drive her away, remember?

"You killed him."

"Yes. I shot him where he stood."

"Because you thought he deserved it."

"Yes, since I'd just found my sister's body in his bed."

No sense in trying to make her understand why. It was

enough that she knew he'd done it. That first shock in her eyes had told him everything.

And who wouldn't feel that way? She'd just been in bed with a killer who hadn't told her he'd done murder.

Why didn't she get out of this truck?

But no, she truly was stubborn. She kept on trying to put together the man she'd thought he was and the killer he really was.

"Are you sorry now?"

"For the years in prison, I am."

He reached for the gearshift.

"This is incredible," she said, stunned.

"Believe it."

"Did you try to get away?"

"No, and I didn't lie about it, either."

Another heartbeat passed with him trapped in the headlight of her look. Then he got a grip.

"I gotta ride," he said.

She opened the door and got out, but as she closed it again she kept her hand on it and looked at him through the open window. He spoke before she could.

"Life lesson," he said. "Be careful of the company you keep."

She gave a shocked, rough little laugh as if he'd said something rudely inappropriate. At least it made her step back from the truck.

He drove away and left her there.

ANDIE LEE TURNED, ran into the house and up the stairs blindly, not stopping to answer Goldie the housekeeper, who called to her from the kitchen.

"I've got to go to the hospital," she yelled back and kept going.

I've got to get my mind around this.

All the while she stripped and showered, she could think

of nothing but Blue's confession. A killer. She couldn't take it in.

Yet she hadn't doubted it from the minute he said it. He had been in prison. He had murdered a man.

She had trusted her child, already troubled and addicted, to a *killer.*

She had trusted her body and a little part of her heart to him, too.

He was right. This was a life lesson. She had trusted him way too much while knowing way too little about him.

When she stepped out of the shower and picked up a big towel, she wrapped it around her and walked to the mirror to meet her own gaze. To look herself in the eye and make herself believe it: Blue Bowman was a killer. Self-confessed killer.

Believe it, he had said.

She did.

But how could she? When she was standing here this minute regretting the loss of his scent from her hair? Wanting the smell of him to still linger on the curve of her shoulder where it had fit like a charm tucked underneath his arm?

In his arms and in his bed, she had slept in a deep sleep for the first time in weeks. Months.

She stared at herself. She had made love with a killer.

With his arms around her, she had felt safer than she'd felt for a long, long time.

Except, of course, for the shiver of a whole different kind of danger that came from the excitement he roused in her every time he looked at her.

Andie Lee grabbed another towel and began wringing the water out of her hair. She'd been right, there in the hospital waiting room, when she'd thought that a relationship with Blue would be a hard, long road.

At least her instincts weren't totally gone.

What must it take, what anger, what depths of fury, what frustration to actually kill another person?

She tried to imagine it. She was a passionate person. She knew anger and fury and frustration and how they lived in her blood like old, old enemies.

Yet, she didn't think they could drive her to killing another human being…unless it was in self-defense or defense of her child. But killing his dealer would be defending him, and…

She jerked her mind away from that path of justification.

Contrary to all her instincts, she must have trusted the wrong man. Desperate, she'd been too desperate. Just because Shane looked up to him didn't make him worthy of admiration. What did Shane know, with the condition he was in?

Yet…horses trusted Blue. The roan horse, with all his natural wildness and his history of bad treatment from men, trusted Blue.

So he wasn't evil. Animals didn't trust people who were evil.

That thought was the only comfort she had as she dressed and left the house with a hurried goodbye to Goldie. She was in her truck with the motor running, getting ready to drive the long miles back to the hospital when it hit her: Micah!

Did *he* know Blue was a killer? Micah always knew more about everything and everybody than he told.

How much did he know about his wrangler, anyhow?

How selfish could she be if she hadn't thought of him the minute Blue confessed to her? After all, Micah was living in the same house with him.

She sat there for a long minute staring toward the little log house on the bluff. What a time for him to be gone! Micah never would carry a cell phone. He had called in on the ranch radio to ask about Shane but she certainly couldn't call him back about this and blab it all over the air.

He'd said that they'd be camped at the Manuel place for several days.

An hour off the highway, but in the same general direction as the hospital.

She threw the truck into gear and drove away from headquarters while she called Shane's room to say she'd be late. He was watching a movie and he sounded fine, so she relaxed about him.

All the way to the haying crew camp, she tried to keep her mind blank and just be. She made a plan, which was to just enjoy the scenery and her time alone but the doubts about herself in relation to Blue wouldn't leave her be.

How could her instincts be so wrong? This should teach her a lesson.

But then if hers were wrong, so were Micah's. Her stomach clutched. What if Blue were to harm him? She couldn't do without Micah.

Blue wouldn't. But he *had* taken the life of another human being. That was beyond the pale.

She couldn't think about it. She'd made a mistake in judgment that she'd never make again. "Life lesson" was right.

She'd warn Micah and be done with it. She'd tuck the loving time with Blue into her memory, and someday when she was an old woman she'd take it out and look at it for itself alone.

Someday, after years of being back in her practice with all its horses waiting for her to solve the mysteries of their different problems. With the owners, likeable and unlikeable, interesting and boring, stupid and smart, and all the hustle and bustle of the horse shows where the horses passed through her treatment trailer and her hands. Someday that would be her life again.

With no killers in it. No Blue.

But now…Shane was definitely in a different frame of mind and what he talked about was the roan horse and Blue. What should she do?

A small part of her couldn't help but trust Blue anyway. She tried, but she couldn't imagine his harming Shane in any way. Or Micah.

One thing, though, was certain now. She could never go to bed with him again. And she would never let herself love him.

She bent and, holding the wheel with one hand, reached under her seat for the big wallet of CDs she carried at all times. No way could she have gotten through these last hard years without music.

Nothing else soothed her imagination. Nothing else opened her up to the reality of so many possibilities.

Flipping through the pages and glancing down at each, she chose an Ian Tyson CD and slipped it into the slot. The rest of the way to the Manuel place, she rolled along, listening to him sing about purple starlight and a coyote's call on the wind. Letting him pull her into another place and time.

BLUE INTENDED to ride as soon as he got back to the barn, but instead he went to the roan colt's stall and looked at his wound again and put the halter on him. If the colt would lead calmly to the stock and back, he would probably lead all right outside the barn. Roanie had been cooped up so long he needed some fresh sights and interesting winds.

Blue needed the comfort of companionship. He finally admitted that truth to himself as he led the colt down the aisle and out into the waiting sunshine. That was the real crux of the deal. He needed the trust the colt gave him.

He needed the affection he felt when he laid his arm around the colt's neck and Roanie nuzzled into his hand or rubbed his head against Blue's shoulder. Big problem. He truly was getting attached to the horse.

Well, then, he'd just have to plan well enough to make sure he got to keep him.

He also needed some time to regain his balance before he went on with his day. He'd done the right thing by telling Andie Lee where he'd been and what he'd done, but that empty feeling was still haunting him. That, and a rawness that felt as if something had been ripped from his skin.

He would take just a little while to find his focus again. He should not *ever* have taken Andie Lee to bed in the first place. He'd known better. And now here he was missing her already.

Get used to it, Bowman. You'd have to choose between her and your sworn vengeance somewhere down the line, anyhow.

No, he wouldn't. Since he'd told her his secret, she'd be the one to make the choice—and that had happened the minute the words left his mouth.

He stayed at the colt's shoulder and hand-walked the roan, who limped badly. The horse ignored the wound to dance on the hind end a little bit, though, and his snorty, ear-pinning spirit seemed intact. They rambled through the unfenced meadow, disagreeing and fussing a little bit now and then without getting too serious about it and stopping every once in awhile to let Roanie sample the tall grass. Mostly they felt the warm sun growing ever hotter on their backs, and smelled the wind off the pines.

When they got to the edge of the bluff, the colt was tired and they stood for a long time looking across the valley and the river to the snow-capped mountains. Then Roanie dropped his head to graze a little more and Blue set his eyes on the headquarters, on the big, old house that his ancestors had built. From here, it looked like a dollhouse.

But it was Gordon who lived there and Gordon he had come to this ranch to deal with. He would stay focused on Gordon. He would forget about Andie Lee and Shane.

He was glad that he'd told Andie Lee when he did. The truth took away the temptation for them both. Temptations, actually—to talk more and get to know each other besides the one to make love again. Yes. It saved them both from more involvement and more heartache down the road.

After all, when he'd done what he came to do at the Splendid Sky, she wouldn't want to know him anyhow.

ANDIE LEE SAW that Micah had his chuckwagon set up and a fire going in the yard of the old Manuel family house. He sat awkwardly on a bucket, his stiff leg sticking out to the side, raking coals out of the fire when she drove in off the road.

She rolled down the window and yelled as he struggled to his feet.

"It's okay. Shane's fine. Nothing's wrong. Don't worry, Micah."

"Then why the hell are you here, if you'll pardon my French?"

She got out as fast as she could. He was hobbling toward her anyway.

"Looking for a dish of dried apple cobbler," she said, going to hug him. "Is that what you're baking?"

He shook his head and then turned it away from her to spit.

"Fresh apple. We done moved uptown."

He looked at her.

"How come you ain't at the hospital? What's goin' on?"

"Come over here and sit by me a minute," she said, heading for the canvas chairs beside the wagon.

They sat down facing each other and she came right to the point, telling him what Blue had told her. He showed no surprise.

"Did you know you hired a killer, Micah? Has he told you that, too?"

"I knowed it from the start, yes," he said. "But Blue don't know I know."

"Then how'd you find it out?"

He squinted at her for a minute.

"Never mind trying to figure out how much to tell me," she said. "Spill it."

"Friend of mine put me on to Blue comin' outta prison about the time I was needin' some help," he said. "He knowed all about him bein' a hell of a horseman. Said he was a good kid that never crossed the line except to kill that drug dealer."

"What else?"

"Said it happened over Blue's sister's dead body in the dope pusher's motel room."

"Go on," she said.

"That there's what I know."

"Who's your friend?"

He shook his head. He wasn't telling.

She knew him well. Badgering would get her nowhere.

They sat in silence some more.

"You knew it all the time," she said, "but still you asked him to let Shane come and ride."

"I'd judged Blue was honest, and you see it, too. He told you this flat out, didn't he? And I reckoned he ain't no murderer. He had a reason. He was a twenty-five-year-old hot-blooded kid with one hell of a provocation."

She thought about that.

"Gotta go with your gut," he said. "Montana and the rest o' this country was built by many a man with a past."

EVEN BEFORE Andie Lee pushed open the door to Shane's hospital room, she heard his laughter rising over the lower hum of the television set. It put a smile on her face and she stopped for a second to listen. Probably the cute red-haired nurse was flirting with him again.

It'd be great to see Shane's face with a smile on it, so she slipped inside the room. Maybe he'd be laughing much more often from now on. Maybe he would even embrace life for good and not slide back into his wretched existence of the last couple of years.

She took two steps, halted in her tracks, and let the door swing closed on its own.

Chase! It was Chase making Shane laugh.

Something inside her relaxed a little. Chase cared. He really did love Shane.

Chase turned his head, swept his lazy, sexy glance from the television set to her face and welcomed her with his trademark grin.

A woman would have to be dead not to feel a lift in the pit of her stomach from that look, that smile.

Andie Lee grinned back at him.

Then he was unfolding his long legs and getting up to come to her, coming to take her in his arms. They held each other and rocked a little back and forth.

"I'm so sorry I couldn't get here sooner, babe," he said. "And I'm so *damn* sorry this had to happen to our boy."

Our boy. That sounded so good to her. Help. Help at last.

But not for long. Of course.

"I can stay a couple of days," he said. "Help you get him settled at Gordon's. He said they're letting him out of here tomorrow."

She pulled back to look at him. "If there are no more complications," she said.

"Mom! Dad's here," Shane said, his voice full of excitement.

Mom. Dad.

God help her, she ought to tell him the truth. For Chase's sake, especially.

And Shane needed to hear it from her. Someday, somehow he'd find out. That always happened, didn't it?

She'd been an idiot not to marry Chase long ago. Long ago, before she began to love him like a brother instead of a lover.

"I know, darlin'. Isn't it great?" she said

"And he can stay for two days!"

No, she'd been right not to marry him. Two days? Was that not pitiful?

But even two days would be better for Shane than any medicine.

"He brought me a present," Shane said. "Look here."

She went to his bedside and smoothed back his hair as she took the nice leather sheath from his hand.

"Mmm," she said, "basket-stamped. Same color as your saddle. Silver concho snap. Very, very nice."

"That's for when he wants to wear his knife on his belt," Chase said, going around to the other side of the bed. "I was askin' him if he's remembered yet how he lost it."

Andie Lee looked from Chase's bright brown eyes to Shane's weary gray ones. They were getting lighter and brighter every day, though.

"Have you?" she asked Shane.

His gaze slid away from hers. "Only little flashes," he said. "They don't make any sense."

"Anything about the shooter?" Chase asked.

"No."

That had been Shane's story the whole time. And the whole time Andie Lee had known he was lying.

But she and Chase exchanged a look that said not to push him and the three of them talked about other things for a few minutes until the crew came in to give Shane's bath. Then they left the room and drifted toward the coffee shop.

"He still won't let me pat on him or hug his neck," she said. "Did he let you touch him?"

He shrugged. "He's bound to be sore all over."

While they waited for the elevator, Chase put his arm around her shoulders and pulled her close to lean against him.

"You worry too much, Andie. He's gonna be fine when he gets over this. I taught him to be tough, didn't I? He's my boy."

Andie Lee stood up, away from the warm, solid comfort of his body.

"You're his daddy, Chase, but not his biological father and I need to tell him that."

"What the hell's the matter with you? Look what kind of a shape he's in. You can't lay that on him, too!"

"Not right now. But he's going to find it out from somebody else one of these days."

"How? It's my name on his birth certificate."

"Gordon. That day Shane was running away, saying he was going to find you, Gordon yelled, 'You don't *have* a dad to do jack for you, boy.'"

"That arrogant son of a buck. He never did have a thought for anybody else's feelings."

"Shane's never mentioned it to me, but then he's barely been speaking to me for months. He argued with Gordon at the time, and he may not remember it at all now because of the drugs, but I wouldn't put it past Gordon to drill it into him, with details, one of these days."

"I'll go see him when we take Shane home."

"Go ahead. You can't make Gordon hold his tongue and you know it."

"Yeah. He never had a thought for anybody else's feelings."

Chase jammed the elevator button again.

"You saved our lives, mine and Shane's both, before he was born," she said. "And I don't want him to hate you, deep down, the way he does me. You're his hero. I can't let him keep on resenting you for not making a family out of the three of us. It's not fair to you."

"He doesn't resent me."

"'Why won't Dad *make* you marry him? Or at least move in with us like a long time ago? Or take me with him on the road? I'm *his* kid, too, so why won't he?'"

Incredulous, he stared at her. "He said that? When?"

"Six or eight months ago."

He shook his head.

"It's not right for him to blame you, Chase. It's not right for him to go through his whole life thinking that. And still thinking it after you're dead, every time he remembers you."

"Forget it for now," he said. "Let Shane get well. Enjoy his attitude toward you now. And whenever it crosses your mind, think about this: Shane's liable to want to hunt up his so-called biological father and tell him he's his son. Stir up a basket of snakes. Do you want that?"

She laughed a little.

"It's not his 'so-called' biological father, Chase," she said. "It's a scientific fact."

"There's your trouble," he said as the elevator opened again and he took her by the arm, "too many facts and not enough truth."

TRUTH WAS that if a man set out to live by a code of honesty, then it had to apply not only to how he dealt with others, but also to how he dealt with himself.

So Blue acknowledged, when the three of them drove up to his barn and he saw Andie Lee in the front seat of the little rental car where she sat beside a big, good-looking, starched-and-creased cowboy and Shane in the back seat, for all the world just like a cozy little family, that the first thing he felt was jealousy. He couldn't deny it because the sharp blade of it sliced through his body faster than through his mind.

Must be the famous Chase Lomax, Shane's dad—as far as Shane knew. Well, power to him, was all Blue could say. If he could whip the little junkie into shape, he was welcome to him.

Chase, if that's who it was, walked around and opened Andie Lee's door for her and they both went to the trunk of the car to take out a wheelchair. They set it up and helped Shane into it just like two parents taking care of a child.

It was good for Blue to see all that. And to realize he was

jealous. It told him he'd done the right thing by telling Andie Lee the truth about himself and stopping all that "lovers" nonsense before it really got started.

This would help him stop remembering her in his bed.

He sat the bay colt just outside the barn and waited to see what they were up to.

"Hi, Blue," Andie Lee called. "Shane wants to see the roan."

They walked toward him with Chase pushing the chair.

"He has to save his strength for a while," she said, walking along beside them as they approached.

Blue nodded. He looked at Shane instead of at her.

He talked to Shane instead of to her. "When did you get back?"

The kid looked better out of his eyes than he'd ever seen him. He met Blue's gaze head-on, too.

And he actually answered a civil question in a civil tone.

"Late yesterday. How's Roanie?"

"Coming along on the wound. Don't know yet about the lameness."

Shane looked stricken. He did have some feeling for the colt.

Blue stood in the stirrup and swung down, determined to show he had some class, ex-con or not. It was his barn, after all. He walked to the bay horse's head and took down his reins.

"Blue Bowman," Andie Lee said, "Chase Lomax."

The two men shook hands. Chase's grip was firm and strong. He gave Blue a clear, straight look. His smile made a person want to smile back at him. Blue hated to admit it, but he'd like to find fault with him if he could at all.

Jealousy was a sneaking, low devil of an unworthy feeling. It made him feel petty and he tried to dispel it. There was no reason for it. He had no connection to Andie Lee or Shane, either one.

"I'll take Shane in," Blue said. "He can sit in the aisle and we'll see if Roanie'll come to the door for him."

He put the bay into an empty stall and went back outside. As he took hold of the wheelchair and began to push, he said to Andie Lee and Chase, "Y'all are welcome to come in. But stay on this end of the barn away from Roanie's stall."

As he pushed Shane into the aisle, a truck came growling and purring into the yard.

Blue looked out. Ranch truck, crew cab, Gordon.

Great. A whole convention of visitors. Where was Micah when you needed him? Blue sure as hell didn't want to talk to any of them.

Andie Lee, telling Shane about Roanie and how the wheelchair might scare him and how some animals didn't like medical and hospital smells, opened the door to her gray horse's stall and took Chase in to see him. Her sorrel mare nickered to him from the next stall.

Evidently horses, too, were susceptible to the famous Lomax charm.

Blue went into Roanie's stall and, with a hand beneath his chin, led him to the door. Roanie looked down at Shane and nosed at him, sniffing. Shane reached up and touched his muzzle.

"I'm sorry, Roanie," he said. "I didn't do it. I'm not the one who hurt you."

Typical addict. Blame somebody else. Of course, technically it was true. Shane hadn't tied himself to the saddle.

The colt let the boy pet his nose.

"I hope he won't blame me for being in pain," Shane said, looking at Blue.

When Blue didn't say anything, he said, "Do you think he will, Blue?"

Blue shrugged. "So far, so good. He's not biting at you."

Gordon walked in at the east door as if he owned the place. Which, of course, he did.

Hatred and frustration and anger swirled up in a dizzying mix with the jealousy, making Blue feel as if he'd totally lost control of his emotions as well as his barn.

Gordon started down the aisle with a touch on the shoulder for Shane and not a glance at Blue.

"Andie Lee," he said, as he walked up to the gray's stall, "you should've waited. I told you I'd bring Shane up here in my truck. That little tin can piece of shit is liable to jar his ribs apart again."

Chase turned around and went out of the stall to greet him. "Hey, that's the only car I could rent. You're not turning into some kind of a snob, are you, *Mr.* Campbell?"

To Blue's surprise, Gordon smiled—actually smiled—and held out his hand. He and Chase shook.

"I expected a five-time world champion to drive something a little better than that," he said. "You've done okay for yourself since you left here, Lomax."

"Well, you know what they say," Chase said. "A man's only as good as his last ride. I have to admit I didn't make it to the bell on that one."

So. He wasn't a braggart. The tone of his voice was sincere. Blue didn't like himself very much for wishing it wasn't, but he ran the words through his mind again, listening.

"Sorry I missed you at breakfast," Gordon said. "Had a problem over on the Little Creek section and we're shorthanded. Can't hire decent help these days 'cause nobody wants to work."

A cold, green hand twisted Blue's gut. Chase at breakfast in the main house. Chase sleeping at the big house.

Which last night had housed not only Chase, but Andie Lee.

Gordon glanced at Chase's belt buckle. It was the dinnerplate size trophy kind.

"I was looking forward to some Vegas finals stories with

my bacon and eggs," he said. "Micah always raves about watching all those wins of yours on TV."

Yeah. Everybody liked a champion. Even Gordon.

"I'm sorry to miss the old coot," Chase said. "Andie Lee says he's still getting around pretty well."

Andie Lee came out of the gray's stall and walked past them both, coming toward Blue. No, to Shane, of course.

She watched him for a minute, then she said, "Let me roll you over here now, so I can go in and look at Roanie's wound. You want to go talk to Dad and Gordon?"

He gave the colt a last pat and nodded. "I can roll myself."

"Remember your ribs."

"How can I forget?"

Then he was gone and Andie Lee was waiting for Blue to move the horse back so she could come into the stall.

"How's he doing?" she asked.

The soft tone reminded him of her hands on his skin.

"You're the doctor," he said, clucking to the colt to move him into a better light.

She bent over and looked at the wound closely.

"Good," she said. "You did a good job cleaning it."

Blue nodded his thanks.

She straightened up and looked at him directly. He made himself meet and hold her gaze, but he couldn't read her eyes.

He didn't need to be thinking about her. He wasn't *gonna* think about her anymore.

Gordon was still talking to Chase. Chase was famous and used to lots of attention, no doubt, but this was Gordon. Probably when he'd been Gordon's horse trainer he'd been treated like the rest of the peons. It took a world championship to make him Gordon's equal.

Well, not quite. Gordon didn't consider anyone his equal. But he could lower himself to visit with a world champion, even if he had once been a saddle bum.

Roanie shifted his hind end and shook his head with a restless snort, moving away from them toward the window.

"The colt's had enough," Blue said. "Let's leave him alone."

He let Andie Lee out, then followed her, turning to fasten the stall door behind him.

Gordon and Chase were walking slowly toward the west door, Chase pushing Shane's chair.

Gordon stopped and looked back at the roan colt.

"The wound's healing?" he said to Andie Lee.

"Right," she said. "And it's made him learn to tolerate me a little bit."

"I rode him all the way up the mountain," Shane said, turning to look at Chase. "He let me catch him. I remember he came to the fence for me."

Blue caught the glance that passed between Chase and Andie Lee.

Like they were a couple. Good. That was great. That was the way it should be. The boy needed a strong hand in his life.

"Go look at him, Dad," Shane said. "Blue, just from the aisle. Can't Dad look at him from the aisle?"

At Blue's nod, Chase walked back to where he could look at Roanie without going close enough to make him feel crowded. He was thoughtful, too. Nothing less than a saint, no doubt.

"Don't you like the look of him, Dad?"

Chase nodded. "He's a handsome devil."

As Blue moved away from the door, Roanie whirled awkwardly and kicked the wall beneath the window.

Shane laughed. "You nailed him. Sometimes he is a devil, but not to me."

They all started walking out the west door.

"He's a two?" Chase asked Blue, who answered with a nod.

"I'd like to ride him again," Shane said.

"It'll be a while before you're able to ride," Andie Lee said. "And before he's able to be ridden."

Shane turned around to talk to Blue.

"Maybe in a few days, can I work with him from the ground?"

"Well, I don't know about that," Gordon said. "From what I hear, you got thrown out of this barn, even before your big escapade."

He walked up to where he and Shane could see each other. "I'll find you something to ride, boy. I've got some fine young ones, if that's what you want. I'll help you get one started right and if you like him, I'll sign the transfer papers to you."

Well. That was a shock to Blue. Gordon must be going soft in his old age.

It'd be a shocking sight to see, too: Gordon yelling and cussing at Shane and the horse. He'd probably be throwing things at them. Maybe even taking a whip to them both.

Shane didn't reply. He looked at Blue.

Gordon stared at the kid.

It was weird, but Gordon really did seem to care about Shane and Andie Lee and want to help them—today. Maybe it was because Shane nearly died. Or because his behavior was different now and Gordon took that as a sign he was all cured and he'd be sober forever.

If so, there was a lot Gordon didn't know about addiction.

Or maybe Gordon just wanted to show off to make points with Chase the champion.

"Thanks," Shane said. "But I don't want you to help me."

"Not even for a free horse?" Gordon asked.

"I want to be with the roan colt."

Gordon was not pleased. Everyone waited to see whether that had destroyed his good mood completely. Everyone but Shane.

"Blue," Shane said, wheeling around to look up at him

like one of those big-eyed kids in a drawing, "what would I have to do for you to let me ride with you again?"

Nothing. There's nothing you can do that would make me take you back.

The boy was pale as chalk. His arms were trembling a little—from fatigue or withdrawal, Blue didn't know.

He was pitiful. And Blue didn't want to humiliate him in front of his dad and mom. Or Gordon.

Especially since Blue had called the tyrant on that very thing more than once.

"There's all kinds of young horses on this ranch," Blue said. "Gordon's are the best. You can have your pick of his and own it. The roan's not for sale."

"I don't care. I want to help you with him. Nobody thinks he'll amount to anything."

"They don't, huh?"

"No."

Blue's mind raced, looking for a tactful way to refuse Shane.

"You broke the rules, Shane," he said. "We had an agreement."

The boy interrupted. "I know. I know. But I was using then. And now I'm clean. Won't you give me a chance to prove it?"

I'd be a fool to take you on again. You're a charmer now but all addicts are charmers when they need to be.

Damn. Damn. Why didn't Andie Lee step in? She must be screaming inside at the thought of Shane with Blue again.

Blue looked at her. She was looking at Shane.

Shane, who had the natural cunning of any child playing two adults against each other.

"Gordon said you might be able to get a little use out of Roanie," he said, "but he'll never be really broke unless other people can ride him, too."

Blue looked at him and waited.

Shane continued to confide in him. "Roanie is crazy, Gordon said, and it'll come out again real soon."

Great. Here was a new way to go about this.

"Well, then, aren't you scared to get on him? Being hurt may make him meaner and harder to ride than ever."

"I'll do everything you say," Shane promised. "Won't you give me a second chance now that I'm not a junkie anymore?"

Damn. The kid sounded like a pitiful orphan asking for a crust of bread.

Blue played the last card in his hand, even though it made him feel like a helpless coward.

"You'll have to ask your mother."

That would do the trick.

Everyone waited for what Andie Lee would say.

Hurry up. Get it over with. Tell him any reason, tell him I'm not fit company for him, or don't even give him a reason. Just tell him no.

"All right," she said slowly, her eyes fixed on Shane's. "But you know that if you mess up this time, it's the last chance you'll have with Blue and the roan colt. You know that, don't you?"

What?

Blue couldn't believe his ears. Surely that wasn't what she said.

But it was. Shane's face broke into a smile that lit him up from inside and he turned his big, hopeful eyes on Blue.

He was pitiful. An addict who was trying to get clean and needed some hope to even have a chance to do it.

A messed-up boy, trying to get with a horse he loved.

Everyone waited to see what Blue would say.

Finally, he found his voice. Gruffly, he muttered, "One more shot."

Shane's wan face broke into a smile that proved how young he really was.

"One's all I need."

Then, to Blue's great surprise, he added, "Thank you, Blue."

CHAPTER SIXTEEN

AFTER THAT, Shane started talking excitedly, telling Chase about the individual horses and how he'd be riding all of them soon. He, Chase and Gordon drifted off to look at the ones in the pasture. Blue turned on Andie Lee.

"What the hell were you thinking? What's the matter with you? Have you lost your mind? You're sending your kid to hang out with a murderer?"

She paled a little under the onslaught but she snapped back.

"You saw his face," she said. "If I'd killed that hope, he'd have been at loose ends again and probably right back on the drugs. He has a goal, Blue! For the first time since he started all this trouble. What would happen to his recovery if I took that away?"

"What if I killed *him* instead of his hope? Aren't you afraid of that?"

"I don't think so," she said.

"You'd better damn well be sure, don't you think?"

"I'm as sure as any person can be about another."

"What the hell's that supposed to mean?"

"Look," she said, glancing toward the others as if to see if they were watching, "I've been in a fury with Gordon for making Shane take such consequences. You know that. But what if it's working? What if this really is Shane's road to redemption? We can't screw it up now, Blue."

He threw up his hands. Literally.

"Shane's talking about you and the roan," she said quickly. "Blue and the roan. He rode the horse that couldn't be rode and he has to prove he can do it when he's sober. And he thinks he can work hard enough to make it all up to you. Isn't that what we want children to learn—to take responsibility and make amends?"

"Andie Lee…"

"Andie Lee," Gordon called. "Come here. This filly's out of that Sunshine mare you used to love so much."

"Let's just give it a chance," she said to Blue. "Okay? Please excuse me."

"You're out of your mind," he said, as she walked away. "I won't be responsible."

He looked up to see Gordon's glance go from him to Andie Lee and back again.

THE NEXT MORNING early, Andie Lee walked Chase out to the rental car to say good-bye.

"Tell Shane 'bye' again for me," he said. "I'm glad he decided to sleep in. We stayed up talking until after midnight."

"Did he tell you anything I should know?"

He thought about that as he opened the car door and threw his bag into the back seat.

"Nah. Mostly it was, 'I'm gonna prove I can ride the rough ones so I can rodeo' and 'Blue's gonna teach me how to start colts so I can do that when I retire from rodeo.'"

They laughed.

"One extreme to the other," Andie Lee said. "He's gone from not caring what happens to him in the next minute to planning his retirement."

He straightened up and turned to her, mimicking Shane's voice.

"Does this mean I don't have to go to school anymore, Mom?"

She laughed. "It does not. But let's take it one step at a time, okay?"

"That's the secret of life," Chase said. "One step at a time."

He took her into his arms and gave her a lingering kiss on the mouth.

Then he pulled back and looked into her eyes. "Just like we've always done."

She felt safe in his arms, too, she really did. And she knew Chase through and through. She should've married him long ago.

"What d'ya say, Andie Lee?" he said. "Maybe one more step? When Shane's able to get away from the rehab deal, y'all come to my place for a while."

She reached up and touched his face. He was the one who'd been through the fire with her. Part of the time.

"Problem is, you'd probably not be there," she said, and it came easy to smile at him. "Go, Chase darlin'. Ride the life out of every minute…"

Together they finished their old saying, "…eight seconds at a time."

They laughed and he shook his head.

"Them seconds is gittin' longer every year," he said.

Behind Andie Lee, the screened door slammed.

"Gordon," Chase said, lifting a hand to him. "Thanks for the hospitality."

"Can't stay for breakfast?" Gordon called, boot heels clattering across the porch. "Well, come back anytime."

He strode up to them, his usual stainless steel insulated mug of morning coffee in his hand. He switched it to the left one and shook hands with Chase.

"Good luck," he said. "Ride safe."

And then, with one last brush of his lips against hers, Chase was in the car, had it fired up and was gone with only a wave when he turned up the road to the highway.

"Maybe you should've married him," Gordon said. "He made something out of himself after all."

"Oh yeah, you've got twenty-twenty hindsight," Andie Lee told him. "But don't flatter yourself. It wasn't because you called him a saddle bum that I didn't marry him."

"Damn," he said lightly and took a sip of coffee, "and I thought you always listened to me."

"I'm not going to wrangle with you today, Gordon. I'm feeling good about my child and grateful for my blessings. You're getting too mellow to be any fun, anyhow."

That made him bark his scratchy laugh.

"Miss Sass," he said, and threw her a look as he started to his truck. "Any chance that another one of your blessings is that good-looking Indian, Blue?"

He laughed some more at the look on her face. He was still grinning at her as he drove away.

BLUE HAD EXPECTED it to be a couple of weeks, at least, before Shane felt strong enough even to come up and hang around the barn, much less do any of the work. Instead, after four days and nights at the big house, he had his mother drop him off one morning. He was a help, although for the first couple of days Blue kept him away from the horses, even on the ground, so he could judge how strong he was. He had decided to accept Shane philosophically, in memory of Dannah, and simply to stay away from Andie Lee.

That first day, Shane lasted until noon before he called his mom to come pick him up. Gradually, as he felt stronger, he stayed longer and longer, mostly hanging out with the roan colt, who was accepting him—and no one else, to Shane's great satisfaction—and watching what Blue did with the other horses.

He didn't talk a whole lot and when he felt the need to rest, he sat staring off into the mountains. Finally, Blue began to give him light chores, which he did without a word of protest.

Micah—and according to him, Andie Lee—were beginning to truly believe that Shane was coming to his senses and well on his way to being completely clean and sober for the rest of his life. Blue didn't talk to either one of them about it. He couldn't forget how many times Dannie had taken a step forward, only to slide two or three steps back.

He couldn't complain yet, though. Shane was truly sorry about hurting the roan colt, was trying to learn all about everything Blue was doing, and did more work every day.

One morning, Shane arrived even earlier than usual. Blue leaned against the edge of the barn door and watched him climb down out of Andie Lee's truck, trying to keep from tangling his feet and his spurs. She stayed there and let the truck run until Shane looked back and motioned for her to go on.

Blue had to smile. Shane wore chinks as well as the spurs. He was trying to tighten the strap on the short chaps, keep the saddle pad that he carried folded over his shoulder from falling off and walk like a cowboy at the same time.

"The doctor said I can ride today," he called to Blue.

"Yeah."

Shane stopped in his tracks.

"I told Mom not to say anything!"

"She didn't."

"I bet she told Micah and Micah told you."

"You told me."

Shane walked faster.

"What?"

"The gear."

Shane glanced down at himself. Then he gave Blue a nod and a grin.

"We got any coffee?"

"Fresh pot."

Today must be special all around. Shane didn't like coffee. He usually wrangled a couple of Cokes out of Micah every day and drank water the rest of the time. Maybe he thought coffee went with chinks and spurs.

The thought widened Blue's smile. He laughed to himself.

He turned and walked with him into the barn, down the aisle to the tack room. Shane went to his saddle, threw the pad over it, and carried them both out to an empty saddle rack in the aisle.

Blue poured two mugs of coffee from the pot on the rickety table in the tack room and followed him out. He offered one of the cups and Shane took it.

"Saddle pads around here not good enough for you?"

Shane was sipping at the coffee. He shrugged.

"It's for Roanie. The holes let more air to the horse's back and the stuff it's made out of takes more of the weight of the saddle."

"Pretty pricey," Blue said.

"My dad gave me some money."

He grinned at Blue, raising his eyebrows as if to invite him in on the joke. "This time I didn't use it to get high."

"You can save a lot that way," Blue said dryly.

"And buy a lot of stuff," Shane said.

He took a drink of coffee and looked Shane over. He appeared to be happier. His skin had lost its pallor.

What was really different was that his eyes had come alive. They'd been so flat before he got hurt that there'd been no expression there—not even hopelessness. Now they were still twinkling with the humor of his joke. Which he'd made himself.

And he'd lost his sloppy look.

It hit Blue then. Shane looked distinctly like him. Chambray shirt, denim jeans, hat creased the same as Blue's, chinks and spurs exactly the same type as Blue's.

The kid was drinking Blue's coffee when he didn't even like it.

Damn. Look at it that way, and the morning wasn't starting out to be quite so funny.

Damn it to hell, he didn't want another impossible responsibility. Hadn't he done everything in his power to keep away from it?

This just made it even more of a mistake that he'd taken the boy back into the barn. God knew, he didn't want—or deserve—to be anybody's hero.

He could still remember how hard and deep a fifteen-year-old's hero worship could go. He hoped Shane's wasn't as fierce as Blue's own had been for Robert Cornsilk.

Robert had been a rounder, but as far as Blue knew, he'd never killed anybody. He had stuck to every bronc and bull he rode like a tick on a dog and had won every rodeo he entered, and Blue had thought he could do no wrong. He'd won every fight, he'd held his liquor and he'd danced with the most beautiful cowgirls at the rodeo dances Blue had snuck into long before he was old enough.

The fifteen-year-old Blue had been so hungry for a father that he tried to do anything Robert did. He'd imitated his dress and his manner and his walk and he would've died for him, although the most attention Robert ever paid to him was a brief slap on the shoulder and a "How's it going?" when he barely noticed him hanging around.

Blue didn't want that kind of power over anybody. But that was the rub. The person wielding it had no control in that kind of a deal.

It must be born into every boy to hunt for a hero to teach him how to be a man. Why didn't Shane stick to his dad? *Chase* should be his hero.

The only thing he could do was to keep this whole thing horses only.

"I'm thinking you might do that bay colt some good if you want to get on him today," he said.

"I was thinking more about Roanie," Shane said.

His tone was exactly like the one Blue had just used.

Somewhere, deep inside, in spite of all his misgivings, that warmed a tiny corner in Blue. But he wasn't going to let that warmth grow. If he had influence over Shane, he'd use it, not to build a friendship or anything personal at all, but to try to make a horseman of him.

And to try to solidify this turn of his away from the drugs.

That'd be one for Dannie.

He could hold the kid at arm's length and still get that done.

"But if you want me on the bay, then that's okay," Shane said.

"Good. I don't want anybody on Roanie yet. Let's give him a little more time."

They saddled, mounted, and rode for half an hour or so with Blue coaching Shane and keeping an eye on both mounts' progress.

"Let's start getting them used to standing still while we're mounted," Blue said. "They need to learn to wait and listen for what we'll ask them for next and it'll rest them, too."

He nodded at the little clutch of aspen trees on the east side of the pasture.

"How about over there?"

They sat their saddles quietly for a few minutes enjoying the breeze and watching the play of the clouds' shadows on the valley. Shane stared across it at the mountains for a while and then he broke the silence.

"I've decided," he said. "I'm gonna kill him."

The words hit Blue like pellets of hail on a beautiful day. *"What?"*

"Jason," Shane said, meeting Blue's eyes without a waver. "Remember him?"

It took a second.

"The guy Gordon fired from the Center?"

"Yeah. That Lininger cabin? That's where he keeps his stuff."

Blue drilled him with his eyes. "What stuff?"

"You know. Crack. Grass, meth, pills, whatever."

"He's a dealer?"

"Yeah. The whole time Gordon was paying him to keep the ranch drug free. That's how stupid *he* is."

In spite of a little laugh at Gordon, the flat determination was still in his voice. And in his eyes. This kid was serious.

"Jason's the one who shot me and hurt Roanie. I'm gonna blow out his lights."

The words bounced around inside Blue's mind like gravel in a concrete culvert. What the *hell?*

What *was* this? A *boy*. Just a boy, fifteen years old, sitting a fine horse in a soft breeze on a warm, sunny day looking out over spectacular mountains and a beautiful valley... talking about killing another kid.

Jason might be in his twenties, but from where Blue was sitting and where he'd been, he was a kid like Shane. He pierced Shane with a look.

How could that be? To be young and strong and free to do anything you were smart enough and man enough to do, and what you chose was to take another kid's life?

That went on all the time. Shane had probably seen it on TV.

What he hadn't seen was the concrete years that followed. Take another kid's life and lose your own.

And what he didn't see was that if he really did kick his habit, his future could hold anything he wanted.

Instead of even trying to see that, he sat there mouthing off like some stupid con already in the pen for life. Like Pitbull Crawford, making a vow to a buddy in the prison yard. A vow Blue had overheard, a vow Pitbull had kept.

But Shane saying it out here in the wonderful, wide open space was so insane as to be laughable. Shane's tone of voice and the look in his eyes, though, told Blue that he was every inch serious.

His guts shrank against his backbone. It was like hearing his own words come out of a baby's mouth.

Shane couldn't know he was imitating Blue in that, too.

"Why tell me?"

"Advice. I've gotta figure out how to do it. Where's best, when, stuff like that. And how to get there, since I don't have a car and Mom's a witch about not letting me drive without a permit. If I take her truck, she'll call the police. She told me that and she means it."

Blue stared at him.

"If you kill Jason, somebody might call the police about that, too."

Shane didn't want to hear it.

"I don't think Jason'll come back to the cabin, so I'll have to hit him at the Crazy Creek or the convenience store or at a rodeo or a concert—someplace he meets his customers. Or I'll have to find out where he's living. You can help me decide."

"Me?" Had Andie Lee told him that Blue killed a man? No. Surely not.

She wouldn't. Not knowing that her child looked up to him.

"I can trust you not to tell. You know stuff. You've been around."

"Where do you think I've been?"

Shane shrugged. A shrug like Blue's.

"At least from Oklahoma to here, Micah said. And you know just about everything and you're not scared of anything."

Blue sat, his whole body wanting to shiver in the saddle. He sure as hell was scared of this.

"Have you thought about what could happen when this killing's all done?"

"Nothing will happen to me," Shane said. "The police will think it was one of his customers. A drug deal gone bad."

"The police know he's a dealer?"

"No. But they'll find out when somebody calls in that they found his body."

"Why don't you call in now and let them pick him up? Save yourself a lifetime in the pen. Or death."

"He'd snake his way out of it. I mean to make him pay for saying I should get on my horse and ride away and then shooting me in the back."

He looked up the mountain that rose behind Butte Hill, glowering as if he could still see Jason.

"You could get put to death for murder."

Shane set his jaw.

"If I call the police, I'll end up in jail again for horse theft and gun theft. They won't believe what I say because I'm a thief and they won't even look for Jason. No. I know his schedule. I can stalk him. I'm gonna make sure he gets his."

When Blue said nothing, he added, "It's *Roanie*, Blue. Think about it. He's the one who put your horse through hell and nearly killed him."

"Prison's worse than jail. Revenge wouldn't be worth going there. You don't have a clue what you're talkin' here, Shane."

"I know what it's like to be in jail and I'm *not* goin' back there, much less to prison."

More of Blue's own words. The kid must've been stalking him.

Shane met Blue's gaze again with an unwavering one of his own.

"I'm taking care of this," he said flatly. "For me and Roanie. Whether you help me or not. All I want's a little advice."

It wasn't going to be easy to change his mind. Blue tried to think of exactly the right thing to say. In the right tone.

"Could be a dicey proposition if he got the drop on you," he said. "He's a fair hand with a crossbow."

"He's jerked me around for the last time," Shane said. "He'll not get the drop on me again."

Blue's mouth felt too stiff to speak. His *brain* was too stiff. Here was another situation, like with Dannie, where he was trying to clean up after a parent's mistakes. It made him mad as hell. Hadn't he sworn never to do that again?

Shane copying his clothes and his gear and his methods and his tone of voice were one thing but this was another. An inexplicable thing.

How could he be imitating something he didn't even *know* about Blue?

Was Blue wearing the mark of Cain on his forehead for wannabe killers to see? Or MURDER branded into his hide like in the legend of the murder steer?

Was this some kind of a sign?

BLUE STOOD IT as long as he could, then he said he had an errand in town and borrowed Micah's truck. He went into the house to change his shirt and called the number for Andie Lee's cell phone that the old man had at the top of his list beside the phone.

She sounded pretty happy when she answered. He hated to burst her bubble, but it had to be done. Face to face.

"I have to run into town," he said. "Want to ride along?"

There was a silence.

"Blue?"

She was probably afraid to go out with him alone.

No, if that were true she wouldn't let her son spend every day with him.

He should've identified himself, for God's sake. And it was a pretty strange invitation, considering that they'd both been avoiding being alone with each other every day when she came to the barn to ride.

Before he could say "sorry," she was saying, "If we can grab some lunch. I skipped breakfast."

"Deal."

"Want me to come up there?"

He had to move, had to do something this minute.

"No, I'll pick you up. At the main house?"

"I'm here now."

"Meet me out front."

And then he was in the little truck cab with her, breathing her scent and thinking about how she'd looked and felt in his bed and glancing at her beautiful profile while he drove the old truck up out of the valley and headed for the highway. Listening to her and talking to her and trying to think where to start when he told her—again—to take her son off his hands. That he didn't want any part of trying to keep Shane from killing someone.

By the way, Andie Lee, your kid is plotting a murder.

He had to tell her. He would tell her, right now, in just a minute. She had a right to know.

But all the unaccustomed feelings and dark thoughts roiling in his gut had sealed his lips. They'd brought up memories that had thrown him back into the old habits of not wanting to talk, the habits forged by ten years of speaking only briefly to only a few other men and never saying anything important.

This was important. And it had to be said.

He just wanted to get it over with and be rid of Shane. He had enough guilt already.

But he couldn't even form the words on his tongue. Andie Lee was happy right now but she wouldn't be for long.

They talked about the horses and Roanie's wounds and one of Gordon's best broodmares who had colicked the night before. Blue drove beneath the crosspiece of the gate and out onto the highway. He needed to tell her now and get it over with.

As they drove along, she was chattering on about how hopeful she was getting to be because Shane was still clean and sober. How much Shane was enjoying riding with Blue. How much he looked up to Blue.

Blue lowered his foot on the gas and gave thanks for all the engine noise. Then he lifted it again.

Up there, on the side of the road, a sign on top of a log building. Neon sign: THE CRAZY CREEK. Cars and trucks outside. He had promised her lunch.

Blue slowed and pulled into the parking lot. Shane had named this as one of Jason's hangouts.

"Good choice," Andie Lee said. "The food's better here than any place around."

Stepping into the Crazy Creek was like stepping back in time. A long, mirrored mahogany bar ran along the wall facing the front door. Heads of elk, moose, deer, buffalo, longhorns and bighorn sheep loomed above and all around it. And on the side wall. A large dance floor stretched in front of it.

The rest of the place was a warren of secluded, highbacked booths and tables in corners. Perfect for conducting private business.

Blue looked around for Jason as they followed the hostess to a booth. If he saw him, what would he do? Tell him to watch his back? Kill him himself?

They sat down, looked at the menu, and ordered buffalo burgers and seasoned fries. Once the waitress was gone, Blue let himself lean back into the padded leather of the seat. He took a deep breath and let go a little.

They could eat first. She hadn't had any breakfast and he felt like he'd been through some kind of an emotional wringer this morning.

Plus he'd do a better job of telling her if he had something in his stomach besides butterflies. And she'd be in better shape to hear it.

Andie Lee shifted around and curled her legs up under her on her side of the booth, then folded her long arms on the table to lean across it toward him.

"You look great," she said. "I hate it when you avoid me."

He laughed. It was so unexpected but so typical of her usual directness that he shouldn't have been surprised at all.

"I thought you were avoiding me," he said.

She laughed at that.

"You are so full of it," she said, smiling, teasing him. "You know you're the one who started it."

"Andie Lee."

He just shook his head. He couldn't think what to say with her looking at him, smiling that way. Why did he have to catch her in this great mood? Now he'd have to be the one to ruin it.

"You know who I really am, now," he said. "You ought to have more sense."

"One bad mistake doesn't make you who you really are," she said, getting serious.

"I don't understand why you aren't afraid of me," he said. "I expected you to jump out of the truck and go running to the house or at the very least tell me never to speak to you again."

Her solemn gray gaze held his.

"Why did you do it, Blue?"

"He needed killing."

She was looking at him like she wanted to see into his soul.

He turned up his open hands helplessly. "I don't know how to put it into words," he said, "but sometimes a man has to do the hard things."

She waited for him to go on.

He didn't know whether he could talk any more about the feelings that went so deep they lived in his bones and drove his life.

"To bring justice," he said. "To protect the weak ones. To keep the good so evil won't take over."

"But it didn't save your sister," she said. "And you went to prison."

"It stopped one scumbag," he said.

She nodded. "There've been times I've wished with a passion that I could take revenge on whoever got Shane started," she said. "I mean, I hated him. But I was thinking more along the lines of calling the police or the DEA."

"Yeah," he said dryly, "that'd be another way to go."

They smiled, but the dark memories were lapping at the edges of their minds. They both saw it was true for the other. Andie Lee reached across the table and took both his hands.

He knew it well: that deep, long yearning to find something to hold on to.

"I definitely would've turned them in—every last one who ever sold Shane one gram of anything—but I never could find out where he was getting it."

Let me tell you where he's been getting it lately. And what he's planning to do about it.

But the waitress brought their tea right then and said the food would be there soon and there was no sense ruining a nice lunch.

"What've you been doing this morning?" he asked. "How come you missed breakfast?"

She shifted her fingers in his palms so she could caress the back of his hand with her thumb. The slow rhythm of it started sending a calmness into his gut.

And a steady thrum of excitement, too.

"I was painting," she said. "Trying to catch the dawn on the mountains right at the minute it turns them rose. And then I just kept on going."

His hands tightened a little on hers, although he didn't intend it.

"I didn't know you're a painter," he said.

Bowman, you idiot. There are a million things you don't know about her.

"What?" she said. "Do you paint, too?"

She knew by the way he said it. As soon as he said it, she knew. And there was nothing in the words themselves to tell her.

That means nothing. Stop looking for signs in everything that anybody says. And stop this getting interested in her. All you have is a few minutes more, because when you tell her the news, she won't be smiling anymore.

"I'm a rank amateur," she said. "And not much good. But it takes me away from my real life and I love it. Some counselor suggested it early on in my troubles with Shane."

He nodded.

"What about you?" she asked.

For ten years, it was my life. It saved my sanity.

"I've done some. Did you get the rose?"

"Let's say I'm working on it," she said. "But I came closer than I've ever done."

"That's all you can hope for," he said as their food arrived. "To come closer every time."

They ate heartily and talked about painting, which made him miss it and soothed him at the same time. That refuge had always been there. He could always fall into it and forget.

When they got back into the truck, Andie Lee said, "Where's your errand?"

Blue stared at her, blank for a moment.

"You said you have to run into town."

"Oh. Yeah. My errand."

She knew him too well.

She laughed. "It's okay, Blue. You're a terrible liar. There's nothing wrong with a workaholic wanting to get away from the job on a beautiful day like this one."

If only you knew what a liar I am. I do it best without saying a word.

He drove slowly back toward the ranch. They talked

some, but the sun through the windshield and food in their stomachs made them drowsy and the time together had made them comfortable with each other again.

Just like that. It was so strange how he could feel so good, so…right…when he was with her.

He would give anything to while away the long afternoon with her in his bed. Or out of it.

It would upset her so much, what he was about to tell her. He'd wait until they were back on the ranch.

When he drove beneath the crossbar of the gate at the highway and started down the winding road, he watched for a good spot to pull off and talk. Three or four different creeks ran near or across the road and when he came to the spot where he'd glimpsed the deer the day Micah had brought him onto the Splendid Sky, he saw a beautiful little open spot on the opposite side.

He drove off into it.

"Let's get out and walk a little," he said. "Look at the creek."

She looked at him. He made his eyes meet hers.

Was she wanting to while away the long afternoon the same way he was?

She sensed something coming, he could tell. But without a word, she just nodded and opened her door.

They walked along the creek to a big rock outcropping and stopped. He leaned back against it and then he couldn't stop himself from taking both her hands. This would be so hard for her to hear.

"Andie Lee," he said. "I have to talk to you."

She moved up closer, her eyes wide.

"No, you don't. I understand. There at the Crazy Creek, when I said that about calling the police, I didn't mean that to sound sanctimonious."

She squeezed his hands as if to make sure he was listening.

"There's not a family member or a loved one of *any* addict that hasn't wanted to kill the pusher. Not one. And not one who'd have hesitated to do it, given the right moment, the weapon and the opportunity all at the same time."

It took him a heartbeat or two to change gears. Then when he could hear what she was saying, he yearned toward her voice. The loyalty in it. Loyalty to him. He didn't even care what the words were.

He wanted her in his arms, in his bed, laughing with him, making love with him at that very moment.

And she wanted it, too. He knew it.

What made him happiest was that she understood. She knew him. She liked him. For more than sex. The real truth about him hadn't run her off the way he'd intended it to do. She still trusted him. She still wanted him.

There was a real possibility trembling between them— in the look they shared, in the very air. They might, just might, have something that could grow and last a long time. Maybe forever.

A terrible realization washed through him with the force of a tidal wave: he would have to choose between her love and his revenge on Gordon. *That* she would never forgive. He slammed his mind against the thought.

"Evidently, some recovering addicts feel that same way," he said.

Honesty, Bowman. Blurt it out.

"Shane told me this morning that he's planning to kill Jason."

Her eyes widened and her face paled as she tried to get her mind around the totally unexpected. She gripped his hands tighter and came closer to him still.

"*What?* Shane? Jason?"

"The director of the Center who called the cops on Shane that day. The one Gordon fired. Remember him? Shane says he was a pusher in disguise."

Her mouth fell open.

"And *Shane's* wanting to kill him?"

"He's trying to make plans. Jason's the one who shot him up on the mountain. Shane knew he kept his stash at the Lininger cabin and went up there to steal it."

Andie Lee pulled her hands away and stepped back, but she listened with her eyes as well as her ears, nodding yes and then no, never saying a word, while he told her everything he knew about the whole story.

"I can't be responsible for him, Andie Lee. I can't be the one to try to keep him from becoming a killer. You'll have to take him to ride with somebody else. Gordon said he'll help him and give him a horse, to boot."

She seemed not to hear him.

"Shane *told* you all that? Why?"

"He wants me to give him advice. Help with his plans."

It took a few seconds for that to sink in.

"Oh, Blue! He *can't* know. I didn't tell him what you told me. I *wouldn't*."

She reached out and took his hand. Hers was trembling.

"*Please* don't think that I did. Do you think that?"

"No," he said.

Then she jerked away to bury her face in her hands.

"What I think is that I'm the only person he could turn to for help. Micah would go straight to you."

He was trying to keep her from crying. He did not want her to cry.

She didn't. She stiffened her back and looked at him straight.

"You're still the only one," she said. "I can't talk to him because we can't let him know that you broke his trust. You have to turn him around, Blue."

"No. I'd feel too guilty if I couldn't get it done."

"You'll feel *really* guilty if you don't even try."

CHAPTER SEVENTEEN

"THAT'S MY PROBLEM," Blue said.

Andie Lee blocked the words from her ears while she tried to control her rising panic. This was on a whole new level of trouble—Shane planning to kill someone. She couldn't even think about Jason. Her son, the son she'd loved so much and gone through so much to birth and nurture was serious about *murder?*

Was this why he was being so good lately? He was staying clearheaded to plot a murder?

Talk about helplessness! She'd thought she lived with it but she never even knew the meaning of the word until now.

"I know you said you didn't take him to raise…"

Her voice left her. It didn't break, it just left her standing there with a whole new dread beating its drum in her mind and deep in the pit of her stomach. She didn't have a clue what to do and she had no right to badger Blue to take this responsibility. She turned away from him and walked down to the edge of the creek, trying to see the grass and the rocks and the water through eyes so dry she couldn't bear to close her lids over them.

Beyond tears. She'd never known exactly what that meant until now.

She saw a large, flat rock that jutted out over the fast-running stream and headed for it. She sat down and stared at the glittering water rushing by, totally oblivious to any pain.

After a long time, Blue said, "Andie Lee?"

She didn't turn to him. For one thing, she couldn't move and for another, she didn't want to beg for help.

"Leave me alone," she said.

She felt him, though. He didn't go away. After a minute or two, she thought he might've sat down on the other end of the rock.

"Go away."

"I'm not walking to the house," he said. "And you're in no shape to, either."

That made her look at him. It made her try to smile a little.

"A remark from a whole different world," she said.

He looked a question at her.

"Like when you have a broken heart and your mother tells you you have to eat," she said.

She lifted her open hands and let them fall empty into her lap.

"I've screwed up so bad I don't want to ever eat again," she said. "I've loved him so much. How did I raise a child who wants to kill somebody?"

Blue's gaze held hers gently.

"I thought he was getting a whole new attitude," she said. "Every day he was in that hospital, and every day since he got out of it, his outlook has been getting better and he's been acting and talking as if he's more and more normal. I was getting my hopes up like crazy."

He still didn't say a word.

"But it was only his addict's cunning at work," she said, the cold fear in her gut starting to flow into words. "He's only fooling so he can get enough freedom to move on up into bigger crimes. All he's doing is scheming his way into the big leagues."

Blue waited.

"What's wrong with him?" she said, hearing her voice getting more desperate. "What wrong with me? What did I do wrong? All I ever did to Shane was try to be a good mother to him and I've raised a heartless monster-child."

She tried to read the answer in his eyes. Tried to read the true response Blue was thinking. After all, she told him with the look, he ought to know.

"My mother never did anything to cause me to kill a man," he said at last.

The tone of his voice told her that he wasn't accustomed to talking about this. She waited, never letting him break the look that held them locked together.

Tell me.

"And I'm not a monster," he said. "It's like you said. Probably just about everybody could kill, given the right circumstances."

Andie Lee nodded.

He began to speak a little faster, as if it felt good to him to talk about it.

"Especially somebody young. I'm not saying it's all right. You and I talked about it back there and we excused me from killing that creep. I'd like to leave it at that. It would be so easy. But it wouldn't be honest."

"So you *are* sorry now? Besides for the prison time?"

"It changes a man to kill another man," he said. "Whatever the reason. No way around it—it's final, it can't be changed, that human will never *be* again. A man isn't God and has no right to act like he is. And yet we have to do what we think's right at the time."

"Do you think now you were less right?"

He turned and stared off into the trees.

"Hindsight's always different. A man's a different person at fifteen or twenty-five, as I was, and then at thirty-five. Life looks different."

He looked at her again.

"Sometimes I think about that kid I was then and he seems like a stranger to me."

She watched the fire come into his eyes.

"Yet when I remember the fury I felt that had nowhere to go—the rage at how wrong it all was that he stood there breathing in front of me, evil in the flesh—and poor, innocent Dannie, who never had a chance against him, lying there between us, I'm glad to this day that I did it."

She knew he wasn't finished.

"Justice," he said. "Bringing justice, when there's so little of it in this world. That's sweet."

They looked at each other for a long heartbeat.

"Shane's ten years younger than you were then," she said. "He's not strong in himself. Not yet. He never will be if he goes to prison."

Blue looked off again, this time down. Into the sparkling water of the creek.

"I'll talk to him," he said.

THE ROAN COLT WAS a little funny about water. He hadn't shied much at the tree limbs scraping him or even at the elk horns lurking on the trail ahead where they'd been scraped off in the spring. But they'd crossed three creeks so far this afternoon, and he'd resisted at each one. For a shorter time with each try, yes, but it was still a deep resistance. He would get better and he would finally get over it, but he'd taken that first step into a running stream only because of his trust in Blue.

Like Shane's.

Which would disappear if Shane ever found out Blue had betrayed him. Would Andie Lee accidentally let it slip? Or would she grow so desperate that she'd try to talk to him herself?

He didn't think so.

You don't know her, Bowman. You don't know her anywhere near well enough to predict what she'll do.

That was true. He knew her some, though. And he wanted

to know her better. Because knowing her better made him want her more, every time. That peace he'd felt with her in his bed had been rare and precious.

He still couldn't believe he'd talked to her about his feelings the way he'd just done. That had given him such relief. Relief he'd never admitted he needed.

Which, like the lovemaking, made him want more. Made him *need* it.

He would have to choose between that wanting, that need for Andie Lee and his bone-deep vow of revenge against Gordon. The purpose of his life, held for ten long years. The intent to bring sweet justice one more time.

It had been stupid to tell her what Shane was up to, although a parent needed to know something like that. All he'd accomplished was heaping more worry on her and destroying the small bit of happiness she was clawing from her life, which just went to prove he never should've started this babysitting business in the first place.

That's what had been stupid. If he hadn't been drawn into trying to help Shane, he'd never have gotten to know her enough to be in this trap.

Yes, she'd had a right to know, but he must've also hoped, in some small corner of his mind, that she could do something to stop Shane. Which had been stupid, considering that she hadn't been able to stop him from doing the drugs.

Every time Blue had a flash of her walking away from him to the rock along the creekbank, he wished he'd never told her. She'd moved with that long, strong stride of hers and the square shoulders that said she could handle anything, keeping her head up so she'd give no hint of the pain she carried inside.

She was a gallant woman. Like his mother.

That was much the same way Rose had walked out of the visitors' room the two times she'd come to visit him in prison. The strength at her core had comforted him then.

But he'd finally broken that, too, just as he had Shane's trust.

That was the problem with a code against betrayal. It didn't make allowances for foolish teenagers.

Roanie walked away from the creek along the foot of a hill. All the hand-walking had done him good, had helped him heal with less of a limp—one that might eventually completely go away. The scar would be wide and deep and permanent, but maybe he'd still be able to use the leg normally.

Roanie seemed to read Blue's thoughts. He began trying to break into a trot, so Blue let him do it for a short distance. A slow trot. He'd worried about riding him for the first time today, but Micah had come home and he'd had to get horseback and get away from the talking. He'd needed the company of only this horse and Roanie had been restless in his stall. He'd been right. It was time.

And it was right that he had told on Shane. The boy had no clue about the misery he'd be bringing on himself if he did succeed in getting to Jason and killing him, so it was worth taking any chance and breaking any code to try to stop him. It was Andie Lee's job to figure out how. He would just do what he could, as another human being, and then not worry about it anymore.

Now that he thought about it, one thing making Shane's eyes bright and alive again was his passion for killing Jason. Andie Lee might be right that his recovery was only an act so he could get free to do murder. Talk about irony—kick the habit so you can kill your dealer.

Move yourself out of one hell only to end up in another.

The roan spooked sideways and Blue's legs tightened on him. A hawk, screaming somewhere. Horse and man together threw up their heads to look for it.

Against the enormous bright blue sky, it swooped down toward them, dipping low, then away. Roanie danced all the way over under the trees and into some loose rocks while he was making sure it was gone. The pine duff made the footing a little tricky, but he didn't get any more excited and it only took a minute to get him calmed down again.

"Good job, good job," he said, patting Roanie's neck as they walked out into the sunshine.

The hawk's cry still rang in his ears. Squinting, he picked it out in the southern sky and watched it as long as he could see it. With such a wingspan he'd soon be halfway to Oklahoma.

This, too, could be a sign. Hawks always caught his interest because of his name and Auntie Cheyosie.

The Blue Hawk brings trouble with it.

That's what she used to say every time when, as a little boy, he got into trouble. It was the first line of an incantation to separate people she'd told him, but she had never recited the rest. That was all she knew, she'd insisted, but he had not believed it.

That had been a red-tailed hawk screaming at him. Blue was the blue hawk. And he did bring trouble.

He must stop thinking about the look on Andie Lee's face when he'd told her about Shane. They were not connected to him. They were already separate from him and from each other.

What he must think about was the man who'd separated Blue from his mother and his sister. He had to think about bringing trouble to *his* door. That was why he was here.

But the mountains caught his eye and he couldn't hold that thought, either. The hawk had pulled him out of himself as surely as if he'd been a mouse to pluck out of the grass.

This was a magnificent country and he had eyes and ears. A nose to smell the wind and skin to feel it.

He was riding into a big clearing full of yellow daisies backed up by a wall of old-growth lodgepole pines. The sky arched endless and blue.

A good horse between his legs and a covey of partridges whirring up from the long grass murmuring in the breeze.

Peace held the whole world in its arms.

He'd been to hell. This was heaven.

HE RODE UP to Micah's barn on the west end and dismounted. He led Roanie in and stopped to unsaddle, hating for the afternoon to end. If it hadn't been for Roanie's recovering condition, he would've ridden even farther.

Faintly, he heard voices outside the barn somewhere and hoped that whoever it was wouldn't come in. He hadn't felt this calm and balanced for a long, long time, if ever. It was as if he could feel the blood moving smoothly in his veins and hear his own sure, unhurried heartbeat.

It was enough just to *be.* No thinking, no planning, no past, no future. Just for this little while.

He took a deep, long breath of the good smells. Old barns, probably because they were made of lots of wood and not so much metal, had a mellow resonance all their own.

"And so do you," he murmured to the roan, who was nosing at him as he unbuckled the halter. Blue brushed the back of his hand across the soft muzzle after he slipped the bit out. The horse stamped one foot and rolled an eye at him.

Mellow? Don't take it for granted, man.

The look brought Blue a smile and then a chuckle while he put away the saddle and bridle, slipped the halter on, and picked up a currycomb and a brush. He led Roanie down the aisle to his stall.

As they walked into it, the sounds of hoofbeats and voices floated through its open window. Damn. He wished they'd go away. He tried not to hear them.

But one of the voices was Gordon's.

"Open your ears," he yelled. "I said for you to throw back those scrawny shoulders and straighten that spine, Shane."

That was new. Usually it was "boy" or "you little idiot."

Blue glanced outside to see Shane riding around between the barn and the round pen on a good-looking, young black horse that Blue hadn't seen before.

Oh. So Gordon wasn't giving up. Shane had rejected his offer of a free horse and free advice, and he was going to make him change his mind.

Gordon ruled. Didn't Shane know that?

"Damn it! Why don't you listen?"

"I *am* listening."

"You're not *hearing*. You've fried your brains taking all that shit and ruined your hearing into the bargain."

He was glaring at Shane.

"Or else you've always been that stupid."

"At least I never paid anybody to cheat me," he yelled back. "So who's stupid now?"

That wound Gordon up a notch louder and into his nasty, most sarcastic tone of voice.

"Don't be a smart-ass with me, boy."

Aha. Back to normal.

"What're you talking about? Who do you think cheated me?"

Shane stopped the horse.

"You don't have a clue, do you?" he said in a tone that gave weight to the words. "You're always yelling insults and bossing people around but you don't know jack shit."

Blue walked closer to the window and began to watch in earnest. He remembered when Gordon had yelled those same words at Shane the day he tried to run away. Did Gordon remember that, too?

Gordon took a step toward Shane and the horse.

"Know *what*? What are you talking about? Come right out and say it. I've got no time for riddles, you little pill-head."

Shane slouched in the saddle as if to defy Gordon's early

orders as well as this last one. He laid his arm across the horn and smiled.

"Spit it out or shut up," Gordon said.

Shane took his time. He got down from the horse, picked up the reins and led the black toward Gordon.

The kid had more guts when he was sober than he did stoned.

"Remember Jason?" he asked, smiling again. "Remember how you cut him a paycheck every month to get us off drugs?"

Gordon nodded. One abrupt jerk of his head.

"Jase was making five or ten times as much as you were paying him by selling crack and pills and everything else, too."

Shane let that soak in.

Then he said, "To us. He sold them to us. At *your* rehab center. We all thought that was pretty funny."

Speechless. For once, Gordon was speechless, staring at Shane as if he'd drill the truth out of him with his eyes. But he already knew it was true. Shane's tone and his manner left no doubt.

Shane held out the reins. Gordon ignored them.

"I'm gonna kill him," he said. "'Cause Jase's the one who shot me and messed up Roanie's shoulder."

That froze Gordon in place.

"What?"

"I was stealing his stash that he kept up at *your* Lininger cabin. He'd been living there ever since you fired him off *your* place."

He waited a beat after that, too, to let that thought sink in.

"But don't worry about it, Gordon," he said, his voice full of disrespect, "I'll kill him for you."

"If you're lying to me, I'll pull your head off."

The cold menace in Gordon's tone would've made most kids lose their nerve.

"I'd rather not own a horse than take your insults," Shane said, offering the reins again.

Absently, Gordon took them.

Shane turned and walked away.

"Hey," Gordon called. "Wait a minute. I need some details. What kind of proof can you give me?"

Shane just kept walking.

The kid had way more sand than Blue would ever have thought.

Gordon stared after him, then turned and looked all around, as if looking for somebody else. He headed toward the east end of the barn, leading the black horse.

He came in the door scanning the place for Blue. Or maybe Micah. His face was flushed and he was hunting for *somebody* to question, somebody to help him start getting to the bottom of this unbelievable tale that a lazy kid like Jason had scammed him so thoroughly. The set of his shoulders and his walk, even more arrogant than usual, announced his determination.

"Micah!" he bellowed, just the way he had done that first time Blue ever saw him.

Then, "Blue!"

He spotted Blue then.

"What the hell's going on up here?" he roared. "Shane says Jason pulled the wool over my eyes, big-time. Says he's gonna *kill* Jason. Have you heard anything about all this?"

Blue continued rubbing the roan's back with the currycomb.

He shrugged. "Maybe."

It always made a man look bad to be out of control when the other man was not. Gordon recognized that and lowered his voice.

"Do you think he's telling the truth?"

"About Jason?"

"Yeah." The one word was filled with the wonder and

shock that must be flowing through Gordon like a river. "Was Jason really bringing drugs in all the time I was paying him to get those kids off them?"

Blue shrugged again. "Shane oughtta know."

Gordon walked to the door of the stall and Blue started toward it with the rubber currycomb still in his hand. It made him feel trapped to be in that small space with Gordon blocking the door.

He couldn't stand it. Too many years on the wrong side of the bars.

Gordon moved away to give Blue room, then walked on down the aisle to give his horse room to turn around. When he came back, Blue stood in the aisle, leaning back against the stall door.

"Do you think the boy's all talk about trying to kill Jason?" Gordon asked.

"Not after what I've just seen out that window."

"I don't, either."

It was the strangest feeling in the world to be talking something over with Gordon this way, much less agreeing with him.

"Andie Lee thinks you're a good influence on him," Gordon said. "If so, you'd better lean on him about this. Stop the foolishness."

He searched Blue's eyes with such a sharp focus that it stabbed Blue with a thought. Had Gordon guessed from where Micah picked him up that he'd been in prison? Had he bothered to go check and find out why Blue had been there?

"Shane makes his own decisions," he said. "I don't control him."

Their eyes held for a long minute in the dusky gloom of the barn.

"What's Shane planning?" Gordon asked. "He gonna ride up to the Lininger and get himself shot again?"

"We haven't got down to details."

Blue wasn't going to betray any of Shane's confidences to Gordon. If Gordon wanted to find Jason, he could put pressure on his local lawmen to do it. But he couldn't resist twisting the knife a little.

"Jason sure could still be living up there, though. He'd probably like to, since you threatened him with his life if he didn't get off your place."

Gordon hated that.

"My men searched that whole area up there when Shane got shot," he snapped. "*They* didn't find any sign of somebody living there."

Blue shrugged.

"Well, maybe Shane was pulling your leg on that. The cabin may be nothing but a cache for Jason's merchandise."

Well. Whichever, it was a direct insult to Gordon. He set his jaw, drew up the reins on each side of the black's neck and stepped around to the side. He turned the stirrup with his toe, ready to mount.

Ready to get back to headquarters and get started finding and squashing this sneaking coyote that had once invaded his ranch.

"Nothing but more hell for Andie Lee," he said. "Stupid kid. It'd be long odds if he got the job done, but he could get himself locked up for a long time just for trying and that's all it would take to kill that girl."

There was an unintentional note of sympathy in his flat, impatient tone that struck at Blue. At least Andie Lee was one person he cared about.

But naturally, Gordon's biggest concern was avenging this damage to his ego and his reputation. If Shane talked or if one of his men saw Jason up there and found out he'd either been living there or stashing drugs there, the jokes and the gossip would be wilder even than the talk about Shane breaking into his house and stealing his gun right from under Gordon's nose.

Gordon settled into the saddle, his eyes drilling into Blue's. The very same color. Their eyes were the exact same shade of cobalt.

"Talk to him, Blue."

"Not my job," Blue said.

Gordon's face reddened a shade more. He locked his gaze on Blue's but Blue didn't waver.

"By God, you're as big a pain in the ass as he is."

Gordon turned the horse around again, as if to prove he was the one in control—of the horse, at least—and rode out the west door.

Blue stood looking after him.

That last remark had made him sound like a kid. Gordon's kid.

It stopped Blue for a moment. Why had he even thought that? He'd had thirty-five years to realize that Gordon would never be a father to him.

On a rare occasion or two, he'd heard Gordon call Shane "Son," and Micah often called Blue "Son" but there would never be an occasion rare enough for Gordon to call Blue "Son."

Just like Newt in *Lonesome Dove*. In prison, he'd read that book many times. Like Newt, he would never hear his father acknowledge that he was his son. Not even if he held a gun to his head.

BLUE HAD FINISHED brushing out the roan and was nearly done with the feeding when Shane came in the east door with a can of Coke in one hand and a large bag of chips in the other.

"Micah will have your hide," Blue said. "You know that's his favorite kind."

"I won't eat 'em all."

Blue dumped the scoop full of sweet feed into Roanie's feeder, came out of the stall, and closed the door behind him.

"Grab a bale, Shane."

He nodded at an unopened bale of hay lying along the wall at the side of the aisle. Shane threw him a puzzled look, but he sat down on it.

"Gordon made me mad and I told him I'm going to kill Jason," he said, raising his voice a little so Blue would be sure to hear as he walked back to the feed room. "I didn't mean to. But it's okay. He thought I was just blowing smoke."

"You sounded pretty serious to me," Blue said.

He threw the old wooden scoop in the barrel, set the lid back in place and used both hands to click it closed all the way around.

"You *heard?*"

"Through the window. I was in Roanie's stall."

"Well, anyhow, he can't stop me. I won't tell any of the plans we're gonna make."

When Blue walked back out into the aisle, Shane popped another chip into his mouth and smiled at him.

"He can't prove anything, either," he said around the crunching in his mouth. "It's my word against his and even if he does have a lot of influence and the police listen to him, it's what happens in court that counts."

Blue's skin went cold all over. Fury flashed through his blood like a runaway fire.

"Listen to yourself," he snapped, covering the distance between them in three or four long strides. "This is real life for God's sake, not some fantasy of a TV show."

Shane stared at him, eyes wide with surprise.

Blue set one boot up on the end of the bale, propped his arm on his knee, and leaned over to get in Shane's face.

"First of all," he said, "there *is* no 'we.' I never said I'd help you make plans to kill Jason and I sure as hell won't. Second of all, you don't know shit about doing it yourself, so you *are* going to prison, whether you succeed or fail. All you have to do is try it."

"You don't know. I'm a good shot."

"You used to be, maybe, before you fried your brain and burned hell out of your nerves. How many rounds have you shot lately?"

"Uh. Not any, yet, but…"

"You ever been inside a prison?"

Shane shook his head.

"You ever washed the soap out of your eyes in the shower and opened them to see four big pumped-up gorillas surrounding you and you gotta fight 'em, one at a time or lose your manhood? Be their girlfriend? You know what I'm talkin' about?"

Shane nodded.

"Or maybe lose your life instead."

He had his attention now.

"Think about it. Look at the muscle on me and on you. Could you handle me, Shane? If we really got into it?"

Wide-eyed, the boy shook his head. "No," he said.

"So you couldn't handle four bubbas bigger than me. Is that fair to say?"

Shane agreed.

"You wanta eat whatever slop somebody slaps onto your plastic plate, every day, year in and year out, and nothing else?"

He gestured at the can frozen in Shane's hand halfway to his mouth.

"No soda pop, no potato chips, no candy? How about never seeing a beautiful thing? Like the moon or the stars or a thunderstorm or green trees and grass? How about being locked in, day after day, until an hour is as long as a year used to be on the outside of that wall?

"Never seeing a woman, never touching one. Never feeling a tender hand on your skin like your mom's on your forehead checking for a fever. Never a touch or a hug or a kiss.

"Never talking, for days on end, until you don't even

know if your voice still works or not. Silence except for the racket of the dining hall when you go there. *Always* silence when it comes to somebody saying something *to* you, except when somebody gives you an order.

"You want to be a person? You don't want to be an animal in a cage?"

He stopped for a moment to take a deep breath and slow the racing of his pulse. He felt he might explode.

"You're not allowed to talk to the other prisoners?"

"I didn't *want* to talk to them." The question made him despair. He wasn't getting through to the kid at all.

"Look at these horses and think about how they'd feel and how they'd act if we never let them out of these stalls."

"They'd come out over the top," Shane said.

"Maybe. Some would. But there'd be no top to *your* bars. Your cell'd have another one right on top of it. And horses would be nothing but a memory. You'd never *see* a horse, much less smell one or run your palm over a muzzle or stroke a smooth, silky neck or slap your hand on a sleek-muscled rump."

Shane's eyes went to the roan, looking out over the top of his stall.

"If you do go after Jason, Shane, you're gonna find out all this stuff up close and personal. Think about it. If you can't figure out how to get off this ranch to look for him, you can't figure out how and when and where to shoot at him, much less how to get away afterward."

"I can so," Shane said with a stubborn set to his chin. But his tone said he knew he couldn't. "Just because you've been watching too many prison movies—"

"I was *there,*" Blue growled. "I lived it for ten years."

"What did you do?"

"I killed a man."

Blue straightened up, dropped his foot to the floor and spun on his heel. He walked out of the barn and into the night, dark now with stars sparkling by the millions overhead.

Every word he'd just said was ringing in his ears as if he'd never heard it before.

CHAPTER EIGHTEEN

THE WORDS WERE still screaming through his consciousness like an eagle diving, making him want to duck for cover. Yet he couldn't bear a roof over him or walls around him. Out in the enormity of the Montana night, he was safe.

He walked, slowly, farther from the barn as if he could get farther from the horrors he'd brought to life in there. Always, always, for ten endless years, he'd believed that he could take it if he had to go back inside again.

Now he'd nearly convinced himself that he couldn't.

Blue walked toward the edge of the bluff. Dew was beginning to wet the grass and the smell of the pines rode the wind from the mountains. The fresh wind, the sweet wind.

He could stand being in prison again. After all, when he got out, he'd been expecting to serve five more years right then. He could do anything he had to do.

Every word he'd said to Shane had brought back a hundred memories and every one of those was so real his hands were shaking. It was because he hadn't ever said them out loud before. And, actually, the memories had been leaving him alone for a while until he'd brought them up again.

He walked on, away from the barn and the boy and the words, through the new night air, drawing it in deep to calm him. He pulled down his hat to make sure the wind didn't take it and headed out to be alone.

That was what he was used to. That was what he needed most—time to himself.

The thought made his lips move in an ironic smile. Hadn't he just had ten years of alone time?

But being alone was his natural state of being. He was a loner. It was nothing but stupid that he'd gotten so worked up over a kid that wasn't even his.

Shane had to make his own decisions. Shane would do what Shane decided to do. No one could control him. Blue'd said those things over and over again to Andie Lee.

And then he'd gone and gotten involved and let himself really care what happened to the kid.

Shane. He was like Blue in that he had a passion for the payback, that was for sure.

Revenge. It was only human to want it. But was going after it worth the price?

What had it accomplished for Blue the first time? For one thing, it had saved who knows how many other kids like Dannie from dying young. From getting addicted in the first place.

But it had also taken the last spark of life from his mother. He'd seen that when she came to see him in prison, but he'd tried to deny it.

What would it accomplish for him this time?

There Gordon had been, trying to take Shane over as if he could do him some good. Yelling insults at him and tearing down his confidence and pretending he was teaching him horsemanship when all he was doing was proving his power. That kind of treatment crushed Shane's spirit more.

Blue thought again about how Shane had stood up to Gordon. Had he been able to do that because he'd thought Blue was on his side?

Well, Blue *was* on his side, but not as a conspirator the way Shane thought. Kids never understood things until it was too late. It'd be a miracle if the rant he'd dumped on Shane just now actually did stop him.

Gordon was more guilty for Rose's death than Blue was.

Rose had loved him for all those years and Gordon hadn't cared a damn thing about her. He'd proved that by forcing her to raise his children all by herself.

Blue walked to the edge of the bluff, to the spot where he'd been standing the first time he saw the sun rise over the Splendid Sky. Now it was the moon coming up behind him, with its light starting a glow on the granite cliffs across the river. The wind talked in the trees. A beautiful night in a beautiful place.

Lights dotted the valley, each one signaling a home for someone or a building where somebody worked. Places where people lived life.

If he got sent back to prison, he probably would never see such a sight again as long as he lived. He'd be in the ugly place where life stopped.

Where death lived in minds and hearts.

He tried to push the memories away. Why was he thinking like this?

He didn't have to go back. He'd take revenge on Gordon, then he'd disappear with the roan horse, never to be heard of again.

He'd haul the roan back to Oklahoma and vanish into the rough hills that were the last bastion of his people.

He would *not* get caught.

A bird sang from somewhere very near him, the song Andie Lee had called a nightsong, when the two of them used to lean on the fence and watch the horses graze while sunset washed Montana in scarlet and gold. What would she say if she knew he was planning vengeance on Gordon?

She would not understand his thinking and she'd lose trust in him and she'd only want to get away from him. That'd be a whole different deal from telling her that he'd killed a drug pusher over his sister's death.

A terrible hand clutched his gut. This was his choice: revenge on Gordon or friendship from Andie Lee. Or maybe even love from Andie Lee. It was such a fragile idea with such a powerful draw on his heart that he hardly dared think it.

Was it possible? Could it be that someday he and Andie might love each other? His mind shied away from such an enormous possibility, but he couldn't help but linger on it, just for a moment.

Don't be foolish, Bowman. You're a loner.

He wrenched his mind away.

Move on. Think about something else. The boy.

And what would Shane think of him? If Blue went through with his plans for vengeance, from now on, throughout the boy's life, what would come to him first when Blue crossed his mind?

Revenge didn't change things for the target and the avenger only. It changed every life it touched.

BLUE WASN'T SURPRISED when Shane didn't appear at his usual time the next morning. He'd figured the kid might be mad at him. Shane would probably see Blue's refusal to advise him on killing and then his hard lecture about the consequences as Blue turning on him or going back on his word.

He might not show up at all.

Well, so what? He'd been trying to get rid of Shane, hadn't he? Maybe he'd finally done it. Wasn't that what he'd been begging for? It would be a relief.

Yet, it'd be a shame, too, because the boy was learning a lot and getting connected with the horses.

Oh, well, there were lots of horses in the world and lots of good teachers. He and Shane would be better off apart.

Come to think of it, though, he probably *would* show up, after all.

After the grit Shane had showed yesterday with Gordon, it'd probably be a point of pride with him to come to the barn and quit Blue face-to-face.

Sure enough, when Blue had barely started the chores—before he could even get the hay all thrown—he heard a truck's motor and the door slam. A minute later, Shane came in.

"I overslept," he said. "My mom wouldn't wake me."

Blue took a second to look him over. He looked a little drawn up around the edges.

"Trouble sleeping?" he asked.

"Yeah," Shane growled. "Thanks to you."

Working in tandem, they finished the feeding and watering, and then walked together toward the pens to get some of the colts to ride.

Halfway there, Shane spoke. "You really think I'd get caught?"

Blue nodded.

Shane stopped in his tracks and turned to face Blue, squinting a little in the fresh sunlight.

"I can't let Jase get away with it," he said. "He was supposed to be my friend, but he's the one who called the cops that day they took me to jail. And then, on the mountain, he shot me in the back *after* he told me if I'd get out of his sight he'd forget I was ever there."

He clenched his jaw against the tears that threatened.

"He said he sure couldn't go to the cops about me trying to steal his stuff. Then he laughed his head off."

Blue studied the fury in the lines of Shane's stance. And in his face.

"How about you taking the cops to him?"

Shane's eyes flashed disappointment at Blue's stupidity.

"And put myself back in jail? What was all that crap you were giving me last night about staying out of prison?"

"Everything I told you was the God's truth," Blue said. "And you know it or it wouldn't have kept you up all night. You won't go to jail."

Shane's jaw dropped.

Then he recovered. "Hel-lo," he said sarcastically. "Horse theft is a big crime, too, in case you've forgotten. Breaking and entering is another one and so is stealing a gun."

His eyes narrowed.

"Not to mention I was using at the time and it was drugs I was after up at the Lininger. And I told Gordon with my own mouth that I'm plotting murder. Isn't that a crime? A big one?"

"The horse is mine. I won't press charges."

"But the house and the gun are Gordon's."

Blue shrugged.

"He would've already pressed charges if he was inclined to."

"No. He was probably waiting for me to get well. And I pissed him off good yesterday. You heard me."

Blue shook his head.

"You know Gordon has a lot of power," Shane argued. "He told the police how long to keep me in jail, and he told me he makes lots of political contributions. He's a big man around here."

"Gordon cares about your mother. He got his gun back. You're behaving yourself. So what's his problem?"

"He's an SOB. You know, like you say about each one of the horses having different true natures? That's his true nature. And he hates me."

"But he likes your mother. And she's happy for the first time in a long time. Gordon won't wreck that."

Shane thought about it.

Blue took a chance on one more push.

"Gordon's got a lot of influence with the law around here. You know that firsthand."

"Yeah."

Shane thought about it, wanting to do it, and then he gave it up.

"I can't talk to that bastard."

"You talked right up to him yesterday."

"Yesterday I wasn't asking him for a favor. Plus, what about conspiracy to commit murder, like they're always talking about on TV?"

"He'll not breathe a word of that if he can get Jason. Jason made a fool out of him, Shane."

Shane thought some more. Blue could almost see his brain working, trying to get used to this crazy idea that would never have popped into his own head.

"If he wants Jason bad enough, Gordon can make a deal for me as a cooperating witness," Shane said. "Isn't that what they call it?"

Blue nodded.

"And I'll be okay and Jason'll get to meet the four gorillas?"

Blue nodded again. He waited.

Finally, Shane said, "I'll think about it."

He turned and they walked on toward the pretty, grassy pen with the trees in it. They were through the gate and standing in the middle of the pen before Blue realized he'd been holding his breath.

THE NEXT DAY, Andie Lee drove into Micah's yard, raising a big cloud of dust. Blue and Micah, on the porch for their noon break, sat up and settled their hats on their heads.

"Well, we can kiss our naps goodbye," Micah drawled.

As soon as she killed the motor, she got out, slammed the door, and strode toward them with that purposeful walk of hers.

"Are y'all keeping something from me?"

Blue watched her come and just the sight of her, determined and beautiful, gave him an overwhelming urge to get up and go meet her.

"What're you talkin' about?" Micah said.

She walked up and stood in front of the porch, bending one knee to rest it on the edge.

"Shane's gone somewhere with Gordon in his new truck," she said. "What in the world's going on around here?"

Blue went still. Even his lungs quit. Could it be? Could it possibly be that Shane had decided to do what he'd suggested? Had the kid actually *listened* to Blue?

"We seen Gordon's truck go by," Micah said. "Them damned old tinted windows, we couldn't see Shane was in there, too."

"Aren't y'all his employers? He's supposed to be working, isn't he?"

"He took the paint colt for a little trail ride," Blue said. "Said he'd get a sandwich from you for his lunch."

"I thought my eyes were deceiving me," she said. "Barry called me over to palpate a mare and when I drove by the indoor, I saw Shane and Gordon walking out of it together. They went to Gordon's truck, still all buddied-up, climbed in, and drove off up this road. Did they go on toward the highway?"

"Yep," Micah said. "Didn't even slow down at the corner."

He shook his head, mystified, and lifted his gnarled hands, open and empty.

Andie Lee's stormy gray gaze left him and moved to Blue.

"Anything I could tell you would be only a guess," Blue said, and glanced at Micah.

"It's okay," she said. "Micah knows everything."

Of course. They both had told him more than once: Micah was the closest thing to a grandpa she'd ever known.

"So," she said. "What's your guess?"

"I told Shane to ask Gordon to take him to the police and let them find Jason."

She stared at him while she absorbed that. Her eyes never left his. The look in them turned from worried to admiring. Happy. Grateful. Admiring.

He felt a new heat spring up in his gut. And along his breastbone. How long had it been since a beautiful woman admired him?

She smiled like the sun coming up at midnight.

"How could you possibly get him to do that?" Andie Lee asked. "He hates Gordon."

"Both of them hate Jason and want him punished," Blue said.

Her smile grew even brighter.

"You are *brilliant*, Blue! Thank you!"

He could sit there all day and let her look at him like that. He could fall into her eyes and never come out. He could stand up and walk to her and kiss her luscious, smiling mouth—smiling at him—until they both were senseless.

Time to move on.

He stood up.

"All right," he said, "I better ride."

He took two steps and dropped down off the porch, which put him directly beside her. She turned to him and laid her hand on his arm.

"I can never thank you enough for doing this," she said.

"No problem."

But there was a huge problem. He didn't want to walk away from her. He couldn't even move one foot.

"I want to hear more about how you did it," she said. "What you said to him."

He wanted to brush back the strand of hair that blew across her face. He wanted to make love to her.

"I told you a long time ago," he said, "that my conversations with Shane are between him and me."

"Okay," she said in a final tone that said she was dropping the subject. "The main thing is that you got it done."

That was another bad thing about sticking to a code. He'd wanted to hear some more about how brilliant he was.

"Right," he said. He tore his gaze from her face and turned away.

"Bye, Micah," she said. "I think I'll go ride, too."

She walked toward the barn beside Blue, keeping pace with his long stride. He should tell her he didn't want company. He should tell her he wanted to ride alone.

"I've been trail-riding the roan some," he said. "I found a pretty spot."

"Take me there," she said.

They saddled up out in the aisle. Blue took the bay colt, since he'd already ridden the roan that morning. Andie Lee took her big gray horse.

"I don't like it that Sinn Fein is named for a terrorist," she said, "but I think it's bad luck to change a horse's name."

Blue looked at her over his horse's back.

"You know that line of Billy Joe Shaver's. 'It's bad luck to be superstitious.'"

That made her laugh and they bantered a little more as they led the horses out into the sunshine and mounted them. As they rode away and lost the barn and the house and every sign of anybody else behind them, they looked at each other.

"It's a field of yellow daisies," he said. "Surrounded by lodgepole pines."

She smiled. She just smiled at him and let her gaze linger on his.

All he could think about was getting her into his arms.

He couldn't hold her again. He'd promised himself that one time in his bed would be the only time. Any more making love with her and he'd grow to want it so much he'd be miserable without her.

Any more making love with her and he'd be hard put to go on with his plans. His plans that had kept him alive for ten years while they grew into his bones.

Making love again wouldn't be fair to her, either. She liked and admired him now, and she thought she knew everything about him, but she didn't know him at all. He was nothing but an imposter of the man she thought he was.

But the red hawk or the eagle might as well have swooped down and snatched that thought from his head because he couldn't hold it. He couldn't hold any thought. Once again, all he could do was *be*.

All he could do was just sit here on this slow-trotting horse and watch Andie Lee riding beside him and look at her smile.

Which, at the moment, was turning into a teasing grin.

"And you thought you couldn't do anything with Shane," she said, shaking her head in wonder.

"Maybe that was because I couldn't do anything with you," he said.

"Ha," she said scornfully. "You've only wrapped me around your little finger since the minute we met."

"*Ha!* I've done whatever you wanted since the minute you jumped into Micah's truck and smashed me into the gearshift."

"You're only playing to my sense of power and flattering me hoping to get another kiss," she said.

Her voice was light, teasing him. He could tell she didn't even care what she was saying, she just wanted to make him grin back at her.

He gave her a slanting, heavy-lidded glance instead.

"No," he said. "I *know* I can get another one."

She raised her eyebrows.

"You're mighty sure of yourself, cowboy."

He held her gaze, which was heating up as fast as his blood.

"You gonna tell me I'm wrong?"

That made her laugh and toss her hair flirtatiously over her shoulder. She was wearing it loose today. He liked it that way.

Good God, what was he doing? He hadn't even known he remembered how to flirt.

He was going over the edge. A drumbeat had begun in the back of his mind: *This is the last time. This is the last time.*

So. He'd decided to break his word to himself. Everybody knew it was good intentions that paved the road to hell.

But life was short. A man had to grab a little bit of heaven when he could, right? This would be goodbye to her. He had to make a move, and do it soon.

That's right. Think about Gordon. Think about anything except Andie Lee. Get serious, Bowman.

"I didn't sleep much last night," he blurted, "for thinking about Shane."

What shameless pandering for more praise! He hated himself the minute the words came out of his mouth. What was the matter with him?

"He didn't sleep, either," she said. "I heard him rustling around in there half the night and I wondered if it was because you'd talked to him by then."

She shook her head in wonder, never taking her eyes off him. She looked like a girl, pretty and happy. And like a woman, beautiful and content.

He had done that. He'd put that look on her face.

"I knew you were the one to help Shane turn around," she said. "I picked you."

I picked you.

The words flowed through him with his blood and washed his strength out of his body through his fingertips where they rested on the reins.

She's only talking about her son, stupid. She's been desperate about him since the day you met. Remember?

"I *knew* you could get through to Shane when nobody else could," she said. "This may not be the end of his troubles, but it's a huge move toward the good."

He ought to turn back. He ought to put a stop to this right now. Because, no matter what the little voice in his head said, there was plenty in the look in her eyes that had nothing to do with her son.

And really not much to do with gratitude.

"Did you tell him you've been in prison?"

He didn't answer, only looked at her, but she knew him well enough to read his face.

"Thanks, Blue," she said. "I know that wasn't easy but I'll bet that's what did it."

Go back. Go back to the barn. You want this too much.

But the Splendid Sky was splendid indeed and the day was incredibly blue. They'd never have another. He swore that to himself. This was his last one time with her.

"Oh," she said, as they came into the meadow, "I thought this might be the place you were talking about. I used to come here with Micah when he cut wood. I made daisy chains until I couldn't even carry them all home. I wore as many as I could and put a bunch on my horse's neck and hung the rest on the bushes for the birds and squirrels."

They rode into the tall flowers, the yellow faces brushing the horses' hocks. The look between him and Andie Lee held and grew stronger. The horses slowed.

Andie Lee stood in her stirrup and leaned out to him. He leaned to meet her and brushed her lips with his, greedy for their sweet, wild taste. And, for that fleeting moment, he was helpless to resist her.

But only for that instant. He could still put a stop to this. But the look in her eyes was fast turning hot and truly tantalizing instead of teasing.

It was there, vibrating between them, all the desire and need that they weren't putting into words. It was in both of them, just there through no conscious will of either one, raw and certain, naturally in them and in the air between them.

"Let's unsaddle," he said. "We didn't bring any other blanket."

"We can use your shirt, since I intend to rip it off you."

"Whoa, now," he said. "I think you're scaring me."

They laughed at that and because the sky was endless and the smell of fresh-cut grass was blowing to them from a hay field somewhere. They got down and secured the horses, then came together like two magnets and kissed until they could barely stand.

Every time a thought or a caution tried to find him, he slipped away from it.

Andie Lee tried to make good on her threat, but when her fingertips first touched his skin, she began to take her time between each button to run her hands over his chest and rub his nipples and brush her own pearling ones against him.

"One shirt," he said, dragging in enough air to talk, "ain't big enough. Need yours, too."

He started on her buttons while she nipped at his neck and the lobe of his ear and rained small kisses all around his mouth.

"Good thing…" she said. "…I didn't…wear a…little bitty T-shirt…"

They lost the thread of the conversation then and all desire to talk. They fell into each other's arms and helped each other strip out of the rest of their clothes and spread out the shirts, not going more than a few seconds without a kiss.

As he discarded the last boot, Blue propped himself on his elbows and looked into her eyes. He stroked the spread of her bright hair around her face, a pool of shining light on the thin, ragged bed of blue chambray.

"Andie Lee," he said, savoring her name on his tongue. "We'll never have another day like this one."

Not for them there wouldn't be. Not for him.

She smiled up at him dreamily, her lids half-closed with the anticipation of what he was about to do, but the look hot with need.

"No," she said, "and there'll never be another man like you."

Never be another man like you.

He wouldn't think about that now. He couldn't. Anyhow, she was just saying that.

Never be another day.

No sense in rushing it.

He brushed the edges of her hair, pushed it back from her face, and tried to memorize her beautiful bones and eyes and brows and nose and mouth in one long look. Finally, the contours of her mouth drew him so strongly that his fingertip had to trace the shape and then his tongue had to taste it.

She moaned, deep in her throat, and wrapped her arms up around his back, stroking his shoulders, kissing him with a passion. Every sound she made and everything she did begged him never to stop, begged him for more than the kiss.

Her need—her need for *him*—opened every pore of his body, wakened every nerve. He slipped one hand underneath her head to cradle it so he could deepen the kiss and caressed the curve of her body with the other, his thumb just brushing the side of her breast as his palm claimed her rib cage, her waist, the flare of her hip and her thigh. He let his hand wander, pressing close everywhere, absorbing the feel and the heat of her silken skin through his calloused roughness.

That heat went straight to his blood, which was already hot enough to burn.

His. He wanted her to be his. And for now, she was.

He concentrated on her breast, then cradling it in his palm and teasing the nipple with his thumb. She pushed into his hand for more of that. He broke the kiss and looked to see the heat in her eyes, the look in her eyes that was for him.

That heat was building with every move he made.

Then he bent and took her breast with his mouth while desire exploded in his blood. The cry of delight she gave made him feel ten feet tall.

"Blue," she said. "Blue..."

She was limp with need and then she was strong, reaching for him, touching him everywhere, melting his flesh into his bones until he could hardly breathe. Could hardly hold back anymore.

Never be another man.

For this moment, he'd let himself believe that.

He changed to the other breast. She cried out all over again. He loved the sound of his name on her lips.

He loved every touch she gave him, every inch of her sweet flesh that his hands found, loved the kisses she was dropping on to his head as she took it in both her hands and held it to her breast. Finally he raised his head and looked at her so he could see her pleasured face.

She smiled. With the most perfect mouth he'd ever seen. In the most perfect face.

Never be another day.

He would live this moment as if that were surely true.

He let his palm trace the shape of her one more time, for the perfect way she fit his hand, then he slipped one thigh between hers and knelt between them. He met her blazing gaze for one long moment, then he bowed and kissed her smooth flat belly.

She gave a wordless gasp that touched him in a deeper place, even, than her cry had done. He looked deep into her eyes to see what she was feeling, too, so he could remember it.

And so he could answer it, something he'd never be able to do with words.

Then he surrounded her and covered her with himself and gathered her up in his arms so close she could never go away. She guided him into her and purred, deep in her throat, as their bodies melded again, perfectly.

Perfectly together.

With the whisper of his name, over and over again, in his

ear and in the heat of the kisses she burned into his skin, Andie Lee told him she wanted to stay right there. She wrapped her arms and legs around him and buried her face in the hollow of his shoulder while they clung to each other, skin to skin, as if they might fall off the mountain.

He held her even tighter as they found their way together. The westerly wind lifted then, and swept down through the meadow to cool the sweat on their skins and bring them the smells of wild places and far distances. Slowly, deliberately he thrust into her; she arched to meet him and they moved together in the rhythm of that ancient dance until they flew off instead.

Into the endless blue of the sky.

BLUE WOKE with a start, lying on his side with Andie Lee's head tucked into the hollow between his neck and his shoulder and her arms around him as if she would never let him go. The sun slanted across them. The air was cooling.

He caressed her shoulder, then ran his hand along her side and cupped her bottom in his hand. For two long heartbeats he let himself press her even closer to him so he could feel every inch of her that was touching him.

He let himself admit that he never, ever wanted to move away from her.

What he wanted didn't matter. He *couldn't* move away. He was too drunk with her nearness.

Thank God he was too drunk with it to think.

She stirred in his arms and murmured, "Blue," her lips light as a butterfly against his skin.

"Andie Lee." He took in a deep breath, just for the scent of her hair.

She rolled onto her back and opened her eyes. He settled her head carefully in the crook of his arm. They looked at each other.

Her eyes cleared from the sleep and from the sex but she

kept on looking at him, with her soul showing clear as the sky.

"I love you," she said. "I love you, Blue Bowman. No matter what ever happens, I have to know that you know that I love you."

His heart stopped beating. This mustn't happen.

No. No.

But even as that word sprang to his lips, his heart cried a wondering, victorious "yes!"

He silenced it. He couldn't let this happen.

Maybe she didn't really mean it like that. That was it. She meant it lightly.

He could handle it lightly.

"You're only thinking that because you're so happy I talked to Shane," he said, trying for a careless smile. "And because you just had your way with me."

She smiled a little but she didn't even bother to shake her head. She just held his eyes with her soul-searing gaze and made him believe she had not meant it lightly.

"I do love to get my way," she said, "but that has nothing to do with how I feel about you."

He tried to quit looking at her, tried to quit seeing what was in her eyes, but he couldn't look away. He needed it so much that he wanted to drown in it.

"Aw," he said, using his drawl, "I'll bet you say that to all the guys."

She shook her head slowly "no," while she caressed his face with one slender hand.

"I know my own mind," she said. "And my heart. I used to love Chase, but not like this."

He stared at her, stunned.

Her fingertips brushed his temple, along his hairline.

"Never like this," she said. "If you felt the same way about me that I feel about you, I could even run my fingers through your hair."

Walk in my soul, Andie Lee.

He couldn't let her do this. He didn't have the slightest idea how to truly love a woman or let her love him.

He was a loner, meant to be alone.

His heart dropped out of his body into the bed of yellow flowers. He'd waited too late to stay away from her. This was his punishment. This was his hell that he'd have to live in from now on.

It was going to wrench the guts out of him to take his arms away, much less never to hold her again. Not to mention what it would do to her if she really did love him.

He wasn't good enough for her to love. She didn't know him.

And he cared for her more than he wanted to admit.

He'd fooled around and put off what he had come here to do, and now he had more than his freedom and his life to lose. He had her happiness in his hands, or at least, she thought he did.

Which was the same damn thing when it came to heartbreak.

Better to do it now than to get deeper and deeper into this desire and this closeness with her—deeper, where she would love him more.

What a marvelous, unspeakable gift! Andie Lee loved him.

He couldn't love. All the ability to love had been burned out of him in the hell of prison.

And when he took revenge on Gordon, that would burn the love out of *her* in a heartbeat.

He gave her a kiss on the mouth. One time. Light and sweet.

He didn't look into her eyes again. Gently, he removed his arm from underneath her head and sat up.

He picked through the scattered clothes and found his. Now he felt too vulnerable naked.

"You don't know me, Andie Lee."

He made himself go on in a rush of words as he pulled on his jeans and, then, for the sake of his own pride, made himself turn to meet her startled gaze while he said it.

"I'm Gordon's son. He never married my mother and he never helped her when she was struggling to raise me and my sister. He's never acknowledged us at all. He refused to pay for Dannah to get treatment for her addiction."

He gave her a second to absorb that while he reached for his boots.

She gasped. "You're his *son?* Why didn't you say so? Why didn't *he* say so? Why didn't Micah tell me?"

The shock and growing coolness in her voice closed his throat. He found his socks and pulled each one on, then the boot that went over it.

Before he was done, he had to turn and look at her. He had to.

Her eyes were wide with shock and their color was definitely growing stormier by the second. Her lips parted.

"You all have kept this a secret from me? What is this?"

She stared into his eyes demanding answers. Now.

"Micah doesn't know who I am," he said. "And neither does Gordon."

"Then what are you doing here, Blue?"

"I'm here to kill him, Andie Lee."

CHAPTER NINETEEN

"ANDIE LEE, you don't want to love me."

She paled so fast it scared him.

But what scared him more was the chasm opening inside him. What had he done?

He'd just held heaven in his arms and then thrown it away. Love. She loved him. She'd said it and she meant it and it was true because he'd seen it in her eyes, felt it in her every touch, and known it in the core of his being by the way she wrapped herself around him and held him inside her as if she would never let him go.

The world was full of men who would kill for that kind of love. Who would kill for any kind of love.

And *he* was going to kill the love itself. He'd already done it.

"Do you want to say that again?" She sounded dangerous enough to kill *him*. "Are you telling me that you have spent ten years locked up in prison and come out to this—" she made a wide gesture with her long, graceful arm that included the earth and the sky and the makeshift bed they'd just slept on "—and you are intending, *deliberately,* to get sent back there?"

"I won't get caught," he said.

He sounded as foolish as Shane had, saying the same thing. But he had to say it aloud to counter her. Spoken words could make predictions come true.

"*Now* you say 'Andie Lee, you don't want to love me'?

Now you say it, when you know I already do." Her voice broke a little on the last word, but she recovered.

"After you make such sweet love to me that no woman could ever forget it—or get over it. *After* you make me crazy for you, Blue Bowman!"

The words thrilled him through while the scorn that was burning so hot in her eyes scorched him where he sat. He was a fool. Forty kinds of a fool. People just didn't get this kind of love. Not one in ten thousand. In a hundred thousand.

Especially not after living the life he'd lived. He'd never known anyone who'd had a love like this.

Except for Rose, loving Gordon all her life.

Gordon. Who had to die for what he'd done to that good woman's heart.

"I feel so betrayed," Andie Lee cried. "All this time you've been Gordon's *son,* and you never told me! I thought we were friends, Blue."

She held him with a piercing look.

"You've been a fake all along, hiding behind your horse-manship, pretending to care about Shane and your colt and Micah and every two-year-old in the ketch pen when all you were here for was plotting murder. You could've just left me out of it, Blue. You didn't have to make love to me and stomp all over my heart!"

"I haven't been hiding," he said. "I've been honest with you."

Her eyes blazed. "Up to a point! Honest about your past sins, but not your future ones."

She glared at him for a long minute.

"You've got to be kidding me, right? Gordon's son? Plans to kill him?"

She shook her head no, her bright hair catching the sun and throwing it into his eyes.

"You can't be serious, Blue. You can't be truly meaning to do this."

"He deserves to die. My mother loved him her whole life and he killed her. He made her want to run her car into a tree."

"And I don't suppose your being incarcerated for *murder* had anything to do with her feelings of depression?"

Her sarcasm cut him like the blade of a knife.

He tried to ignore it.

"He killed Dannie, too," he said. "I told you he refused when my mother asked him to pay for her treatment. If he'd said yes he could've saved her."

She waited, her fuming silence demanding more.

It did sound a little weak to his own ears, but that was because he was thinking of Andie Lee and how she was hearing it.

Killing that SOB has been your life's purpose—your reason for living—for ten endless years, Bowman. You know it has to be done.

"That's all that got me through prison," he said. "Planning to kill him."

"And now you're out," she snapped. "And free. And you just can't wait to get back inside those walls and bars so they can throw away the key. What'll get you through the *next* ten years in there? And this time it'll be more than ten, I'll bet you."

It did sound like a stupid mistake he was about to make, instead of like one of the hard things of life that needed to be done.

But he didn't know how to love her.

And he did know how to kill.

"I'm not going back in," he said stubbornly.

Andie Lee acted as if he hadn't said a word.

"We have just made love like this…"

She connected him, her, and the bed between them in one graceful sweep. The movement outlined the creamy curve of her breast against the blue sky in an image that would stay in his eye forever.

"...yet you're choosing to go where there's no love at all?"

"I don't have a choice," he said.

"Bullshit," she said. "Then why'd you tell Shane that *he* had one?"

"This is different," he said, getting to his feet, stomping into his boots. "Gordon could've saved Dannie and, at the same time, saved me ten years in hell. He could've saved Rose, but he didn't. He was too damn selfish."

It was a groove in his mind. In his bones. It was the only way he knew how to think.

"Killing him won't bring them back."

"Somebody has to do the hard things," he said. "Dannie and Rose deserve to be avenged. I have to give them justice."

"The troubles of this world are nothing to them now," she said. "And even if they were alive they wouldn't want you to do this. Gordon is what he is and what he's always been."

"He's the reason I'm alone in the world."

"You don't have to be alone in the world," she said. It was a challenge.

"Andie Lee, I can't love anybody."

He reached for his shirt as he got to his feet.

"Have you ever?" Another challenge.

"Only my mother and sister. All that's past for me."

He threw the shirt on and looked down to button it. The relief of escaping her disdainful stare was almost physical.

"I never meant to make love with you again," he said. "I didn't mean to lead you on."

"Go," she said, in that low terrible voice. "Get out of my sight. Stay away from my son."

She got up then, like a whirlwind, and stepped into her jeans.

"If you are going to throw away what we could have together so you can go back to hell, get out of my sight. Never come back."

She snatched up her shirt off the grass as he turned away.

BLUE GOT BACK to Micah's but it was the bay colt's doing that brought him there. By the time he dismounted at the barn, he couldn't remember one sight or sound since he left Andie Lee.

He couldn't feel anything, either, except for a strange constriction in his chest and a sharp pain in his gut. Desperately, he looked around for something to do, something to channel his mind on to something else.

The chores were already done. He took care of the bay and then went to see Roanie. He caressed the soft muzzle and let the horse snuffle at his hand. Then he drooped his arm around the colt's neck and laid his weary head against it.

Roanie tolerated him only for a moment, then he pulled away and moved restlessly around the stall. He kicked the wall.

"I thought you'd quit that," Blue said. "I was thinking you were half-civilized by now."

The horse pinned his ears and eyed Blue, curling his lip a little.

"You're right," Blue said. "I'm no better. People were thinking that about me, too."

He felt the tug toward Andie Lee. Strong as ever. Stronger. Something in him wanted to go to her, stay with her, bury his face in her hair and wrap his arms around her. Hold on tight. Forever.

Give up this revenge. This killing.

But he couldn't give it up. It was his purpose. It was all he had.

Roanie snorted and grabbed hold of the top of the wall with his teeth. Blue shushed at him and waved him away from it.

He jerked his thoughts away from his impossible dream.

"Don't start taking up new bad habits," he said. "You're like me on that, too. You've got enough old bad ones."

He would take the roan and go. Tonight. He was bound to see Andie Lee if he stayed on the place and besides, it was time. Past time. He had come here for a purpose. He wouldn't even think about her anymore.

What a deal. He'd turned Shane around so he wasn't breaking her heart anymore and then Blue had broken it himself. But she didn't love him—she only thought she did. He wasn't lovable. It was lust and she couldn't tell the difference.

He would not think about her. Or try to imagine what the rest of his life would be like if he chose to change his plans and accept her love.

He would think about Gordon instead, and justice.

First thing he had to do was warn Gordon. He'd never feel right if he didn't. It would go against his code.

His code was all he had.

BLUE REACHED for the horseshoe on the door knocker, then dropped his hand. What the hell was he doing? Come to warn a man for his life and knocking on the door? Might as well shake the old bastard up by proving he could surprise him.

He pulled open the screen and walked in onto the stone-floored entryway of the big house. The headquarters house of the Splendid Sky Ranch. The main house of the Wagontracks brand. The heavy oak door, standing wide, was branded at eye level with the two curving S's.

"Gordon!"

The answer came instantly.

"In here!"

Of course he wasn't surprising him. Gordon would've heard him drive up, since Micah's truck wasn't exactly a stealth bomber. Probably he'd even watched Blue get out of it—his voice and plenty of light were coming down a narrow hallway from a room fronting the porch.

Blue went in Gordon's direction, glimpsing the old house surrounding him but not wanting to see it. Outside, the summer evening still held plenty of light, but inside it was almost dark. Some ancient photos in bowed-glass frames hung on the walls—probably Blue's Campbell ancestors—and covering the wall all around the lighted door were some more recent pictures. Champion horses and prize cattle.

All of it might as well be on the moon, for all the time and inclination he had to look at them. Too late. It was all too late to do him any good.

Blue stepped into the lighted room.

Gordon sat behind an enormous desk piled with papers and folders, a large calculator and assorted stacks of mail, some opened and some not. He tilted his chair back and looked up at Blue.

For a long minute they looked at each other. Gordon gave no sign that it was unusual for Blue to be here.

"Sit," he said, pointing to a leather-covered chair angled into the corner.

Blue said, "This won't take long."

Gordon cocked his head and raked Blue up and down with his bright eyes. Then he let out a big sigh and leaned toward him, crossing his arms on the sheets of paper spread out in front of him.

"Spit it out."

"I'm the son of Tanasi Rose Bowman. Remember her?"

Gordon kept on looking at him without a flicker of feeling.

"The woman who had two children for you before she was twenty," Blue said. "And raised them alone, barely making ends meet. The one who called you ten years ago asking for help for your daughter and you turned her down."

Still no response.

"She ran her old car into a tree shortly after that. The impact killed her."

No reaction.

Blue tried to be just as dispassionate, but the old rage in him was rising fast.

"She loved you all her life, you son of a bitch, and you killed her. That's as sure as if you'd had hold of the wheel."

Gordon leaned back in his chair.

"Why tell me this now?" he asked.

"To warn you for your life. I'm not the kind to shoot you in the back. I'm leaving tonight, but not for long. I came here to the Splendid Sky to kill you, Gordon."

He looked Blue over again as if he'd never seen him before. Then he threw back his head and laughed.

"Gonna put me out of my misery, huh?"

He flicked one of the piles of letters with his finger.

"One more batch of bills like this one, and I don't much care if you do."

"Fine."

Blue turned to go.

He heard the squeak of the chair's springs and the thump of heels on wood. He turned back, thinking Gordon was coming after him.

But the old man had fixed his boot heels on the desk, ankles crossed, and leaned the chair back as far as it would go.

"Sit down," he said, slanting his knowing glance up at Blue. "Next time we meet there'll be no time for talk. Let me tell you about your mother."

Blue froze.

Of course Gordon had to get the last word. And he knew just which word would do it.

But he was right. There'd never be another chance to hear about the mysteries that had dogged Blue all of his life. Rose was dead and Gordon soon would be.

Blue turned around and sat down in the chair.

"What about my mother?"

"I'll get to that in a minute," Gordon said, lifting one cautionary finger. "First, I'm not afraid to die but I want to give you some things to think about while you're gone to get ready to try me."

Their eyes locked as they took each other's measure now that this threat lay open between them.

"I hope to God *I* don't kill *you*," Gordon said. "But that'd be about my luck, since all I want now in this world is for you and this ranch to be my legacy, living on after I'm gone."

Blue stared, trying to get his mind around those words. He couldn't.

"*I* brought you here, you bozo," Gordon said. "I vouched for you as a parolee and got you out of prison and sent Micah to pick you up."

A million unnamable feelings rose in a choking cloud in Blue's gut.

"Why?"

"Because I had to see if you're man enough to run this ranch."

"I wouldn't take it," he said. "I wouldn't take a crumb from you if I was starving to death."

"You're not thinking right," Gordon said. "Pretty soon you will be."

He grinned.

"This is a hell of a note. I offer to give you the world on a string and you say you're out to kill me—and not for the inheritance, either."

Blue's head felt light and strange. His brain whirled to try to process it all.

"Don't be an ass. You never acknowledged that I existed for thirty-five years."

"Age and the specter of death can change a man."

"You called me a jailbird that day on the hill. How do you know I wouldn't sell every damn inch of this place as fast as I could sign the papers?"

Gordon shrugged.

"I don't. It's a guess. A hunch. I hired people to check you out seven ways to Sunday when I got this idea. I know every detail about your life, both before and after you killed that bum. I've seen some of your paintings."

Blue felt the floor fall away beneath him.

"You had no right."

Gordon ignored that. "I bought some of 'em. A man who paints the land and the sky the way you do—and from memory, too—he's gonna take care."

"You don't know squat about me."

Gordon waved that away. "Maybe not. But I know me. I want to leave this ranch to a child of mine and you're the only one left."

"What about Andie Lee?"

"She's my child, too, and she'll be well taken care of but I already told her: no woman can run this ranch. Besides, you're my blood."

"Fine time to acknowledge that," Blue said sarcastically. "No. Leave it to somebody else. Anybody."

Gordon's gaze bored into Blue. "Anybody else is gonna divide and sell to the goddamned California crowd or the developers. I've worked my guts out to hold on to what my dad and granddaddy left me and add to it. I poured my life into taking care of the land and breeding my lines of cattle and horses."

All I want now in this world is for you and this ranch to be my legacy.

That was an acknowledgement from Gordon that Blue was his son. He listened to it again in his mind.

Too little, too late.

"Breeding a new line of cattle or horses, either one, that takes a man's whole lifetime," Gordon said.

"So does raising the children he bred in five minutes," Blue said.

He wished he'd kept his mouth shut. It sounded like he was begging for attention.

"It's not like I never did a damn thing," Gordon said. "I built that rehab center over there out of remorse for Dannah."

Fury touched the cold lump that had filled Blue in these last few minutes.

"Yeah," he drawled sarcastically. "After you wouldn't spend five grand for my mother to get help for her before it was too late."

Gordon didn't flinch.

"Why else would I build such a thing and have all those squirrelly strangers on my place?"

His voice was as level as his look.

"Part of the reason I told Rose I wouldn't help her with Dannah is that it made me mad as hell to hear from her *then* after she wouldn't let me come near her *or* you and Dannah your whole lives," he said.

Blue stared at him. Disbelieving him.

"Her pride," Gordon said. "Her goddamned pride. That's why she left me. Left Montana. Said if she couldn't be my wife, she wouldn't have another thing to do with me and neither would her kids."

Gordon glowered at Blue.

"It didn't matter to her that I loved her best. It didn't mean a thing that she was the love of my life and I was hers. She knew that and said so. But did that move her, once she got that beautiful Cherokee head set to leave me?"

He shook his head, staring into the distance as if reliving that moment.

"No. It did not. Not come hell or high water."

He looked at Blue again. "She thought I wouldn't divorce and marry her because she was Indian."

"Was it?"

"No, goddamn it. I had a wife who'd have taken me for everything I had! And a young son. I wouldn't do that to him and let his mother take him away from here."

He squinted at Blue, as if to gauge his reaction, and waited.

"You married Andie Lee's mother. Why not mine?"

"I didn't have the guts to risk my heart again after it was buried up there on the side of the mountain under three tons of snow. Besides, your mother wouldn't even talk to me. Or listen to me."

His face hardened into a bitter mask and he stared into space.

"I told her when she left Montana that she'd have to live with the consequences of her decision."

His eyes caught Blue's again.

"So *my* pride—not just hers—killed her. But that's always been my code: people have to live with the consequences of the decisions they make. That's another reason I wouldn't send money to Dannah."

He held Blue's gaze ruthlessly.

"It's the same reason I left you in prison for so long. Now I'm sorry about that, too. You're a good man."

A lump sprang up in Blue's throat, which was stupid. This whole tirade was probably a pack of lies Gordon had thought up to save his life.

"You're a top hand, Blue. With the horses and with Shane. You could keep this ranch together and make it even greater," Gordon went on. "He really stood up that day I took him to turn Jason in to the police. He's the only reason they caught him so fast, and that's all your doing."

Blue said nothing.

"Pass the ranch down to your son and make it eight generations in the same family."

That was the first compliment Gordon had ever given him. And the first time he'd ever spoken his name with respect. The sound struck Blue's heart with a clear power like the toll of a bell.

All kinds of tantalizing pictures of the future flashed before Blue's eyes. Which was also stupid. Gordon couldn't be trusted as far as he could throw him.

"I'm proud you're my son, Blue."

Listen to him now. After thirty-five years.

The words twisted in Blue's gut like the blade of a knife.

"Blood's not all that makes a son," he said. "You're years too late."

He held Gordon's gaze just as ruthlessly as Gordon had done his.

"You've made this ranch a coffin for yourself, Gordon," he said, "by being totally selfish every day of your life. You've never given five minutes' thought to anybody else. The fact that you're still mad at my mother for not spending her life as your mistress proves that. And your precious rehab center over there is nothing but a sop for your guilt."

But truth be told, Rose's death wasn't all Gordon's fault. Her only living child being locked up in a prison hadn't helped her situation any.

By his personal code, which was all Blue would ever have, he had to acknowledge that.

The phone on Gordon's desk rang but he didn't move.

"Now it's you who'll have to take the consequences of your decisions," Blue said. "Going soft and sentimental in your old age won't save your hateful hide."

The phone kept ringing. Gordon picked up the receiver without taking his eyes from Blue's. He listened for a second, then stood up and reached for his hat on the wall rack.

"Coming," he barked. "Call Lupe to send her kids over here to ring the bell."

He dropped the phone.

"Let's go. Barn fire."

They ran together, down the hall and out across the porch, talking in snatches of words.

"Which one?"

"Micah's."

The roan colt. Blue's blood chilled, deep, like it hadn't

done for a long, long time. No way around it, he cared for that colt. A lot.

"Jason started it," Gordon said, as they ran down the steps toward his truck. "He escaped. Same damn junkie friend of his smuggled him a knife. I'm gonna see to it that some heads roll over this."

The smell of burning was already threading the air. Bitter-sweet. The sweet scent of burning wood mixed with the bitter odors of leather and hay and all the other things that were not made to burn. Blue looked back over his shoulder.

The worst of it was on the west end and the roan was stalled on the east end. Maybe he could get there in time.

Flames were eating the roof, sending the popping, crackling sound of their greed riding the wind even this far down into the valley.

"Damn him. Trying to get back at me by torching every barn on the place. Thank God Micah caught him at the first one."

"*Caught* him? Or *saw* him?"

"Caught. He's got 'im tied to the hitching post."

The kids ran across the road as Blue and Gordon reached the new truck and threw themselves in. Gordon turned the key and the motor roared to life.

"Every barn on the place," Gordon said, throwing it into reverse, talking loud over all the noise. "Stupid-ass kid. What would that accomplish? Nothing but suffering and dying for a bunch of innocent animals."

That surprised Blue. Gordon talking about animals suffering and dying? Realizing that animals had feelings, too? Normally he didn't seem to know other *people* had feelings.

Gordon backed around, shifted into drive, and stomped the gas pedal. Every move he made seemed slow, impossibly slow, to Blue.

Roanie must be going crazy with fear.

The wide-axled dually surged out onto the road as the

bell began to ring. Up on the hill, flames were bursting higher and higher from the west end of the barn, reaching up against the sky like they were wanting to be part of the sunset.

"Vengeance," Gordon growled. "Payback. As a rule, that's damn cold comfort."

The remark cut straight to Blue's heart. Once he killed Gordon, would he feel satisfied? Would his mind and heart rest, feeling he'd righted the old wrongs? Or would that vengeance, too, be damn cold comfort?

Would he be on the run for the rest of his life, or locked on death row with no comfort to be found anywhere?

The truck shot up the road like an enormous bullet, but Blue still leaned forward, willing it to do more, trying to get there and get to his horse.

Nothing was worse than a fire in a horse barn. He'd only been around it once, but he'd never forget the screams of the horses and the smell of burning horseflesh. He clenched his fists and mashed his foot against the floorboard as if he were the one driving.

Andie Lee's horses. He had to get them out, too. There was another heartbreak for her if he didn't.

How could she even think she loved him? How could she think he was good enough for her to love?

She had to be mistaken. She'd said it'd been a long time for her, too, since she'd had a lover. She was mistaking that heavy, sultry desire they felt for love. It hit them like heat lightning every time they saw each other.

She was a giving kind of person and she just thought she loved him.

Where was she? Could she have been in the barn when this started?

Fear took him by the throat with both cold hands.

He had left her in the meadow and that hadn't been all that long ago. Or had it? He'd lost all track of time.

No, it hadn't, because the sunset still glowed.

He loved her.

He loved Andie Lee. That truth pierced Blue with a blade so sharp it sliced through the ten-year-old wall around his heart. He loved her. He didn't mean to, he didn't want to, but he did.

Even though he would've sworn that he could never love anybody, ever again. That he *would* never love anybody.

But his will had nothing whatever to do with it. His iron will was nothing but melting wax over the heat of his passion for Andie Lee.

It wouldn't matter whether her love for him was real or not. He loved her. He couldn't help it.

This must be the same way Rose had loved Gordon. She'd had no choice at all.

Gordon took the corner at full speed, slammed the truck across the ditch into Micah's place and blasted on to the other end of the yard.

"No sense taking a chance on burning up this truck," he muttered.

He cut the motor. They both fell out of the cab and started for the barn at a run.

Smoke was gathering and drifting in clouds everywhere—over and above and around a few people. Ashes blew in the wind and the fire whipped higher.

Dimly, Blue glimpsed Shane, struggling to hold Andie Lee's big gray horse and lead it away from the barn. It kept trying to go back to the stall that still felt like a refuge from the chaos. From the corner of his eye, he saw a couple of hands trying to hook up a hose to the outside faucet at the house.

But still he didn't see Andie Lee.

Then he did. Andie Lee. A wash of relief went through him as he ran.

She was struggling out through the east door to safety,

leading a plunging horse with each hand, digging in her heels for balance, fighting to hold them both and keep them from turning back. She kept turning her head to see Micah, who was following her with two heads of his own. Flames leapt and danced deep in the barn aisle behind them—Blue saw them when the smoke cleared away for an instant. Then it was back again like a thick curtain.

Andie Lee kept coming through the smoke toward him, brave and strong and completely determined with her jaw set to show it. The smoke stains on her face and the sparks of fire in her hair only made her more beautiful when she broke through into the clear again.

He loved her.

He ran on. Toward her.

"We couldn't…lead Roanie," she yelled, gasping for fresh air. "I'm sor…sorry, Blue. All I…could do…get his…halter on."

"I'll get him," Gordon yelled, and rushed past Blue into the burning barn.

That took Blue's eyes away from her, and he went after him. Gordon was an old man and the roan wouldn't like him, to boot. No way could he handle the colt.

It was an inferno in there. The lack of good air shocked Blue breathless. He wished for a wild rag or a handkerchief, for water, and then he slipped out of fantasy and into the chaos of reality.

The roan screamed and reared, clawing at the sides of his stall, but he wasn't on fire. Yet.

Burning pieces of the rafters were falling everywhere and the far end of the barn was in a blazing roar. The wind was picking up and whipping flames into walls in front of it. The rafters were on fire, the tack room was a memory and the stacked hay was next.

Gordon was too fast for him—he ran in through the door of Roanie's stall before Blue could get there. Andie Lee and

Micah must've left it open on the off-chance that the horse would run out when the fire got closer.

No such luck. The roan colt had been tamed too much: now he trusted the safety of his stall the same way he trusted Blue.

Gordon reached for the halter. Andie Lee hadn't been able to buckle it completely, but the tongue through the hole looked good enough to hold.

The roan jumped back, rearing to strike.

"Gordon! Get out!"

The horse was squealing, slamming himself against the wall, rear hooves slipping in the shavings. He struck at Gordon, missed him by a hair, came down on all fours and lunged at him, knocking him down with his shoulder. Then, instead of letting his momentum carry him on and out into the aisle to Blue, he whirled back.

Blue went in, slowly, so as not to panic him more, wanting to talk to him, needing to soothe him. Instead, he had to keep his mouth shut and his breathing shallow. The fire, cracking and popping, starting to roar, was making too much noise for the roan to hear him, anyhow.

He took his eyes off the colt to look at Gordon, intending to signal him to lie still. No need. His head had hit the hard oak post at the door of the stall. He lay with eyes closed, unmoving.

Damn. Now Blue had to get them both out.

He reached out slowly and laid one hand with a reassuring pat on the roan's sweaty rump. The colt was dripping now—from the heat, but from nerves, too. He whirled again, narrowly missing Gordon, and then he recognized Blue. He lowered his head enough to let Blue take hold of the halter.

With every nerve in his body screaming for hurry, Blue made himself keep moving slowly, steadily. He led the horse forward, chanting inside his head, easy, easy.

He walked close in beside the roan's shoulder and got him

around Gordon in spite of the horse spooking two or three times at the man on the ground and offering to paw him. Blue got him to the door and through it, although Roanie was jumping around and swinging his rear from side to side, first on one hind foot, then the other, bumping into the wall, nearly hitting Blue, nearly stomping Gordon's frozen frame.

In the aisle, Blue looked back. Gordon still hadn't moved.

Well, he couldn't possibly lift him with one arm to carry him out and he sure as hell wasn't going to turn loose of the roan. If he did, he'd never be able to catch him again. He might run straight into the flames.

Damn Gordon, anyhow. He should've had more sense than to rush into the stall like that. He knew the roan's reputation in normal times, and any horse would go wild in a fire.

But Gordon always thought his own reputation was bigger than anybody's, outlaw horses included. He was the horseman of all time, Gordon was, to his own thinking.

He was the rancher and breeder of all time, too. With a large legacy and no one to leave it to.

Blue pushed the horse's shoulder, heading him toward the door. He'd take the roan out and come back for Gordon.

Or not.

That thought fell into his head like the devil's own plan.

Why should he save him? Why, when Blue's own life was devoted to taking Gordon's? His whole purpose in living was to see this man dead.

The roan jerked his rear around and went up on his front legs to kick the stall across the aisle. Blue had to grab the halter with both hands. The horse pulled sideways, eyes rolling, dragging Blue around in a circle.

Just in time to see one of the rafters burn in two and fall with a huge cracking sound, onto the hay. Wildfire.

It would be in this end of the barn in seconds. No time. He had run out of time.

The west wind freshened in one huge lifting push, driving the fire in the roof toward him faster and faster. A piece of burning wood fell onto Blue's shoulder.

He knocked it off and glanced at Gordon as another piece fell onto his chest.

No one would ever know. No one would ever fault Blue if he came out with the horse, thinking Gordon was right behind him.

All he had to do was let Gordon die. He didn't even have to kill him.

His purpose would be accomplished and, at the same time, he could forget about making plans for murder and maybe being shot at by Gordon in self-defense.

He could lose the worries about getting caught and getting life. Or death.

Gordon would be dead, Rose and Dannie would be avenged, and Blue would be truly free at last. He could make a life with Andie Lee.

She loved him. He loved her.

All he had to do was get out of here alive.

But that was the coward's way to go. If he took that path, he would never respect himself again. He wouldn't deserve Andie Lee.

His code would be ashes, and all the times he had made himself adhere to it would be worthless.

Because she loved him and he loved her, he had to do the right thing.

Choose love over hate.

He urged the horse closer to the stall door, maneuvered his own body to where he could hold on to the halter and bend to grab Gordon's shirt collar. The fire roared and reached for them all.

No way could he hold on to the roan and pick Gordon up. All he could do was to drag him.

Blue jerked him out of the stall and started for the door,

desperate for a good breath, praying that neither of his arms would be pulled out of its socket. The roan could do it with one good lunge.

Sparks flew in a swirling tornado, the flames whipped at them from behind. His lungs were seared, his back was burning, and all three of their lives would be gone in another minute. Gordon's shirt was on fire.

The roan panicked more and more the farther they got from his stall and he got harder to hold. Gordon got heavier and more awkward to drag.

All Blue had to do was uncurl his fingers and let him drop. Then he could run out with the roan.

He was risking the life of a fine horse. He was risking his own life. He was risking Andie Lee's happiness and his own, all in order to save the son of a bitch Blue had been vowing for ten years to kill.

He tried to let go but his brain refused to send the signal to his hand. Both of his hands, all of his fingers, stayed curved like claws, holding on, holding stubbornly on while his legs kept driving on, his eyes pouring and blind in the smoke.

It was decided. They would all three get out together or none of them would. He'd get them out. Or die trying.

After a lifetime of flames chasing him and the world burning around him, he plunged out into the fresher air. Not clean, full of smoke, but fresher. By far. He gasped, gulped in a big lungful that nearly choked him.

Shane appeared out of nowhere at the roan's head with a leadrope in his hand. A bunch of men ran to grab Gordon, tearing Blue's fingers loose and carrying him away toward the stock tank while one of them slapped at the burning shirt with his cap.

Blue and Shane looked at each other while Shane clasped the lead to Roanie's halter. Neither could speak aloud and be heard.

You're a good kid, Shane.

Thanks, Blue.

Blue forced his hand open and it fell from the halter.

Then Shane was leading the horse away and Andie Lee was all Blue could see. Running toward him.

He opened his arms. She ran into them and threw her own around his neck.

He folded her so close not even smoke could come between them and pressed his face to the top of her head. She thrust her fingers into his hair.

Walk in my soul.

He was alive.

She loved him. He loved her.

Free. He was free. He was home free.

He was home.

CHAPTER TWENTY

ON THE OUTSIDE, Blue was shaking. His whole body convulsed to drag in one breath after another and his arms and legs trembled from exhaustion. On the inside, though, he felt a stillness and a peace that amazed him.

He'd made the right decision. He felt as if a terrible burden had been lifted, a burden that he'd carried all his life.

And Andie Lee's arms were wrapped around him. Her love for him was real—he could feel that and let himself know it.

She was starting to cry now, lifting her head to lay her cheek against his, sealing their faces together with her tears.

"I thought I would die…before you came out of there. I was so scared. I'd never…see you again."

The words were nothing but whispers that his ear could barely catch. Her lips brushed his cheek and then she just stood there, tightening her hold on him even more.

Then she started running her hands over his back. "Your shirt's got hot coals all over it," she said. "Come on and let me see about you."

She took his arm and turned him toward the house. The first step he took, he stumbled. She grabbed him.

"You may be hurt. Blue. Are you hurt?"

He would never get accustomed to her—or anybody—taking care of him, actually caring how he felt.

She propped one hand under his elbow and started trying to unbutton his shirt with the other.

"Every time I see you, you try to get my shirt off," he drawled. "I'm beginning to think you might be one of those women my mama warned me about."

She chuckled. He loved that sound.

"What I am is a *doctor*," she said primly.

"Yeah, a *horse* doctor."

She steered him around a ranch hand dragging a hose toward the barn and jerked his shirt off one shoulder at the same time, walking so close to him that her hipbone bumped his leg. She was sticking with him, ignoring all the chaos.

"I'm also qualified to work on mules," she said, jerking it down across his back and turning loose of him to get it off his arms, "which comes in handy right about now."

That made him laugh and when they got to the porch of Micah's house, he let her set him down on the edge of it, although he didn't need that much help. He was still desperate for clean air, though, and he threw his head back to lean against the post and take some deep breaths.

"Stay right here," she ordered. "I'm going for my bag and a flashlight and then we'll see if your back's burned or not."

He let his muscles relax a little as he stared through stinging eyes at the vehicles bringing more help from other parts of the ranch, and the firetrucks of the rural volunteer fire department coming over the hill on the road from the highway. They had enough help. He didn't need to try to do anything else right now.

Blue sat, letting his breathing slow and deepen, listening to the sirens winding down, to the shouts and yells and crackling of the fire and the whinnying and calling of the horses and thinking about Andie Lee. He smiled to himself. Something like joy was rising in him.

He let it. He leaned his head against the post and looked out at the fire where nobody, horse or human, had died, and smiled. It was a good day. A good night. The sunset had faded completely and the flames leapt orange against the black sky. The old barn would be a total loss but the old round pen where he'd started the roan was going to survive.

So was Gordon. And that was all right, too.

He was up and walking around with the lights of a pickup truck trained on him, over by the stock tank where they'd dunked him to put out the fire. Imagining that, Blue's smile broadened. Ol' Gordon had probably come to madder than a hornet. He was a little wobbly now, but he was slapping away everybody who tried to steady him.

It hit Blue then, with the force of a moving train. He had been trying to kill his *idea* of Gordon all these years. The father who never came when a little boy dreamed that he would show up one day and prove that he loved him by buying him a horse of his own.

Now he was offering him an enormous spread and hundreds of horses. For his own ends, of course, because Gordon was a single-minded, selfish man. But Blue believed him when he'd said Rose was the love of his life. That he'd tried to keep her here in Montana. Rose's pride had ruled her, and she'd clung to it with a stubbornness that never let go. It had made her life harder in many other ways besides keeping her children from Gordon. Maybe Gordon might have come to see them growing up, helped them financially if Rose had allowed it.

And he believed Gordon did care for Andie Lee and Shane. He hated it, but he had to be fair to the man. He might've been no father to her when Andie was little, but that was past. He might've been destructive in the way he talked to Shane but he'd offered him a good horse and free rehabilitation. He had built the Center out of remorse over Dannie.

Gordon may have made himself a coffin out of the ranch, true, but Blue had made *himself* a coffin out of the image of Gordon he'd made in his mind. Out of his stubborn pride and desire for revenge that were so like his mother's. Those traits had caused her to wrong him and Dannie. She should never have told them anything about Gordon if she wasn't going to tell them everything.

Rose hadn't been perfect. Gordon wasn't all bad. Blue felt he was leaping a mile-wide chasm, and even as his belly sank at the thought of the drop below him, his heart reveled in the freedom of flight.

He was the last of Gordon's blood. The next generation to take care of the Splendid Sky—if he took it—and he didn't even know the ancestors that had gone before. He could hardly comprehend it.

Just then Andie Lee came out of the house with her bag and a canteen and some towels, the screen door slamming behind her.

"I'm going back to shut the wooden door," she said, coming to drop everything by Blue, "but the house is already so full of smoke everything'll smell like it for months to come."

Blue turned around for the pleasure of watching her move across the porch to the door and back again, which she did with her usual competent grace. Every move she made said she knew exactly what she was doing.

"Shane's over there at the hitching post lambasting Jason," she said, kneeling behind Blue and opening her bag. "Using a little psychological torture on him, telling him what he can expect when he gets to jail."

Blue grunted.

"Yeah," she said, "that's what I thought. He's passing on the word he got from you."

"Better than killing him," Blue said.

The words hung in the air between them as she began cleaning and putting medicine on the many small burns scattered over his back.

"I'm so glad you've come to that conclusion," she said. "I cannot tell you."

He nodded. The depth of the feeling in her voice made him speechless.

Finally, he said, "You probably oughtta go see about Gordon. He was burned worse than me."

"Barry's over there with him," she said. "Nothing like having plenty of veterinarians around to take care of all the old mules."

He winced at the pain of her treatment and twisted his head around.

"Hey, now, watch it," he said. "I'm not *old*."

"Well, that's progress," she said. "At least you admit to being stubborn."

"No," he said. "Loyal, smart, surefooted, hardy and interesting. All the *other* characteristics of a mule."

Another siren sounded on the hill and they watched the lights as another car turned onto Micah's road.

"Highway patrol," she said. "Come to pick up Jason. The tables have turned. I wonder if he'll think about the day he called them to come for Shane."

"Probably not," Blue said. "Jason strikes me as pretty self-centered."

"Which reminds me of Gordon," she said. "How come you and he arrived here together?"

"I went down to the house to warn him for his life," Blue said with a shrug that sent pain all across his back. "And we got to talking."

Andie Lee gasped, laughing. "Get out! You can't be serious."

"I am. That's exactly what happened."

"Okay, then, spill it. I want all the details, every single word."

And he told her, amazing her and himself, too, all over again at the things Gordon had told him.

"Do you believe that about him and your mother?" she asked when he was done.

"Yes," he said. "From the way he said he loved her, and from knowing how stubborn and prideful she was."

He shrugged again. "Of course, if she had said she'd let him, I don't know whether he'd have come to see us or not. I'll never know."

"What are you going to do? About the ranch?"

He sat up straighter and turned a little at the urging of her hands so that she could see his shoulder better. He stared off past the burning barn and the flaring light it threw into the dark of the night where the mystery of the mountains waited.

"I love it," he said. "Like no other place I've ever seen."

"Then take it."

"And do what Gordon wants? What he schemed up and meddled in my life and brought me here like a piece in a chess game to do? Just because he was The Man and had the power to do it?"

She laughed. That low, throaty chuckle that made him want to grab her and lay her down and look at her laughing face beneath his.

"I thought you'd learned to quit cutting off your nose to spite your face," she said. "What about the big lesson of the day, cowboy?"

He laughed, too, a gruff sound that could barely rasp out of his throat.

Joy, again, and fear grabbed him in the gut. Could he really do that? *Was* he man enough to run this ranch? Was he solid enough to settle down and stay in one place and take on all that responsibility of the other people who lived and worked here?

There they were, out there fighting fire and risking themselves—for Gordon's sake. Ultimately, for Gordon's property. Did he want that kind of obligation on his shoulders?

Andie Lee finished with his back and climbed down off the porch to stand in front of him. To walk in between his open legs and touch his face. She looked deep into his eyes and then, without saying a word, went to work on a couple of small burns on his forehead.

"Well?" she said. "How *much* do you love it?"

He told her what he'd just been thinking.

"Ranching on a big scale means a lot of hired help," he said, "and this is a huge operation. All these people would be my responsibility."

"They have to work for somebody," she said.

"If I want to start and train horses and paint a little bit on the side, managing all this is too much to handle by myself."

She pulled back and looked into his eyes again.

"You wouldn't have to do it by yourself."

A thrill shot through him at the steady gaze of her gray eyes. She meant it. And she was talking about more than running the ranch.

"You're sure?"

She nodded. "Never more sure."

She put both her hands on his shoulders.

He pulled her to him and buried his face in her breasts while she wrapped her arms around his neck and held him there. He felt her long legs against his manhood. It started to swell.

He stood up and pulled her even closer against his body, held her inside his arms and fenced her in with his legs and tucked her head into the hollow between his neck and his shoulder. To get them as close together, all the way up and down, as they could get.

As close as they could be.

All they needed was to *be*. Together.

"What about Shane?" Blue asked.

She turned back and locked eyes with him for a long, long minute. She knew what he was thinking.

"Give him time," she said.

Blue's gaze never left hers.

"Give us all time," he said.

She thought about that.

Then she gave him a smile that lit up the night. One that matched his. The joy was there. He could see it in her, too, as bright as it burned in him.

"Right now, don't you just feel that together we could do anything?" she said.

It made him laugh.

"I love you," he said, shaking his head in wonder. "I love you, Andie Lee."

She loved him, too, with her eyes. And her smile.

That gave him all the courage in the world. And all the certainty.

"Andie Lee," he said, low and easy, caressing her with his voice, "will you walk in my soul?"

She took his face in both her strong, capable hands.

"I will, Blue," she said, lifting her mouth to his, "if you will walk in mine."

"I will," he said, but his words were only a whisper against her lips before they sealed their bargain with a kiss.

CHAPTER ONE

FARRELL TOOK THE FIGHT to the bull. She ran between him and the rider he was going after while the announcer was saying, "Chase Lomax! Yes, there's the score, folks. How's eighty-six points for a thirty-eight-year-old bull rider? Come on, let 'im hear from you, rodeo fans!"

She felt the air moving as the mass of the bull created a wind behind her, and then Joe's voice and the crowd's noise faded away. A whole new surge of adrenaline pumped through her blood in a river of power that held her flying feet off the ground and her mind in the zone.

She could do anything. She could make *him* do anything. This big, snorty beast was all hers.

He stopped and she turned in that instant to see the huge head wobbling to focus on her, horns shaking, front hoof pawing the dirt, fixing her with an evil eye. She wasn't going to let him think he could decide what came next, even if he did outweigh her a hundred times over. She was the boss. *She'd* be the one to say how this little rendezvous ended.

She flew to him, in close, and raced past his nose again, just the way she'd done a thousand times, in and out in less than a heartbeat, using the move she thought of as her "hummingbird." He came after her so close she could feel his breath and smell it. She ripped off her hat and slapped him in the face with it at the same time she reversed directions. Her heart lifted, went lighter than the cloud of fine dust she was running through, and the shaking ground behind her roused her blood to a fever's heat.

She whirled to face him again. The tip of a horn thrust at her and missed but the keen edge of danger touched her mind. She danced away, running backward now, speeding up to angle sideways. She loved this job. It was like she was in her own house. Despite having her heart beating hard as anything, these were the most calming, peaceful, private times she ever had.

The bull rider was safe because she'd gone into the maelstrom of the whirling bull and jerked his rope loose when he had that little hang-up. That was a thrill in itself. She loved helping the cowboys in danger, loved feeling that she might've saved somebody's life. Now this bull was hers.

It was just her and the bull, mano a mano.

She felt a huge smile come over her face as she backed up, took a running jump into the air, over the bull's head, landed on his back and took a couple of steps before she leapt over his tail and off to the ground again, still running. Somebody rode horseback in between them, and then drove the bull toward the out gate.

That was when she finally heard the roar of the crowd again.

"Miss Farrell Hawthorne, ladies and gentlemen," Joe yelled. "How about them apples? Little bitty girl, great big bull. Y'all won't see a better protector for these brave cowboys, nowhere, no way, and she sure can entertain a crowd, too. Tell her how you feel about her!"

The roar got even louder. It picked her up on a wave of noise and washed the joy she was feeling into an explosion in her veins. She swept off her hat and threw it into the air the way the cowboys did when they made a great ride.

Then she looked for Rocky, the painted clown who'd been acting silly all night, and Junior, who'd been inside the barrel for the bulls to butt around. She beckoned the crowd to acknowledge them, too. Joe began announcing their names and talking about their years of experience.

They ran to her and Rocky clowned around, gesturing for more applause from the fans. Farrell turned to one side of the grandstand and then to the other, bowing and then holding her arms out to embrace the fans while they screamed and yelled and stomped even louder. Smoke 'Em had been the last bull of the evening.

Once again, way too soon, the rodeo was over. People were already pouring into the aisles, and, as always, the audience seemed to vanish in a heartbeat.

"You done good, kid," Junior said as they began to gather up their equipment.

Rocky agreed.

"Yep. Mighty fine bullfightin', girl."

"I like it better than being a rodeo clown," she said. "Lots better. And I'm not about to get in that barrel, so y'all get ready. This is my job from now on."

"Nope, gotta share," Junior said. "Didn't yore mama ever teach you to share?"

They teased and joked with each other but the fun was draining away from the evening for Farrell. In only a moment the arena and the area behind the chutes were as empty as the grandstands. All gone.

All the life, all the noise, all the excitement and the danger and the people. Gone. It was that quiet, lonesome moment that Farrell hated every time. Nobody around, the animals back in their pens, the big lights shining down on vacant seats, dusty dirt and deserted pieces of trash slapping against the fence to glare white and ugly against the night.

This was the letdown she always felt.

Now, instead of electricity and excited voices, the thud of hooves and snorts of challenge, the clatter of the chute gates and the clang of the bull bells, the only thing filling the air was the wind. The whole world felt empty and hopeless.

The end of a rodeo always gave her a little chill.

CHASE LOMAX walked into the swirl of music and laughter that was Larry's Steak House after a rodeo and grinned because somebody yelled out his name the minute he came through the door. Tater Gibbons, a calf-roper he'd known for years, waved him over to shake hands.

"Eighty-six points, huh?" Tater said. "Congratulations, Chaser. Reckon you just might make a bull rider in your old age, after all."

Chase couldn't stop smiling. Getting into bull riding, going for the All-Around had put the excitement back in his life.

"You're my inspiration, Tate," he said. "Seeing as how you're living proof a man can still cowboy when he's 102."

Everybody at the table laughed and jeered, joining in.

"Yeah, but I ain't gettin' on no roughstock," Tater said when he could be heard again. "Gotta hand it to you, man."

Chase slapped him on the shoulder and moved on among the tables looking for Robbie. The place was full of people, pulsing red-dirt music and smells of steak and onions sizzling over mesquite coals. His mouth watered and his stomach growled. He never ate much before he rode and afterward he was ravenous.

Somebody all the way over by the dance floor stood up. Robbie. Smiling all over his good-looking Brazilian face because they'd both had great rides tonight. Good old Robbie. Without doubt, the best buddy he'd ever had and one heck of a bull rider. They'd had a lot of fun since they'd partnered up for traveling, hitting the big rodeos and competing on the professional bull-riding circuit, too.

Chase headed that way, stopping here and there to shake hands and hear compliments about his bull ride and bronc ride, too, to swap jokes and good-natured insults. He knew, at least by sight, probably half the people in Larry's tonight and some of the ones he didn't know were watching his progress, too, smiling, pointing him out. He'd probably sign some autographs before the night was through.

Robbie was rustling up another chair from somewhere and the dozen or so friends around the long table were moving over to make room for Chase when he reached them. The first thing he spotted was Farrell Hawthorne among them.

The welcoming flash of her smile before she turned to say something to her friend Missy Jo gave him a little prickle along his spine. He'd never met her. It'd be interesting to see what she was like out of the arena. A woman who wanted to be a bullfighter—no, who *was* one—was bound to be a whole lot different from all the other girls.

He wasn't prejudiced. He believed that anybody, man or woman, ought to do anything they were big enough to do, but maybe women should do anything they wanted *except* be bullfighters.

Once they got chairs arranged, somehow the empty one ended up so that he sat directly across from her. She looked right at him, direct and sassy, and sizing him up.

"I think you two have never been introduced," Robbie said in his soft, lilting accent. "Farrell Hawthorne, this dangerous cowboy is Chase Lomax. Chase, this is Farrell. Now you can see her beautiful face, my friend, instead of only a blur in the arena."

She stuck out her hand and Chase stood up to shake it. *Beautiful* might be a bit of an exaggeration, with that dusting of freckles across her nose.

Or not. Her smile was a hundred watts and her eyes were something else.

"Pleased to meet you, Chase," she said. "Are you truly dangerous?"

"Some say so," he drawled, returning her smile with his

own most charming one. "But then, you look like you can handle a little danger, Farrell."

Robbie favored her with his famous grin.

"Come to me, Farrell," he said, "if you need any help. I know how tricky he is."

"Now that right there is a trick," Chase said to her. "He introduces me, but then he tries to keep you for himself."

"That's life, right?" Farrell said, grinning. "Always something to watch out for. If it's not a bull, it's a cowboy."

She grinned at them both. "Or, as Missy Jo says, if it's *full* of bull, it's a cowboy."

They all laughed and then she turned to her right and started talking to Tim Traywick.

As if *he* were the interesting one. Nothing against Tim, but any other woman would've been all over Chase and Robbie instead. Face it: Tim was still a rookie and looked hardly old enough to be away from home alone.

Then the waiter came by and when Chase had finished ordering, he saw that she was really laughing it up with Tim. Far as Chase knew, the boy wasn't known for being a wit. He overheard something about one night when Cooder Graw was playing live at Billy Bob's. They could be dating, for all he knew. Or cared.

But when he turned to listen to whatever it was that Robbie was trying to tell him, he decided he'd dance with her. He wanted to talk to her, although he didn't quite know what he wanted to say. Or maybe it was that he didn't know *how* he could say it. No way did he want to get out of line, but yet, he needed to let her know.

In a minute, the band switched to the lively Alan Jackson song "Burnin' the Honky-Tonks Down." Chase looked back to Farrell. She was busy with Tim, but too bad. Chase didn't care if they *were* dating.

"Come on, Farrell," he said, pushing back his chair, "dance with me."

She looked up at him, startled, but he held her gaze and she didn't try to look away. She grinned and stood up, too. "How do I know you can dance?"

"You saw me gettin' clear of old Smoke 'Em tonight."

That made her laugh. "I hate to hurt your ego, Lomax, but I didn't have time to watch your footwork."

Well, you certainly had time to interfere with my dismount.

He didn't want to say anything in front of anybody else, though.

He met her at the end of the table, which was at the edge of the dance floor, took her hand, and they went with the music.

She was a dancer who put her heart in it, no holding back, reading his mind like a gypsy woman and adding plenty of flourish during the guitar, and then the fiddle and finally the mandolin breaks. He got a whole new respect for her.

Farrell Hawthorne was one of a kind. She threw herself into play as hard as she did into work.

When the song ended, they just stood there for a minute, grinning at each other, pretty proud of themselves.

"I love a partner who's not afraid to dance," he said.

"Me, too."

So when the band struck up a slow one, she just naturally moved into his arms. He started to say something but then he didn't. He didn't want to ruin this with a lot of talk. He wanted to enjoy it while he could.

She was warm in his arms, small and just the right height to lay her head on his chest. She didn't, though. She kept a little distance.

He pulled her closer and brushed his legs against hers as they danced. She let him. She even moved her free hand higher onto his shoulder.

Then she glanced up, looked into his eyes and held the look like she was thinking him over.

"You've got the moves," he said.

That made her grin.

"Yeah," she said dryly. "*I* have the moves."

"In the arena, too. I watched you and Smoke 'Em after I got off."

"Thanks," she said. "You made a good ride. What's the score? Something like only five riders stuck him in seventeen outs."

"Sheer luck," he said modestly. "When he started that really hard whippin' around with his hind end, he came within a hair of scooting me down off my rope and onto his head."

"Yeah," she said. "He is one big, strong boy who loves his work with all his big old ugly heart."

She shot him an impish grin. "Nearly as much as you."

He raised his eyebrows at her. "Are you saying I'm big and ugly? Or big and strong?"

"Whatever," she said with a definitely flirtatious tilt of her head.

Her soft laugh mingled with the music.

"You looked like you were having a pretty good time," he said.

She nodded. "I love it. Everything and everybody fades away and it's just me and *el toro*."

Then she bit her bottom lip—a really nice bottom lip—as if she'd said more than she meant to.

"Me, too." Then *he* said way more than *he'd* meant to. "I don't know what I'll do when I can't ride anymore."

She shot him a look.

"I noticed the announcer mentioned that you're thirty-eight, like you're the old man of rodeo or something."

He laughed. "I'm gonna jump him out about that. I'm sick of hearing it."

And he was. He still had the want-to and he still had the talent.

"To be fair," she said, "earlier, he called you a great champion."

A cold finger touched his mind.

Would they be saying that about him as a bull rider, too? Or was he making a fool of himself by trying for the All-Around?

Maybe it was true that the older a man got the more it took to get the adrenaline flowing, but that was because the more experienced the cowboy, the more he'd been there, done that. He wasn't as scared. It was as simple as that.

It still flowed in him all right, even if most of it was from desire and determination instead of fear. And, since he'd gotten into bull-riding, the fear was coming back stronger, too.

"Fear's what makes a rider good," he said lightly, "and I'm scared."

He took the conversation back to tonight's ride. Which was what he'd wanted to talk to her about in the first place.

"I was really glad when Smoke 'Em finally started to spin. I couldn't believe how high he could kick and how hard he could buck."

"Yeah, the spin's what kept you on," she said. "I sure thought you were hung up there at the end, though."

Good. Great. She'd brought it up herself. Maybe he could get his message across without offending her.

"Yeah, you did come in too soon," he said. "I was okay."

She stiffened and gave him a narrow-eyed look.

"You're the first customer I ever had that complained I tried too hard to keep him alive and healthy. And you looked pretty much hung-up with your hand there in the rope and your feet trying to find the ground."

"I wasn't."

He brought out his most charming smile.

"I don't mean to be critical," he said. "I just like to be in control as long as I can."

She was looking at him like he had two heads. "What happens after the buzzer doesn't get you any more points. I could drag you away from the bull by your hair and it wouldn't change your score."

The image sent a quick shot of anger through him. Wasn't it always the cave*men* who did the dragging?

"I'm not *talking* about points. I'm talking about control. Winning is all about control."

"You're talking about *image*," she said, and now she was mad, too. "This is the most ridiculous thing I ever heard. Tuff Hedeman or Ty Murray or Donnie Gay or any of the *best* bull riders in history never felt any shame at *running* from a bull, much less being helped to get loose from one."

"Look," he said, "I'll run from a bull with the best of 'em. I'm not proud. I just don't want any help if I don't need it."

She studied him, eyes full of fire, but her body still moving flawlessly with his.

"What *is* the deal here? Tell me this, would you be saying this to Rocky or Junior?"

"Of course."

"Of course *not*."

She glared at him. "I'm thinking you just don't like to be rescued by a woman."

"I *wasn't*," he snapped. "You didn't rescue me because I didn't need to be rescued."

"You're criticizing me because I'm a woman in a man's job. It's as simple as that. I know it."

He shook his head and opened his mouth but she was too quick for him.

"Since when does a cowboy criticize a bullfighter? At least to his face? If he's not a woman? I can tell you right now that I intend to win the title in Vegas and I'll do it *next* October. I'm gonna be the best in the world."

"I don't doubt that. I'm just telling you I like to do all I can on my own."

"I never saw such an ego," she said. "And I've known some real jerks."

"I'm just trying to save you until I really need you."

She was giving him a furious, narrow-eyed look, reassessing what she'd originally thought of him, no doubt.

Her body wasn't reassessing anything, though. It was like his, still dancing on, in sync with his, as if they were longtime lovers.

Insane thought.

She was only a kid.

"It's hard to run from a bull and look cool at the same time," he said, grinning. "What I need is for you to come in right when I start to run and distract the audience with your guts and skill."

She kept on giving him that look.

"Since, as Robbie pointed out, you're such a blur in the arena that they can't be distracted by your beautiful face."

"You wouldn't say that to a male bullfighter, either," she snapped. "You like to be in control, but you can't manage with flattery."

She sounded like she was about to get really mad again.

Lomax, get a grip. This is not worth a big blowup. This is stupid and you should've kept your mouth shut.

He smiled at her, trying to get back on the easy footing they'd had at the beginning. He wanted to accomplish something here, not alienate her or get talk started among the bullfighters that he was disrespecting them and the bull riders that he was stepping out of bounds to the detriment of them all.

"I can't help it," he said lightly. "I have to hang on 'til the buzzer in case the bull decides to jump back under me right at the last second. It *has* happened, you know, so you'll have to cut me some slack."

She scowled at him. *Fiercely* scowled at him.

"Get over it, Lomax. I'm not going to have it on my conscience that you got hurt or killed when I could've saved your life."

Quick anger tried to take him again. That was the proof right there—women did not belong in a bullfighting job. By nature, they were overprotective.

"If I get hurt or killed, that's just bullriding," he said. "I hate to break it to you, Farrell, but you can't save everybody. Somebody's gonna get killed and somebody's gonna get hurt while you're fighting bulls and it will *not* be your fault. You won't have anything to do with it."

She bowed up again and snapped at him. "I know I'm not God."

"You don't talk like it. You talk like a naïve, little-girl greenhorn out to save the world."

"Don't 'little girl' me, buddy. I may only be half as old as you are but I've had more than twenty-four years' worth of trouble to face up to and I know what my job is and how to do it."

"I don't need a nursemaid," he said. "And I am *not* twice as old as you are."

They glared at each other, those words hanging in the air, then they both laughed.

"Sorry," she said.

The song ended and Farrell stepped back, out of his arms. The front man announced that the band was going to take a break.

"You *can* dance," she said, with a grin. "Sorry I doubted you, but with an old man, you never know."

HQN™

We *are* romance™

Catch the second SIZZLING read in the HOT ZONE
trilogy from *New York Times* bestselling author

CARLY
PHILLIPS

Win a free makeover! See inside book for details.

Sports publicist Micki Jordan has always been just one of the
guys. But enter Damian Fuller—professional ballplayer and
major league playboy—and suddenly it's time for Micki to retire
her tomboy ways and reveal the hot number that she really is!

He'll never know what hit him.

Pick up your copy of
Hot Number

**in August for further details on how
YOU can become a hot number, too!**
www.HQNBooks.com

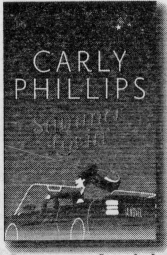